"HOPELESSLY ADDICTIVE . . . DEFINITELY THE SEASON'S GUILTY PLEASURE."
—*Time Out New York*

"A wonderful new thriller . . . Comparisons to [Donna] Tartt will understandably abound . . . but this work stands on its own. . . . Goodman pinballs from present day to flashback, slowly weaving together the similarities of tragedies in deliciously escalating, well-written tension."
—*The Dallas Morning News*

"Genuinely haunting . . . The suspense is so pervasive."
—*New York Daily News*

"Goodman debuts strongly with this intricately plotted and captivating tale of buried secrets. . . . The dark and shocking secrets of Jane's adolescence, revealed gradually in flashbacks, progressively absorb the readers into the final disquieting denouement. . . . Goodman weaves ancient mythology with modern legend into a chilling and evocative story of deception and complicity."
—*Publishers Weekly*

"*The Lake of Dead Languages* holds its secrets to the end. If it weren't for Goodman's keen ability to weave a mystery of multiple layers, each revealed with exquisite timing, her picturesque prose would be reason enough to keep the reader turning the pages."
—*BookPage*

"An outstanding novel by a marvelous new talent. Carol Goodman's use of language and her ability to let a story unfold naturally reflect a writer at the top of her game. Goodman uses the lake and its characters to lure you into a story so compelling you won't want it to end. This is a must-read for anyone who loves good writing."
—*Rapport*

The
Lake of
Dead Languages

• • •

Carol Goodman

Ballantine Books • *New York*

To my mother, Margaret Goodman,
and in memory of my father,
Walter Goodman
1924–1999

Acknowledgments

I would like to thank the early readers of this book whose support and encouragement were invaluable: Laurie Bower, Gary Feinberg, Wendy Gold Rossi, Scott Silverman, Nora Slonimsky, Mindy Siegel Ohringer, and Sondra Browning Witt.

To my teachers whose vision and advice guided me, Sheila Kohler and Richard Aellen.

For a work of fiction, I had a lot of factual questions. Thanks to Ann Guenther, Mohonk naturalist, who told me how lakes freeze, and to Joan LaChance, Marion Swindon, and Jim Clark for talking to me about ice harvesting at Mohonk. To my brother, Robert Goodman, for answering questions about the physics of freezing, and my daughter, Maggie, who invented the corniculum.

Thanks to Loretta Barrett, my agent, and her assistant, Alison Brooks, for taking a chance on me and steering the book toward its present incarnation.

For Linda Marrow—I couldn't have dreamed up a better editor.

Most of all, thanks to my husband, Lee Slonimsky, whose love and wild, improbable faith made all the difference. I wouldn't have written this book without you.

THE LAKE IN MY DREAMS IS ALWAYS FROZEN. IT IS NEVER the lake in summer, its water stained black by the shadows of pine trees, or the lake in fall, its surface stitched into a quilt of red and gold, or the lake on a spring night, beaded with moonlight. The lake in my dreams reflects nothing; it is the dead white of a closed door, sealed by ice that reaches sixty feet down to the lake's glacial limestone cradle.

I skate over that reassuring depth soundlessly, the scrape of my blades absorbed by a pillowy gray sky. I feel the strength of the deep ice in the soles of my feet and I skate like I've never skated in life. No wobbly ankles or sore thighs, I skate with the ease and freedom of flying. I skate the way skating looks, not feels.

I lean into long, languid figure eights and arch my back in the tight spins, my long hair shedding sparks of static in the cold dry air. When I leap, I soar high above the silver ice and land straight and true as an arrow boring into its mark. Each glide is long and perfect and crosses over the last, braiding tendrils of ice and air out of the spray which fans out in my wake.

Then comes the moment when I am afraid to look down, afraid of what I'll see beneath the surface of the ice, but when I do look, the ice is as thick and opaque as good linen and my heart beats easier. I am weightless with relief. I pirouette as effortlessly as a leaf spinning in the wind, the fine lines my blades inscribe in the ice as delicate as calligraphy. It is only when I reach the shore and look back that I see I have carved a pattern in the ice, a face, familiar and long gone, which I watch, once again, sink into the black water.

PART ONE

•

Overturn

Chapter One

●

I HAVE BEEN TOLD TO MAKE THE LATIN CURRICULUM RELE-vant to the lives of my students. I am finding, though, that my advanced girls at Heart Lake like Latin precisely because it has no relevance to their lives. They like nothing better than a new, difficult declension to memorize. They write the noun endings on their palms in blue ballpoint ink and chant the declensions, *"Puella, puellae, puellae, puellam, puella . . ."* like novices counting their rosaries.

When it comes time for a test they line up at the washroom to scrub down. I lean against the cool tile wall watching them as the washbasins fill with pale blue foam and the archaic words run down the drains. When they offer to show me the undersides of their wrists for traces of letters I am unsure if I should look. If I look, am I showing that I don't trust them? If I don't look, will they think I am naive? When they put their upturned hands in mine—so light-boned and delicate—it is as if a fledgling has alighted in my lap. I am afraid to move.

In class I see only the tops of their hands—the black nail polish and silver skull rings. One girl even has a tattoo on the top of her right hand—an intricate blue pattern that she tells me is a Celtic knot. Now I look at the warm, pink flesh—their fingertips are ten-der and whorled from immersion in water, the scent of soap rises like incense. Three of the girls have scratched the inside of their wrists with pins or razors. The lines are fainter than the lifelines that crease their palms. I want to trace their scars with my fingertips and ask them why, but instead I squeeze their hands and tell them to go on into class. *"Bona fortuna,"* I say. "Good luck on the test."

When I first came back to Heart Lake I was surprised at the new girls, but I soon realized that since my own time here the school has become a sort of last resort for a certain kind of girl. I have learned that even though the Heart Lake School for Girls still looks like a prestigious boarding school, it is not. It is really a place for girls who have already been kicked out of two or three of the really good schools. A place for girls whose parents have grown sick of drama, sick of blood on the bathroom floor, sick of the policeman at the door.

Athena (her real name is Ellen Craven, but I have come to think of the girls by the classical names they've chosen for class) is the last to finish washing. She has asked for extra credit, for more declensions and verb conjugations to learn, so she is up to her elbows in blue ink. She holds out her forearms for me to see and there is no way to avoid looking at the scar on her right arm that starts at the base of her palm and snakes up to the crook of her elbow. She sees me wince.

Athena shrugs. "It was a stupid thing to do," she says. "I was all messed up over this boy last year, you know?"

I try to remember caring that much for a boy—I almost see a face—but it's like trying to remember labor pains, you remember the symptoms of pain—the blurred vision, the way your mind moves in an ever-tightening circle around a nucleus so dense gravity itself seems to bend toward it—but not the pain itself.

"That's why my aunt sent me to an all girls school," Athena continues. "So I wouldn't get so caught up with boys again. Like my mother goes to this place upstate when she needs to dry out—you know, get away from booze and pills? So, I'm here drying out from boys."

I look up from her hands to her pale face—a paleness accentuated by her hair, which is dyed a blue-black that matches the circles under her eyes. I think I hear tears in her voice, but instead she is laughing. Before I can help myself I laugh, too. Then I turn away from her and yank paper towels from the dispenser so she can dry her arms.

I let the girls out early after the test. They whoop with delight and crowd the doorway. I am not insulted. This is part of the game we play. They like it when I'm strict. Up to a point. They like that the class is hard. They like me, I think. At first I flattered myself that it was because I understood them, but then one day I retrieved a note left on the floor.

"What do you think of her?" one girl had written.

"Let's go easy on her," another, later I identified the handwriting as Athena's, had answered.

I realized then that the girls' goodwill did not come from anything I had said or done. It came because they knew, with the uncanny instinct of teenagers, that I must have messed up as badly as they had to end up here.

Today they leave shaking the cramp out of their hands and comparing answers from the test. Vesta—the thin, studious one, the one who tries the hardest—holds the textbook open to read out the declension and conjugation endings. There are moans from some, little cries of triumph from others. Octavia and Flavia, the two Vietnamese sisters who are counting on classics scholarships to college, nod at each answer with the calm assurance of hard studiers. If I listened carefully I wouldn't have to mark the tests at all to know what grades to give, but I let the sounds of sorrow and glee blur together. I can hear them all the way down the hall until Myra Todd opens her door and tells them they're disturbing her biology lab.

I hear another door open and one of my girls calls out, "Hello, Miss Marshmallow." Then I hear a high nervous laugh which I recognize as that of Gwendoline Marsh, the English teacher. It won't be Gwen, though, who complains; it's Myra I'll catch hell from later for letting them out before the bell. I don't care. It's worth it for the quiet that settles now over my empty classroom, for the minutes I'll have before my next class.

I turn my chair around so that I face the window. On the lawn in front of the mansion I see my girls collapsed in a lopsided circle. From here their dark clothing and dyed hair—Athena's blue-black, Aphrodite's bleached blond, and Vesta's lavender red, which is the same shade as the nylon hair on my daughter's Little Mermaid doll—make them look like hybrid flowers bred into unnatural shades. Black dahlias and tulips. Flowers the bruised color of dead skin.

Past where the girls sit, Heart Lake lies blue-green and still in its glacial cradle of limestone. The water on this side of the lake is so bright it hurts my eyes. I rest them on the dark eastern end of the lake, where the pine tree shadows stain the water black. Then I pick my homework folder up off my desk and add the assignments I've collected today, sorting each girl's new assignment with older work (as usual, I'm about a week behind in my grading). They're easy to sort because almost all the girls use different kinds of paper that I've come to recognize as each girl's distinctive trademark: lavender stationery for Vesta, the long yellow legal-size sheets for Aphrodite, lined paper with ragged edges which Athena tears from her black-and-white notebooks.

Sometimes the page Athena gives me has something else written on the reverse side. A few lines at the top that look to be the end of a diary entry. I know from the scraps I've read that she sometimes writes as if addressing a letter to herself and sometimes as if the journal itself were her correspondent. "Don't forget," I read in one of these coda. "You don't need anyone but yourself." And another time: "I promise I'll write to you more often, you're all I have." Sometimes there is a drawing on the back of her assignment. Half a woman's face dissolving into a wave. A rainbow sliced in two by a winged razor blade. A heart with a dagger through its middle. Cheap teenage symbolism. They could be pictures from the book I kept when I was her age.

I recognize the paper she uses by its ragged edge where it's been pulled out of the thread-stitched notebook. If she's not careful, pages will start to come loose. I know because I used the same sort of book when I was her age, the kind with the black-and-white-marbled covers. When I look down at the page I think I've got another piece of her journal, but then I turn it over and see the other side is blank. Athena's homework is on a separate page at the bottom of the stack and I've lost track whether the page I'm holding is one that was just handed in or was already in the folder. I look back at the page I thought was her homework. There is a single line of tiny, cramped writing at the top of it. The ink is so pale that I have to move the paper into the light from the window in order to make it out.

You're the only one I can ever tell.

I stare at the words so hard that a dim halo forms around them and I have to blink to make the darkness go away. Later I'll wonder what I recognized first: the words that I wrote in my journal almost twenty years ago, or my own handwriting.

I MAKE THE STUDENTS IN MY NEXT CLASS RECITE DECLENSIONS until the sound of the other words in my head is a faint whisper, but as I walk to the dining hall the words reassert themselves in my brain. *You're the only one I can ever tell.* Words any teenager might write in her diary. If I hadn't recognized my own handwriting there would be no cause for alarm. The words could refer to anything, but knowing what they do refer to I can't help but wonder how someone has gotten hold of my old journal and slipped a page of it into my homework folder. At first I had thought it must be Athena, but then I realized that any of the girls could have handed me the page when she handed in her own assignment. For that matter, since I left the homework folder on my desk overnight and the classrooms are unlocked, anyone might have slipped the page into my homework folder.

I know that that particular page is from the last journal I kept senior year, and that I lost it during the spring semester. Could it have been on the property all this time—hidden under the floorboards in my old dorm room perhaps—and Athena or one of her friends has now found it? The thought of what else is in that journal floods through me and I have to actually stop at the foot of the mansion stairs and lean on the railing for a moment before I can start up the steps.

Girls in plaid skirts and white shirts coming untucked from the blue sweaters tied around their waists stream around me as I make my way up the stairs toward the massive oak doors. The doors were designed to intimidate. They are outside the human scale. The Crevecoeur family, who donated the mansion to the school, also owned the paper mill in the nearby town of Corinth. India Crevecoeur ran a tea and "improvement society" for the female mill workers. I picture those mill girls, in a tight gaggle for warmth as much as for moral support, waiting outside these doors. My own grandmother, who worked at the mill before working as a maid for the Crevecoeurs, might have been among them.

When I won the scholarship to come here I wondered what the Crevecoeurs would have thought about the granddaughter of one of their maids attending their school. I don't think they would have been amused. In the family portrait that hangs in the Music Room they look like dour, unhappy people. Their ancestors were Huguenots who fled France in the seventeenth century and eventually made their way here to this remote outpost in upstate New York. It must have been a shock to them—this wilderness, the brutal winters, the isolation. The fanlight above the door is plain glass now, but when I went here it was stained glass: a red heart split in two by a green fleur-de-lis-handled dagger and the family motto in yellow: *Cor te reducit*—The heart leads you back. I've always imagined them waiting for some deliverance from this savage place, to France, or God perhaps. But since I have found myself back at Heart Lake—a place I swore I'd never return to—I've begun to think the heart in the motto is the lake itself, exerting its own gravitational pull on those who have once lived on its shores and bathed in its icy green water.

• • •

THE FACULTY DINING ROOM IS IN THE OLD MUSIC ROOM. When I went to Heart Lake the scholarship students worked in the kitchen and served the teachers at meals. Some years ago the practice was discontinued as it was considered demeaning to the scholarship students. I never minded though. Nancy Ames, the cook, always gave us a good meal. Roasts and potatoes, creamed vegetables and poached fish. I never ate so well in all my life. She saved us the rolls she baked fresh for every meal. She gave them to us wrapped in thick linen napkins embroidered with the Heart Lake crest, which we were to remember to return. Walking back through the cold dusk— that last year at Heart Lake resides in my memory as one endless winter dusk—I felt the warmth of them in my pocket, like a small animal burrowed for shelter against my body.

Now the school uses paper napkins and the teachers serve themselves from a buffet. Tuna fish salad and packaged bread. Carrot sticks and hard-boiled eggs. What hasn't changed, though, is the mandatory attendance for all faculty. It was a tenet of India Crevecoeur, Heart Lake's founder, that the teaching staff be a community. It is an admirable goal, but on days like today I'd give much to be able to take my sandwich out to a rock by the lake with no one but Ovid for company. As I enter the room I give India's image in the family portrait a resentful look, which she, snug in the bosom of her large family, disdainfully returns.

The only empty seat is next to Myra Todd. I take out a stack of quizzes to grade and hope they will keep her from commenting on third period's early dismissal. Half the teachers at the long table have a similar stack of paper-clipped pages at which they peck with their red pens in between bites of tuna fish. When I take out mine, though, I see I still have the journal page with my handwriting on the top of the stack. I hurriedly fold it and stick it into the pocket of my plaid wool skirt just as Myra leans across me for the salt shaker. I have to remind myself that she'd have no reason to think anything of those enigmatic words even if she did see them. Unless she's the one who found my old journal.

I steal a glance at her to see if she's paying undue attention to my stack of papers, but she is placidly chewing her sandwich and staring into the middle distance. Under the smell of tuna fish and stale coffee I catch her distinctive smell—a whiff of mildew as if she were one of her own science experiments left too long in the supply closet over Christmas break. I've always wondered what peculiar health condition or faulty laundry procedure is the cause of this odor, but it's hardly the kind of thing you could ask a person as prim and proper as Myra. I try to imagine what she would do if she came upon my old journal, and I am pretty sure she'd take it straight to the dean.

I try to imagine what Dean Buehl would make of my old journal. Celeste Buehl was the science teacher when I went to Heart Lake. She was always kind to me when I was her student—and she was more than kind when she gave me this job—but I don't think that kindness would survive a reading of my senior-year journal.

When she comes in today I notice how much she's changed in the twenty years since she was my teacher. I remember her as slim and athletic, leading nature hikes through the woods and skating on the lake in winter. Now her broad shoulders are rounded and her short, cropped hair, once dark and springy, looks lifeless and dull. Myra Todd picks the moment of the dean's entrance to mention third period's early dismissal.

"Jane," she says loudly, "your third-period class disturbed my senior lab this morning. We were at a very delicate stage of dissection. Mallory Martin's hand slipped and she nicked her lab partner with a scalpel."

I know Mallory Martin by reputation. My girls call her Maleficent. I somehow doubt the incident with the scalpel was an accident.

"I'm sorry, Myra, I'll tell them to be quieter. They get so keyed up for these exams."

"The thing to do is give them extra problems when they finish their tests. That way they won't be so anxious to finish early." Simon Ross, the math teacher, volunteers this pedagogical advice and resumes scoring a pile of quizzes with a thick red marker. The tips of his fingers are stained red with the marker, and I notice the color has bled onto his sandwich.

"I let the girls write in their journals," Gwendoline Marsh offers in a small voice. "It helps them to have an outlet and it's part of their grade."

"And just how do you grade these journals?" asks Meryl North, the history teacher who already seemed as ancient as her subject when I was a student here. "Do you read their private thoughts?"

"Oh no, I only read the parts they want me to—they circle the parts I'm not supposed to read and mark them *private*."

Meryl North makes a sound between a laugh and a choke and Gwendoline's pale skin reddens. I try to catch Gwen's eye to give her a nod of encouragement—she is the closest thing to a friend I have here at Heart Lake—but she is resolutely staring down at a worn volume of Emily Dickinson.

"They do seem to be under a lot of stress," I say, more to cover Gwen's embarrassment than because I want to open this particular line of conversation. There were two suicide attempts last year. In response, the administration has instituted weekly faculty seminars on adolescent depression and "How to detect the ten warning signs of suicidal behavior."

"Anyone in particular?" The question comes from Dr. Candace Lockhart. Unlike the rest of us at the table she has no stacks of papers to grade or texts to study for next period. Her fingers are never stained with ink, her exquisitely tailored dove gray suits never tainted with the ugly yellow chalk dust that the rest of us wear like a wasting disease. She's the school psychologist, an office that did not exist in my day. There is an aura of secrecy surrounding her appointment here. I've heard some of the faculty complain that Dean Buehl hired her without going through the proper channels. In other words, without giving the resident faculty a chance to gossip about her credentials. There's a whiff of jealousy about the complaints, to which I am not immune. The rumor is that she is conducting research for a groundbreaking study on the psychology of adolescent girls. We all suspect that once her research is done she will leave us for private practice, a glamorous lecture circuit with appearances on "Oprah," or perhaps a tenure-track post at an Ivy League college—some existence more appropriate to her wardrobe. In the meantime, she resides among us with her pale, almost white, hair, blue eyes and thin, ascetic figure, like a lilac point Siamese slumming with drab tabbies.

Poor Gwen, in her faded Indian print jumper and fussily old-fashioned high-necked white blouse, looks especially dowdy in comparison. Although Candace Lockhart and Gwen Marsh are both in their early thirties, the effects of teaching five classes a day, not to mention sponsoring half a dozen clubs, have left their mark on Gwen. Her complexion is muddy, her hair limp and going gray at the roots, her blue eyes washed out and bloodshot. Candace, on the other hand, clearly has time to get her hair done (that platinum blond can't be entirely natural) and *her* blue eyes are as clear and cold as lake water.

I am sufficiently unnerved by those blue eyes to make a mistake. Of course, I should say, "No. No one in particular." But instead I name a name. "Athena . . . I mean Ellen . . . Craven. I noticed today that she has an awful scar on her arm."

"Well, yes, I know about that of course. That's old news and not surprising given Ellen's history."

I should be glad for her dismissal, but something in the way Dr. Lockhart's blue eyes glaze over, already looking past me toward whatever illustrious future fate has in store for her, irks me. I am forever thinking I am past such vanities and finding that I am not.

"Some of the pictures she draws on the back of her homework assignments are . . . well . . . somewhat disturbing."

"You let your girls turn in homework with pictures on the back?" Myra Todd looks up from her stack of papers, appalled, only to meet Dr. Lockhart's cool look of disdain. Gratified to have someone else silenced by those eyes, I go on. It has occurred to me that this is exactly what I should be doing. My responsibility as Athena's teacher, as an especially trusted teacher in whom the girl confided, demands that I seek help for her emotional problems. To whom else should I refer those problems than the school psychologist?

"Disembodied eyes with tears turning into razor blades, that kind of thing. I suppose the images aren't unusual . . ."

I notice that the rest of the table has grown quiet, and it occurs to me that I shouldn't be talking about my student in front of the entire teaching staff. Dr. Lockhart must think so, too.

"Perhaps you should come see me in my office to talk about Athena. I'm in my office by seven. Why don't you come in before your first class?" Dr. Lockhart suggests.

She no doubt sees my reluctance to agree to this early appointment—I am thinking of the lake swim I try to take each morning before class—and so she adds this last piece of admonishment.

"It's crucial we address any preoccupation with death or suicide immediately. These things have a way of turning into trends, as I'm sure you know from your own experience here, Miss Hudson. Don't you agree, Dean Buehl?"

Dean Buehl sighs. "God forbid that happen again."

I feel blood rush to my cheeks as if I had been slapped. Any thoughts I had of protesting the early-morning meeting are gone now, and Dr. Lockhart seems to know that. Without waiting for my answer she rises from her chair and adjusts a pale blue shawl over her suit jacket.

"I especially want to know if that Crevecoeur sisters legend . . ." The rest of her words are drowned out by the bell ringing to signal the end of lunch hour and the scraping of chairs being pushed back from the table.

Dr. Lockhart, unencumbered as she is, glides out of the dining room while the rest of us gather books and shoulder heavy canvas bags. Gwen especially seems to list to one side from the weight of her book bag. I ask if she needs some help and she pulls out a thick manila envelope and hands it to me.

"Oh, thank you, Jane, I was going to ask if someone could type these student poems up for the literary magazine. I'd do it but my carpal tunnel syndrome's acting up." She lifts up her arms and I see that both forearms are wrapped in ace bandages. All I'd meant to offer was to carry something for her, but what can I say?

I transfer the heavy folder from her bag to mine. Now I'm the one listing to one side as we leave the Music Room, and Gwen, lightened of her load, hurries on ahead to class. I trail behind the rest of the teachers thinking about what the psychologist had said about preoccupation with death and suicidal trends. I picture my students with their skull jewelry and kohl-rimmed eyes.

The nose rings and skull jewelry and purple hair may be new, but this preoccupation with suicide is not. Like many girls' schools, Heart Lake has its own suicide legend. When I was here the story would be told, usually around the Halloween bonfire at the swimming beach, that the Crevecoeur family lost all three of their daughters in the flu epidemic of 1918. It was said that one night the three girls, all delirious with fever, went down to the lake to quench their fever and drowned there. At this point in the story, someone would point to the three rocks that rose out of the water off the swimming beach and intone solemnly, "Their bodies were never found, but on the next morning three rocks appeared mysteriously in the lake and those rocks have from that day been known as the three sisters."

One of the seniors would fill in the rest of the details as we younger girls nervously toasted our marshmallows over the bonfire. India Crevecoeur, the girls' mother, was so heartbroken she could no longer live at Heart Lake, so she turned her home into a girls' school. From the school's first year, however, there have been mysterious suicides at Heart Lake. They say that the sound of the lake lapping against the three rocks (here the speaker would pause so we could all listen to the sound of the water restlessly beating against the rocks) beckons girls to take their lives by throwing themselves into the lake. They say that when the lake freezes over the faces of the girls can be seen peering out from beneath the ice. The ice makes a noise like moaning, and that sound, like the lapping of the water, draws girls out onto the lake's frozen surface, where the sisters wait to drag the unsuspecting skater through the cracks in the ice. And they say that whenever one girl drowns in the lake, two more inevitably follow.

If the legend is still circulating, as Dr. Lockhart fears, there are a few things I could tell my girls. I could tell them that the Crevecoeur family did lose their youngest daughter, Iris, but she didn't drown. She caught a chill from a mishap during a boating party with her two older sisters and died of the flu in her own bed. I could also tell them that nineteenth-century drawings of the lake show the three rocks, which were called, by early settlers, the three graces. But I know that the harder you try to dispel a legend the more power it gains. It's like Oedipus trying to avoid his fate and running headlong into it at the crossroads. And once I begin to talk about the legend they might ask if there were any suicides when I went to school here. Then I would either have to lie or tell them that during my senior year both my roommates drowned in the lake.

I might even find myself telling them that since then I have always felt the lake is waiting for the third girl.

Chapter Two

●

BETWEEN TEACHING AND TAKING CARE OF OLIVIA AFTER school, the question of who has found my old notebook recedes to background noise. I can hear the question whispering at the edge of my consciousness, but I push it away until I can concentrate on it.

That night I scramble eggs for Olivia and me. After dinner we wash out the eggshells for an arts and crafts project for her nursery school. Olivia holds the shells under the running tap water and then hands them to me. I surreptitiously scoop out the transparent jelly that still clings to the hollow cups and set them into an empty egg crate. She explains to me that not just birds come from eggs. Snakes and alligators and turtles also come out of eggs. Even spiders.

"Charlotte made a sack for her eggs and Wilbur carried it home from the fair in his mouth," she tells me. I remember that her preschool teacher, Mrs. Crane, is reading *Charlotte's Web* aloud in class. They'll study spiders and eggs at the same time and visit a local farm to see pigs. It's an excellent preschool program, one of the perks of working here.

I set the crate aside on the counter to dry.

"And then Charlotte died," Olivia finishes.

"That's a sad part, isn't it?"

"Uh huh. Can I watch some TV before bed?"

"No, it's time for your shower."

Olivia complains bitterly about no TV, about the fact she has to take a shower because the cottage we've been given by the school has no bath, and, for good measure, she throws in the fact that her father isn't here to read to her. It's on the tip of my tongue to say that he hardly ever read to her anyway, that he was usually at work far past her bedtime, but of course I don't. I tell her that her father will read to her when he sees her the weekend after next, which requires a lengthy consultation with the calendar before she grasps the time frame of every other weekend visitation.

By the time her shower is finished it is past nine o'clock and my throat is raw from teaching all day and arguing with a four-year-old. Still, I can't really weasel out of reading to her after that remark about her father. I go into the spare bedroom where I've stacked the boxes of books and papers and find one of my old children's books, a collection called *Tales from the Ballet*.

Olivia is intrigued with the idea that this is a book I had as a child.

"Did your mommy give it to you?" she asks.

"No," I tell her, and wonder how I could possibly explain to her that my mother would never have spent money on anything so frivolous as books. "One of my teachers. Here, she wrote something to me."

Inside on the flyleaf my kindergarten teacher had written, "To Jane, who dances on ice."

"What's that mean? Dance on ice."

"Ice skating. Mommy used to be a pretty good ice skater. I used to skate on this very lake when it froze in the winter."

"Can I skate on the lake when it freezes?" she asks.

"Maybe," I say. "We'll see."

I flip through the pages of the book looking for a story she'll recognize—"Cinderella" or "Sleeping Beauty" perhaps—but then the book falls open to a page marked with a dried maple leaf, its once vibrant scarlet faded now to palest russet. "This one!" Olivia demands with that odd certainty of four-year-olds.

It's "Giselle." My old favorite, but not the one I would have chosen for Olivia.

"This one has some scary parts," I say.

"Good," Olivia tells me. "I like scary parts."

I figure I can edit out anything too scary. I stop to explain why Giselle's mother won't let her dance and then I have to explain what it means to have a weak heart. She likes the part about the prince disguised as a peasant—"Just like in Sleeping Beauty"—and is sad when Giselle dies. I am thinking I will just leave out the part about the Wilis—the spirits of girls disappointed in love who seduce young men and make them dance until they die—but when I turn the page to the picture of the wraithlike girls in their bridal dresses, Olivia is instantly in love with them. Just as I was at her age. This had been my favorite picture.

So I read on. Through the part where the girls dance with the gamekeeper, Hilarion, and lure him into the lake to drown, and up to where the queen of the Wilis tells Giselle she must make Albrecht, her false lover, dance to his doom.

"Will she?" Olivia asks, her face pinched with concern.

"What do you think?" I ask her.

"Well, he did make her sad," she says.

"But she loves him, let's see. . . ."

Giselle tells Albrecht to hold fast to the cross on her tomb, but he is so entranced by her dancing that he joins her. But because of Giselle's delay, he is still alive when the church clock strikes four and the Wilis return to their graves. "And so she saves him," I tell Olivia, closing the book. All I've left out are the last two lines of the story, which read, "His life had been saved, but he has lost his heart. Giselle has danced away with it."

· · ·

When Olivia has fallen asleep I take out the piece of paper folded in my skirt pocket. As I unfold it I am sure that I will see now that the handwriting is Athena's, or Vesta's or Aphrodite's, anyone's but my own. But as I stare at the words again there is no escaping the truth. I recognize not only my own handwriting, but the ink—a peculiar shade of peacock blue that Lucy Toller gave me, along with a fountain pen in the same color, for my fifteenth birthday.

Still holding the paper, I go into the spare bedroom to find the box marked "Heart Lake." I tear at the packing tape and rip open the box so hastily that the sharp edge of the cardboard slices into my wrist. Ignoring the pain, I pull out the stack of black-and-white notebooks inside.

There are three of them. I started them in the ninth grade when I first met Matt and Lucy Toller, and faithfully kept a new one each year through our senior year at Heart Lake.

I count them as if hoping that the fourth one will have miraculously rejoined its companions, but of course it hasn't. I haven't seen the fourth notebook since spring semester senior year, when it disappeared from my dorm room.

At the time I thought someone in the administration had confiscated the notebook. I spent that last term at Heart Lake sure that it was only a matter of time before I was called into the dean's office and confronted with the truth of everything that had happened that year, and what I had said at the inquest. But the summons never came. I attended the graduation ceremony and the reception on the lawn above the lake, standing apart from the other girls and their proud families, and afterward I took a taxi to the train station and a train to my summer job at the library at Vassar, where I had a scholarship for the fall. I decided that the notebook must have gotten lost. Sometimes I told myself that it had slipped out of my book bag and fallen into the lake and the lake had washed away all the blue-green ink until its pages were as blank as they were on the first day of senior year.

I open the first notebook and read the opening entry.

"Lucy gave me this fountain pen and beautiful ink for my birthday and Matt gave me this notebook," I had written in a flowery script that tried to live up to the fancy pen and ink. There were blotches, though, where the pen's nib had caught the paper. It had taken a while to get used to that pen. "I'll never have any other friends like them."

I almost laugh at the words. *Other friends.* What other friends? When I first laid eyes on Matt and Lucy Toller I had no other friends.

I take out the folded paper and smooth it out next to this page. The handwriting is surer and blotch-free, but the words are written in the same beautiful shade of blue-green.

I go outside to watch the moon rise over Heart Lake. I think, not for the first time, that I must have been crazy to come back here. But then, where else had I to go?

When I told Mitch I wanted a divorce he laughed at me. "Where will you go? How will you live?" he asked. "For God's sake, Jane, you were a Latin major. If you leave this house you'll be on your own."

And I had thought of Electra's line, "How shall we be lords in our own house? We have been sold and go as wanderers." And right then I knew I'd go to the only homeland I'd ever had: Heart Lake.

I started to work on my Latin, which I hadn't touched in years. At night I studied from my old Wheelock textbook, picking away at case endings and verb conjugations until the unintelligible jumble of words sorted itself out. Words paired up like skaters linking arms, adjectives with nouns, verbs with subjects, inscribing precise patterns in the slippery ice of archaic syntax.

And always the voices I heard reciting the declensions and conjugations were Matt's and Lucy's.

When I had reread Wheelock twice, I applied for the job at Heart Lake and learned that my old science teacher, Celeste Buehl, had become dean. "We've never really been able to replace Helen Chambers," she told me. I remembered that Miss Buehl had been good friends with my Latin teacher. No one was sadder than she when Helen Chambers had been let go. "But then we've never gotten an old girl in the position." "Old girl" was how they referred to an alumna who came back to teach at Heart Lake. Celeste Buehl was an "old girl," as were Meryl North, the history teacher, and Tacy Beade, the art teacher. "Your generation doesn't seem interested in teaching. I haven't interviewed a graduate since I became dean, but I can't think of anyone better to take the job than one of Helen Chambers's girls. Luckily my old cottage is free. It will be perfect for you and your daughter. You remember it, the one above the swimming beach." I remembered it all too well.

And although the idea of living here was at first disturbing, I've come to treasure my view of the lake. It's only a few yards from my front door to the Point, the stone cliff that bisects the lake, giving it its heartlike shape. From where I stand now I can see the curve of the swimming beach, white in the moonlight, and the stones we called the three sisters rising out of the still, moonlit water.

I go inside and look at Olivia sleeping. The moonlight comes through her window and falls on her tangled hair. I smooth back her hair from her forehead and rearrange the twisted sheets so she'll be cooler. She stirs and moans softly in her sleep, but doesn't call my name as she would if she were anywhere near waking. I know she might wake up later, at two or four perhaps, but I'm almost positive she'll sleep undisturbed for the next few hours.

I go back outside and down the steep stone steps that lead from our house to the lake. Every night I do this and every night I'm amazed at myself for taking the chance. Of course I know I shouldn't be leaving Olivia alone for even these few minutes—fifteen, twenty minutes, at most, I tell myself, what could happen? Well, I know what could happen. Fire, burglars, Olivia waking up and getting frightened when I don't come to her call, wandering out into the woods . . . my heart pounds at the images of disasters my mind so easily conjures up. But still I walk down the steps barefoot, feeling through the soles of my feet when the stone steps become damp from the mist off the lake and then slimy with the moss that grows over the stones.

At the foot of the steps the ground is hardpacked mud. I can hear the restless slap of water on the rocks. I wade through the cold water until I am standing, calf deep, next to the first of the three sister stones. I lean my shoulder against the tall rock and it feels warm. Like a person, I think, although I know it's only giving off the heat collected through the unseasonably warm day. The three stones are made of a hard, glittery basalt, different from the soft surrounding limestone. Lucy said they're like the tors in England, foreign stones carried from afar and erected in the lake, but Miss Buehl said they were probably deposited by a retreating glacier and then eroded into their present shapes. Each one has been molded differently by water and time, and the freezing and unfreezing of the lake. The first stone, which I am standing by, is a column rising six feet high above the water, the second is also a column, but it leans in the direction of the southern shore. The third stone is a rounded dome, curving gently out of the deep water.

If you look at the rocks in succession—in the right light or through a faint mist like the one that rises from the lake tonight— you can imagine that the first stone is a girl wading at the edge of the lake, the second is the same girl diving into the water, and the third is the girl's behind rising above the water as she dolphin dives into the lake.

The lake feels deliciously cold. The weather has been unseasonably warm for early October, but I know this Indian summer can't last much longer. Any day now a cold front will move down from Canada and it will be too cold to swim. Suddenly I notice how sweaty and sticky I feel, how sore my neck and back are from standing at a blackboard all day and leaning over stacks of papers. I remember that I won't be able to take my swim in the morning and the thought is like a physical pain. I could leave my clothes on the rock and swim for just a few moments. The cold water would wash away all thought of that lost journal and what is in it.

I am about to take off my shirt when I hear a rustle in the trees behind me. Instinctively, I move into the shadow of the second stone as if I were the errant schoolgirl caught out of her dorm at night. From there I can see three white shapes pass by me and into the lake. They move smoothly into the water, like spirits, and I am reminded eerily of the Wilis in the story I had been reading to Olivia. White sheets billow up around them like the Wilis' bridal gowns, and then, like animal brides in a fairy tale discarding their skins, they emerge out of the white billows and stroke naked out to the farthest rock.

A white clump floats past me and I pick up its corner and read the laundry marking, which identifies it as the property of the Heart Lake School for Girls.

One of the girls has pulled herself onto the farthest rock. She stands stretching her arms above her head as if reaching for the moon.

"We call on the Goddess of the Lake and make offering to honor She who guards the holy water."

The two girls in the water giggle. One of them tries to heave herself onto the rock and lands on her chest with a painful-sounding thud.

"Damn, I smashed my boobs."

"Oh, like they could be any flatter."

"Thanks a lot, Melissa."

With their giggling and bickering the three girls are transformed from mysterious Wilis to three awkward adolescents: my students, Athena (Ellen Craven), Vesta (Sandy James), and Aphrodite (Melissa Randall).

"Come on," Athena says, her hands on her naked hips. "You're ruining it. How can the Lake Goddess take our offering seriously with you two messing around? I told you we shouldn't have gotten high first."

With the last comment I am transformed from innocent

bystander—amused voyeur—to responsible teacher, if only in my guilty conscience, because I still don't reveal my presence. But now I've been given some information I should act on. The girls have been smoking pot. And yet, why should this alert me to my role while the sight of my students skinny-dipping at night fails to? Perhaps because skinny-dipping and making offerings to the Lake Goddess are both old Heart Lake traditions. In my day the girls routinely made sacrifices to the spirit of the lake. Sometimes we called her the Lady of the Lake (that was when we were reading Tennyson), which we later translated as Domina Lacunae, and in our senior year we called her the White Goddess. Over the years we offered her half-eaten S'mores, beads from broken necklaces, and locks of hair. Lucy said that if you gave her something at the beginning of the term you wouldn't lose anything in the lake that year. Girls are always losing things in the lake. I imagine the dark floor of the lake as faintly glimmering with broken ID bracelets, tarnished hairclips, and hoop earrings.

At the thought of the lake bottom I am suddenly cold. I remember Olivia alone in the house and I wonder how much time has elapsed. I want to go back, but if I let the girls see that I have seen them, I will have to report them to Dean Buehl. I remember her expression today when Dr. Lockhart mentioned the Crevecoeur legend and know that the last thing I want to do is remind her of girls making sacrifices to the lake. Also I am afraid to leave them here. What if one of them slips on the rocks or gets a cramp swimming back? Having witnessed them I feel they are now my responsibility. So I wait while they finish their "rite." I can tell they are cold now, their skin goosefleshed in the moonlight, and impatient to be done. I can't see what they hold up in their hands as offerings, but I can hear their "prayers."

"Let me maintain a B average this term so my mom gets off my back," Vesta says.

"Keep Brian from falling in love with someone else while he's at Exeter," Aphrodite pleads.

Only Athena says her bit too quietly for me to hear, but I see that as she whispers her plea she holds up her left arm, bending the wrist back so that her empty palm is flat to the night sky and the long scar on her forearm shows up livid in the moonlight. It's as if her offering were the scar itself.

Chapter Three

●

"ANOREXIA, SELF-MUTILATION, SUICIDE . . . THREE SIDES of the same picture. Teenage pregnancy, STDs, drug abuse, you name it. It all begins when puberty strikes. Look at your ten-year-old girls—they're bright and confident. Then look at your fifteen- and sixteen-year-olds. Girls' IQs actually plummet during adolescence. And it's getting worse. Did you know that the suicide rate among girls age ten to fourteen rose seventy-five percent between 1979 and 1988?"

Dr. Lockhart leans back in her swivel chair and waits for my reaction. It is difficult to read her expression. She sits with her back to the window so that her body is silhouetted against the silver mirror of the lake. A light rain had begun not long after I returned to my house last night and continued through the dawn, consoling me, somewhat, for the loss of my morning swim. Now the rain has stopped and the sky, though overcast, is a bright, burnished pewter, against which Dr. Lockhart is a darker, blurrier gray. Neither the swimming beach nor the two rocks closest to the shore are visible from her second-floor office in the mansion; they are obscured by the steep rock wall of the Point. I can just make out, however, the third rock where I saw Athena standing last night.

I tell her I hadn't been aware of a rising suicide rate after 1979. I don't mention that by 1979 I was immured at Vassar, poring over my Latin books in the library until midnight. Girls got drunk at the campus bar; my dorm reeked of marijuana; boys wandered in and out of the hall bathroom; girls drove each other to the clinic in Dobbs Ferry for abortions. You could get a prescription for the Pill at the school clinic and no one had heard of AIDS. I memorized Horace and struggled over Latin composition.

"Diderot said to a young girl, 'You all die at fifteen.' "

I am startled by her statement until I realize she isn't speaking literally. I am somewhat familiar with this line of thought—that girls suffer a loss of confidence with the onset of puberty. I recognize the titles of the books that line Dr. Lockhart's shelves. *Meeting at the Crossroads, Reviving Ophelia.* I think of what I had hoped for my life at fourteen, and it isn't so much as if I had died as that I had fallen into a long sleep like a girl in a fairy tale. But I had thought of my case as unique.

"A girl like Ellen is particularly at risk," Dr. Lockhart says.

"Why a girl like Ellen?"

Dr. Lockhart wheels herself over to a gunmetal gray file cabinet and pulls a light green file folder from the middle drawer. She looks at it briefly and slips it back into place.

"The girl's parents are divorced—the father is almost entirely out of the picture and the mother's an alcoholic who spends most of her time in rehab clinics." Dr. Lockhart rattles off these facts as if she's reciting a recipe. I remember what Athena said about her mother *drying out.* "There's an aunt who's the legal guardian, but her solution has been to shuttle the girl from school to school."

"That's too bad," I say. "I knew some girls like that when I went to school here."

"Did you?" Dr. Lockhart studies me for a moment and then smiles. "Maybe you asked them home to spend the holidays with you."

I start to laugh at the idea. Those girls from Albany and Saratoga in their shetland wool sweaters and graduated pearls might have been neglected by their wealthy relatives, but I could only imagine what they would have made of my mother's Campbell's soup casseroles, the plastic covers on the one good couch, the view of the mill from the living room window. I look at Dr. Lockhart and see she's no longer smiling. "No," I admit. "I never thought to ask them home. I guess it *was* lonely here for some of them."

"Imagine every time you got settled at one school and made some friends having to start all over again. A person would eventually give up."

The dry tone has vanished. She really does care about these girls, I realize. "Did you go to boarding school?" I ask.

"Several," she answers. "So I can guess how lonely it's been for Athena—switching schools so often. It's that loneliness that makes a girl susceptible to depression and suicidal urges. It's essential to curb any such tendencies in our girls. Once the idea of suicide breaks out . . ."

"You make it sound like a contagious disease."

"It is a contagious disease, Jane. I've seen it happen. One girl might be playing with the notion of suicide, or indulge in cutting herself as a way of coping with emotional pain, then one of her friends might emulate her and succeed in killing herself. The inevitable drama surrounding such tragedies exerts a morbid pull on these girls. Notice their fascination with death—skull jewelry and black clothing, the whole 'Goth' look."

"Yes, my senior Latin class looks like something out of the Middle Ages, and they almost all have scratches on their arms."

"Do you remember *The Crucible*?"

"The play by Arthur Miller? Of course, but why . . . ?"

"Remember how the Salem girls accused their tormentors of pricking them with pins? When the judges examined the girls' bodies they indeed found scratches and cuts, bite marks, pins sticking in their flesh . . ."

I flinch and Dr. Lockhart pauses. "I know it's not a pleasant topic, Jane," she says, "but it has to be faced. Most of our girls engage in some form of cutting or self-mutilation. Most people don't realize how long such practices have existed."

"No," I say, "I had no idea. How did you . . . ?"

"My thesis topic," she explains. "Self-Mutilation and Witchcraft in Puritan New England." She leans back in her chair and looks out the window at the silvery surface of the lake.

I follow her gaze and once again I think of Athena standing on the rock, holding her arm up to the moon like an offering. A sacrifice.

"Fascinating," I say.

"Oh, it is," she agrees. "The connection still exists. Often the same girls who indulge in self-mutilation practice some form of witchcraft. It's all an attempt to gain control over a world in which they have no power. Even their own emotions, their own bodies, seem out of control. Spells, rites, initiation ceremonies . . . these are all strategies to order the chaos of adolescence."

I think of my three students standing naked on the rock in the lake, asking for help with boyfriends and grades. I think of the S'mores and bangles we used to offer up to the Lady of the Lake.

"Don't adolescent girls always play with this sort of thing? I mean witchcraft and spells? Ouija boards and cootie catchers."

"You're saying you practiced witchcraft with the girls you went to school with?"

"The girls I went to school with?" The question takes me by surprise. "I'm sorry," I say. "I've been thinking about Athena all morning. What does this have to do with my schoolmates?"

Dr. Lockhart wheels her chair in closer to her desk, out of the glare from the lake, and I see her blue eyes narrow on me. She touches the edge of a folder that lies on her desk as if to open it, but then she rests her long, slim fingers on its surface.

"Wasn't there a rash of suicides during your senior year?"

"I wouldn't exactly call it a *rash*," I say perhaps a little too indignantly. I feel as if she has accused *me* of having a rash. I hear the defensive note in my own voice and apparently she can, too.

"Are you uncomfortable talking about this?" she asks.

"I just don't see what it has to do with Athena," I say.

"I had hoped we could draw on your own experience with troubled, suicidal adolescents. Perhaps what you witnessed back then could throw light on your present students' troubles."

I think of what happened during my senior year and instead of light I see murk, the kind of brownish-green murk I see when I open my eyes in the lake. But perhaps Dr. Lockhart is right. Perhaps talking about what happened back then might help me to understand Athena better. And I do want to help Athena.

"There were two students who committed suicide my senior year," I say.

Dr. Lockhart shakes her head sadly. "That must have been very hard on you. What is so unfortunate in these situations is that one suicide—or suicide attempt—spurs another. As I keep trying to tell you, it becomes almost a fad. An epidemic. The girls were roommates, I believe. Weren't you all roommates?"

"We shared a suite, yes. Lucy Toller and I shared one room and Deirdre Hall had the single."

"I believe there was an unsuccessful suicide attempt first."

"Yes, Lucy slit her wrists over Christmas break. She and Deirdre were alone here on campus. It could be pretty bleak."

"The notes I have from the school nurse at the time indicate that Deirdre Hall was particularly upset by the event, especially since Miss Toller chose to slit her wrists in Deirdre's bed."

"Deirdre had the single. I guess Lucy wanted privacy. But yes, I think Deirdre was upset about that."

"Upset enough to make her own suicide attempt. Only hers was successful."

"Yes, she fell from the Point and broke her neck on the ice." I can't help but look up at the outcropping of stone as I speak. Dr. Lockhart follows my gaze. And there we are, both staring at the forty-foot cliff as if we expect to see Deirdre Hall appear on its height and perform her last swan dive. For a moment a picture does appear in my mind: Deirdre standing on the point, her face contorted with rage and fear. I blink away the image and turn my gaze away from the window and back to Dr. Lockhart. "Some people thought it was an accident," I say.

"According to my files her journal indicated otherwise." She flips open the folder on her desk and reads silently for a moment. A breeze from the lake stirs the pages and I can tell they are of the light onion skin we used to have in typing class, not the smooth sheets that people use nowadays in computer printers.

"And then Lucy tried again. She drowned in the lake?"

"Yes, she went through the ice. . . ."

"That could have been an accident as well?"

"Yes, but it wasn't. I was there."

"I see. Why don't you tell me what happened."

I look out at the lake. A fog is rising from the water, whitening the surface of the lake. I can almost imagine it is winter and the lake is already frozen.

"She had a terrible fight with her brother," I say. The words come tumbling out before I can consider whether I really ought to relate this information to Dr. Lockhart. Maybe it is because they are words I rehearsed and repeated so many times. "And then she ran onto the ice, which was breaking apart. . . ."

"What was the fight about?" she asks.

"I only heard part of it and I didn't understand it all." I'm amazed that the well-rehearsed lines are there, tripping off my tongue as if the twenty years that have elapsed since I first delivered them had never passed. Like my Latin declensions, they'd stayed in my memory all these years. "But it had to do with a teacher here."

"Helen Chambers." I notice that Dr. Lockhart doesn't need to consult her notes to produce the name.

"Yes, Helen Chambers. She taught Latin and Greek. She was an amazing teacher. She had us all reciting Greek plays. Our senior year, she put on an aquatic version of *Iphigenia in Aulis* in the lake."

"*In* the lake?"

"Yes, in the lake."

"She sounds remarkable. But why would Lucy and her brother have been arguing about her?"

I shake my head. "I don't really know, but Lucy idealized *Domina* Chambers. We all did. It was thought that Lucy had an unhealthy obsession with her."

"*It was thought?* What do you think?"

The question is eerily like one that Helen Chambers herself would pose. If you tried to hide behind someone else's opinion—the introduction in your Penguin edition of *Antigone*, say, or some predigested litcrit babble from Cliff Notes—she would nail you with those icy blue eyes of hers and ask you—no, demand of you—*What do you think?* And if your answer failed to measure up to her standards for original thought she would look heavenward and shrug her elegant shoulders. "Perhaps you really haven't thought at all, Miss Hudson. Come back to us when you have."

"She could be a bit harsh," I tell Dr. Lockhart.

Dr. Lockhart smiles. "Don't you ever find, Jane, that sometimes a teacher has to be a little harsh?"

"Yes, I agree," I say, but I wonder if I do. I've never been much good at the "tough love" school of teaching. "But it was thought—*I thought*—that she sometimes went too far."

"Well, then perhaps you should think of Helen Chambers when you're dealing with your students. As I'm sure you remember, she was let go."

AFTER MY MEETING WITH DR. LOCKHART I WALK TO THE LODGE for my first-period class. The rain has cleared and the girls who run past me have tied their regulation navy school windbreakers around their waists so that they stream out behind them like shiny, rustling tail feathers. A raucous crowd of eighth graders parts to make way and then regroups behind me never losing the thread of their shouted conversation. I might be a stone parting a stream for all the notice they take of me. It makes me feel good. Like a part of the geography.

It's all I've ever wanted. To feel a part of something. I wonder if this was how Helen Chambers felt, when she came back to teach at

Heart Lake. I know that to me she always seemed the defining spirit of the place.

On my way to my class I pass the art room. I stop just outside the door and watch Tacy Beade setting up for her next class. The room hasn't changed since I went here—the girls say Beady deducts points from your grade if you don't put the art supplies back in their proper places—and neither has Miss Beade. She moves around the room, arranging palettes and easels like a nun performing the stations of the cross. Is this what I want, I wonder, the comfort of teaching in the same place for forty years? To be one of the *old girls*?

My first class is Language Discovery for Sixth Graders. I trade off with the Spanish and German teachers. It's a new idea of Dean Buehl's. This way the kids will have a basis for picking which language they want in seventh grade.

"Think of it as a recruiting opportunity," Dean Buehl had told me. "Make Latin fun. Build up the Latin program and you'll have a job for life."

When I went to Heart Lake Latin was mandatory. The idea of Helen Chambers recruiting is absurd and slightly offensive. I can't imagine Helen Chambers spending two minutes worrying about how to make Latin fun. And yet we all loved her. We would have done anything for her.

I wonder what Helen Chambers would think of how I teach this class. I use a textbook called *Ecce Romani*. Here are the Romans. The title always makes me think of a TV sitcom. Oh, those goofy lovable Romans, with their charming villa in southern Italy and their colorful, perky slaves. There's even an episode in which one of the slaves escapes. When he's caught, he's beaten with a stick *(virga)* and branded on the forehead with the letters FUG, short for *fugitivus*, runaway.

When Dean Buehl first showed me the new books my mouth went dry. All those nights studying declensions and memorizing Catullus hadn't prepared me to talk about the weather in Latin *(Quaenam est tempestas hodie? Mala est.)*

I spent hours in front of the mirror practicing conversational gambits like a nervous teenager preparing for her first date. *Salve! Quid est praenomen tibi? Quis es?*

Now, when I enter my first-period class, I am greeted by a dozen loud voices. *Salve Magistra! Quid agis?* And though I know that *quid agis* means, idiomatically, how are you, this morning, after my meeting with Dr. Lockhart, I hear instead its literal meaning: What are you doing? Why didn't you tell her about what you saw last night? And I have to stop myself from telling my cheerful, beaming, *prepubescent* sixth graders, *"Nescio."* I don't know. I have no idea.

IN THE ADVANCED CLASS THAT DAY I TRY NOT TO STARE AT Athena, Vesta, and Aphrodite, but I find myself stealing surreptitious looks while they read their translations. I think I can detect blue circles under Athena's eyes, but then I know that the girls often affect this sleepless look by smudging kohl under their eyes, which matches the shade of blue lipstick they all favor.

She fumbles, though, in her translation, which is not like her.

"How are you translating *praecipitatur* in line six?" I ask her.

"She fell under the water."

"She?"

"It's the light, not she," Vesta interrupts. "But I don't get it: The light throws down its head under the water? Doesn't *praecipito* mean, like, to fall on your head?"

Aphrodite giggles. "I think you must have fallen on your head last night, Vesta."

Vesta and Athena exchange dangerous glances with Aphrodite, and I find myself, of all things, blushing, as if it were my secret that was threatened. Maybe it is. If they knew that I was there last night what does that say about my authority as a teacher?

"Tace," I tell Aphrodite. *"Praecipitare* means to cast down headlong. In the middle sense it can mean to cast oneself down headlong. In this case it means the light casts itself below the water, or, more idiomatically, the light sinks beneath the waves."

"That's a lot of English words for one Latin word," Athena points out.

"Well, Latin is an economical language, especially when it comes to destruction."

Athena gives me a smile that chills me like a rush of lake water. "That's exactly why we like it," she says.

AFTER CLASS, I WALK TO THE PRESCHOOL TO PICK UP OLIVIA. I am early, so when I come around the corner of the building and see the children on the playground I step into the shadows of a large sycamore so Olivia won't see me yet.

I look for Olivia in the brightly colored knots of children playing together in twos and threes, running and climbing in the mottled shade of the playground. And then I see her, apart from the others, dancing and singing to herself under the pine trees.

She doesn't look unhappy, but the sight of her alone worries me. It reminds me of something I can't at first put my finger on. Maybe, I reason, it's just that she reminds me of myself at her age. Until I met Lucy Toller in the ninth grade I had no friends.

Olivia's dance is punctuated now with little swipes to the ground, as if she were picking flowers, only I can see from here that her fingers barely graze the pine needles. It's a charade of flower-picking, no doubt part of some make-believe. She is so absorbed in her game that she is wandering farther and farther from the playground, into the deeper woods that surround the school grounds and slope down to the lake. And that's when I realize what she reminds me of: Persephone, straying from her companions to pick flowers on the shores of Lake Pergus, where she was snatched by Hades.

I step out of the shadows to call her, but just as I open my mouth I hear one of the student aides call her back to the playground. It takes a minute for the sound of her name to penetrate her daydream, but then she skips toward the older girl eagerly. I see the aide lean over to tell Olivia something and Olivia nodding. I can tell by the

way Olivia's eyes slant away from the aide that she is being reprimanded for straying away. Good, I think. But I'll have to talk to her
myself tonight.

I follow the children as they leave the playground. Dismissal is
from inside and I'll have to wait while they sing their good-bye song
and collect their artwork. I find myself wandering under the same
trees Olivia had been playing near. I can see why she likes the spot. It
is cool under the pines and the ground is golden with dried pine
needles. I kick the needles and unearth something thin and gold and
metallic.

Stooping down to pick it up, I am reminded again of Persephone picking her flowers, only it isn't a flower I retrieve from the
pine needles, it is a hairpin, or, rather, several hairpins linked together. When I lift them up into the light I recognize the pattern.
Two U-shaped hairpins linked together with a bobby pin bisecting
the top one. It looks like the head of a horned animal holding something in its mouth. I shiver, not because of the shade now but
because I've seen this particular configuration before, but not for
twenty years.

Chapter Four

●

WE CALLED THEM *CORNICULA*, WHICH, AS LUCY FOUND
in Cassell's *New Latin*, meant little horned ones. Deirdre
used to say she had invented them when she found Helen Chambers's hairpin in the love seat in the Lake Lounge. I have always
thought, though, that they were a truly cooperative endeavor, prod-
uct of a tripartite genesis.

We were in the suite's one single room, Deirdre's room, studying
for our Latin midterm, fall semester, junior year, drinking Deirdre's
tea to stay awake. She had the single in our suite because of a note
from her mother's psychiatrist saying Deirdre had boundary issues
and severe migraines. Lucy used to say it was overkill, that she ought
to have stuck to one thing or the other: boundary issues or migraines.

Deirdre's habits, which Lucy viewed as affectations, could be
annoying. Her parents had something to do with foreign affairs
and she'd spent her childhood in various remote corners of Asia.
She wore an antique kimono to the shower room instead of the
frayed and stained terry robes the rest of us shuffled around in. She
liked to dress in outfits composed entirely of silk scarves clinging provocatively to her well-developed figure. It used to make me
nervous looking at her in class because I always thought some piece
was about to slip off, but the only time they came off was on our

nocturnal swims, and then our path down to the lake would be strewn with her discarded silks.

She kept two large China tea tins on her bureau, one filled with pot, the other, and this was considered odder by Heart Lake standards, filled with loose tea. She was as particular about her teas as she was about her marijuana. Sometimes, listening to her rattle on about estate provinces and curing processes, it was difficult to know which she was talking about. I suspected she mixed more than her talk about the two, and there was many a morning I spent dazed and light-headed after drinking a cup of her dark smoky tea and many a night I spent sleepless after smoking one of her exquisitely rolled joints.

On this night Deirdre's tea had a minty bite to it that set my teeth on edge and made the objects in her room glow around the edges. In between lines of Catullus I found myself mesmerized by the texture of the hemp mats on the floor and at one point the ceremonial dancers on a Balinese tapestry seemed to take a spin around the floor.

We were translating Catullus's poem 2, the one where Catullus says he's jealous of Lesbia's pet sparrow. Deirdre claimed that the poem was really about Catullus's jealousy of Lesbia's female sexuality. Lucy, as usual, was annoyed by Deirdre's reduction of nearly everything in Latin to sex. Having failed to interest Lucy in her interpretation of Catullus, Deirdre cast about the room for something that might capture Lucy's approbation. Her eye alighted on a bit of folded paper stuck between the pages of the Tantra Asana that Deirdre kept on the night table beside her bed.

She slipped the paper, which had been folded into the shape of a flower, out of the book and held it up in front of Lucy.

"Do you know what's in this?" Deirdre asked.

"Some illegal substance, no doubt. Honest, Deirdre, you're going to be dead by twenty if you keep this up."

"Better a short life full of glory than a long inglorious one," Deirdre quoted. Deirdre was fond of quotes having to do with death. After sex, death was her favorite subject. She kept a silk-covered notebook filled with quotes from the ancients and moderns on the subject of early death. "Anyway, it's not drugs." Deirdre tugged at one petal of the flower and the whole thing blossomed in the palm of her hand, only to reveal another packet folded in the shape of a grasshopper. Deirdre loved this sort of thing, secrets within secrets, Chinese boxes, *sanctum sanctorum*. She knew Lucy did, too. With a flick of her long lacquered fingernail, the grasshopper sprang open. In the center of the folds lay a single hairpin.

I started to giggle. The unveiling had been so theatrical; the result was anticlimactic. Lucy, I noticed, wasn't laughing.

"Where'd you find it?" she asked, touching one finger to the coppery wire.

"Behind the cushions of the love seat in the Lake Lounge. Where *she* always sits."

Lucy lifted the hairpin out of its paper grasshopper carcass and held it aloft. A single strand of gold hair clung to the metal for a moment and then slipped to the floor where it evaporated into the straw mats. We all three leaned forward at the same time to catch it, but Deirdre plucked it from the matting with a quick dart of her fingers, nimble as a child picking up onesies at jacks.

She held it up to Lucy's short hair.

"See, it's the same color."

"You can't tell from one strand," Lucy said, but I knew, with a pang, that she was pleased. That Deirdre had pleased her. To be like Helen Chambers in any small way was all any of us wanted. To find some hidden affinity, or to acquire one by emulation, we studied her more carefully than we studied our declensions and conjugations (and we worked on those hard enough, if only to please her). If Helen Chambers left a cardigan draped over a chair back one of us was sure to read its label. If she left her teacup in the Lake Lounge after four o'clock tea, we read the tea bag she'd chosen and studied the lipstick smudge left on the rim. Later, when we were invited to her apartment in Main Hall, we memorized the book titles on her bookshelves, the album covers stacked by her phonograph, and the perfume bottles on her dresser. We amassed our common knowledge into one eclectic but (to us) cohesive portrait: She wore Shalimar and read a Dickens novel every Christmas. She had gone to Vassar and always stayed at the Vassar Club when she went into the city, which she did twice a year to see the ballet (*Giselle* was her favorite, too) and shop at Altman's for the simple but beautifully cut black jersey dresses she favored. Her favorite novel was *Persuasion* by Jane Austen and her middle name was Liddell, which, Lucy felt sure, must be her mother's maiden name. We liked to think she was related to the Liddell of Liddell & Scott's Greek Lexicon, the father of Alice Liddell— the model for Alice in Wonderland. Wouldn't it be fitting, we thought, if she were related to Alice! But the one thing we never knew was how long her hair was because she always wore it twisted into a knot at the nape of her neck.

Deirdre held the strand of hair between the thumb and forefinger of each hand. "I already measured it," she said, "twenty-seven inches long. It must hang below her ass."

I thought Lucy would be most interested in the hair, but instead she held up the hairpin so that its prongs faced up. The metal was crimped halfway down each side.

"That's to hold the hair better," I said. "Look." I took a pin out of my own hair. I had started wearing it up that term because Lucy said it made me look more scholarly. The pin was shaped the same but was darker to match my plain brown hair. I took my pin, prongs down, and linked it with the one in Lucy's hand. It dangled there limply. Lucy took the single bobby pin she used to hold back the bangs she was growing out that year and slipped it over the prongs of the top hairpin—Helen Chambers's pin. Then she held the thing up by the end of the bobby pin.

"It looks like some kind of animal," Deirdre said. "A goat, maybe."

"It's a talisman," Lucy said. "Of the Horned One. A . . ." she paused, looking into the middle distance, a look she often had right before she read her Latin translation, as if a page invisible to all but her was unfurling in the air. "A corniculum. A little horned one. From now on this will be the sign we leave for each other."

"A sign of what?" Deirdre asked. "What will it mean when we find one?"

Lucy looked at both of us. I became conscious of how we were sitting, cross-legged in a tight triangle, our knees nearly touching, each of us leaning into the middle. Out of the corner of my eye I thought I saw the tapestry dancers take another spin around the room and then Lucy's gaze brought me back, told me to pay attention, made the room still again.

"A sign that we're always here for each other," Lucy said.

I saw Deirdre smile. It was what she wanted, a sign of affirmation from Lucy (I knew that I was beside the point, but she'd take me because I came with Lucy). It's what I wanted, too, of course, but there was something in Lucy's tone that unnerved me, that made what she said less a promise of friendship than a threat of constant surveillance.

IT'S A SENSE OF BEING WATCHED THAT I HAVE NOW, holding the little hairpin totem up so it catches the light slanting down through the tall pines. I look toward the lower school, but all the children have gone inside to collect their things. I can hear, faintly, the good-bye song they sing at the end of each day.

"So long, so long, it won't be so long till we see each other again. . . ."

Deirdre and I used to wait here to meet Lucy when she worked at the lower school as an aide. The younger girls would follow her out the door, begging for another song, or another story. I remember there was one girl in particular, a skinny girl with pale, colorless hair like dried straw, who would trail after Lucy dejectedly until Lucy would go back and promise that she'd be back the next day.

"Do you really *promise*?" the girl, standing at the edge of the woods, would yell.

"Yes, Albie, I *promise*," Lucy would yell back, drawing out *promise* as if it were a magic word that could bind the speaker just by its utterance.

I look behind me toward the lake, which glitters between the tree trunks like slivers of a broken mirror. The water pulses so brightly that when I turn away my vision is slashed with dark jagged shards. I have a hard time spotting Olivia in the crowd of brightly dressed children coming out of the school now. For a moment my heart pounds with the fear that she's not there, that when I go up to her teacher she will look at me blankly and tell me that someone else has taken her . . . didn't I send a note saying it was all right? A ridiculous thought. I saw her go into the school five minutes ago.

Still, I am so panicked that the faces of the children blur into bright spots and I can't make out Olivia's face until she rushes right into me. I can barely hear what her teacher is trying to tell me, something she doesn't want Olivia to hear, I guess, from the exaggerated mouthing adults use when they're whispering secrets in front of children.

". . . a bad day . . ." I make out. ". . . overwrought . . ." I nod and say something about Olivia not getting much sleep the night before, how we're still getting used to the new house, excuses that come easy and are, in their way, true.

"She's probably just tired," I conclude.

"I am not," Olivia snaps, as tired children will when told they're tired.

"Okay, sweetie," I say, taking Olivia's hand. "Let's go home." I steer her away from the school. "Let's go home and have a snack. We'll make cookies . . ." I say before I remember I don't have the supplies for baking. In my mind we were heading home to the kitchen in our old house where the matching ceramic canisters were filled with flour and oatmeal and chocolate chips.

"I want to go down to the magic rock and look for tadpoles," she says.

"Okay," I say, glad to get out of the baking promise. Tomorrow I'll go to the store and buy flour and baking powder and cookie sheets.

". . . and then the tadpoles turn into frogs," Olivia is telling me, "and Mrs. Crane says we'll have tadpoles in our class so we can watch it happen. . . ."

Olivia drops my hand and runs ahead on the path, chattering all the while about frogs and tadpoles. I'm left alone in the woods I used to wander with Lucy and Deirdre. We often came down this path to the swimming beach, and yes, sometimes we came at night and swam out to the farthest sister stone. We made our own sacrifices to the Lake Goddess. And once Deirdre introduced us to it, we were often stoned.

Olivia disappears around a bend in the path, but I can still hear her voice. She is singing one of her made-up songs.

When my students ask me what the school was like when I went here, I know they expect to hear that we worked harder, the rules were stricter, more was expected of us. Some of that is true. It was a given that you'd go from Heart Lake to a Seven Sister college. Our teachers even hinted to us that after our preparation at Heart Lake we'd find the work in college easy. They were right about that. No test I ever took in college was harder than *Domina* Chambers's Latin final, or Miss North's history orals, or the slide test in Tacy Beade's art class. But what the girls don't guess—and I can't tell them—is that when I went here in the seventies the rules were already changing. In some ways, things were looser. The Pill had become available, but no one had heard of AIDS yet. There was no war on drugs, because the teachers didn't even suspect we had access to them. Cigarettes were vaguely tolerated as a bad habit, like chewing your nails or wearing laddered tights. Even the school uniform had given way to a haphazardly enforced dress code that specified skirt length but neglected to make bras mandatory.

I've come to a bend in the path where the path divides in two. To the left the path goes up to our house, to the right it slopes down steeply to the lake. I stop here and realize I don't know which way Olivia has gone. She'd been talking about seeing the tadpoles, so she probably went straight down to the lake. I stand still and listen for her voice, but the only thing I hear is the wind sifting through the dry pine needles on the forest floor.

I still the flicker of panic that licks at my brain like a small flame. Panic. I hear Helen Chambers's voice telling us the word originated from the god Pan. The Greeks thought he inspired the unreasoning fear that sneaked up on mortals in wild places.

I head down the path to the lake. The sun has gone behind the clouds again and the water looks flat and gray. If she went to the house, I figure, she'll be all right for a minute or two, but if she went to the lake . . . I decide not to finish that thought.

The swimming beach is empty. I look down at the sand for footprints and see some, but they're too large to be Olivia's. I realize that they're probably my own, made last night when I watched Athena, Vesta, and Aphrodite on the rocks. I am about to turn back to look for Olivia at the house when I hear a small splash. The sound seems to come from the farthest edge of the Point and when I look in that direction something white flashes briefly and then is gone. Just the sun glinting off the rock, I think, turning back toward the steps, but then I see her. Olivia is standing on the farthest rock. Her back is to me and she stands on the very edge of the far side of the rock. I start to call her name, but then think I'll startle her and she'll fall into the water. The lake, I know, is deep on the other side of that rock.

I kick off my shoes and wade into the water, moving slowly so as not to make any noise. The water is warm at the shallow edge, but as soon as I'm up to my waist I can feel the icy cold currents from the underground springs that feed the lake. I stroke out, keeping my head up, eyes on Olivia, just like Miss Pike, our gym teacher and swimming coach, taught us in Lifesaving.

I approach the rock from the shallow end because I am afraid that if Olivia sees me she might be startled and fall into the water. I am too scared to take my eyes off Olivia even for an instant to look down for a place to put my feet, so I feel the rock with my toes. My feet hit something hard and slimy that falls away when I try to put my weight down. I try again and find a flat rock where I can get enough purchase to lift myself up onto the rock, but my foot, numb from the cold, slips just as I'm pulling myself up.

I hit the rock hard with my stomach and make a sound like "ooof." Olivia hears me and turns. For a moment I see fear in her face, but then it dissolves into giggles.

"Mommy, why are you swimming in your clothes?"

I crawl over to her and pull her down to the rock before answering. "Well, Miss, I could ask you the same question." I try to make my voice sound light, a gentle reprimand for getting her good clothes wet, but when I pick up the hem of her dress I notice that her dress—and her sneakers and white ankle socks—are bone dry.

Chapter Five

●

AFTER I DROP OLIVIA OFF AT SCHOOL THE NEXT MORN-
ing I go back to the swimming beach. It is getting late in the
year to swim—already the water by the shore is coated with a skin of
dead leaves and a cold mist, which I push away to enter the water—
but I am determined to keep to my routine as long as this spell of
Indian summer lasts. The lake is cold even in summer, but since I've
been back I've gotten in the water as often as I can. And, I tell myself, I need to have a look at those rocks again to figure out how
Olivia got to the farthest one without getting her clothes wet.

When I asked her she told me, first, that she flew. Then she told
me that it was the Queen of the Wilis who came in a magical boat
and carried her to the rock. Maybe Mitch was right when he said I
read her too many fairy tales. When I demanded that she tell me the
truth she burst into tears and said I was mean for not believing her. I
told her Mommy was tired and couldn't have this argument right
now. (Talking about myself in the third person is a clear sign that my
patience is slipping.) She responded by throwing her chocolate milk
on the floor. I screamed at her to go to her room and she told me she
couldn't because her room wasn't in this house. I pulled her up by
the armpits and said, "March, young lady." She folded her arms across

her chest and stamped her foot. I gave her a little push, just to get her going, and she crumpled to floor, screaming that I had shoved her.

Things went downhill from there. Afterward I thought of what she might say to her father.

When I think of how our fights might sound, or look, to an outsider I go hot with shame. The cold water of the lake is a relief, the impact of the cold draining my body of any feeling but the rush of the cold. I stroke out past the first two rocks and then to the third, measuring the distance with my eye. There is no way that anyone, let alone a four-year-old child, could jump from the second rock to the third rock. My head is dizzy with trying to solve the problem of how Olivia made it to the rock. I float on my back, arching my neck so that the lake soaks the top of my scalp, and then I turn over and strike out for the deep water.

The lake is a half mile across from the swimming beach to the south end. When Lucy and I were here it was a graduation requirement to swim back and forth twice. Now the swimming area is roped off and the girls are only permitted to do a lake swim accompanied by a lifeboat.

My girls believe that this rule is because of the three sisters and their suicidal pull on Heart Lake girls. They tell stories about the girls who have drowned in the lake since the Crevecoeur sisters and claim that their spirits still haunt the lake. They say you can see their ghostly forms in the mist that comes off the water on an autumn morning like this. Their faces have been seen, the story goes, peering out from beneath the ice in winter.

When I look up I see I am off course. I always swim with my eyes closed because there is something about looking into that bottomless green that unnerves me. Even with my eyes shut I see it—a sunlit grass green so bright you could imagine the light came from the bottom of the lake and not the other way around.

Halfway across the lake I pause and tread water. The lake is seventy-two feet deep here and I can feel the cold of that depth pulling at my feet. When they pulled Deirdre Hall out of the lake she had only been in the water a few hours. She didn't look so bad, considering. But when Lucy and her brother Matt drowned in the lake it took longer to find their bodies. The night they drowned the temperature dropped to ten below zero and a blizzard blew down from Canada and held the school snowbound for three days. When the police could finally start looking for their bodies they had to bring an icebreaker from the river to tear up the ice before they could dredge the lake. It took five more days for them to find the bodies. They had died clinging to each other, their arms and legs wrapped around each other and then they had frozen like that. Their mother told me later that she had to have them buried together because they would have had to break their bones to pry them apart.

This is the coldest part of the lake—Miss Buehl used to tell us there was an underground spring that fed into the Schwanenkill at the south end of the lake. In the winter it makes a thin spot in the ice and in the summer it makes a cold spot in the water. It is almost unbearable staying still in it, but I do this every morning as a kind of penance. I think of it as an appeasement to whatever local genius inhabits Heart Lake. I don't believe in the Lake Goddess we gave our S'mores and bracelets to all those years ago, but the Romans have taught me something about *lares et penates*, household gods and nature spirits, and the importance of giving them their due. Instead of offering them crumbs and bangles I offer myself—my body flayed by the cold water.

There's a spot in my left arm where my shoulder was once dislocated that begins to ache in the cold water. When I feel I have stayed long enough—when the ache in my arm feels like icy fingers pulling at my flesh—I stroke forward with my arms and kick my legs out behind me. And hit something solid in the water. I spin around and see, directly in front of me, a white forehead—hair slicked back and pale eyes—rising out of the water. An arm arcs out of the water and grabs my hair. Icy cold fingers graze my scalp with a touch I've felt in nightmares. I open my mouth to scream and swallow water instead, the cold mineral taste flooding my brain with fear. I feel myself slipping under and grab the arm and twist it away from my hair. It's only when I see the blue spiral on the hand that I realize who it is.

"Athena," I say in the same voice I'd use if she were talking out of turn in class.

"Miss Hudson!" Her lips are at water level and she spits a little as she says my name. "Oh my God, Miss Hudson. I didn't see you. There's the fog and I was swimming with my eyes closed."

We've pulled away from each other, beating the water with our arms.

"Well, you would hardly expect to run into someone in the middle of the lake. Don't you know you're not supposed to swim alone."

I think only to admonish her, but she turns her head fractionally toward shore and I think I might hear someone else moving in the water, but the fog is so thick now that I can't be sure.

"Yes," she says, "I know. You won't tell, will you? I mean about me swimming across the lake."

I had forgotten for a moment that it was against the rules.

"Well, you know it's very dangerous to swim alone, Athena." I mean only to withhold my cooperation for a moment—just long enough to preserve my teacher's authority. I've been thinking since my talk with Dr. Lockhart that I ought to be a little stricter with the girls.

"One more infraction and I'm out of here," she says.

I notice that Athena's chin is trembling and I'm afraid she's about to cry, but then I realize that it's her teeth chattering from the cold. Her lips are bluish-purple, the color of dead skin. I know why I subject myself to this cold water every morning, but I wonder what self-punishing instinct brings Athena into the lake. Perhaps it's only a teenage dare.

"It's OK," I say. "I won't turn you in."

The blue lips press together in what might be a smile or just an attempt to keep her teeth from chattering. I feel the beginning of a cramp in my right calf muscle and it makes me wonder what I would do if Athena got a cramp out here. Would I be able to get her to shore? We took lifesaving training every year with Miss Pike, but it has been years since I practiced. I was never any good at it. Once when I was "saving" Lucy I kicked her in the side so hard she wasn't able to play field hockey for two weeks.

"We'd better swim back," I say.

Athena turns her head, not in the direction of the swimming beach but toward the opposite shore. I wonder if she is supposed to meet someone there. I remember that on the south end of the lake, just across from the swimming beach, is the Schwanenkill icehouse where Lucy and I used to go meet her brother, Matt. I wonder if there is some boy from town that Athena has arranged to meet there. Well, whoever it is would just have to wait. I am not about to leave Athena out in the lake alone. I feel responsible for her. If I don't turn her in and she keeps swimming out here I *am* responsible for anything that might happen to her.

"Come on," I say in as stern a teacher's voice as I can muster between chattering teeth.

Swimming back I stay a little behind her. I swim with my head up so I can keep an eye on her. She is a good swimmer, but I know that is no guarantee. Good swimmers can drown, too.

When we approach the swimming beach Athena swims to the west end of the cove, to the place under the Point where there's a shallow cave in the rock. It's where I left my clothes this morning. Athena reaches behind a rock and pulls out a sweatshirt and jeans. I find my clothes behind another rock. I feel her watching me, taking in my hiding place and the secrecy it implies. I am not supposed to be here any more than she is.

I pull my sweatshirt over my wet suit and climb into my jeans without toweling off. I feel the wet seeping through the seat of my pants almost immediately. When I turn to Athena she is finger-combing her wet hair, the blue spirals on her hand weaving in and out between the wet ropes of hair. The color has returned to her lips. I have a sudden, unbidden image of Helen Chambers in her apartment in Main Hall taking down her hair and combing it while Lucy and I watched. She had handed the brush to Lucy and asked if she wouldn't mind combing her hair out.

I remember, too, what Dr. Lockhart said at the end of our meeting the day before.

Think of Helen Chambers when you're dealing with your students.

I'M FIVE MINUTES LATE FOR MY NINE O'CLOCK CLASS. I quickly scan the hall to see if anyone has noticed, but luckily Myra Todd is off first period and Gwen Marsh is also late—when I stick my head in her class her girls are either writing in their journals or reading. I go into my room and tell my ninth graders to translate the next lesson in *Ecce Romani.* When they finish that I let them read—*Gwen does,* I think—because I'm not up to much in the way of teaching. I can't help myself from doing what Dr. Lockhart advised—I think of Helen Chambers.

Specifically I think about how she ended her tenure at Heart Lake.

After two of her students, and the brother of one of her students, ended up dead in the lake, an inquest was held to look into Miss Chambers's professional behavior. The effects of the two dead girls were examined and students were interviewed. Deirdre Hall had kept that journal with quotes about premature death and suicide. Several of the quotes were either attributed directly to Helen Chambers or Deirdre had credited her teacher as the supplier of the quote. Lucy hadn't kept a journal but she had written a letter to her brother the week before their deaths. In it she told Matt that *Domina* Chambers had opened her eyes to a secret that had changed everything for her, *for the both of them,* she wrote. *When I tell you what it is you'll understand why we have always felt different from everybody else. The ordinary rules of the world don't apply to us.*

The board asked Miss Chambers to explain what her student meant by this enigmatic letter. Into what secrets had Miss Chambers initiated this young girl? Miss Chambers declined to answer the board's questions. She said it was a private matter between her student and herself and she couldn't discuss it.

Miss Chambers's students and colleagues were called in for questioning. We were all called in. We waited in a row of chairs that had been placed along the wall outside the Music Room. The cold weather and storms that had delayed the dredging of the lake had broken and it was unseasonably warm. The school grounds were awash in melted snow and slush. The foyer floor was gritty with mud and broken glass (someone had broken the fanlight over the front doors) and we sweated in our Fair Isle sweaters. We were told not to speak with one another. No one was allowed to discuss the questions they had been asked in the Music Room. Whenever a girl came out of the Music Room she went out the front door without looking back at the rest of us. Wet, *lakey* air gusted into the foyer and we all sniffed the breeze like dogs scenting game until the door slammed shut and we were left in the stale, overheated hallway, the boarded-up fanlight staring back at us like the blinded eye of the Cyclops.

I was the last to go because, I assumed, as the roommate of the two dead girls I would know the most. When it was my turn I went into the room and sat at the single chair that had been placed in front of the long dining room table behind which the members of the board sat. Helen Chambers was there, a little apart, in a chair in front of a window. A dark figure silhouetted in the bright glare of the melting lake ice.

It was odd seeing her sitting apart. The board was made up almost exclusively of "old girls." Truly a jury of her peers, it was a club to which she'd not only belonged, but seemed to epitomize: women of indeterminate ages, who favored frumpily elegant dresses and wore their hair in untidy buns or cut boyishly short. They'd all gone to good women's colleges after graduating from Heart Lake and gone on to get a master's degree or some apprenticeship in the arts. There was Esther Macintosh, the English teacher, who had gone to Mount Holyoke and was supposed to be working on a book about Emily Dickinson. She even dressed like Emily Dickinson, in high-necked white blouses, her lank brown hair parted severely in the middle. Tacy Beade, the art teacher, worked her way through Sarah Lawrence as an artist's model. There was a certain slide—shown only in Honors Art—of an abstract expressionist nude that was purported to be of her. Dean Gray, Celeste Buehl, Meryl North, and even Elsa Pike, the chunky gym coach, were all there in almost identical black dresses and graduated pearl necklaces. Silhouetted against the windows they looked like a row of crows perched on a telephone wire.

I fixed my eyes above their heads on the portrait of India Crevecoeur and her family, but instead of looking at India I found myself looking at Iris Crevecoeur, the little girl who'd died of the flu. She stood a few feet away from the rest of her family, small and dark where her sisters were tall and blond, fussed over by a family servant who seemed to be trying to tie the sash at her waist. She looked as miserable and as lost as I felt.

And for the first time I realized that even though Helen Chambers was one of them—one of the old girls—she also stood apart. The black dresses she wore were cut better, her pearls had a softer gleam. She was a little smarter and much more beautiful than any of them. And now they would make her pay for that. Even before the first question I knew what the board members believed. I knew what they wanted to believe.

Did Miss Chambers encourage drug use? Miss North asked.

Only for sacred, not recreational purposes, I answered.

Did Miss Chambers encourage free sex and homosexuality? Miss Beade asked.

She said the same rules didn't apply to everybody—like in *Antigone*—and, I quoted, proud to have remembered the words, "Which of us can say what the gods hold wicked?"

Had my friends been unhealthily obsessed with their teacher, Miss Chambers? Miss Macintosh asked.

I told them about the strand of hair we found. I told them about the used tea bags we stole and the lists we kept of things we knew about *Domina* Chambers.

Did Miss Chambers encourage this obsession? Miss Pike asked.

I told them about the private teas that she invited Lucy and Deirdre and me to and how she then invited just me and Lucy and, finally, just Lucy. I told them that Lucy had stopped sleeping. She seemed upset when she came home from these teas, but she wouldn't tell me why.

Miss Buehl picked up a piece of thin blue paper. I noticed that her hand was shaking. *This is what Lucy wrote to her brother the week before she died: "Domina Chambers has told me something that changes everything. When she told me, I understood why I've always felt different from everybody else. The ordinary rules of the world just don't apply." Do you know what she meant?* Miss Buehl asked.

I told them no, I didn't know. That was true enough. I didn't know what she'd meant, but I knew what it sounded like.

Is that what she was fighting about with her brother when she ran out onto the ice?

I didn't answer right away. I couldn't tell them what Lucy and Matt had argued about on the lake. So I did what was easier. I agreed with Miss Buehl. I told them they had been arguing about *Domina* Chambers, but that I hadn't really understood what it was all about.

I saw Miss North and Miss Beade exchange a knowing look. Then they told me they didn't have any other questions and that I should go and finish studying for my finals. *We see you have a scholarship for Vassar for next year,* Miss Buehl said kindly. *You're a smart girl; you shouldn't let these unfortunate events interfere with your future plans.*

I left without looking in Helen Chambers's direction. I kept my eyes on the floor as I walked past the line of chairs in the foyer even though they were now empty. I saw specks of red and blue and yellow glass glittering on the floor—tiny fragments of the stained-glass heart and the school's motto: *Cor te reducit.* Not me, I thought, I'm never coming back here.

Outside the wind was blowing off the melting ice in the lake. I never saw Helen Chambers after that day. Dean Gray announced at dinner that night that all of us at Heart Lake must put the incident behind us and never talk about it again, lest the reputation of the school be irrevocably damaged. (Of course the damage was done. Already parents were pulling their daughters out of the school, not even waiting for the end of term.) She said that Miss Chambers had been *let go*. When I heard the words I imagined a hand releasing its grip on another hand and I felt something slip away, and that was as much as I knew about how Helen Chambers had ended up.

Athena doesn't come to class. I ask Vesta and Aphrodite if they know where she is and they both shrug. I assume they're covering up for that early morning swim Athena took. It may be my imagination, but the advanced girls seem sullen today. Perhaps it is the weather. This spell of Indian summer we have been enjoying seems to be drawing to a close. A fitful wind rattles the windows of the classroom and I can see storm clouds massing on the eastern shore of the lake. There hasn't been a glimmer of sun since yesterday afternoon. The thought jars something in my memory—a flash of white on the Point just before I saw Olivia stranded on the rock. I'd thought it was the sun glinting off the rock, but now I remember that the sky had been overcast. Could it have been a rowboat just rounding the Point? Could it have been one of my students—maybe three of my students?—who rowed Olivia out to that rock? I look at Vesta and Aphrodite, noticing the deep circles under their eyes that look real, not kohl-induced. If they're sneaking out to the rocks at night, might they also take a boat out onto the lake? They look edgy to me, but then, so do all the girls. When called on, the girls whisper their translations, which are lost under the hiss of the steam heat. When I ask them to speak up they get nervous and seem to think they have translated their pieces wrong. They turn their sentences around and come up with unintelligible messes. When I try to unravel their syntax I can hear an irritation in my voice I hadn't even known I was feeling. I give up and tell them to read quietly until the end of the period. Several of them put their heads on their desks and fall asleep. I let them, hoping Myra Todd doesn't come by and peep through my door window.

At lunchtime I commit the unpardonable sin of dining alone. I purchase peanut butter crackers and a Coke from a vending machine in the lodge basement and go down to the swimming beach. I stare out at the three sister rocks and across the lake to the south shore, where I can just make out the shape of the icehouse. The county extension agent used to keep her boat there. During Christmas break senior year, Lucy and I took the boat out and rowed it all the way across the lake almost to the Point. I'd written the whole episode down in my journal. The journal that I'd lost.

A wind from the north is whipping the water against the three sisters. I watch a flock of Canada geese land on the lake and take off again. When I walk back to the lodge for my last class of the afternoon I think I have gotten things into perspective.

One of the girls—one of my students—has perhaps found my journal and realized that I was involved in two deaths during my senior year, three if you count Matt Toller. I have to face the fact that it might very well be Athena. The "rite" I witnessed on the three sisters indicates an interest in the suicide legend. Although I can't figure out what she hopes to gain by bombarding me with these relics of my past—the journal entry, the corniculum—and luring my daughter out onto one of the rocks, I can only assume she has some plan to blackmail me or somehow compromise my authority as a teacher. Let's face it, my authority has already been compromised.

I think of what Dr. Lockhart said, that sometimes a teacher has to be a little harsh.

I decide to go to Dr. Lockhart and tell her everything. Then we'll go to Dean Buehl. I imagine that I will be reprimanded, but I don't think I have done anything to merit my dismissal.

With a clear plan in my head, I feel better already. When I open my classroom door, though, my calm dissolves at the sight of Dr. Lockhart seated at my desk leafing through my homework folder.

When she looks up and those cool blue eyes narrow on me I feel a chill gust of arctic air.

"Bad news," she says. "Ellen Craven has tried to kill herself. She's been taken to the hospital in Corinth."

I almost ask *who?* before realizing she's talking about Athena.

Chapter Six

●

I FIND ATHENA SHROUDED IN WHITE. SNOWY WHITE SHEETS are pulled up to her chin. Her arms, which lie on top of the sheets, are bandaged from the tips of her fingers to the crooks of her elbows. Both arms. She is sleeping, or at least I hope it is sleep and not a coma.

Outside the hospital window I can see that the sky above the paper mill has gone blank and white as well. Driving here in Dr. Lockhart's car, I noticed that the sky in the west was growing overcast. Now it looks like it might snow. Only this morning Athena and I swam in the lake and now the sky is threatening snow. I know from growing up here, on the edge of the Adirondacks, that such shifts of weather are possible. (The night Matt and Lucy drowned had been as warm as a spring night and the next day we got one of the worst snowstorms in the area's history.) Still, I find the change *stunning*, although perhaps not as stunning as the change in Athena—from the strong swimmer of this morning to this pale shrouded invalid.

"Is she sleeping?" I ask Dr. Lockhart, who is standing at the window looking out at the clouds gathering above the lake.

"She's not in a coma," she replies. "She regained consciousness briefly after her stomach was pumped. She didn't take enough sleeping pills to put her in a coma."

"She took sleeping pills *and* slit her wrists?" In my mind I hear Lucy's cool, assessing voice: *overkill.*

"Yes, I find that distressing as well. Many experts believe that the more violent the means of suicide the more it's meant as a kick in the face to the survivors. 'This is how badly I hurt,' the victim is saying, 'this is how badly I want out.' "

"But she's alive," I remind Dr. Lockhart. Or perhaps I am reminding myself. Saturated in white, her skin pale as the sky outside, her lips still stained with the bluish lipstick she habitually wears, my student looks dead.

Dr. Lockhart dismisses my comment with an impatient wave of her hand. "Only because I decided to check up on her when she didn't show up at breakfast today."

For all my concern about the girls it had never occurred to me to seek them out at meals.

"You found her?"

"Yes, so I can attest to the violence of her attempt. She used a steak knife we think she stole from the kitchen when she did her clean-up shift last night. She severed both arteries. Thank goodness it happened before the weather got worse." Dr. Lockhart gestures toward the lowering sky outside the window. "I can't imagine what we would have done with her if we'd been snowbound. I've heard that happened once."

I nod. "When Lucy cut her wrists. We couldn't get her to the hospital. Celeste Buehl herself had to suture them."

Dr. Lockhart shakes her head. "I didn't think Ellen would make it, not with all the blood she lost. They'll have to pull up the floorboards in that room to get it all out. I don't know what to do about my dress."

I give her a puzzled look and she opens the long charcoal gray coat she has been wearing since I found her in my classroom, and had kept closed during the drive here. Under it she is wearing a dress I take to be burgundy. I think it is an unusual choice of color for her until I realize it's blood.

"I haven't had a chance to change," she says, no doubt seeing the horror on my face. "I had to call her aunt, who's at a spa in California, and then I wanted to talk to you."

"Me?" I want Dr. Lockhart to close her coat, but she leaves it open.

"After our conversation about Miss Craven I thought you might be able to help me explain *this* to her aunt." She says *this* and gestures to Athena's somnolent form. "When was the last time you saw Ellen?"

"Ellen?"

Dr. Lockhart looks at me as if I've taken leave of my senses and I do just about the worst thing I could do. I laugh.

"It's just that I think of the girls by the Latin names they take. She's Athena to me."

"Hm. That's not a Latin name."

"I know, but I let them pick classical names and this year the girls all wanted goddesses."

"That's very interesting. Are they into goddess worship? Do you talk about that in class? Goddess worship? Pagan rites? Wicca covens?"

"*Wicca covens?* What would that have to do with Latin?"

Dr. Lockhart shrugs. Her coat slips off one thin shoulder and I see that the blood goes at least halfway down her sleeve. It is hard to imagine how Athena could have lost that much blood and still be alive, but then I remember another white room with blood: It was Deirdre Hall's room, where Lucy had slit her wrists on Deirdre's bed. When I first came into that room after Christmas break I thought Deirdre's mother had sent her a red bedspread for Christmas.

"You'd be surprised what some teachers—teachers I'm sure must mean well—consider relevant to the curriculum. The digressions they indulge in—"

"I haven't been preaching New Age witchcraft to my students, Dr. Lockhart."

"I'm not saying that, Jane. I know you care about the girls, but you might not realize how much influence you have over them."

"Are you saying that it was something I said to Athena that made her do this?"

"Why are you getting so defensive, Jane?"

"I'm upset," I tell her. "I can't believe Ellen would do a thing like this."

"But you know she tried to kill herself once before. And just yesterday you told me that she leaves drawings of razor blades on the homework she turns in to you. Did it ever occur to you that she might be asking for your intervention?"

I shake my head. I had thought the pictures were left on her homework by accident, but I can see how lame that would sound now.

"Did you ever try to talk to her about the scars on her wrists?" Dr. Lockhart asks.

I remember the conversation I had with Athena before her last exam, when she saw me looking at the scar. She told me that her aunt had sent her here to *dry out from boys*. I had laughed and turned away from her. Then there was this morning's swim. I realize now that I may have been the last person to see her before she went back to her room, swallowed her roommate's sleeping pills, and took a steak knife to her arms. Was she afraid I would turn her in?

I look up at Dr. Lockhart and remember that I had been planning to tell her about seeing Athena in the lake. I will tell her now. It is not too late.

Only it is. Dr. Lockhart reaches down and touches the collar of my shirt. I flinch as if she had been about to strangle me, but when she draws her hand away I see she has, magicianlike, pulled a long green ribbon from inside my shirt collar. Only it's not a ribbon, it's a strand of grass. The kind that grows on the lake bottom.

"Interesting," Dr. Lockhart says, holding the long strand in the light from the window so that it glows like a shard of green glass. I notice that the white sky outside has broken apart. It has begun to snow.

"We found a piece of grass just like this in Ellen's clothing. We surmised that she might have tried to drown herself in the lake first, but for some reason couldn't go through with it. I thought it was odd to be brave enough to slit your wrists but not to drown. But then, maybe someone stopped her."

She raises one eyebrow and looks at me. I feel the blood rush to my face and for a second I think how the color red must look, in this deathly white room, on her dress and in my face. The nurse comes to the door and Dean Buehl and Myra Todd are with her. I feel caught, as if the blood in my face has something to do with the blood on Dr. Lockhart's dress and the slim blade of grass she holds in her hand is the murder weapon. What can I do, confronted with such incontrovertible evidence? I tell them about meeting Athena in the lake this morning. I tell them, too, about seeing the girls on the rock two nights ago. The only thing I don't mention is the page from my old journal. Because, I tell myself, I can't see what it possibly has to do with Athena's suicide attempt.

I DRIVE BACK TO THE SCHOOL WITH DEAN BUEHL AND SPEND the rest of the afternoon in her office. All afternoon classes are canceled so the girls can attend a "Support Meeting" in the Music Room. After I have told my story about what I saw at the lake the night before last and my encounter with Athena in the lake this morning, Dr. Lockhart excuses herself so that she can change her dress and meet with Vesta and Aphrodite—Sandy and Melissa, I remind myself to say—Athena's roommates. Dean Buehl thanks her for "handling everything."

"If you hadn't found the girl . . ." Dean Buehl's voice trails off and I notice how haggard she looks.

"It's what you hired me for," Dr. Lockhart replies, "to watch after these girls."

As soon as Dr. Lockhart leaves, Dean Buehl regains her official briskness. "Of course, you should have notified me immediately when you saw the girls in the lake," she tells me. Myra Todd nods and I get a whiff of her moldy smell. It makes me think my clothes are wet, but it is only that I am sweating in the dean's overheated office and the mold reminds me of how the changing room would smell after we swam in the lake. "You say they were naked?"

"Yes," I tell her for the tenth or eleventh time. "Of course I should have told you. I was planning to tell you after my classes today. I didn't realize it was urgent."

"You say they were making some kind of sacrifice on the rocks," Myra says. She makes it sound as if the girls were beheading chickens. "Well, I think that sounds urgent."

"We all used to do it." I hate the way my voice whines. I know I shouldn't try to explain, it just sounds like I'm trying to excuse myself, which I'm not. I've accepted the blame. "It's an old Heart Lake tradition," I appeal to Dean Buehl, who is herself an old girl, as if I were talking about founder's day or singing the school song and wearing our school colors, rose and gray. "You'd throw something in the lake for good luck. It's like . . ." I grope for a harmless analogy, "like tossing three pennies in the Trevi fountain."

Myra Todd snorts. "Naked? In the middle of the night?"

Dean Buehl shakes her head sadly. "It's that three sisters story that has plagued us from the beginning. Surely you, of all people, Jane, should know how dangerous the story is. But there's something that upsets me even more than your failure to report your students' nocturnal activities. Although I hope you understand now that you should have come to me immediately . . ."

I nod vigorously. I can hear Myra twisting in her seat impatiently. She wouldn't let me get off so easily, that's for sure, and I imagine that what she's thinking is that I'm receiving this lenient treatment because I'm an alum. I wish suddenly that I'd kept the fact that I went to school here to myself. But how could I have? Aside from Dean Buehl there are Meryl North and Tacy Beade—old girls—who remembered me. Or at least they remembered me once I had reminded them who I was.

"What I need to know, though," Dean Buehl continues, "is if you have shared what happened in your senior year with your students?"

I look up, trying not to show my relief. "Absolutely not," I say with conviction. "I mean, I've thought about it, when I've heard the girls telling the three sisters story, just to dispel the legend. I know that only one of the Crevecoeurs' daughters died—and of the flu, not drowning—from what was said at the inquest, but I knew if I started talking about it they might ask me other questions . . . and so, I've avoided it because it's unhealthy, I think, for them to hear about other girls who killed themselves. I know how that kind of thing can spread."

I am breathless from this little speech and disappointed to see that Dean Buehl looks unimpressed. Unconvinced.

"Are you sure you're telling me the truth?"

I nod.

"Then can you explain this." Dean Buehl holds up a piece of lined notebook paper with a ragged edge. I can see I'm supposed to come get it from her but I suddenly feel weighted to my chair, as if my clothes were indeed drenched and they were pulling me down into deep water. Myra Todd stands up and hands the page from the dean to me.

I am surprised, first off, that although it is clearly a page torn from a bound notebook, the words on it are typewritten instead of handwritten.

"Dear *Magistra* Hudson," the note, which I understand is meant to be Athena's suicide note, reads, "You've been a real friend. I'm sorry that you'll lose another friend in the same way you lost Lucy and Deirdre. I just want you to know that *I* don't blame you. *Bona Fortuna. Vale,* Athena." The *I*, I notice, is underlined, by hand, three times. There is a bloody fingerprint in the lower left-hand corner.

I look up from the note. "She's the one," I tell Dean Buehl. "She's the one who has my old journal."

• • •

WHEN I LEAVE DEAN BUEHL'S OFFICE I SEE VESTA AND Aphrodite sitting on folding chairs in the hall outside the Music Room. I would like to stop and talk with them, but I am already late for picking up Olivia from preschool. Besides, they look so pale and nervous I figure they don't need an extra interrogation. Aphrodite looks like she's been crying. Vesta looks like she would like to throw up. I rip out a piece of paper from the back of my grade book and hand it to Vesta.

"Write down your dorm room number," I tell her. "I'd really like to talk to you both later."

Vesta nods and writes down a number on the paper and hands it back to me folded in half. "Yeah, we'd like to talk to you, too, *Magistra*. Dr. Lockhart told us you saw us the other night and didn't tell anyone."

"Well, yes, I did see you and I was wrong not to tell."

"We think it was nice of you," Aphrodite says. I think of Athena's note: *You've been a real friend.*

"I've got to go pick up my daughter now, but I'll come by the dorm later. Good luck in there." I almost say *Bona Fortuna*, but think better of it.

WHEN I GET TO THE NURSERY SCHOOL I EXPECT TO FIND Olivia in tears, angry that I'm late. But instead I find Mrs. Crane, alone in her room, sorting eggshells. I am out of breath from running and can barely form the words "Where's Olivia?"

She looks up at me with the blank look I have always feared. "Her father picked her up. I figured it must be all right, since you weren't here."

"Her father?" Mitchell's visitation isn't until next week. "But I wrote on her form she's never, ever, to be released to anyone but me. You know I'm divorced. He may have kidnapped her."

Mrs. Crane pulls herself up. "There is no need to yell, Miss

Hudson, we're all upset today about what happened to that girl." It takes me a moment to realize she means Athena. "I thought you'd probably be at the hospital with her since she was your student and . . ." She stops herself from saying whatever she was going to say next. I wonder what stories are being told about my relationship with Athena. "I thought you might have called Olivia's father to come take care of her. I'm sure you'll find them at your house. Olivia said she wanted to show him her rock collection."

"Her rock collection?" Mrs. Crane shrugs and spills a carton of eggshells onto a sheet of newspaper. She lays another sheet of newspaper on top and takes a small rubber mallet and slams it on the table. I jump.

"For our mosaic project," she explains. I think she's still talking about the rock collection, but then I realize she's talking about the eggshells. I think about how carefully Olivia and I washed out those eggshells. Then I understand about the rocks. Olivia meant the magic rocks. The three sisters. I leave without saying thank you or good-bye and I can hear Mrs. Crane muttering something to herself as she pounds away with her mallet.

They are standing on the swimming beach and Mitch is showing Olivia how to skip rocks on the water. Olivia is more interested in catching snowflakes on her tongue.

"Do you think it will stick?" Olivia asks the minute she sees me. "Will the lake freeze? Can we go ice skating? I want to skate around the sister rocks."

When did she start calling them the sister rocks? I don't remember telling her that story, but if I did, and forgot it, maybe I also told the same story to Athena. Or could it have been the person who took her out to the rock who told her the story?

"No, honey, the ground isn't cold enough and the lake won't freeze for a while," I tell her. The temperature is dropping fast. I zip Olivia's thin sweatshirt up and huddle her against me.

"She ought to have a warmer jacket," Mitch says, turning to me at last.

"It was seventy degrees this morning. And I had planned to take her home right after school. I wasn't expecting you."

"Well, I had some business up this way and I thought I'd come check up on you. I would have taken Olivia home, but you were late picking her up, and I don't have a key to your house."

"I wanted Daddy to see the magic rocks," Olivia says. She points at the rocks. I notice that the snow is coming down so hard now that I can barely see the farthest rock. "They're supposed to be sisters," she tells Mitch. "They drowned like Hilarious and now they're together all the time."

"Hilarious?" Mitch asks me. "What kind of bedtime stories have you been reading her, Jane?"

"I think she means Hilarion. It's from Giselle. But I don't know about the sister part. You know she has a very active imagination."

"The Wili Queen told me." Olivia sounds angry, as if I had accused her of lying.

"OK, honey, we'd better go home and get you warmed up. I'll make some nice warm soup for dinner."

Olivia heads up the path and Mitch signals for me to walk a few paces behind with him. "I thought I'd take her for dinner," he says.

"Well, all right, but I wish you had told me. This isn't the visitation schedule we talked about . . ."

"There are a few things we didn't talk about. We didn't talk about you leaving Olivia alone at night when you go meet your boyfriend down here at the lake."

"What in the world are you talking about?"

"I guess you still keep a diary, Jane. You ought to be more careful about who sees it. This came over my fax today."

He hands me a piece of slippery white paper. The top line is typed with the sender's phone number, which I recognize as the school's fax number. The rest of the sheet is handwritten.

"Tonight I will go down to the lake to meet him and I'll tell him everything. I know I shouldn't go, but I can't seem to stop myself. It's like the lake is calling me. Sometimes I wonder if what they say about the three sisters is true. It's like they're making me go down to the lake when I know I shouldn't.'"

The page is shaking in my hands and it takes me a moment to realize it's my hand and not the wind that's causing it to shake. It's as if I can feel the hatred of whoever sent this to Mitchell in the paper itself. I have to remind myself that whoever sent the message never even touched this paper. I check the time and date of transmission: 8:30 A.M., today's date. I got back from my swim a little after 8:00 this morning. Dr. Lockhart found Athena at a little before nine. But why would Athena send this and then go back to the dorm, type me a note saying I've been "a real friend," and then slit her wrists? It doesn't make any sense.

I look up from the white paper to Mitchell's face. We've reached the top of the path and we have both paused to catch our breath. He's waiting for a reaction. A denial. But what should I deny? Should I tell him yes, I wrote this, but twenty years ago, and yes, I do leave Olivia alone to go down to the lake, but certainly not to meet this boy who has been dead for nearly twenty years?

I look back down over the lake, at the snow falling onto its placid gray surface, and although I know the snow must melt when it touches the water I imagine the white flakes drifting like white stars though the dark water. The only thing that is clear to me is that whoever sent this message to Mitchell wants to hurt me. And there is no better way to hurt me than to hurt Olivia. Someone—not a fairy, not the Wili Queen—took Olivia out to the farthest stone and left her there. One false step and she would have been in the water. . . . I have a sudden, unbidden image of Olivia's light hair fanning upward in the dark water as she sinks, her face a pale white star extinguished in the black water.

"Maybe I should take her for a while," Mitchell says.

I can tell from the combative tone in his voice that he's bluffing.

He's expecting me to tell him no, call my lawyer, tell him I've done nothing to justify his taking her. But instead I say the last thing he expects me to.

"Yes, maybe that's a good idea. Maybe you should keep her for a little while." Because even though it breaks my heart to see her go, I am beginning to think that Heart Lake isn't a very safe place for little girls.

Chapter Seven

●

THE COTTAGE, WITHOUT OLIVIA, IS TOO QUIET. AFTER DIN-
ner (I scramble eggs and throw out the eggshells) I decide to go
over to the dorm to talk to Vesta and Aphrodite. Their dorm is next
to the lot where my car is parked. I can see if there's anything they
think Athena would like before I drive to the hospital for visiting
hours. It seems like a good plan. The dorm and then the hospital. It
seems like a good way to fill the evening.

I walk along the edge of the lake because, I tell myself, it's a beautiful night. Today's snow shower has left only a faint white gloss on the
ground and a clear moonlit sky. It is cold, near freezing, I think. The
moonlight lies on the water like a premonition of ice. It will be many
weeks before the lake freezes, but tonight I sense something stirring in
the lake. Matt Toller once explained to me how a lake freezes. He said
that when the surface water grows colder it also becomes denser, so it
sinks to the bottom. When the warmer water rises to the top, it's
chilled by the colder air temperature and sinks. The water circulates
like this for weeks—a process called overturn—until the moment
when the lake is all one temperature and then the surface begins to
freeze. Matt said that if you could be at the lake on that night, the
night of first ice, you could see ice crystals forming. I imagine the lake
now like a giant mixing machine, stirring old things to the surface.

I pause on the Point. There are ledges on either side of the Point, carved out of the same soft limestone that lines the lake bottom, but the rock here on top is made of something harder—granite I think Miss Buehl told us. Its curved surface is bare except for the cracks and scorings—chattermarks, they're called—left by the last glacier ten thousand years ago. I think of how even this rock, so impermeable that it bears the scars of a ten-thousand-year-old event, was once under the surface of the earth.

Looking straight across the water I can see where the lake narrows and flows into the Schwanenkill and from there into the Hudson and the sea. Below me to the right the three sisters march into the water off the swimming beach. To my left I see the lights of the mansion and the dorm.

The journal pages, the corniculum, the three sisters story that have come to light are just floating debris, flotsam from a wreck that happened twenty years ago. But now the wreckage itself seems to be surfacing. Events that happened twenty years ago are happening again.

During our senior year Lucy Toller was sent to the infirmary with two slit wrists. A few weeks later our roommate Deirdre Hall was found in the lake, her neck broken. It was determined at the inquest that she jumped from the Point, landed on the ice, and then slipped into the water. A month after that I watched as Lucy, followed by her brother, Matt, walked out onto the thawing lake and vanished beneath the ice.

Could it be that there is something about this place that makes these events recur? Are all the deaths, from Iris Crevecoeur's to Deirdre's and Lucy's and Matt's, written on the landscape of Heart Lake like the glacier scores left on the rocks? Or is somebody re-creating the events, following a script written twenty years ago?

IT'S ONLY WHEN I AM IN THE DORM STANDING IN FRONT OF the security desk that I realize I don't know what room Vesta and Aphrodite are in. I dig in my pocket and find the piece of paper

Vesta gave me. I show it to the matron at the desk without looking at it and she tells me the room is up the stairs, second door on the left. And so I find myself standing in front of my old dorm room, the one I shared for three years with Deirdre Hall and Lucy Toller.

I knock and a voice from inside calls, "It's open." My students, Vesta and Aphrodite (or Sandy and Melissa as I try to think of them now), are sitting cross-legged on the same bed facing each other. I smell cigarette smoke and feel a cold draft. The bed is under the window. If I checked the sill beneath the window blind I am sure I would find an ashtray, but I don't.

"*Magistra* Hudson," Vesta says. "*Salve*. What a surprise." There isn't a trace of surprise in her voice. I realize that I am probably one of a long line of adult visitors the girls have entertained tonight. I imagine the grilling they must have received this afternoon in the Music Room and the well-meaning sympathy calls from teachers.

I notice a book of poems by Emily Dickinson on the bed and detect a faint whiff of mold in the air. Gwendoline Marsh and Myra Todd must have preceded me.

"May I sit down?"

Aphrodite shrugs, but Vesta at least has the good grace to gesture to one of the two desk chairs. I sit in the maple Windsor chair and wonder if it's the same one I sat in twenty years ago. The desks look the same: soft, dark wood scored by generations of Heart Lake girls' initials. If I looked hard enough I might find mine. Instead I look down and notice the dark stain on the floor.

"I think we should put something over it, but Sandy says that'll only make it worse." It's the first time Aphrodite has spoken since I came in and I can hear from the hoarseness in her voice that she has been crying. I look at her and take in the dark smudges under her eyes, darker than the ones she used to draw with kohl.

"I'm sure if you asked the dean would let you switch rooms. No one would expect you to stay in here with . . . that."

"Yeah, Dean Buehl said we could move and Miss Marsh says we ought to move to another room. She said it would be like living with a ghost staying here and we shouldn't have to . . ." Aphrodite's voice trails off and she looks, I think, as white as a ghost herself. I'm sure Gwen meant well, but the ghost image certainly wasn't well thought out.

"But Dr. Lockhart says we should stay and face our fears. She says that it's not good to bury the past," Vesta says. "I think she's right. What do we have to be afraid of? That we're going to suddenly decide to off ourselves just because Ellen went round the bend? I don't think so."

"Yeah," Aphrodite nods eagerly. "It's not like we believe in that three sisters story."

"Who told you that story?" I ask.

The girls look at each other. Vesta is scowling at Aphrodite, as if she is mad at her for bringing it up.

"Everyone knows that story. It's one of our great Heart Lake traditions like tea in the Lake Lounge and ringing the bell on top of the mansion so you don't die a virgin."

I laugh before I can stop myself. "You all still do that?"

Vesta and Aphrodite smile, relieved, I think, that they've gotten me to laugh. "Yeah, although it's not such a big issue with some girls," Vesta says. Aphrodite slaps her playfully on the arm and steals a look at me to see how I'm taking it. I smile at her. I remember what she asked the Lake Goddess—to keep her boyfriend at Exeter faithful.

"Did Athena have a boyfriend?" I ask. "She told me that she was upset last year when her boyfriend broke up with her. Did something like that happen this time?"

The girls go quiet. I can feel them shrinking away from me.

"How could she have a boyfriend here?" Vesta asks. "There are no boys here."

"Sometimes girls meet boys from town. When I was here . . ."

I see the sudden interest in their faces and stop.

"What? What did you do when you were here? Did you meet boys out in the woods when you were here?" Aphrodite asks. "Maybe on the swimming beach? You know, you can't see the swimming beach from the mansion."

I feel suddenly hot and I notice that the high-intensity desk lamp is beating down on my shoulders. I remember what I came for—to find out if Athena had my journal and, if she had it, do Vesta and Aphrodite have it now. I look around the room. If I had left it hidden in this room twenty years ago they could have found it. I would like to look in my old hiding place—under a loose floorboard behind this desk, but then I had looked there twenty years ago. It had occurred to me at the time that Lucy might have hidden my journal, on that last night before she followed me to the lake, and Lucy was awfully good at hiding things.

Ignoring Aphrodite's question with the smile I give my students when they ask something too personal, I stretch my leg and touch my toe to the edge of the bloodstain. I notice a gouge in the wood that has been worn smooth by time.

"I wonder if they'll tear up these floorboards," I say. "They're old and loose as it is. I'll tell you something we used to do when I was here. We used to hide things under the floorboards."

I look up to see their reaction, but I can't read their expressions. They look like they're hiding something, but they've looked like that since I came in. It is a not uncommon look for a seventeen-year-old. At any rate, they've got nothing to say to my question.

"I bet you could find stuff that girls hid over the years," I say, deciding to take a more direct route. "Have you ever? Found anything?"

The girls do not look at each other, but I have the feeling they are not looking at each other *on purpose*.

"No," Vesta says evenly. "Did you lose something?"

I swivel the chair toward the desk, away from Vesta's gaze. Does she know this was my old room? Suddenly I feel like I'm the one who's being interrogated and I start to sweat under the heat of the desk lamp. I push it away from me, knocking over an empty teacup.

"We should get rid of that," Aphrodite says. "You're the second one who's knocked it over tonight. At least now it's empty."

I right the teacup and set it next to a history textbook. I idly flip open to the first page and read "Property of Heart Lake School for

Girls" printed on the inside cover. Under the school's seal are places for students to put their names and the year. The names go back to the mid-seventies and I look to see if there's anyone I knew, but I don't recognize any of the names. I was never much good at remembering my classmates' names, mostly because I hadn't bothered to get to know anyone that well except for Lucy and Deirdre. On the bottom line is Ellen Craven's name.

"Is this Athena's desk?" I ask.

"Yes," one of the girls answers; I don't notice which one.

I am looking for a black-and-white notebook; I don't know which notebook I'm looking for, hers or mine.

"I'm going into town to see Athena now. I was wondering if she'd want any of her books."

"Like her Latin books?" The note of sarcasm in Vesta's voice sounds vicious, but when I turn around her face is bland and innocent.

"No. I don't expect her to do her Latin work right now. I thought something more personal. Her journal, maybe. She did keep a journal, didn't she? I remember seeing a black-and-white notebook."

"Yeah, she had a bunch of those," Aphrodite says.

"But you're too late," Vesta adds. "Dr. Lockhart came and took them all away."

ON MY WAY TO THE PARKING LOT I NEARLY SLIP ON THE ICY path twice. I keep my eyes on the ground to avoid the icy patches, but the moonlight coming through the pine branches strews the path with black-and-white blotches that dazzle my eyes. The pattern of moonlight and shadows begins to look like the black-and-white cover of my old notebook—of Athena's journals, too—so that I feel as if I were skating over the slippery cover of a book.

A bunch of those, Aphrodite said. If Athena had my old journal then it's possible Dr. Lockhart has it now. I have to find out from Athena if she had it, but will she even be conscious?

When I get to the hospital, I am relieved to find that Athena is awake, but disappointed to see that she is not alone. Dr. Lockhart is sitting in a chair by the window with an open book in her lap. The room is dark except for the small book light attached to her book. When she sees me come in, she closes the book and rises. The book light moves with her and throws lurching shadows across the room. Athena turns her head on the pillow and smiles when she sees me.

"*Magistra* Hudson," she says in a painfully raspy voice that makes me think of razor blades. "We were just talking about you."

"You look like you're going to sleep," I say. "I can come back in the morning."

"Oh no, I was just telling Dr. Lockhart that I wanted to talk to you."

"Yes, Ellen says that Latin's her favorite subject. I was just keeping her company until she fell asleep, but now that you're here, I'll go."

Dr. Lockhart comes around the bed and motions me to come with her. "I just want to have a word with Miss Hudson, Ellen, then I'll leave her to you."

Athena turns over on her side to watch us move into the hallway. I can see her bandaged arms in the moonlight from the window. They remind me of a horse's legs taped for a race.

Dr. Lockhart takes me by the elbow and steers me down the hall. "I wanted you to know that she's in a denial stage," she whispers. "Don't take anything she says about the suicide attempt too seriously. It would be better if you didn't ask her too many questions about what happened."

"I won't," I tell her. "There's just one thing I wanted to ask you."

Dr. Lockhart lifts one eyebrow and crosses her arms over her chest. The book light shines up onto her face ghoulishly the way the seniors used to shine a flashlight on their faces when they told us the three sisters story at the Halloween bonfire.

"Athena's roommates told me you took some journals from her desk, I wondered if . . ."

"If any of them were yours?"

I nod.

"No, I checked carefully. If she is the one who has your note-book, she's hidden it well. Maybe someone else has found it." She pats my arm reassuringly, making the light wobble over the dimly lit hall. The effect is like water reflected on the walls of an underwater cavern. "Don't worry, Jane," she says, "surely there's nothing so bad in your teenage diaries." She turns and walks down the hall, the light attached to her book wobbling weakly beside her like Tinker Bell in *Peter Pan*.

Athena's eyes are closed when I enter her room, but when I sit on the edge of her bed she opens them.

"Oh, *Magistra* Hudson," she says, "I've been wanting to talk to you all day. You're the only one I can tell."

The words sound familiar and I realize they are the ones I found on the journal page left for me two days ago.

"What do you want to tell me?" I take Athena's bandaged hand and try not to hold it too tight.

"I didn't do it," she says.

I think for a second she's trying to deny taking my journal, but then I realize I haven't accused her of that.

"Do what?" I ask.

"Slit my wrists. I didn't try to kill myself. Someone tried to kill me."

Chapter Eight

●

"PARANOID DELUSION BROUGHT ON BY DRUG OVERDOSE," Dr. Lockhart says when I tell her about Athena's claim that someone tried to kill her. "It's what I was afraid of."

We are back in her office with its panoramic view of Heart Lake. Although it's only been days, it seems like months since I sat here thinking longingly of a swim in the lake. Since yesterday's first snow the temperature has dropped into the twenties.

"Denial of a suicide attempt is common," Dr. Lockhart tells me. "In fact, I wrote a monograph on that very subject when I was doing my residency." She glides backward in her desk chair and reaches for a file drawer behind her. I notice her chair's sleek ergodynamic design as she arches back in it and how well its charcoal gray velour upholstery complements her clothes. I wonder how she got the school to order her such an expensive chair while the rest of us make do with creaky, straight-backed desk chairs.

She hands me a slim sheaf of paper that I expect is her monograph. I am about to utter some polite assurance that I'll read it as soon as I catch up on my grading, when I notice it's not a monograph at all. It is a letter, handwritten on pale blue stationery, from Lucy Toller dated February 28, 1977. The letter is to her brother, who had been sent, that last year of high school, to a military school in the Hudson Valley. True to her fashion she starts out with a quote, one I recognize from Euripides' *Iphigenia in Tauris*: "A greeting comes from one you think is dead." She then goes on to assure her brother that the official report of her suicide attempt over Christmas break was false. "I can't explain now, Mattie, but please believe that I'd never willingly take my own life. You see, *Domina* Chambers has told me something that changes everything. When she told me I understood why I've always felt different from everybody else. The ordinary rules of the world just don't apply. 'Which of us can say what the gods hold wicked.' " I remember that it was this passage that had been so damning to *Domina* Chambers at the inquest.

At the very bottom of the page she had copied a line from a poem, "And sin no more, as we have done, by staying, but, my Matthew, come let's go a-Maying." I remember the Robert Herrick poem from Miss Macintosh's English class.

I read the letter twice and lift it to see what the rest of the papers are, but Dr. Lockhart reaches across the desk and pulls the sheaf of papers out of my hands.

"As you see, even your friend Lucy denied that she tried to kill herself, and if the dean's notes are to be believed, the blood from her slit wrists soaked through two mattresses."

At her words my vision is flooded with red. I see the blood-soaked bed, the tangle of crimson sheets.

"And we know that suicide attempt was real. After all, she eventually succeeded. She walked out onto the ice and deliberately drowned herself. You saw it yourself, right?"

I nod, but realize from Dr. Lockhart's continued silence that she expects more of an answer. "Yes," I tell her, "she deliberately drowned herself."

"She didn't try to hang on to the ice? You couldn't help her?"

"She didn't want my help," I say, "she practically dived under the water. She wanted to die."

"And she didn't call for you to help her?"

"No," I say, trying unsuccessfully to keep the irritation out of my voice. "As I said she went right under. She couldn't very well call for help from under the water."

"So we can assume that first attempt was real as well. Besides it would be too awful if your friend Lucy hadn't meant to kill herself that first time."

"Why?"

"Because it was the precipitating factor in your other roommate's suicide. Deirdre Hall?"

Dr. Lockhart extracts another sheet from the stack of papers on her desk. This one is a Xerox of a lined, handwritten page.

"Whatever happens now, it's all because of what Lucy did at Christmas," I read aloud. The last lines on the page were cut and pasted from a mimeographed handout. I read them to myself: "I will arise and go now, for always night and day / I hear lake water lapping with low sounds by the shore; / While I stand on the roadway, or on the pavements gray / I hear it in the deep heart's core." Yet another of Miss Macintosh's favorites: Yeats's "The Lake Isle of Innisfree."

"Deirdre Hall's last journal entry before she drowned herself in the lake," Dr. Lockhart says. "No, Jane, I don't think we should believe that Ellen didn't try to kill herself. I think we should watch her very closely. And her roommates, Sandy and Melissa. I consider all three girls at grave risk."

FOR THE NEXT FEW WEEKS I DO LITTLE BUT WATCH MY GIRLS. I tell myself that I am watching them for signs of depression and suicidal tendencies, but truthfully I am also watching them for hints that they have my old journal. They seem, though, if anything, less troubled. Perhaps it's only the change of wardrobe brought on by colder weather. By the time Athena returns to class all my girls are huddled in layers of sweaters, scarves, and flannel shirts. The sweaters hide the bandages on Athena's arms and scratch marks on the other girls' wrists. The girls look more normal, less sepulchral, in their bright red plaids and fuzzy angoras. It's hard to look like a Goth lumberjack.

The snows begin in earnest early, even for the Adirondacks. By Halloween the ground is covered, by Thanksgiving the mounds on the sides of the paths are knee-high. The campus takes on that enclosed feeling it gets in winter. I know that by January the feeling may be claustrophobic, but for now it feels cozy.

I speak to Olivia each night on the phone and visit her every other weekend. As long as I don't say anything about her coming back to live with me, Mitchell says nothing about seeking permanent custody. I think it is better to leave things be for the time being.

I receive no more notes from my past. When I look at the lake I can tell it will freeze soon and I find myself looking forward to it, as if the past could be sealed under ice as well.

I go down to the lake every night, hoping to be there for the first ice. One night I find Athena, Vesta, and Aphrodite there and I almost turn back on the path, but then I see that Gwendoline Marsh and Myra Todd are with them along with a few other girls. They have blankets and thermoses of hot chocolate.

"*Magistra*," my girls call when they see me. "Join us. We're waiting for the lake to freeze. Miss Todd says if there's a moon when it happens we'll see the crystals forming."

They call it the first ice club.

"It's a Heart Lake tradition," Vesta says, handing me a mug of hot chocolate.

I nod and burn my tongue on the hot liquid. Myra Todd gives a lecture on the physics of lake freezing and Gwen reads the Emily Dickinson poem that begins, "After great pain a formal feeling comes . . ." I wonder why until she comes to that last stanza, "This is the Hour of Lead— / Remembered, if outlived / As freezing persons, recollect the Snow— / First—Chill—then Stupor—then the letting go."

It's as good a description of freezing as any I've ever heard and it's not Gwen's fault if it makes me think of Matt and Lucy's last moments. *First—Chill—then Stupor—then the letting go.* Only they didn't let go. They had each other to hold on to.

I WONDER IF THEY ASKED THE DEAN'S PERMISSION TO MEET. I wonder if Dr. Lockhart knows about the club. I find I can no longer judge the difference between a club meeting and a pagan rite.

When the girls start stomping their feet in the cold and the hot chocolate runs out we all leave. Gwendoline Marsh and Vesta sing "Silent Night" on the walk back. *Club meeting,* I think, definitely *club meeting.*

In the second week of December I notice a change come over Aphrodite. She arrives in class late without her translation done. She's no good at sight reading, so she can't fake it. Vesta and Athena try to cover for her. I can tell they are giving her their translations because they are too alike. If I stop Aphrodite to ask her how she got a particular translation or to identify a case ending, she flounders aimlessly amid the syntax. Out of six possible cases she makes four wrong guesses. It's painful to watch, so I stop calling on her, but still the littlest thing makes her burst into tears: Catullus's poem about his girlfriend's infidelity, Book Four of the *Aeneid,* the definition of the verb *prodere.*

"What's wrong with Aphrodite?" I ask Athena after class.

"She's getting notes from Exeter about her boyfriend, Brian. You know, like that he's cheating on her and badmouthing her. She's on the phone with him every night and he swears none of it's true."

"She seems to be taking it pretty hard."

"Well, yeah, they've been going together since the ninth grade. She says they're going to go to college together. Only the way she's going, she's never going to make it to college."

"You mean you think she might kill herself?"

Athena stares at me.

"No. I mean her grades really suck. Haven't you noticed?"

• • • •

I DECIDE I'D BETTER TALK TO DR. LOCKHART ABOUT APHRO-
dite. She listens to my story quietly.

"Of course I'll have a word with her," she says when I have finished, "but I doubt if it's anything serious. The important thing is
not to plant the idea into anyone's head that her sadness might be
suicidal. Whatever you do, don't discuss it with any other student."

I remember my conversation with Athena and the way she stared
at me when I asked if she thought Aphrodite might kill herself. I
thank Dr. Lockhart for her time and leave quickly.

That night when I call Olivia she tells me all about her new
baby-sitter who watches her after school, about how pretty she is and
how they bake cookies together. I think that being jealous of the
baby-sitter is the worst I'll have to suffer tonight until she asks me
when she can come back to live with me.

"Soon," I tell her.

I get off the phone and go into her room and lie down in her
bed. On her night table is the *Tales from the Ballet*. I remember the
part of the story when the mother warns Giselle not to dance because of her weak heart. Even with the best intentions, it's impossible to always protect your child. I'm not sure my intentions have
been the best. Did I really consider her welfare when I left Mitchell?
I thought I took the job at Heart Lake because it would be a good
place for her to go to school, but was I really thinking of her? Or
was I following my own desire to return here? I think of the lines I
read in Deirdre's last journal entry: "*I will arise and go now, for always
night and day I hear water lapping with low sounds by the shore; While I
stand on the roadway, or on the pavements gray I hear it in the deep heart's
core.*" The last lines make me think not of a human heart but of the
lake and what lies at its core.

I'm no longer sure if I even trust myself with Olivia. Am I any
good to any of these girls, I wonder, let alone my own daughter? Am
I, as *Domina* Chambers was accused of being, a *corrupting influence*?

I go out of the house and listen for a moment to the lake. *For always night and day I hear water lapping.* The sound tonight is madden-
ing. When, I wonder, will the damn thing freeze?

Instead of taking the path down to the lake I walk out onto the Point. Ice has formed in the glacial cracks. One wrong step and a person could slide off the smooth, curved surface of the rock and into the lake below. When Deirdre Hall fell to her death here some people, her parents, for instance, thought it was an accident. But then the administration confiscated her journal. Deirdre liked to collect quotes about death. She was also fascinated by the three sisters legend, especially after her roommate's suicide attempt. The last quote in her journal, the one from the Yeats poem, seemed to suggest that she felt drawn to the lake in the same way the three sisters legend suggested that Heart Lake girls were drawn to suicide.

I hear a sound to my left and turn a little too quickly. My heel catches in one of the icy cracks and for a moment I lose my balance, but then I feel a gloved hand catch my arm and right me. It's Athena. She must have been on the ledge below the Point and that's why I didn't see her. Behind her, walking up from the ledge, I see Gwendoline Marsh and Myra Todd with my other students, Vesta and Aphrodite. The first ice club.

"Magistra," Athena gasps in the cold air. "What are you doing up here? It's dangerous."

"Yeah," Vesta says. "We saw someone up here from the beach and we thought it might be a jumper."

Athena rolls her eyes. "We did not. We just wanted to . . . you know . . . make sure."

Aphrodite has come forward, stepping gingerly over the icy rock. She peers over the dome of the rock into the darkness. "Wasn't there a girl who killed herself by jumping from here?"

Gwen Marsh puts her hand on Aphrodite's arm to pull her back. "No dear, that's just another silly legend," she reassures her. But Aphrodite is still looking at me for an answer and I can't seem to think of one.

I FIND MYSELF THINKING THAT IF WE CAN JUST MAKE IT through the rest of December to Christmas everything will be all right. Athena is going to stay with her aunt and there's a possibility her mother might even be out of rehab for the holidays. Vesta is planning to read *Bleak House* by the pool at her grandparents' condominium in Miami. Aphrodite will see Brian and realize that those letters have all been lies. After all, I tell her, you can't believe everything you read.

And I will spend the vacation with Olivia. I've rented a room at the Westchester Aquadome for two whole weeks. It's all the salary I've saved so far, but it will be worth it. We'll swim in the hotel pool and I'll take her into the city to see the Rockettes and *The Nutcracker*. We'll go skating at Rockefeller Center. Far better than skating on the lake, I tell her, which at any rate remains stubbornly unfrozen.

Gwendoline Marsh tells me at the faculty Christmas party that the first ice club has been disbanded. Gwen looks almost pretty tonight. She's got on her usual high-necked white blouse, but tonight she's wearing it with a long brown velvet skirt that makes her waist look tiny. Instead of ace bandages, her wrists are encircled by broad Victorian cuff bracelets. She's even teased out a few tendrils from her usually severe bun and curled them into ringlets that tremble as she shakes her head over the lake's unwillingness to cooperate and freeze. Myra Todd overhears our conversation and comes over to commiserate.

"I blame global warming," she says. "The lake was always frozen by mid-December."

Simon Ross, the math teacher, volunteers that the lake was only good for skating four days the previous year.

"It might not freeze at all."

I turn around to see who has uttered this pessimistic prediction and see that it is Dr. Lockhart. She is wearing a silver dress that shimmers in the Christmas lights strung around the Music Room.

"It'll freeze when we're all away on holiday," I tell her. "When we come back, everything will look different. The school always does, after break." It may be the two glasses of champagne I've drunk, but I find myself oddly cheerful.

"Well, it'll do us all good to get away," Gwen Marsh says. "Imagine staying here through the whole break. I hear they used to let the scholarship girls do that to earn extra money."

"How inhuman," Dr. Lockhart says, taking a sip of her drink. "Imagine how depressing that must have been for those girls. Did you ever do that, Jane? Stay here during break?"

I notice that everyone is looking at me. I'm an old girl and so an authority on old Heart Lake customs, but no one has ever publicly mentioned before that I was a scholarship student. I wonder how Dr. Lockhart knows, but then I remember those files.

"In tenth and eleventh grade," I answer. "It wasn't so bad. My roommates were scholarships, too, so we all stayed. Our Latin teacher, Helen Chambers, stayed on campus and so did Miss Buehl." I say the last bit loudly enough for Dean Buehl to hear and she comes over, one eyebrow raised inquiringly. "I was just saying that you were always here over Christmas break. We helped you collect ice samples."

Dean Buehl nods. "Some of the younger girls even stayed with me at my cottage."

"How kind of you, Dean Buehl," Gwen Marsh says. "I wonder if any girls would want to stay here with me over break?"

It occurs to me that I haven't asked Gwen what her plans are for the break. What if she's stuck here all by herself? I know she has an apartment in town, but I certainly hope she isn't spending her Christmas alone.

"Oh, I never minded," Dean Buehl is saying to Gwen. "It was company and I took the girls skating with me. I always wanted to have an old-fashioned ice harvest," she says, "like the Crevecoeurs had."

Everyone is immediately fascinated with the idea of an ice harvest. Meryl North describes the icehouse on the other side of the lake at the mouth of the Schwanenkill and explains how even in summer there would still be blocks of ice packed in sawdust. Tacy Beade remembers that when she was a student here they used the ice to make ice sculptures. I notice that as soon as the older teachers come over Dr. Lockhart slips away from the group. I've seen her avoid them before and I can't say I blame her as they both have a habit of droning on endlessly. When Myra Todd starts corralling people into an ice harvest committee (Gwen, I notice, immediately volunteers to do most of the work), I follow Candace Lockhart over to the drinks table that has been laid out under the Crevecoeur family portrait. She is standing with her back to the room, seemingly absorbed in the photograph of India Crevecoeur and her daughters, posing in ice skating costumes on the frozen lake.

"You'd think after the failure of their first ice club they wouldn't be so gung-ho about an ice harvest," she says as I help myself to some lukewarm Chardonnay.

"Well, it's tricky catching the first ice. We always tried . . ."

"Did you ever see it?"

"I was actually at the lake the night the ice formed my junior year," I tell her, "but, if you can believe this, I fell asleep."

"So you missed it," she says smiling into her drink, something clear and fizzy with ice. "Like you missed that last Christmas break."

"Excuse me?"

She shakes the ice in her empty glass. "You said you spent the break here tenth and eleventh grade, but not in twelfth. And that's when your roommate, Lucy Toller, first tried to kill herself. That's what started it all, wasn't it? You must have wondered at times if things would have been different if you'd been here." She turns away from me to refill her glass with club soda. I hear something crack and think it must be the glass in my hand, but it's only the ice in Dr. Lockhart's drink, settling in the warm liquid.

"I was in Albany," I tell her, "with my mother, who was dying of stomach cancer. In fact, she died the day before New Year's."

"Oh, Jane," she says, "I didn't mean to imply it was your fault what happened. Only that you might feel that way. What is it that the poet says about remorse . . . ?"

I look at Dr. Lockhart blankly, unable to think of any appropriate line, but of course it's Gwen who thinks of one. " 'Remorse,' as Emily Dickinson says, '—is Memory—awake.' "

. . .

ON THE MONDAY BEFORE BREAK APHRODITE DOESN'T COME TO class. I ask Athena and Vesta where she is and they tell me that she went out early that morning to take a walk around the lake and they haven't seen her since.

After class I go straight to Dean Buehl and report Aphrodite's absence.

"We'll go to her room right now," Dean Buehl tells me.

I am not wild about being in my old dorm room with Dean Buehl, but what choice do I have? Walking from the mansion to the dorm I find myself looking at the Point, which blocks our view of the northeast cove and the swimming beach. I pull my collar up around my neck and start to shake.

"This morning's weather forecast says the temperature will be in the single digits by nightfall. If we can't find her by dusk we'll have to call the State Police and organize a search party. She'll never make it through the night in that kind of cold." Dean Buehl and I look at each other and I think we are remembering the same thing—a cold night twenty years ago when I showed up at the door of her cottage. Dean Buehl blushes and looks away first as if she were the one who was embarrassed at the memory.

At the dorm we find Athena and Vesta sitting at their desks with their books open. There is something wrong about the picture, I think. Something stagy about the way their books are laid out and how intently they lean over them. I sniff the air for cigarette smoke and smell, instead, gingerbread. The smell, with its connotations of holiday baking, confuses me. There are no ovens in the dorm. Then I realize what it is: air freshener. The girls were expecting us.

Dean Buehl sits on one of the beds and I stand because the other bed is covered with dirty laundry and it feels strange to sit on the same bed with the dean.

Dean Buehl asks the girls if Melissa seemed upset when she left this morning. The girls exchange guilty glances.

"Um, well, actually we're not even sure she was here this morning.

When we woke up she wasn't in the single. There's something on her bed, but it's not a note or anything—it's just some dumb poem."

Dean Buehl and I both look at the door of the single, which is still closed. She nods to me and I open the door and look inside. The bed is neatly made. On its pillow lies a sheet of paper with blue printing. Perhaps it is the blue writing that makes me realize what it is. Who uses mimeographs anymore? Dean Buehl passes me in the doorway and without removing the page from the bed, reads the first two lines: "I will arise and go now, for always night and day / I hear lake water lapping with low sound by the shore . . ." and I finish the poem aloud: "While I stand on the roadway, or on the pavements gray / I hear it in the deep heart's core."

Chapter Nine

●

"How'd you know that?" Athena asks. "Melissa's been repeating that poem for days. Are you the one who gave it to her?"

Dean Buehl, still standing above the single bed, looks my way.

"No," I say. "It's just something I remember. We read it when I was in school."

Athena and Vesta shake their heads as if to say *Teachers! Who knows what junk they carry around in their heads!*

"Girls," Dean Buehl says, "run down to the matron and ask for a plastic bag, then come right back up. Don't talk to anyone."

The girls scurry out of the room, glad, I think, to be away from us. Dean Buehl moves as if to sit on the edge of Melissa's bed and then thinks better of it and sits on the window ledge. When she looks up at me I think she'll ask the same question Athena asked. *How did you know that poem?* But she doesn't. Maybe she assumes her old girls ought to know their Yeats.

"I'm going to my office to call the police," she says. "You're to follow with Athena and Vesta, but give me half an hour to make the call—no, make it an hour. I don't want them to overhear what I have to say to the police."

"What do you think has happened to her?"

Dean Buehl shakes her head. "I just don't know . . . it's all so odd . . . that poem—it's the same one that girl left in her journal twenty years ago . . . that Hall girl."

"Deirdre."

"Yes, Deirdre Hall. Right before she jumped off the Point. My God. This was her room, wasn't it?" She looks around her and then she looks at me standing in the doorway, noticing for the first time, I think, my reluctance to step over the threshold into the small room. She shakes her head. "What the hell is going on here?"

It is only 3:30 when Athena, Vesta, and I reach Dean Buehl's office, but already the sun is low behind the mansion, its last rays skating across the lake and filling the room with their deep golden light. The State Police officer, in a chair facing Dean Buehl's desk, has to shield his eyes from the glare. All I can make out of him is the copper glow of his hair in the sunlight. I usher the two girls in ahead of me and Gwen Marsh, who is sitting on a couch to the side of the desk, gestures for them to sit on either side of her. She slips an arm around each girl even though both of Gwen's arms are wrapped in ace bandages. Dr. Lockhart, who is standing with her back to the room, looks at the girls, then at me, and then turns back to the window.

"This is the teacher I was telling you about. Jane Hudson," Dean Buehl says to the police officer.

The officer rises slowly to his feet and turns toward me. "Yes," he says, "Miss Hudson and I have met before."

For a moment the air around me seems to shimmer, as if the light the lake throws into the room was lapping up against me. It's that feeling I've had that the lake, as it moves towards freezing, is churning up the past, casting its secrets into the light of day. And now look whom it's cast up—Matt.

But then he takes a step toward me, out of the glare, and the copper hair fades to dark brown streaked with gray, the golden skin ages and sallows. Not Matt. Maybe what Matt would have looked like if he'd lived many years past his eighteenth birthday.

"It's Roy Corey, isn't it?" I ask, reaching out my hand. He takes my hand and holds it for a moment, really holds it instead of shaking it, and I'm surprised and gladdened by the warmth. "Of course I remember you. You're Matt and Lucy's cousin. We met once."

He drops my hand rather suddenly and that warmth is replaced by a sudden chill in the air. The sun has gone down behind Main Hall and the gold glow goes out of the lake like a light that's been switched off. I feel inexplicably that I've disappointed this man, yet, I think I'm doing pretty well to have remembered as much as I have. After all it's been twenty years and we only met that once.

He turns his back to me and sits down. Dean Buehl gestures for me to sit in the other chair in front of her desk. "Detective Corey was just saying we ought to check the Schwanenkill icehouse," Dean Buehl tells me.

"I believe your Heart Lake girls have made a habit over the years of meeting town boys down there."

I find myself blushing. I'm sure he's said this to embarrass me— he knows as well as I do what used to go on in that icehouse.

"This Melissa Randall, did she have a boyfriend?" he asks.

Dean Buehl tells him that she did, but that he's at Exeter.

"Anybody call to see if he's still there?"

Dean Buehl places the call and speaks to the headmaster. Twenty minutes later he rings back and puts Brian Worthington on the line. At a signal from Corey, Dean Buehl hits the speakerphone so we all can hear Brian Worthington swear he hasn't been out of New Hampshire since Thanksgiving break.

"When was the last time you heard from Melissa?" the dean asks him.

"Night before last," he answers. "I knew something was up when she didn't call last night. She calls every night." I can hear the weariness in his voice and I'm not sure whom to feel sorrier for, him or Melissa. "She hasn't done anything stupid, has she?"

Dean Buehl explains that Melissa is missing. She asks Brian to please let the authorities know if Melissa should show up at Exeter and promises to call as soon as she knows anything. When she gets off the phone, Athena raises her hand as if she were in class.

"Yes, Ellen?"

"Melissa said she was going to the hall phone to call Brian at around ten last night. We heard her talking to someone on the phone."

"Did she say she had reached him when she came back?"

Athena and Vesta shake their heads. "She didn't say and we didn't ask. She'd been crying, but that wasn't unusual."

"And did she go out after that?"

"We don't really know," Vesta answers. "She went into her room and closed the door. We just thought she wanted to be alone to . . . you know . . . cry and stuff."

"We went to sleep around eleven," Athena continues. "I noticed when we turned out our lights that her light was off. But I don't know if she was there or not. Her room has a separate entrance."

"So we really don't know how long the girl's been missing," Corey sums up. He slaps his hands on the arms of the Morris chair he's in and then shifts his weight forward as if to get up, but pauses there on the edge of the chair. I revise my opinion about him. Matt wouldn't have looked like this. He'd never have become this . . . solid.

"We'll start the search on the south end of the lake and split into two parties to cover the east and west sides," he says.

"Of course we'll want to be part of the search effort," Dean Buehl says.

"That's up to you, of course, all volunteers are welcome, but I'd appreciate it if you could keep track of your girls. Last thing we need is someone else getting lost." He lays his hands on the arms of the chair and heaves himself up. "Ask me," he says, "the best thing would be if your teachers kept the girls calm and in their rooms."

"We're perfectly capable of keeping the girls calm, Officer," Dr. Lockhart replies.

When Corey is gone, Dr. Lockhart sighs and looks out the window. It is dark outside now, too dark for her to see anything but her own reflection in the glass.

"Thank goodness we're in capable hands," she says.

"I'm sure the police will do their best," Gwen Marsh says. It's the first time she's said anything since I've come in. "I agree with that nice Officer Corey—the girls should stay in their dorms. They've been through enough already."

"That's not fair," Athena blurts out, shrugging herself out from under Gwen's arm. "She's our friend. We want to help."

"A very natural response," Dr. Lockhart says moving from the window and sitting on the edge of the couch next to Athena. "The last thing we want to encourage in the girls right now is a feeling of helplessness." She looks directly at Gwen and I have the feeling that this has been a bone of contention between Lockhart and Marsh before. What surprises me is how warmly Athena and Vesta respond to Dr. Lockhart's suggestion.

"We could organize a search team with teachers and students and work in shifts," Athena says.

I see Dean Buehl considering. "Very well, as long as there's a teacher in every squad."

"Well, of course if that's what you think is best, I'll get working on a schedule right away, but I'll need a secretary," Gwen says, holding up one of her bandaged arms. "Perhaps Sandy will help me."

I see Vesta exchange a desperate look with Dr. Lockhart, but Dr. Lockhart only shrugs and moves back to the window. Gwen has already commandeered a pad from Dean Buehl's desk and put Vesta to work.

THAT NIGHT I WATCH THE SEARCHERS' LIGHTS MOVING THROUGH the woods across the lake.

The shift I am assigned doesn't start until four A.M. I am touched that Vesta and Athena ask to be on my search squad. I know I ought to sleep until then, but I also know that sleep is impossible. I wonder if Athena and Vesta are asleep in their dorm room. I doubt it.

From their window, I know, they, too, can see across the lake to the south shore.

The lights moving through the woods remind me of Wilis, seeking vengeance for earthly betrayal.

At a quarter to four I put on long underwear, jeans and a sweater, gloves and a wool hat and take a flashlight. It is still dark when I walk outside, the moon having set, the woods lit only by faint starlight reflected on the snow. I pause on the Point and look at the lake, which is so still that its surface looks like black marble. It is one of those calm cold nights that don't, at first, feel as cold as they are because there is no wind. But in a few minutes, despite the layers I am wearing, I feel the cold bearing down on me. I shine my flashlight on the scratches on the rock and imagine the mile-high glacier that made them.

I consider taking a shortcut through the woods to the dorm, but already the snow beyond the paths is too deep. Soon the paths will narrow between two walls of packed snow and daily walks from dorm to dining hall to classroom will follow the same ever-tightening pattern.

"Like rats in a maze," Lucy would say.

In our senior year she began at the first snowfall carving out her own paths, narrow deer tracks that meandered aimlessly through the woods.

At the dorm I find Athena and Vesta waiting for me on the steps. They are blowing into their mittened hands to warm their faces. "Miss Marsh was just here," they tell me, "and she says we're supposed to look down at the swimming beach—in case Melissa took out a boat or something."

"When I was a student here," I say slowly and carefully, "I once took a boat out on the lake and rowed to the stones." I am thinking not just of Aphrodite's fate right now, but of that afternoon I found a dry Olivia on the farthest rock and the flash of white I saw vanishing around the curve of the Point.

"Yeah, that's nice, *Magistra*," Vesta says impatiently, "but the boats are all locked up for the winter. If a person wanted a boat they'd have to go down to the icehouse. I think I heard Miss Todd say once that the county extension agent keeps a boat down there to take water samples. At least, that's what I heard."

I remember suddenly the day I met Athena swimming across the lake and the impression I had that she was meeting someone on the other side.

"Well, then, why don't we go there instead," I say.

"You mean deviate from Miss Marsh's carefully choreographed schedule?" Vesta asks, lifting both eyebrows at me.

"Yes," I tell her. "Let's use some initiative. We can walk around the west side of the lake, check the icehouse, and then continue around the east side to the swimming beach. That should warm us up. But remember what Detective Corey said about staying together—I can't afford to lose one of you."

At the mention of Detective Corey's name the girls exchange meaningful glances.

"What?" I ask, feeling suddenly like another teenager, the one not in on the joke.

"Oh, nothing, *Magistra*," Athena says. "It's just that we thought you and Detective Corey would . . . you know, make a cute couple. What do you think?"

I click my tongue and motion for the girls to start down the path, which is too narrow for three to walk abreast. I want to walk behind the girls so I can keep an eye on them. It helps, too, that they can't see me smiling at their matchmaking attempt. It's ridiculous—me and the stocky police officer who clearly seemed not to like me—but it touches me that they're concerned about my personal life.

We call Melissa's name as we go and, at Athena's suggestion, vary our calls of *Melissa* with *Aphrodite*.

"She really liked her Latin class name," Athena tells me. "She said in her old school her Latin teacher assigned names and she got Apia, because *Melissa* comes from the Greek word for bees and Apia means . . ."

"Bees," I finish for her.

"Only the other girls called her Ape and she was . . . I mean she *is* . . . really sensitive about her weight."

"Kids can be so mean," I say. I am thinking about that *was* and wondering if my students are telling me everything they know about their roommate's disappearance. "When I was here one of my roommates threatened to get my other roommate, my best friend, in trouble by telling a secret they shared. She teased her all the time about it, until my roommate, the one who was my friend, was nearly going crazy."

"That's pretty lousy," Athena says. "I mean, no one likes a tattletale."

Tattletale. The word is so childlike that instantly I am ashamed of myself for suspecting these girls of any wrongdoing, but then Vesta says, "Yeah, that must have gotten on your friend's nerves. You could really get annoyed at someone like that."

"It must have been annoying," I say, "to hear Aphrodite crying all the time. I could tell her boyfriend, Brian, sounded worn-out."

Vesta sighs. "God, it's all we've heard all semester. Brian this and Brian that. He's just this little pimply-faced nerd with a trust fund. Girls makes such fools of themselves over guys."

"She should have just trusted him or decided he wasn't worth it. That's what I told her. I mean, a guy's just not worth all that heartache."

"Certainly not," Vesta murmurs. "You know what they say, 'A woman without a man is like a fish without a bicycle.' " I laugh at the old aphorism. At Vassar we had T-shirts made up with that slogan.

"Hey look, we've come to another path. I wonder where that leads," Athena says.

"It follows the Schwanenkill into town," I tell them. "The icehouse should be just past here on the other side of the stream."

I had forgotten that we would have to ford the stream to continue our walk around the lake. Fortunately, the Schwanenkill is mostly frozen.

"There's a place that's narrower, just off the path," I tell the girls. "We just have to go a little into the woods . . ."

"Good," Vesta says. "I have to take a leak anyway. I'll be right back. Can I borrow that flashlight, *Magistra*?"

Vesta takes the flashlight out of my hands before I can think to object and then disappears into the shadows of the pine trees. Athena and I stand at the place where the two paths cross and wait for her. It occurs to me that this might be a good opportunity to talk to Athena without Vesta's restraining presence.

"Vesta sounded pretty annoyed with Aphrodite," I say.

"She just couldn't understand the attraction," Athena says in a normal tone of voice, then she leans closer to me and whispers into my ear, "You know, it's just not her thing."

When she leans away I can feel the warm breath she left on my cheek crystallizing in the cold air. It's not until I watch Vesta walking back toward us through the woods, zipping her fly, that I realize that she's trying to tell me that Vesta's a lesbian.

"Oh," I say, to no one really, because the two girls are walking on ahead of me. What impresses me about Athena's revelation is the lack of malice or censure. When I went to school here girls were teased and called "lezzie," but it wasn't something you could talk openly about. For all our drug use and talk of sexual revolution, we really were still naive. And the suggestion at her inquest that Helen Chambers was a lesbian practically sealed her dismissal.

"I see where we can cross," Vesta calls back to me.

I follow them into the woods, keeping my eyes on the beam from the flashlight which Vesta still holds until I'm forced to watch my footing instead. Off the path the snow is calf deep. I feel the cold and wet seeping into my cheap boots. Each step requires effort and concentration. I watch my feet disappear into the snow and look for places where the snow isn't so deep. There are places where the snow has drifted up against a tree and my legs sink in to my knees. I slip into one particularly deep spot and find, for a moment, that I can't pull out. My hands flutter over the surface of the snow seeking for purchase but finding none. I realize how silly I must look, floundering in the snow, and look up, expecting to find the girls laughing at my predicament, but instead I see nothing but snow and pine trees stretching out around me.

For a moment I do nothing but listen to the silence. And then I panic. It's what they tell you not to do when you're drowning. Miss Pike said if you try to save someone from drowning and they panic, the best thing to do is sock 'em in the jaw and carry them back to shore unconscious. "Never risk your own life," she'd tell us. "That's the first rule of lifesaving."

When all my thrashing has done nothing but sink me deeper into the snow I stop and listen once again to the silence. The night is so eerily calm that not even a breeze moves through the pines. Then I hear, from behind me, the crunch of snow.

I try to turn around but that only makes me sink deeper.

I can hear it clearly now. Footsteps moving through the deep snow toward me. I can do nothing but wait. I imagine a blow to the head and then sinking, drowning, my mouth and lungs filling with ice.

Then I see the lights. Moving through the woods in front of me, they seem to dance among the pines. *Wilis,* I think, they've come to dance me to my death and drown me in the lake just like Hilarious. It's the last thought I have before losing consciousness and it makes me happy. Well, at least it makes me laugh.

Chapter Ten

●

"WHAT'S HILARIOUS?" SOMEONE IS ASKING ME. "FOR God's sake, what's so hilarious?"

The whole thing, I want to say, but my mouth is full of ice.

I open my eyes and see why I'm so cold. I'm in the icehouse. A face leans over me and I realize why I'm so happy. I am in the icehouse with Matt Toller.

"*Magistra,*" another voice says. "We're so sorry we left you all alone."

It must be Lucy, I think, only why would she call me *Magistra*? I'm glad, though, that she has finally apologized after all these years. How could they go and leave me alone. It's all right now though, we're together again.

"Miss Hudson, please try to drink some of this." A strong arm holds me up and I sip from the thermos cup. Matt always remembered to bring the hot chocolate when we went skating.

I take a sip and the bitter, black coffee burns my tongue. I look at the man holding the cup and the wave of sadness that moves through my body is so strong I start to shake all over. I remember that when I gave birth to Olivia I shook like this. *It's because your body has lost all that mass,* the nurse told me, *it makes your body temperature drop.* Yes, I remember thinking, this is what missing someone feels like, like part of your flesh has been torn away. Looking now at the man who is not Matt Toller, who is only his cousin, Detective Roy Corey, I feel that same precipitous drop all over again.

I lean into Corey's arm and immediately he moves it away as if he just noticed he had it around me. No, I think, the girls are wrong. This man can't even stand to touch me.

I take another sip of the bitter coffee and look at Vesta and Athena.

"Your girls led me to you," Corey tells me. "I met up with them here and they were surprised you weren't right behind them."

"I got stuck in the snow," I say.

"You passed out," he tells me. "I was afraid you had hypothermia, but I think it was just fear. How do you feel now?"

"Fine," I tell him. I look around the icehouse. "What are you doing here? I thought you were going to check out the icehouse first thing last night."

"I did, but then all I was looking for was a lost girl. I wasn't noticing what wasn't here."

I sit up and swing my legs over the edge of the wooden ledge. I am sitting, I see, on one of the wide shelves where they used to store the slabs of ice harvested from the lake.

"The boat," I say. "There's no boat."

Corey nods his head and twists his mouth around like a man who's made a big mistake and hates to admit it. I notice that he has the same full lips that Matt Toller had.

"I should have thought of it directly," he says. "But I'd forgotten the county extension agent used the icehouse to store her dinghy."

"You think Aphrodite . . . Melissa took it?"

Instead of answering, Corey looks at the girls.

"We found it at the beginning of the year and took it out once or twice. I guess Melissa could have taken it," Athena says.

"Could she have gotten it down to the water by herself?" I ask.

In answer, Corey swings open the double doors at one end of the wooden hut. At first all I see is blackness, but then I realize that what I'm looking at isn't the blackness of night, but a wide expanse of water—so still it might be air instead of water—spreading out from the edge of the icehouse.

When I have assured Corey and the girls that I haven't suffered any ill effects from my faint in the woods, we walk back along the east side of the lake toward the swimming beach.

We are walking two abreast on the path with the girls in front of us. Corey slows his pace a bit and signals for me to do the same. I realize he wants to leave some space between us and the girls. "We found a boat drifting off the swimming beach, caught between two of the rocks," he says in a voice so low I have to move closer to hear him, "but I wanted to see where the boat came from since the school's boathouse was still padlocked. That's when I remembered about the boat in the icehouse."

"But shouldn't you be looking for Melissa in the water?" Roy pats the air with his hand, meaning for me to keep my voice down. I hadn't realized how loud I'd spoken, or how frightened my voice would sound. It's that image of the empty boat, drifting between the rocks.

"We've called the divers in, but they can't start until sunrise. The girl's parents are flying in from California. I'd like you to get those girls back to their rooms before then. I don't think they need to see this."

"I understand," I tell him. "I'd like to come back. If you don't mind."

He looks at me. "You were there when they took Matt and Lucy out of the lake, weren't you?"

"Yes," I say. "Sometimes I wish I hadn't been."

"Really? I've always wished I had been here. You know, Matt was staying with us the weekend he took off and hitched back here." I nod, remembering that the military school Matt had been sent to senior year was near his aunt and uncle's house. "I knew he was do-ing it. He told me he had to see his sister. That was the last time I ever saw him alive."

So someone else has been carrying the weight of Matt Toller's death all these years. For a moment it makes me feel lighter, and then heavier. This is why Roy Corey is so standoffish with me. He blames me for what happened to Matt and Lucy.

"You shouldn't blame yourself," I say, but what I'm really saying is *please don't blame me.* "You were just a kid."

"That's no excuse," he tells me. "I've thought about this a lot since then. You can't duck responsibility because you're young. You have to take accountability."

"Is that why you became a cop? To hold people accountable for their mistakes? To unmask the villains?"

He stops on the path and looks at me as if I'd slapped him. I hadn't meant to sound so angry, but I'm tired of being blamed.

"Look," I say, laying my hand on his arm. I want to explain to him how I feel, but he moves away from me and walks up the path so quickly I can hardly keep up with him.

AFTER I DROP OFF ATHENA AND VESTA AT THE DORM I WALK back to the swimming beach. The sun hasn't risen yet, but I can see a lightening in the sky across the lake and know that it soon will. I was upset at first after my talk with Corey, but once I got over the fact that he obviously holds me responsible for what happened to Matt and Lucy, I realized how lucky I am to have found him.

Roy Corey saw Matt Toller just before he came back here to Heart Lake that last time. Maybe Matt talked to him about me and, if he did, I might find out what Matt was thinking about me at the end. For the past twenty years I'd felt like I'd been talking to someone on the phone when the lines went down. Right in the middle of the most important conversation of my life. Roy Corey might be able to fill in some of the lost pieces.

When I round the Point and see the police cars and ambulance parked on the road above the swimming beach I feel ashamed of myself for worrying at a time like this about Matt's opinion of me. Vesta is right, we girls make such fools of ourselves over men.

I can imagine what must have happened to Aphrodite. Frantic over Brian's purported faithlessness and feeling powerless hundreds of miles away from him she resorted to a childish witchcraft. What was that Dr. Lockhart said? *It's all an attempt to gain control over a world in which they have no power.* She wanted to go to the farthest three sisters rock and make an offering to the Lake Goddess. Only it was too cold to swim there, so she got the boat from the icehouse and rowed across the lake. It was probably when she was trying to get from the boat onto the rock that she slipped and fell into the water. The cold of the water must have shocked her . . . or maybe she hit her head . . .

From what Vesta and Athena have said, I know that Aphrodite could have gotten the idea to take the boat from their previous exploits. But something else bothers me. Lucy Toller and I once took the rowboat from the icehouse and I wrote about it in my senior-year journal. What if Aphrodite got the idea from my journal? Then I have an awful thought. I think: Maybe Aphrodite had my journal with her when she fell into the lake. If so, maybe my old dream of the lake washing clean those pages has finally come true. It's an awful thought because for a moment it has made me glad.

I walk down the steps to the swimming beach and stop midway. Roy Corey is there, so is Dean Buehl and a middle-aged couple in matching Burberry trench coats. Melissa's parents, no doubt. I find that I don't want to join the group on the beach, so I sit down on the cold stone, about halfway down the steps, and wrap my arms around my knees, trying to make myself small and compact against the relentless cold.

Three men in oily black rubber suits are talking to Corey. They all look at the eastern shore where the sun has just appeared through the pine trees. I can imagine what they are saying. That it's probably better to wait until the sun is higher, shining through the water. But then they look back at the parents. The first morning light hits the woman's face and it's like a blade cracking her open. I imagine this woman looked ten years younger just twelve hours ago.

The divers walk into the water. When they are chest deep they spread their arms over the surface of the water and then they dive. On the beach there is nothing to do but wait. No one talks.

The sun rises above the tips of the pines on the eastern shore and bathes the farthest of the three sisters rocks in light. I notice, for the first time, that the rocks are perfectly aligned with the angle of the rising sun. As the sun rises, the light touches each rock in turn, like a child jumping across stepping-stones. The sunlight glazes the beach and the step I am sitting on, but there's no warmth in it. Instead, I feel as if I, and all the other figures on the beach, have been sealed in ice. The lake is so still that I find it hard to believe that divers are moving below the surface, but then I see a black head surface in the middle of the cove. I see a hand rise out of the water, and Roy Corey, who is watching the diver through binoculars, waves back.

I see Mrs. Randall turn to Corey as if to ask a question, but then she turns back to her husband and kind of leans in on him, like a tree tilting in the wind.

Out in the lake the head is gone. The surface of the water is still again.

We are all still looking toward the center of the cove so we don't notice the diver surface to the left of the swimming beach. He is shoulder deep in the water and his arms, instead of spreading across the water, are below the surface and look as if they are being pulled down as he walks slowly through the water toward the beach.

He's carrying Melissa Randall.

As soon as he lays her down on the beach the paramedics snap into life and try to resuscitate what even I, from this distance, can see is a corpse. The group on the beach contracts into a tight fist around the drowned girl. I am probably the only one who notices the second diver surfacing a little to the left of the three sisters. He is carrying something, too, but something smaller and lighter.

Roy Corey notices and breaks away from the group. He meets the diver at the edge of the water and reaches for the rusty tin box. I am up and moving across the beach, although I don't know what I think I can do about it. Roy Corey is moving his hand over the domed surface of the box, which is a little larger than a shoe box. A webbed belt is fastened around the box. I see him unfasten the brass buckle and the belt falls away, rotting, to the ground. He wipes away the layer of green slime that covers the tin, revealing an improbable landscape of gold mountains that glints in the morning sun. He flicks back a little gold latch and opens the lid.

Inside is a heavy white cloth embroidered with a heart and words I can't make out from where I am. But I don't have to. I know them by heart. *Cor te reducit.* The heart leads you back. Roy Corey lifts the cloth, delicately, with a little flourish even, like a magician culminating his final trick. But there's no flutter of white wings; instead, nestled in a circle of greenish-gray stones, are the perfectly preserved bones of a tiny human being.

I look away from the small skeleton toward the lake and notice that something is happening. I remember again how the nurse said that after birth the mother's body temperature drops precipitously. It is as if now that the lake has given up these two bodies its own temperature has achieved an equilibrium of cold. It's as if that flutter of white handkerchief has produced magic after all because shooting out in all directions at once, brilliant in the morning sun, ice crystals explode across the still surface of the lake. It's what we've all been waiting for: first ice.

PART TWO

•

First Ice

Chapter Eleven

●

WHEN I FIRST MET MATTHEW AND LUCY TOLLER I thought they were twins. Not that they looked all that much alike. He had the sandy red hair, blunt jaw, and stolid build of the Tollers, while she was fair and lithe and sharp-featured like one of the water nymphs in my copy of *Tales from the Ballet*. It was in their gestures and the way they moved their bodies—like one person in two sets of limbs—that they so deeply resembled each other.

I first noticed them the summer before ninth grade. My mother, having decided I ought to meet some West Corinth kids before being thrown in with them at Corinth High School, had gotten me a job as a counselor at the swim club. How she thought spending a summer wading calf-deep in the tepid, citrinous water of the kiddie pool would gain me entrée into the world of doctors' and lawyers' children, I do not know. What it did gain me was a view, through the bitter-smelling box hedge, of the deep end and the high dive where I could watch Matt and Lucy Toller practice their dives and race freestyle in the lap lane. No one ever seemed to win those races; they were more like synchronized swim events. They swam, shoulder to shoulder, their bodies tilting for breath at the same angle like two planets pulled by the same moon, their white elbows cresting the water like the two wings of one enormous swan.

• • •

When I got to high school I found out two things about the Tollers. One was that they were not twins; Matt was thirteen months younger than Lucy. He had been allowed to start kindergarten early because, Lucy told me, he had pitched such a fit when she started school without him. Hannah Toller had gone to the principal and told him she'd either have to keep Lucy back a year or let Matt start early. So Matthew started kindergarten six months shy of his fifth birthday.

The second thing I found out about the Tollers was that although Matt and Lucy lived on the west side of the river (in Corinth it's the river and not the train tracks that divide the haves from the have-nots), they fit in with the West Corinth kids no more than I did. Their father, Cliff Toller, was a paper salesman at the lumber mill—a job only a few rungs above my father's job as factory foreman. Still, the Tollers seemed to live a little better than other salesmen's families. They had a small but picturesque house on River Street where the doctors and lawyers lived. They belonged to the swim club and Matt and Lucy took piano lessons with the music teacher at Heart Lake. My mother assumed that Cliff Toller must do well on commission and she chastised my father for not having the wherewithal to move into a sales job. When Lucy Toller befriended me on that first day of ninth grade my mother was pleased. Perhaps not as pleased as if one of the doctors' or lawyers' children had invited me home to their River Street mansion, but it was a start.

As for me, I was so relieved when Lucy asked me to bring my tray to their table I had to blink away tears before I could say yes. I was standing at the end of the check-out line, balancing a tray heavy with sloppy joes and canned fruit and two waxy milk cartons ("You get two on the lunch program, honey," the cafeteria lady had loudly informed me, "you might as well take them.") The smell of the sweet, orangy meat was making me feel dizzy while kids streamed around me to their places, as sure of where they were going as water knows to flow to the ocean. I saw where I belonged. There was the table with the East Corinth kids: the boys in flannel shirts and jeans cuffed at the bottom for extra wear, the girls in plaid skirts a little too short or a little too long and Peter Pan blouses with darning stitches at the collar. I knew them and I knew they'd make a place for me— not with the enthusiastic hugs and smiles with which the West Corinth kids greeted one another after summers apart at tennis camp, but with the resigned shift of kids from big families making room for one more.

Those afternoons I had spent at the West Corinth Swim Club were shimmering and fading like heat haze just as I felt a cool hand slip under my elbow and pull me out of the current.

"Don't I know you from the pool?" she said, in a small, clear voice I had to lean toward to make out.

I nodded at her, afraid if I talked I might start to cry. I noticed that her pale hair was tinged green from her summer spent swimming in the chlorinated water and her eyelashes and brows were bleached white from the sun.

"Do you want to come sit with us? I think we've got our next class together. Did you sign up for Latin? There's only eleven of us and the rest are all that crowd'll be taking it for their SAT scores and to get into law school." She spoke in a rush I could barely understand.

I followed her to a table in a far corner beneath the cafeteria's only window. Her brother Matt actually half rose from his seat to greet me. They both had brought their lunches—identical brown paper packets of cheese and apples and thermoses of hot cocoa.

"You were right, Mattie," Lucy said, polishing her apple on her sweater sleeve. "She's in Latin."

I couldn't remember telling her, but of course she had known all along.

Matt gave me a long appraising look. "So why did you sign on?" he asked.

He made it sound like I'd joined the foreign legion. The truth was that signing up for Latin, instead of the usual French or Spanish, had been, like most of what I did, my mother's idea. She'd heard that the lawyers and doctors urged their kids into Latin to boost their SAT scores.

"French and Spanish are common," my mother told me. "You'll meet more interesting children in Latin." My mother's ambitions for me were a puzzle, because they didn't seem to come from any belief in my ability. I often felt like a piece in a game that she was moving around on a board. When I achieved some goal she'd set out for me—the best reading scores in sixth grade, a part in the school play—she seemed mistrustful of the success.

"She wants those things for you because her mother wouldn't let her try for anything," my father once explained to me. "Your mother could have gotten a scholarship to Heart Lake, but her mother made her give it up. I hate to speak badly of your grandma, Janie, especially as you're named for her, but Jane Poole was an awful cold woman. She hated the Crevecoeurs after she was let go. Your mother wants more for you, but when you look like you're going to get it, I think she must hear old Jane's voice telling her it'll come to no good."

Of course I couldn't tell Matt and Lucy any of this.

I searched my head for anything I knew about Latin. They spoke it in church, I knew, but we were Presbyterians, not Catholics. There were those movies with chariot races and gladiator fights where the actors' words didn't quite match the movement of their lips, but somehow I didn't think Matt and Lucy spent their Saturdays eating Captain Crunch in front of the TV. They probably went on nature hikes and read books with nice leather bindings instead of the tattered paperbacks mended with yellow tape I borrowed from the town library.

I remembered then that one of those books I had borrowed that summer had been a collection of Greek and Roman myths. I hadn't thought it was as good as my beloved *Tales from the Ballet*, but I had liked some of the stories.

"I like mythology," I said. "The gods and all and those stories of people turning into something else . . . like the one about the girl who turns into a spider . . . ," I blathered on, mashing my fork into my sloppy joe, turning the meat and bread into an even more unappetizing mess.

"Arachne," Matt said.

"Ovid," Lucy said, even more mysteriously.

"Metamorphoses," they both said at the same time.

"That's good." Matt held his apple up between us and closed one eye as if I were a far away object and he was taking my perspective. "Of course we won't get to it first year."

"Oh no, it'll be all grunt work with declension endings and conjugations, but *Domina* Chambers says if we study hard she'll let us read extra bits. I want to do Catullus and Matt's keen on Caesar—just like a boy, right? And she'll help us study for the Iris Scholarship for Heart Lake—only Matt's not eligible because he's a boy. But she says there's no harm in him studying with me as he'll be a help. Perhaps you'll want to join us?"

I felt I was already listening to a foreign language more arcane than Greek or Latin. I hadn't understood half of what she'd said—I had never heard of Ovid or Catullus or *Domina* Chambers—but it was a little like listening to opera on public radio. I didn't always understand the story, but I liked how listening to it made me feel. I liked how the weak sunshine that came through the dirty cafeteria window made Matt's sandy brown hair turn a fiery red and Lucy's pale, greenish hair glow like burnished gold. I liked being with them.

I think that if they had been asking me to join the foreign legion instead of only inviting me to study Latin with them, I would have followed them into the desert willingly.

Chapter Twelve

●

THE IRIS SCHOLARSHIP—NAMED AFTER THE CREVECOEUR daughter who died in the influenza epidemic of 1918—was awarded to the freshman girl from the town of Corinth who scored the highest on her Latin exam. It was a sop, my mother told me when I came home that first day of ninth grade, to the town's resentment of the school. When, in the early seventies, the Corinth Public School Board threatened to cancel the Latin program due to low enrollment and a scarcity of qualified teachers, Helen Chambers, a Heart Lake alum and newly appointed classics teacher there, volunteered to teach the Latin class at Corinth High.

We were her first public school class, she told us that first day, and as such responsible for whatever impression of public education she would take away with her. We also turned out to be her last public school class, so I assume the impression she took away with her was not favorable.

Helen Chambers was unlike any teacher I had ever seen before. The teachers we got in Corinth generally fell into one of two categories. There were the plump, motherly women in shapeless Dacron dresses and cardigans embroidered with ABCs and apples (or whatever was in season: pumpkins at Halloween, candy canes at Christmas) who showed lots of film strips and drew happy faces on returned papers. Then there were the sternish old maids in Orlon sweater vests, scratchy wool skirts, and support hose pooling around their thin ankles who lectured in monotones and gave detention for falling asleep in class. Occasionally, some young woman just out of the State Teacher's College came to Corinth for a few years. Such was Miss Venezia, my kindergarten teacher, who looked like Snow White and gave me *Tales from the Ballet.* But if they were any good they went on, as Miss Venezia did, to better jobs in Albany or Rochester.

Helen Chambers was neither young nor middle-aged. Instead she resided in a suspended state between the two. She was tall and fair, with the sort of blond hair that turns silver instead of gray and which she swept up in an elegant twist like an actress in a French movie. She wore, invariably, black—a color ill-suited for days spent in front of a chalkboard, but then I can't recall ever seeing her use the chalkboard.

She conducted her classes, I realized later, like college seminars. That first day she had the eleven of us pull our desks into a circle, which she joined. She gave us each a plain gray cloth-bound book and told us to turn to chapter one to review the first declension. She timed us on the watch brooch pinned, like a nurse's, above her heart. When five minutes had elapsed she told us to close our books and recite the declension of *puella, puellae,* one at a time, around the circle. She ticked off points in a small leather notebook for each mistake we made. Lucy and Matt were the only ones who got it right.

Afterward she read us a poem by Catullus about a girl who keeps a sparrow in her lap, which makes her boyfriend jealous. Ward Castle made a rude gesture at Lucy and was told he could sit in the hall for the rest of the class. She told us to memorize the first declension and the present indicative active of *laudo, laudare* for tomorrow and dismissed us by saying *"Valete discipuli."*

Lucy and Matt responded by chanting *"Vale, Domina"* and the rest of us muttered some approximation without having the slightest idea what we were saying.

The next day our class size had dwindled to nine, by the end of the week: seven. Aside from Matt and Lucy and me, the rest were the children of doctors and lawyers whose parents had told them they had to stay in Latin to get into law or medical school.

After two weeks I had memorized the first declension, but I hadn't the slightest idea of what a declension was. But I was happy chanting the words with Matt and Lucy walking down River Street after school.

I was happy, truth be told, to be walking in the opposite direction from my own home. I wouldn't have to pass the mill with its sickening smell of fresh-cut lumber and its yellow pall of smoke. My house was down the hill from the mill and every day of my life I had woken up to that oversweet smell and the yellow smoke staining the sky outside my bedroom window. The lumber trucks went past my house, rattling the windowpanes and making the vases of artificial flowers on the coffee table tremble. My mother waged an ever-lasting war against the sawdust that my father brought home on his boots and work clothes. She made him take off his clothes in the mudroom and wash his head under the garden hose even when it was so cold that the water froze in his hair and beard. Still the saw-dust crept in, forming tiny drifts in the corners and speckling the china bric-a-brac and tickling the back of your throat. At night I could hear my father, who breathed that dust all day, coughing so hard that the iron day bed he slept on in the sewing room rattled. When I came home in the afternoons my mother would be dusting and railing against the sawdust and the mud and my father's salary and the cold.

"This is the last place on earth I thought I'd end up," she told me again and again. Since it was the place where she started out, I never understood her surprise over finding herself here.

When I told her I'd be going home with Lucy Toller that Friday I saw her take in the name and roll it around in her mind, measuring its worth like a pound of sugar.

"She's a bastard, you know."

I don't think I had ever heard my mother use a word like that. She always said cursing was common.

"Illegitimate, I mean," she said, seeing I didn't understand. "Cliff Toller's not her daddy. I knew her mother, Hannah Corey, in school. A smart girl. Maybe too smart for her own good. She got the Iris Scholarship." Maybe that was why she didn't like Hannah Corey. "She even got into one of those fancy women's colleges, but she came back after a year with a baby and wouldn't say boo to anyone about whose it was. Cliff Toller married her all the same and gave her a nice little house on River Street. I wouldn't have picked her daughter as first choice for a friend, but you might meet some of her friends on River Street."

I didn't tell my mother that Lucy and Matt didn't seem to have any other friends.

"She'll probably win the Iris this year and then you'd know someone at Heart Lake."

"Lucy says I could have a shot at the Iris," I told my mother. "She says we'll study together."

My mother gave me a long look so that now I felt like the pound of sugar. I couldn't tell if she had never thought of me having a chance for the Iris Scholarship until now, or if she'd been planning for me to go after it all along. After all, I was a good student, although more out of a slavish need to please my teachers than from any innate talent.

"The Iris Scholarship," she said. Like all her goals for me she looked at it with both desire and mistrust.

"Well," she said, "that would be something. But I wouldn't set my heart on it."

From the start, though, I think I did just that: set my heart on the Iris Scholarship. I'd never seen the school even though I'd grown up only a mile from its gates. I'd seen, though, the Heart Lake girls come into town to browse the drugstore for magazines and try on lipsticks at the makeup counter. They'd try on half a dozen shades and then wipe their mouths clean before going back to the school. I thought there must be a rule against makeup, but then I noticed how resolutely plain they were in their dress. Even when the school abandoned their uniform, the girls seemed to be wearing one. Plaid kilts and pastel sweaters. Down vests in the winter, like loggers. Scuffed penny loafers worn down at the heel. My mother always said you could tell a lady by the heels of their shoes, but there was something about these girls—maybe the perfectly straight teeth, the way their hair gleamed, the discrete flash of gold on earlobes and throat, and, most of all, a carelessness combined with confidence— that told me that the backs of their shoes might be worn to the nub but they'd never be, what my mother called, "down at the heels."

It didn't seem such a far leap—from my actual poverty to their assumed negligence.

"You're a cinch for the scholarship," Matt told me walking back to their home that Friday. "The only other one eligible financially is Lucy."

"Well, then Lucy will get it," I said.

"Lucy's lazy," Matt said, loudly enough for Lucy, who was walking up ahead, to hear. I thought she'd get mad, but instead she plucked a scarlet maple leaf from an overhanging branch and, looking coyly over her shoulder, bit down on its stem like a flamenco dancer holding a rose between her teeth. Matt skipped up to her and, clasping her into tango position, spun her around the lawn of one of the big mansions. They waltzed through the neat leaf piles the gardeners had raked together, kicking up red and gold maelstroms, until Matt dipped her low over a bed of yellow leaves and let her drop there in a graceful swoon.

"See," Matt said, turning back to me. I had stayed on the edge of the sidewalk, standing still under the gold waterfall of leaves. "She needs some competition."

Then he grabbed me, one arm firm around my waist, the other holding my hand straight out in front of us, his cheek, cool in the crisp fall air, against my cheek. As he spun me around, the red and gold leaves blurred together like the wings of the Firebird in my ballet book. His breath, against my cheek, smelled like apples.

"Now, repeat after me," he said in rhythm to our dancing, *"Puella, puellae, puellae. . . ."*

I repeated dutifully, shouting the declension as we spun around the lawn. When we came to a standstill, Lucy was on her feet, watching us, red and gold leaves sticking out of her hair like a chaplet of beaten gold. Everything else seemed to keep spinning except for her steady little figure.

"See," she said, "you've got it memorized."

"But I don't know what it's for."

Lucy and Matt exchanged a look and then he plucked one of the leaves from her hair and, with an elaborate sweep of his arm, presented the leaf to me.

"Puer puellae rosam dat," Lucy said.

"What?" I asked.

"The boy gives the girl a rose," Matt translated.

"Boy—*puer*—is in the nominative case, so it's the subject, he's the one doing the giving," Lucy said.

"Girl—*puellae*—is in the dative, so she's the indirect object of the verb—the one who receives the action of the verb. The rose," Matt twirled the scarlet maple leaf between his fingertips so that for a moment I thought I was looking at a rose, "*Rosam* is accusative. It's the direct object of the verb—the thing that's being given."

"See, you can mix it all up," Lucy said.

Matt jumped around me and stood on my right side and held the rose, the leaf, out to his right. Lucy pointed. *"Puellae puer rosam dat.* It still means . . . ?"

"The boy gives the girl a rose," I replied.

Matt transferred the leaf into his left hand and held it between us.

"Puellae rosam puer dat?" Lucy asked.

"The boy gives the girl a rose," I answered.

Matt held the leaf over his head. "Get it?"

I nodded. For the first time I actually did understand.

Matt bowed to me and handed me the maple leaf, which I slipped carefully into my pocket.

"Good girl," he said. "Now, let's get home. It's getting dark." Matt linked his left arm in mine and Lucy linked her right arm in mine and we walked the rest of the way up River Street, chanting the first declension into the cool, blue evening air.

Chapter Thirteen

●

THE HOUSE AT THE END OF RIVER STREET WAS NOT A MAN-
sion, but rather the sort of cottage you'd expect the seven dwarfs
to live in. It had originally been the gatehouse for the Crevecoeur
Mansion. When the estate became a girls' school, the gatehouse was
sold separately to the school's first headmistress. How it passed into
the Toller family I never knew.

The downstairs rooms were always a disappointment to me.
They were furnished in the same overstuffed and overpolished colo-
nial style as my own house. But whereas my mother regarded each
chair and end table as a prized possession, there was an air of disre-
gard and neglect in Hannah Toller's decorating. It looked as if the
furniture had been picked off the showroom floor with no regard for
what my mother called "color coordination." Ugly brown plaids
vied with blue and red chintzes. The curtains were a particularly
horrible shade of mustard. While neat, the place looked unloved.

From that first day we spent as little time as possible downstairs. I
was introduced to their parents and allowed to exchange strained
conversation with them for the length of time it took Lucy to heat
up some hot cocoa and Matt to raid the cupboards for cookies. I saw
immediately why no one could forget that Lucy was not Cliff
Toller's daughter. In fact, it was hard to imagine Lucy issuing from

either of the Tollers. Cliff Toller was large and red-haired; his hands, especially, seemed huge to me. Hannah Toller was small, like Lucy, but looked so dull, with mousy brown hair and unmemorable features, that one could only think of her as a genetic neutral that would require some divine visitation in order to have produced Lucy. I remembered my mother had told me that she'd conceived Lucy in that one year she had gone to Vassar and I imagined some blond scion encountered at a Yale/Vassar mixer.

When Lucy and Matt introduced me, Mrs. Toller's dull brown eyes lit up for a moment. "Jane Hudson," she said my name slowly, much as my mother had pronounced Lucy's name. "Margaret Poole's girl?" I nodded.

"I went to school with your mother," she told me. "Everyone thought she'd be the one to win the Iris Scholarship, but on the day of the exam she didn't come to school."

I shrugged. "Maybe she was sick," I said, but I knew that probably wasn't what happened. My father had told me that my grandmother didn't want her to go to Heart Lake, but I hadn't known until now that she must have kept her home the day of the exam. I tried to imagine what my mother must have felt that day, after studying for the exam, to be kept from what must have seemed her only chance to get out of Corinth and a life of dreary millwork.

"And what do you think of your teacher? *Domina* Chambers?" Hannah Toller asked me.

"Oh, she seems wonderful," I gushed. "So elegant and . . ." I struggled for the right word, ". . . and refined."

"Refined? Yes, I guess you could call her that." And she went back to stirring some pungent-smelling stew on the stove.

"Mother went to school with Helen Chambers," Lucy explained as we trooped up the steep stairs. "First at Heart Lake, and then for one year at Vassar."

"Oh?" I said. I couldn't think of anything else to say and I was glad that Lucy and Matt were ahead of me on the steps or they would have seen me blushing and known I'd heard the whole story about Lucy's birth.

"Yeah, she got the Iris Scholarship when she was our age," Matt said.

"I guess that's why she wants Lucy to have it," I said.

I saw Lucy and Matt turn to each other at the top of the steps. Matt whispered something and Lucy shook her head as if she were angry at what he had said. I was glad to be able to change the subject by exclaiming over their rooms.

"You guys are so lucky," I said a little too loudly. "It's like your own private hideaway. It's like the attic in *The Little Princess*."

"Yeah, Lucy's the princess and I'm the little serving girl she lets clean up after her."

Lucy scooped up a pile of dirty laundry on the landing and tossed it at Matt. "As if you picked up anything ever."

The rooms *were* messy. Lucy's room, on the right side of the stairs, was tiny, with hardly enough room for a single bed and a small bureau. This was why, she claimed, she'd encroached into Matt's room on the other side of the stairs. You'd have thought from the freefall of clothes and books and swimming goggles and ice skates and loose paper and teacups and half-eaten apples that they shared his room.

Lucy had even pushed her desk over to Matt's side so that they could study better. The desks faced each other on either side of the window— "so we both get a view," Lucy told me. "We fought terribly over it." That first day they found an old table for me and placed it between their desks facing the window.

"She'll get distracted looking out the window," Lucy said.

"She won't," Matt countered. "Will you, Jane?"

They both turned to me and I looked out the window from which I could see the river running between tall white birches, their yellow leaves catching the last light, like a band of sapphires set in gold.

I looked back at their eager faces. "No," I told them, truthfully. "I won't be distracted."

●　●　●

I STUDIED WITH THEM EVERY DAY AFTER SCHOOL THROUGH-out the fall term and sometimes on Saturdays until Christmas break. I had been afraid that without the excuse of studying together Matt and Lucy would disappear from view over the long vacation. My re-lief at their invitation to go skating was tempered only by having to admit to them I didn't have skates. I'd always relied on the rented ones at the public rink.

"You can have my old ones," Lucy told me. "Your feet are smaller than my mine." Surprisingly, she was right. Although she was tiny everywhere else, Lucy had unusually long feet. I tried on her skates and found that with an extra pair of socks they fit perfectly.

"Do you think it'll be thick enough?" Lucy asked Matt as we followed a little stream called the Schwanenkill west into the woods, our skates slung over our shoulders. Although we hadn't gotten much snow yet, the temperature had been below freezing since Hal-loween. The Schwanenkill was frozen except for a small rivulet down the middle that scalloped the edges of ice on either side. The ground felt hard to me as I struggled to keep up with them. The stream bank was icy and twice I slipped and broke through the thin ice and felt the cold water seep through my thin-soled sneakers.

Matt and Lucy wore the rubber-soled boots they'd gotten from L.L. Bean for Christmas, so they could crash through the ice and wa-ter heedlessly. I think that if they had noticed I was wearing Keds, they wouldn't have taken me into the woods that day, but they could be unobservant that way. She was careless about how she dressed, more often than not wearing one of Matt's soft corduroy shirts with her faded blue jeans. It didn't matter, though, because she looked good in whatever she wore.

After we had walked about a quarter of a mile we came to a small wooden hut on the southern end of Heart Lake. When I real-ized where we were I grew nervous.

"Isn't this private property?" I asked.

Lucy opened the door of the hut while Matt eased himself down the steep bank to test the ice.

"I suppose so," Lucy answered with a yawn. I followed her into the hut. It was too dark at first to make out much, but then she opened the two double doors at the opposite end and the small space was filled with the late afternoon sun reflecting off the icy surface of the lake, which came up to the very edge of the building. I noticed that the sun was only a little above the line of hills behind the Crevecoeur mansion on the west side of the lake. It would be dark soon. The walls on either side were lined with deep shelves. Lucy stretched herself out on one of the shelves as if she had come for a nap instead of a skate.

"But no one's ever caught us," she said. "And it's the best place to skate. We even have our own skating lodge." She twirled her hand around in the mote-filled air, indicating the little hut.

"What is this place?" I asked.

"It's the old Schwanenkill icehouse," Matt said, coming into the hut and swinging his skates onto the end of the shelf where Lucy was lying. "The Crevecoeurs used it for storing ice harvested from the lake." He swept a handful of sawdust from the shelf and sifted it through his gloved fingers. "They packed the ice in sawdust and it lasted till summer." He pointed to a rotting wooden ramp that led from the double doors down to the ice. "They used that ramp to haul up the ice they cut from the lake. Our father used to help with the ice harvest."

"You're a fund of historical information, Mattie. How's the ice today?" Lucy asked without opening her eyes.

"It's a bit choppy at the mouth of the Schwanenkill. I think there's a spring there that feeds into the stream and it keeps the ice from forming solidly above it. But if we skirt around that we should be all right."

He was already pulling his boots off as he spoke and Lucy, although still supine, brought one heavily booted foot up to her opposite knee and began lazily pulling at her laces.

I looked out at the surface of the lake, which was turning a pale Creamsicle color in the setting sun. It was hard to see well with the glare, but I thought I saw dark patches, like bruises on an apple, which could have been soft spots or just shadows on the ice.

"I hear the lake is really deep," I said conversationally. I'd kicked off my Keds but I was still twisting the skate laces through my fingers.

"Seventy-two feet in the middle," Matt answered proudly, as if he had made the lake, "but this side's pretty shallow near the shore. You stay right behind me, Jane, and if there's a thin spot I'll let you know by going through first." He grinned at me with the utter, un-thinking confidence of a fourteen-year-old boy. "You'd pull me out, wouldn't you, Jane?"

I nodded earnestly, not sure if he were kidding or not.

"Good, because I'm not sure about this one." He jerked his thumb over his shoulder at Lucy. "It would probably be too much trouble for her. She probably wouldn't want to get her feet wet."

Lucy swiped at Matt's shin with the tip of her skate blade. He jumped off the bench and lunged out of the icehouse with Lucy right behind him. When they reached the ice their jerky movements suddenly smoothed and lengthened. I saw Lucy catch up with him and grab his parka hood so roughly I thought they'd both plummet headlong through the ice, but instead he turned around, caught her hands and spun her into a graceful pirouette.

I was tempted to stay in the icehouse. Even if I hadn't been worried about the ice I knew I would never be able to keep up with them. But then I remembered Matt's trusting smile. *You'd pull me out, wouldn't you, Jane?* Of course, he'd been kidding, but I realized at that moment, as I tightened my laces until they hurt, that if Matt and Lucy were in danger there was no point at all to me being safe on the shore.

There's always that first step in skating, from dry ground to slick ice, when it just seems impossible. Impossible that two thin blades of metal will support you, impossible that because its molecules have begun to dance a little slower water will hold you up. There was no railing here, as at the rink, to bridge that gap between solid and liquid, only the imperceptible giving way of earthbound gravity to free fall.

I took a few tentative strokes out onto the ice and then remembered what Matt had said about staying away from the Schwanenkill. I looked for them and saw that they were skating along the lake edge toward the northeast cove, probably to avoid being seen from the mansion on the west side of the lake. I would have liked to get a closer look at the mansion, which I had never seen before, but with the sun setting behind it I could make out little except a low, dark bulk squatting on its rise above the lake. When I looked away there were dark spots burned into my vision, and it took a moment to locate Matt and Lucy under a pine tree that spread its boughs above the lake. Lucy waved at me, but Matt, standing behind her, reached up over Lucy's head and pulled a branch, releasing a shower of snow down the back of her neck. Lucy shrieked and spun around to grab him, but he was already gone, skimming the edge of the lake with a swift hockey player's glide.

Lucy knelt on the ice and gathered together a snowball. When she got to her feet she must have realized she'd never catch up with him. He was already on the western edge of the cove where three rocks broke through the ice. She must have decided that the only way she'd catch up to him would be to cut directly across the cove.

She was halfway across the cove when one of the shadows I'd noticed before darkened and opened beneath her. Matt, on the other side of the lake, was turned the other way. I don't remember deciding to move forward, but I found myself a few feet away from the ice hole.

She was in it up to her waist, her elbows propped on the edge of the ice to hold herself up. I slid one heavy skate toward her and a crack like forked lightning spread between us. Behind her, Matt turned and saw us. He started to skate, not directly toward us, but back along the shore, the long way.

I crouched to my knees and then lay myself down flat on the ice. I moved slowly, but still the ice hit my chest like a wall and sucked all the breath out of my lungs. I reached my arm out but I was still a foot short of her hand. Her fingertips, which had been straining toward mine, relaxed and she shook her head at me. Then one elbow cracked through the ice and her left shoulder slipped under the water. She made a sound like a wounded bird and I thought I heard its echo until I realized it had come from Matt, who was behind me now. I slithered forward, scraping my chin on the rough ice, and caught her right hand. She grabbed my wrist with more strength than I would have imagined existed in those tiny hands.

Behind me I heard Matt's hoarse whisper telling me—*her? us?*—to hold on and then I felt a tug at my feet. As he pulled, she got her left arm onto the ice and I grabbed that one, too, only she had no grip in that hand so I grabbed her wrist. Her wrist felt so cold and brittle I thought it might break, but I held on even after her legs cleared the ice and her body was out of the water.

Matt dragged us like that, both of us flat on the ice, back to the shore. When we were both on dry ground he told me I could let go, but he had to pry my fingers away from her wrist and her fingers away from mine. When she let go I realized I had no feeling in my left arm. I couldn't even lift it to help hold her up on the walk home so Matt picked her up and carried her the quarter mile back.

It was only after Dr. Bard (who lived two houses down from the Tollers) had examined Lucy and given her an injection of penicillin to ward off pneumonia that he happened to notice how I was holding my arm. When he took my jacket off he saw I had dislocated my shoulder—the bone had been pulled clean out of its socket.

Chapter Fourteen

●

ONCE SET, MY SHOULDER HEALED RAPIDLY, AND EVEN though it still hurt, my mother didn't see any reason for me to miss school. It was too bad, she said, that I had always written with my left hand, so this was a good opportunity for me to learn to use my right hand better. I told her I would try, but when I was in school I switched back to writing with my left hand even though the act of writing sent shooting pains through my arm. That arm never felt quite the same.

Lucy was worse off. Despite the penicillin injection, she developed pneumonia from her fall in the lake and was out of school for the whole month of January and some of February. Matt was out of school a lot, too, although I don't think he was sick. I just don't think he could bear to leave Lucy alone all day.

I went to the Tollers' house after school every day to drop off Lucy's homework until *Domina* Chambers told me that she would drop the work off herself on her way back to Heart Lake. I grew shy, then, of visiting even though Matt and Lucy had always acted happy to see me. I thought they had forgotten all about me when, on my fifteenth birthday, *Domina* Chambers gave me a package wrapped in plain brown paper. I waited until my study hall and then sneaked away to an unused corridor where I'd found a window seat looking out over the school's unused courtyard—an air well really—a place I could be alone if I didn't mind burning my bottom on a hot radiator and freezing my arms against the cold windowpane.

There were two packages inside, one contained a beautiful fountain pen and a bottle of peacock blue ink. These were from Lucy. I put those aside and ripped open the second package. It was a notebook, the black-and-white kind you could buy in the drugstore for a quarter. I opened it and read Matt's note on the inside cover, written on the lines provided for a classroom schedule: "To Jane. Still waters run deep. From, Matt." He'd said that to me once when I told him I'd like to be a writer but I worried about not having enough to say. "You're quiet, but you're observant," he'd said. "Still waters run deep."

I filled the pen with ink and wrote on the first page, "Lucy gave me this fountain pen and beautiful ink . . ." The nib of the pen caught on the page and ink splattered on the paper and my blouse. The effort to write made my whole arm ache and I wondered if Lucy realized it would be so hard for me to use it.

". . . and Matt gave me this notebook." I looked at the notebook and tried to think of something poetic I could say about it. It was a cheap exercise book, a brand the town sold because it was made by the paper company that owned the mill. The black-and-white pattern on the cover was supposed to look like marble, but to me it looked like ice on the river in spring, when the ice began to break up and the broken shards traveled downstream to the mill. In the summer the river was choked with logs heading toward the mill to be made into paper—maybe the very paper between these covers and the cover itself—so that holding this book was like holding a piece of the river, and the forests up north, and the ice formed in the high peaks.

I looked out the window at the bleak abandoned courtyard. It was full of the things that kids threw from classroom windows, discarded mimeos and thick felt erasers that had split in the middle and curled up on themselves like small dead animals.

"I'll never have any other friends like them," I wrote. I waited for the ink to dry and then ran my fingers down the page. That's when I noticed the ragged edge along the inside seam of the book. A page had been torn out. I wondered what Matt had written that he had decided to rip out.

I DECIDED TO VISIT THE TOLLERS' HOUSE THAT DAY TO THANK Matt and Lucy for their presents. When I got there I found *Domina* Chambers having tea in the kitchen with Hannah Toller. I shouldn't have been surprised to see her there; I knew she was dropping off Lucy's work, but I had imagined her literally *dropping* Lucy's assignments on the Tollers' front stoop and hastening on her way up Lake Drive to the school. I hadn't pictured her having tea with Hannah Toller. They looked so odd together: Helen Chambers like a Nordic ice queen and Hannah Toller in her housedress like a drab peasant. But there they were, not only sharing tea but apparently sharing intimate conversation. Their heads were nearly touching as they leaned over some large book of photographs.

"Ah, Clementia, we were just talking about you. Come sit down with us." I winced at the sound of my Latin name, which I hated. We didn't get to pick our own Latin names in *Domina* Chambers's class. Rather they were doled out to us according to a strict system. *Domina* Chambers told us what our names meant (I never saw her consult a baby name book; she seemed to know the meaning of all names) and then gave us a Latin name which had an equivalent meaning.

Lucy was easy because it meant, like her own name Helen, light, and so Lucy would use the same Latin name Helen had at school: Lucia.

Jane, she told me, came from the Hebrew for merciful, which was Clementia in Latin. Floyd Miller and Ward Castle spent the rest of the year calling me Clementine.

I sat next to Mrs. Toller and looked down at the table. The book resting between them was a yearbook and it was open to a picture of two young girls with their arms around each other's waists. The girls wore strapless evening gowns and little fur stoles. Off to the side a young man in a tuxedo smiled at the girls. He was blond and handsome and looked, I noticed with a little shock, a lot like Lucy.

"Our freshman winter formal," *Domina* Chambers said, closing the heavy book. I saw the year 1963 printed on the cover. "You knew that Hannah and I were at Vassar together, didn't you?" *Domina* Chambers lit a cigarette and leaned back in her chair. "Only Hannah wasn't so happy there, were you, dear?"

"College is not for everyone," Mrs. Toller said quietly.

"No, of course it isn't. What do you think, Clementia, is college for you? Or should I say: Are you for college? Perhaps the state teachers college in New Paltz? You'd make a very competent teacher, I think, and we always need good Latin teachers."

I nodded. What she described was the pinnacle of my career ambitions, but on Helen Chambers's lips it suddenly sounded dreary and ordinary.

"Now our Lucia on the other hand . . . I see her as a Vassar girl, and then she'll go to the city and work in some arts-related field— publishing, I think, with her preciseness and gift for language. If we can only get her into Heart Lake, she'll be a sure thing for Vassar."

"It's a ways away," Mrs. Toller said.

"Nonsense! Three hours on the train. She can come home on the weekends—when she's not too busy studying or going to football games and mixers at Yale or taking in the museums in the city. We were always encouraged in Art History 105 to spend as much time as we could at the museums."

"Mattie'll half die missing her," Hannah said with an edge in her voice I hadn't heard before. "Have you thought of that, Helen?"

"Well, Mattie will just have to get used to doing without her. He'll get plenty of practice when she comes to Heart Lake next year. Now the thing to do is make sure she's ready for the exam. You're here to study with her, aren't you, Jane?"

I nodded and smiled, glad to be called by my real name for once. "Oh yes, after all, I'm taking the exam, too."

Domina Chambers reached across the table and patted my hand. "Of course you are, dear, and I'm sure you'll do very nicely on it."

I DID DO VERY NICELY ON THE EXAM. IN FACT, I ACED IT. Looking back, I think I set out to do just that—ace the exam—that day sitting at the Tollers' kitchen table with Helen Chambers, if only to prove to her that I was better than she thought I was—better than someone who does *nicely* and goes to teachers college. I wrote in my journal that same night, "Teachers college is OK, but what I'd really like is to go someplace like Vassar. And to do that I have to get the scholarship to Heart Lake. I don't think Lucy would really mind— after all, she's the one who's believed in me all along."

I outlined a study schedule on the back cover of my notebook. I gave myself six weeks to memorize all of Wheelock's Latin. After my parents would go to bed I got up and sat by my bedroom window studying by flashlight. My mother turned the heat down at night so it was cold in my room. When I looked out the window I couldn't see the mill past the ice crystals spreading across the black panes. When the lumber trucks passed on the road in front of our house the glass shook and the ice patterns spread like a flower opening. Sometimes when I looked up from Wheelock and saw the ice crystals on the windowpane I imagined the picture I'd seen in the Vassar yearbook, only instead of Helen Chambers and Hannah Toller I pictured Lucy and me, our arms wrapped around each other, smiling into the camera. And off to the side, handsome in dark evening clothes, Matt looked on. Of course, he'd come visit on weekends from wherever he went to college—Yale, maybe, or Dartmouth because, he said, he liked the idea of going to a college founded by an Indian, and he'd heard they had a big Winter Festival.

Each night I ticked off the declensions and conjugations and *sententiae antiquae* I'd committed to memory in my black-and-white notebook. My fingers turned peacock blue with the ink from Lucy's pen—the same color as the rings under my eyes.

I thought I'd be nervous for the exam, but instead I felt eerily calm and detached—as if I were recalling something I had done a long time ago.

I was frightened, though, when the results were announced, at what Lucy's reaction would be. When Helen Chambers made the announcement at school assembly and the whole school applauded I looked down, as if I were modest, but really it was because I was afraid to look at Lucy or Matt who were sitting on either side of me. But then I felt a small hand creep into mine and squeeze. I looked up at Lucy and saw that she was smiling at me with what I can only describe as a look of euphoria. She was genuinely thrilled for me.

It was then that I started to cry, not, as everyone assumed, out of happiness at winning the scholarship, but because I knew how much *better* she was. Test or no test, she was the one who deserved to go on to Heart Lake and Vassar, not me. I would tell them all that she should have the scholarship. I would tell them all that I had cheated. Hadn't I? If not on the test, then on Lucy?

But then Helen Chambers raised her hand for silence.

"Since the days when India Crevecoeur invited millworkers into her home for educational symposiums, the Heart Lake School has always tried to preserve a friendly relationship between town and gown." There was a smattering of polite applause, which I waited through impatiently. I was wondering if I had the courage to turn down the award in front of the assembly or if I should do it quietly after the ceremony.

"But never has their generosity so overwhelmed me as it has tonight." There was a hush in the audience as we all wondered what she meant. "I've been informed by the Board of Trustees that because of the outstanding performance of another student, this year the Iris Scholarship will be awarded, for the first time since its inception, to two students: Miss Jane Hudson *and* Miss Lucy Toller."

I turned to Lucy and threw my arms around her. Mixed with my genuine joy that we would be at Heart Lake together was craven relief. I wouldn't have to turn down the scholarship. I'd been taken off the hook. Pressing my cheek to hers I could feel that she, too, had begun to cry.

Chapter Fifteen

●

LUCY AND I WERE ASSIGNED TO A THREE-PERSON SUITE, called a "trip" by the Heart Lake girls. All the dorm rooms at Heart Lake were triples. My mother had always warned me to watch out for threesomes. "One always gets left out," she told me in a way that made me understand that the *one* was likely to be me. India Crevecoeur, the school's founder, thought differently. She believed that pairing girls off in twos encouraged "exclusionary friendships inconducive to the goals of community and cooperation."

"They're afraid we'll turn lezzie," our new suite-mate, Deirdre Hall, told us. "Apparently India Crevecoeur never heard of a ménage à trois."

Deirdre Hall came as a surprise to me. She didn't look anything like the Heart Lake girls I'd admired trying on lipsticks at the Corinth drugstore. She arrived in torn, bell-bottomed jeans and a sheer gauzy top through which I could see her nipples.

"They've stuck the scholarship students together," Lucy explained to me. "Although I can't imagine what she won a scholarship for—unless it was for being fast."

"You mean like in track," I asked.

"No, I mean like in bed. Can't you see the girl's a slut?"

Most of what we heard from Deirdre Hall had something to do

with sex. She pulled from her army green duffel bag a veritable li-brary of sex tomes: the Tantra Asana, *The Sensuous Woman* by J., *The Joy of Sex*, *Fear of Flying* by Erica Jong, even a huge tattered copy of the Kinsey Report appeared Mary Poppins–like from the inex-haustible duffel. She decorated the walls *and ceiling* of the single with Balinese tapestries depicting enormously endowed men performing acrobatic sex with pointy-breasted, jewel-encrusted women. Even her seemingly innocent collection of oriental tea tins proved sexual in nature.

"This tea is an aphrodisiac," she informed a horrified Lucy. "Of course the real aphrodisiac is in here." She opened up a large cask-shaped tin that was decorated with a landscape of golden mountains. Inside was a pungent-smelling brownish herb. "Does pot make you horny, too?" she asked us.

Lucy wasn't the only one offended by Deirdre's sexual references. She drove Helen Chambers to distraction by finding sexual refer-ences in every other Latin word.

"Domina?" she said on the first day of class. "As in dominatrix?"

When *Domina* Chambers told her that the translation of *praeda* was booty, Deirdre asked, "Booty? As in ass?"

"No," *Domina* Chambers replied, "as in loot from a conquest."

I am sure that Helen Chambers regretted that the second-year Latin curriculum devoted so much attention to the poet Catullus.

"His girlfriend's name was Lesbia?" Deirdre asked incredulously. "As in . . ."

"No," *Domina* Chambers interrupted, "as in the island of Lesbos, home of the Greek poetess Sappho. Catullus was acknowledging his literary debt to the Greek lyric poets."

"Yeah, but wasn't Sappho like a famous dyke?"

"Sappho did write some beautiful love poems to women. We don't know that her sentiments were expressed . . . er . . . physically."

I had never seen Miss Chambers so rattled.

"I bet she's one," Deirdre told us when we were translating our Latin together that night.

"One what?" Lucy asked.

"A lezzie." Deirdre held up her right hand and wriggled it like a fish. She was wearing a silk hand-painted kimono that her parents had sent her from Kyoto. It was patterned in pale blue and turquoise waves through which swam beautiful red and gold carp. There were slits under the wide sleeves through which I could see Deirdre's bare breasts, like two fish escaped from the kimono's pattern.

"*Domina* Chambers is not a lesbian," Lucy had responded coldly, looking away from Deirdre's exposed breasts. "My mother went to school with her and she says that Helen Chambers was one of the most popular girls at Vassar. She spent almost every weekend at Yale."

"So why didn't she marry one of those Yalies?" Deirdre asked. I could tell that Lucy had piqued her interest. We could all picture, I think, Helen Chambers, in a sweater set and pearls, riding the train to New Haven. A boy in a tweed jacket—or maybe a letter sweater— would meet her at the station.

"She devoted herself to scholarship," Lucy answered, "to the classics."

"Then why isn't she a professor at some college? Or an archaeologist digging up Etruscan artifacts? I mean teaching high school Latin is hardly an exciting career."

I could tell that Lucy was troubled by this question. There *was* something about Helen Chambers that didn't quite add up. Even though there was a tradition of alumnae returning to Heart Lake to teach, Helen Chambers stood out just a little from the other old girls. From Lucy's mother, we knew that after Vassar Helen Chambers had gone to Oxford. She had lived in Rome for several years at the American Academy on the Janiculum Hill and published articles in learned philological journals on Etruscan vases and lacunae in ancient texts. Then she'd come back to New York to complete her doctorate at Barnard. Unlike our other teachers, Helen Chambers was embarked on an illustrious career, but just when it seemed that she had broken free of whatever gravitational pull the school exerted on its alumnae, she had abandoned the doctorate and taken the job at Heart Lake.

"Maybe she was broke," Deirdre said.

"No." Lucy shook her head and wrinkled up her nose. The idea of Helen Chambers's life being determined by base financial considerations was distasteful to her. "I think it had something to do with a failed love affair. I think she was in love with a married man and in order to break it off she had to leave the city."

I remembered the yearbook picture I had seen on the kitchen table. The handsome blond man smiling at Helen Chambers and Hannah Toller. The man who looked like Lucy. It occurred to me that the story Lucy was telling might be Hannah Toller's story. Perhaps she was the girl who left her married lover, bore Lucy in secrecy and shame, and came home to Heart Lake.

"Yeah," Deirdre said. I could tell she liked Lucy's story. She was beginning to be won over by the mystique of Helen Chambers. "Maybe they still meet when she goes into the city. She can't spend all her time shopping and going to the ballet."

Lucy considered. "Perhaps they meet, just once a year, for drinks at the Lotus Club."

"For old time's sake," Deirdre said.

Lucy smiled at her. After weeks of her offending Lucy, I was alarmed to see that Deirdre Hall might also be capable of charming Lucy. But then, as usual, Deirdre went a bit too far (*overkill,* Lucy would say).

"Yeah," Deirdre said, "and then, for old time's sake, they go upstairs and get laid."

THROUGHOUT THE FALL SEMESTER OF THAT SOPHOMORE YEAR Lucy and Deirdre vied with each other like dancers pulling back and forth in some elaborate tango. Although they seemed to hate each other, they couldn't stay away from each other. I understood how Deirdre might be won over by Lucy. Everybody was. At the lower school, where Lucy worked as an aide, the younger girls all adored her. When we met her there after our last class, the children followed Lucy out the door, begging for another story, a song, a hug. One girl, a pathetic-looking creature with pinched features and hair as colorless as dried straw and with the sadly apt name of Albie, used to follow us back to the dorm. It was unnerving the way she'd material- ize in the woods. Deirdre would yell at her and stamp her foot the way you would to scare away a stray dog, but Albie wouldn't even flinch. Only when Lucy would go up to her and whisper something in her ear would she leave, vanishing behind the pine trees as quickly and silently as a cat.

"Poor kid," I said one day, more because I saw that Lucy had been gentle to her than because I really felt sorry for her. "What an awful name."

"Thanks," said Lucy, laughing, "I gave it to her. I told her it would be her Latin name when she started Latin next year, so now she insists everyone call her that. She just needs a little attention. Her dad died when she was little and Albie says her mother's nervous, which I think means she's in and out of mental hospitals. Every time Albie's not doing well her mother thinks it's the school's fault and she switches her to another school. She's only ten and this is her fourth school."

"Please, I'm gonna bawl," Deirdre said, lighting a cigarette. "The kid is creepy and she's getting in our way. It's like she's spying on us."

This was a concern because we had begun to roam the woods when we were supposed to be in evening study hall. Our first forays into the woods were Deirdre's idea. She wanted to find a place to smoke, cigarettes at first, and then pot. I was surprised that Lucy went along with these expeditions—Lucy refused to even try a ciga- rette or a joint—but I soon realized that Lucy felt confined by the regimentation of Heart Lake. She had grown up wandering the woods with Matt, eating when she wanted, sleeping late and missing school if she wished to. She hated, she told me, having to be around people all the time. She hated *the goals of community and cooperation*.

Deirdre, an old veteran of boarding schools, proved to be an ex- pert at subverting and eluding the rules. "Sign into study hall and then excuse yourself to go to the head. We'll meet in the bathroom next to the Music Room and slip out the back door. They'll never miss us."

It seemed to me that we could have done that without Deirdre, but if we were caught, Deirdre always came up with a quick and reasonable cover.

"Jane just got her period, Miss Pike," she explained to the swimming coach one night when we were discovered in the woods behind the mansion. "We're going back to the dorm for a sanitary napkin."

"We're looking for tadpoles, Miss Buehl," she told the science teacher when she found us sneaking down to the swimming beach. "Your lecture on metamorphosis was *so* inspiring."

She had a flair for the dramatic. After we heard the story about the three sisters at the Fall Bonfire she immediately said we had to get out to the farthest rock at midnight under a full moon and say a prayer to the Lake Goddess so we would be spared from the Crevecoeur curse.

"How can we?" I asked. "You can't get there by jumping from the other rocks. Can't we make our sacrifice from the first rock?"

"No, it has to be the third one," Deirdre said.

Lucy agreed. "*Domina* Chambers says that three is an enchanted number. And that the hero must always undergo a series of difficult tests, like the labors of Hercules, to prove himself."

"We'll swim to the rock," Deirdre said. "We do it all the time in swim class."

"But at night? We don't even have suits." We were issued swim suits for class, thick cotton one-pieces that billowed in the water and made all but the slimmest girls look hideous.

Lucy laughed. "Who needs suits? Gosh, Jane, you're so *conventional* sometimes." I saw Deirdre smile. I remembered what my mother always said: "In a threesome one always gets left out."

"If you're scared you can stay in the room," Lucy said.

I was scared, but I wasn't going to stay in the room. For this expedition we needed more time than study hall allowed. Deirdre planned it all. After lights out we would each, one by one, go down the hall in our nightgowns to the bathroom and then we'd leave by the bathroom window, which was at the back of the dorm, facing away from the lake. We'd cut through the woods behind the lower school, and then climb over the rocks on the Point to avoid being seen by Miss Buehl, who lived in the cottage at the top of the steps leading down to the swimming beach.

"But then how will we get down to the swimming beach?" I asked. "The entrance to the stairs is right across from her front door."

"There's a way to climb from the Point down to the swimming beach," Lucy said. "Matt and I did it a couple of years ago when we sneaked onto the campus to go swimming."

"Why doesn't he sneak onto the campus now and join us?" Deirdre asked. "I mean, you miss him so much and all."

"That's not a bad idea," Lucy said. "Maybe another time."

That first night we went out to the rock was unseasonably warm and curiously still for mid-October. I was sure we'd still be cold, so I wore my heaviest flannel nightgown. Deirdre wore the hand-painted kimono, which shimmered like water in the moonlight. The red and gold carp seemed to swim under the tall pines. Lucy wore a plain white T-shirt that came down below her knees and probably had belonged to Matt originally. The two of them, walking ahead of me on the path, looked like figures on a vase. I felt absurd in my stiff flannel gown with its print of teddy bears and hearts.

We stopped in the woods and Deirdre lit a joint. She handed it to Lucy who, much to my surprise, took a long, deep drag on it. She handed it to me and, still holding the smoke in, said in a tight voice, "Remember what *Domina* said about the Delphic oracle?" I remembered Helen Chambers's lecture on the ancients' use of hallucinogenic herbs. *So you condone drug use, Domina,* Deirdre had asked. *The ancients used it for sacred, not recreational, purposes,* our teacher had answered.

I took the joint and placed it, gingerly, to my lips. I wondered if I could just pretend to smoke it, but both Deirdre and Lucy were waiting to see the tip of the joint flame red. I inhaled and held the smoke in my lungs, the way Deirdre said you had to. I also remembered that she said most people didn't get high their first time.

We smoked that joint until it was a tiny, burning nub, which

Deirdre held delicately between her long fingernails. When I was sure it was all smoked down, Deirdre turned the roach around so that the lit side was in her mouth, and motioned for Lucy to come closer. Lucy, who was quite a bit shorter than Deirdre, tilted her face up to Deirdre's, so close it seemed they might kiss, and Deirdre blew a long stream of smoke into Lucy's open mouth. I was amazed at how well they did it. And then I realized it couldn't have been the first time.

I didn't think I was high, but the rest of the walk seemed bathed in a different light. The forest floor, covered with pine needles, glowed golden and seemed to roll up to meet my bare feet. The white trunks of the birch trees flicked by me like the blades of a fan slicing the shadows, spilling splashes of white into the darkness of the woods. It was as if a white figure flitted in between the trees beyond the path, but when I stopped to look for it there was nothing in the dark and silent woods.

When we came to the Point, the domed rock we clambered over glittered as if studded with diamonds. I found myself lost in its rough, crystally texture as we climbed down to the limestone ledge and from there to the swimming beach. It was better than looking over the edge at the sheer drop down to the water.

It took me longer than the others to make the climb down. By the time I was on the beach they were already in the water. Deirdre's pale silk kimono was draped over a rock and Lucy's T-shirt lay crumpled at the edge of the water. I pulled the heavy flannel nightgown over my head and stood for a moment, shivering on the shore.

I could see them, a little ways out in the water, gold and white like the beautiful carp in Deirdre's kimono. They had reached the third rock, which was the only one flat enough to climb up on, and Deirdre was pulling herself up, clumsily flopping on the rock. Lucy turned toward the shore and treaded water. When she saw me she raised her hand to wave and I saw her sink a little, her lips just touching the black surface of the lake. I remembered a line of poetry Miss Macintosh had read to us. *They're not waving,* it went, *they're drowning.* There was something in me that made me want to stand there and see how long Lucy would wave. How far she would sink.

But then I shook myself, dispersing the chill, and walked into the water. I plunged in to get the worst of the shock over with, and swam fast to warm up. I was a good swimmer. One of the strongest in the class, Miss Pike said, although, she would inevitably add, my form could use work.

I swam a little past the rock, showing off a bit. When I approached the far side of the rock, though, I found that the rock was sheer at this end, the water too deep to touch bottom. Lucy and Deirdre had to each take a hand to haul me up.

"Good work, Jane," Lucy said.

"Yeah, Jane, you're braver than I thought," Deirdre said.

We sat on the rock for a few minutes looking out over the still, moonlit lake. I didn't feel cold anymore. The climb and the swim had warmed me up. What surprised me was that I didn't feel afraid either. The third rock was past the Point, and so we could have been seen from the windows of the mansion, but I imagined that if someone, say Helen Chambers who had an apartment on the top floor of the mansion, had looked out her window and seen us, three naked girls on a rock in the middle of the lake, she would have thought it was a vision. I imagined that we looked like the three graces in the painting by Botticelli Miss Beade had shown us.

As if responding to a prearranged signal, we all stood up. Lucy slid her arm over my shoulder and Deirdre, on my other side, slipped her arm over Lucy's. I pulled my arms up to clasp theirs, but instead I kept lifting them—they felt weightless, as if pulled by the moon—until my hands were suspended over their heads. We hadn't talked about what form our "prayer" to the Lake Goddess would take. "We'll let the spirit of the moment move us," Lucy had said. I had imagined it would be Lucy or Deirdre who would think of what to say. They were both better at that sort of thing. But now, with Lucy and Deirdre at my side, I felt stronger than I ever had before. My mother was wrong. Three was a magic number.

"Spirit of the Lake," I said. "We come here in the spirit of friendship. We don't ask for special protection."

I saw Lucy nod. It was what *Domina* Chambers always told us.

The ancients believed they must first humble themselves before the gods. The greatest sin was hubris.

I knew then what form the prayer should take. "All we ask," I said in a high, ringing voice that seemed to echo off the stone face of the Point, which towered above us, "is that whatever happens to one of us, let happen to all of us."

Chapter Sixteen

●

"WE NEED A STAG-KING." DEIRDRE HELD THE HAIRPIN figurine we had recently dubbed a corniculum in her fingers and wriggled it in the light from the window. A minute before she had been dancing around the room to the Allman Brothers singing "Ramblin' Man" on the radio, but then "Seasons in the Sun" came on and she switched it off.

Lucy looked up from Graves's *The White Goddess* and nodded. "Like Cernunnos," she said. "The horned one, the antlered king."

"Like Actaeon," Deirdre said.

"Actaeon was slaughtered by his own hounds," I said. It was junior year. Deirdre had read an article in *Ms.* magazine about matriarchal cultures and goddess worship. She spent most of Latin class pestering *Domina* Chambers about "the patriarchal canon" she adhered to. "At the very least," she told our teacher, "we should be doing Ovid's *Art of Love* instead of boring old *Metamorphoses.*"

I picked up my translation for the next day's class and read aloud: " 'Now they are all around him, tearing deep their master's flesh.' His dogs ate him alive."

Deirdre shrugged. "*Domina* Chambers said he got what he deserved for spying on Diana in her bath."

"But it was an accident," I told her. "Look, even Ovid says so,

'The fault was fortune's and no guilt that day, for what guilt can it be to lose one's way.' "

Lucy sighed. "Don't be so literal, Jane. We're not going to hunt some poor boy down and eat him." Deirdre giggled and Lucy gave her a look that silenced her.

"It's a symbolic rite of renewal. The goddess joins with the stag-king and the community is granted fertility and good fortune."

"Yeah, the goddess and the stag-king get it on."

"Well, are we going to take that part *literally*?"

"I certainly hope so," Deirdre said.

"Then who gets to be the goddess?" I asked.

Deirdre jingled the hairpins so that they sparkled in the sun and she wiggled her hips like one of the Balinese dancers on the tapestries that decorated her room. "Who do you think? Who around here *looks* like a fertility goddess?"

"The goddess is the lake," Lucy said reprovingly. "The stag-king will swim in the lake, like a baptism, and that will appease the Lake Goddess."

"Oh." Deirdre looked disappointed. She tapped the hairpin that dangled from the "mouth" of the top hairpin so that it swung in a wide arc. "Is our stag-king also going to be symbolic or do we at least get a real boy?"

I saw Lucy considering. We both knew which boy Deirdre had in mind. Although Lucy and Deirdre had been friends, more or less, since that night sophomore year when we all swam in the lake, Lucy still hadn't let Deirdre spend any time with Matt. She had met him the couple of times Matt had come to Friday tea and the Founder's Day picnic, but Lucy had always been careful to keep Deirdre from spending too much time with her brother.

"He's adorable," Deirdre had confided to me. "I see why you like him. Have you ever . . . you know . . . done anything with him?"

"He's just a friend," I said, "and my best friend's brother. I don't think of him that way."

Deirdre eyed me skeptically. Just as she had a way of finding sexual meaning in the most innocuous Latin phrase, so she could inject sexual context into the most innocent friendship. Over the year and a half we had all been at Heart Lake she had posited illicit liaisons between the groundskeeper and Miss Buehl, Miss Buehl and Miss Pike, Miss Macintosh and Miss Pike, Miss Beade and three of the senior girls, and the class president and the captain of the swim team. She had taken it for granted from the beginning that I *had a thing* for Matt.

I suppose she was right. Pressed between the pages of my *Tales from the Ballet* I kept the red maple leaf he had given me on that first walk home. It wasn't a rose, but he had *pretended* it was when he gave it to me, so wasn't it almost as if it were a rose? I'd saved other things, too. The pebbles he gave me when he was teaching me to skip stones on the lake, notes he'd written me in Latin class when we were still at Corinth High, and a skate key he'd dropped in the icehouse and thought was lost. I kept them with my journals under a loose board beneath my desk. Not even Lucy knew about my hiding place or the things I wrote in my journal about Matt.

"I think Lucy misses him," I wrote in my journal. I'd used up the first notebook he'd given me and bought a new one that was just the same. I had sat a long time with the fountain pen poised over the lined paper before adding, "I miss him, too."

Since we'd been at Heart Lake we'd seen less of him. I knew Lucy missed him terribly. For the whole first year she had slept in one of his old hockey jerseys, and sometimes at night, after she thought I was asleep, I heard her crying. If she hadn't been afraid of Deirdre going after him I think she would have thought of some way of seeing him more. After all, he lived less than half a mile from the school—only a quarter mile from the far end of the lake—and he knew every inch of the woods surrounding Heart Lake.

"I bet Matt would be interested in the Cernunnos legend," I said.

Both girls looked at me as if they had never heard of a boy named Matt. I half expected Deirdre to say, "Matt who?"

Lucy sighed. "Actually, Mattie's more interested in chemistry and physics these days."

After Lucy and I had gotten the Iris Scholarship, Helen Chambers had given up on her experiment with public education, and Corinth High School had, in turn, given up on its Latin program. Matt seemed forlorn without Latin until he discovered physics.

"All he talks about these days is the temperature/density relationship in water and the molecular structure of ice. He's keen on seeing the lake freeze."

"Well," Deirdre said, "he can watch for the lake to freeze and we can reenact the rite of the horned god. Hey, do you think that's how we got the expression *horny*?"

"We can't make Matt swim in the lake," Lucy said. "It's already too cold."

"They do it in Russia," Deirdre said. "But yeah, it's even getting too cold to hang out outside. If only we had some kind of shelter. The changing room at the swimming beach would be perfect, but they lock it up over the winter."

"There's the icehouse," I said. "We could meet there."

Lucy's head jerked up. Belatedly I remembered that Matt and Lucy had made me promise not to tell anyone that they used the icehouse.

"What icehouse?" Deirdre asked. "It doesn't sound too appealing."

"It's not," Lucy said flatly. "It's just a little hut on the other end of the lake where the Crevecoeurs used to store ice harvested from the lake. It's a good twenty-minute walk away."

"Is there anything in it?"

I shook my head no, but Lucy was nodding. "The county extension agent keeps her rowboat there, but she only comes once a week, on Tuesdays, to take water samples."

I looked at Lucy in surprise. I hadn't been to the icehouse since we had all gone skating last winter. Apparently she and Matt had been there without me.

"A boat?" Deirdre said. "Cool. We could have our stag-king rite on the water. When can your brother meet us there?"

∙ ∙ ∙

I DON'T KNOW HOW MUCH LUCY TOLD MATT ABOUT THE horned god, but he was excited about what he called the first ice club. We met at the icehouse the last weekend in November.

Matt brought a thermos of hot chocolate. Deirdre brought a joint. Lucy brought blankets. We sat in the hull of the extension agent's rowboat using her life jackets for pillows. We'd decided it was too dangerous to take the boat out; someone might see us. Matt insisted that we keep the doors at the end of the hut open so we could look at the lake, even though it made the hut unbearably cold. It was beautiful though. Lying in the hull of the boat, looking out the doors, it seemed as if we were on the water. Across the lake we could see the stone wall of the Point jutting into the lake like the prow of a gigantic ocean liner bearing down on us. After a few hits, I felt as if we were gliding toward it.

"The lake has already begun the process of freezing," Matt told us. "This first stage is called overturn. As water gets colder it gets denser, so it sinks and the warm water rises to the top." Matt made circles in the air with his hands. "But—and this is the part that's really amazing—if water continued getting denser as it froze the lake would freeze from the bottom up."

"It doesn't?" Deirdre asked.

Lucy gave her a scornful look, but Matt continued his explanation patiently.

"If it did that all the fish and other creatures would die. But what happens is that at four degrees Celsius water becomes less dense. That means that ice is actually less dense than water."

"I may be too dense to get this," Deirdre said, passing Matt the joint. "Science was never my thing."

I was surprised at Deirdre putting herself down like this in front of Matt. I thought she would want to impress him. It was weird, too, because Deirdre wasn't dense about stuff like this. She was actually pretty good at science. If she hadn't spent most of her time getting stoned and thinking about boys, she would have gotten all A's. As it was, she did almost no work and still got B's.

Matt took a hit off the joint and passed it to Lucy, then he reached across me and took Deirdre's hands in both of his.

"It's like this." He turned her right hand so that its back lay against the palm of her left. I saw Deirdre wince, but she didn't complain and I don't think Matt noticed he was hurting her.

"This is what a water molecule is like above four degrees Celsius. The two hydrogen atoms fit together like two spoons lying in the same direction. When people lie like that they call it spooning."

I imagined lying next to Matt like that. I imagined what it would feel like to lie against his back, against his broad swimmer's shoulders, and bend my knees to fit into the space where his knees bent. I wondered if Deirdre was imagining the same thing. Why hadn't he used my hands for his demonstration? Why hadn't I said I was dense?

"The oxygen atom lies alongside the two hydrogen atoms," he added, balling his hand like a fist against the palm of Deirdre's right hand. "But at four degrees Celsius the hydrogen atoms flip around." Matt turned Deirdre's right hand over so that her palms were facing each other as if in prayer. "See that space between your hands," he tickled the inside of her palms and she giggled. "There's a little pocket between the atoms now. That's why ice is lighter than water."

"I still don't get it," I said.

Matt dropped Deirdre's hands. I was hoping he would take mine, but instead he made two peace signs with his fingers and held them up.

"Tricky Dick," Deirdre said. She had a cartoon tacked to her wall of Nixon holding his fingers up in two V's.

He lowered his fingers so they were pointing out, into the center of the circle we made inside the boat. "You can also think of it like this. Each water molecule is made up of three atoms—two hydrogen, one oxygen—so it's like a triangle. When water is liquid, the molecules just lie on top of each other like this. He lay one peace sign over another. "But at four degrees Celsius, the hydrogen molecules flip around because they want to touch."

"Oooh," Deirdre cooed. "Lezzie molecules."

"Jesus, Deir," Lucy said, "only you could make hydrogen bonding sexy."

"Well, it is kind of sexy," Matt admitted. "I mean it has to do with attraction. In a water molecule, the positively charged nuclei of these three atoms are stuck together by negatively charged electrons. But the oxygen atom is so greedy for the attention of electrons that it strips the two hydrogen atoms of their negative charge. That makes the hydrogen atoms attracted to other electrons, like the oxygen atom in another water molecule. That's why water is liquid. When water freezes, the hydrogen bonds hold each molecule apart."

Matt reached out both his arms and took my hand and Lucy's. "You guys hold hands, too," he said.

I saw Lucy reluctantly take Deirdre's hand and Deirdre took my hand.

"Now hold your arms out straight."

We had to shuffle around in the boat a little to make space so we could all hold our arms out straight. The boat rocked on the wooden floor of the icehouse. It was a good thing, I thought, that we weren't doing this on the water.

"See how we take up more space now," Matt said. "We're ice."

"My ass is ice," Deirdre said. She released Lucy's and my hands and stood up. The boat lurched toward her and then, when she stepped out of it, careened away from her. Lucy and I both fell against Matt. I felt Matt's arm around me, steadying me.

"Hey, you broke the molecular bond," Matt said.

"I always was a great ice breaker," Deirdre said, shimmying her shoulders and hips. Even under a sweater and down jacket you could see her breasts swaying. I realized she hadn't worn a bra. I looked at Matt and it seemed his gaze also rested on Deirdre at about chest level.

"I think that concludes the science portion of the evening," Deirdre said. "And now for the sacred rite of the horned god. Got your antlers ready, Matt?"

Matt held up his fingers in V's again, but this time he held them over Lucy's head. "I always thought Lucy would make a good deer," he said. "She's about as brave as one."

Lucy shook his hands away and got up out of the boat. She stood at the doorway of the hut and stretched her arms over her head. She was wearing a pale blue ski parka that glimmered against the cold black water. She was like a deer, I thought, leggy and lithe. I thought of a line from Book Four of the *Aeneid*. It's when Dido realizes that Aeneas doesn't love her anymore and he's going to leave her. *"Qualis coniecta cerva sagitta,"* I recited, impressed at myself for remembering the Latin.

With her back to us, Lucy took up the passage, reciting it to the lake. As she spoke Deirdre moved next to her and held her arms up, too. I stayed in the boat with Matt. He had put his arm back around my shoulder.

"Quam procul incautam nemora inter Cresia fixit pastor agens telis liquitque volatile ferrum nescius: illa fuga silvas saltusque peragrat Dictaeos; haeret lateri letalis harundo," Lucy recited.

"Wow," I said. "How'd you remember all that?"

Lucy shrugged. "It's my favorite part."

"Might an ordinary mortal ask for a translation?" Matt asked.

"Just as when a deer pierced by an arrow from some shepherd, who unknowing leaves in her the flying iron, wanders the woods and mountain glades with the deadly shaft still clinging to her flesh," I told him. I had left out a bunch of words, but that was the gist of it. "It's like, even though she runs away the thing that's going to kill her stays with her. She can't escape her fate." I was surprised to hear my own voice quiver. It had always gotten to me, the way Dido was doomed to kill herself from the moment she set eyes on Aeneas.

Matt squeezed my shoulder and I felt his lips brush the side of my face. "You're a sweet kid, Jane," he whispered in my ear, "but I think these two might rip me to shreds, so I better hightail it."

He was gone before I knew it; only the sway of the empty boat and a damp spot on my cheek where his lips had brushed told me he'd been there a minute ago. Deirdre and Lucy ran after him. I could hear them, laughing and shrieking through the woods. I could have caught up with them, but instead I lay back in the boat and watched the moon move from behind a cloud. The rocky prow of the Point, as if awakened by the cascade of white light, seemed to glide toward me, silent as an iceberg in a still, black sea.

Chapter Seventeen

•

ON THE NIGHT BEFORE CHRISTMAS BREAK I CAME BACK to our room from dinner and found a corniculum tacked to the door. I was surprised because it was so cold, but Lucy said we couldn't miss the solstice because it would be a propitious night for the first ice to form. It was a windless night and the full moon seemed unusually close and bright.

"It's going down below zero tonight," Deirdre said. "We could get frostbite. And besides, I feel awful." Deirdre sneezed and blew her nose. She had gone to the infirmary that day and the nurse had excused her from her last final and said she should stay in bed until it was time to catch her train home.

"You don't have to go if you don't want to," Lucy said. "How about it, Jane? Are you afraid of the cold?"

Truthfully, I didn't relish the idea of going out in the cold. I felt like I was coming down with whatever Deirdre had. We'd stayed up late studying for finals all week. Deirdre had produced a white powder that she said was crystal methedrine. She showed Lucy and me how to snort it through a straw. It burned my nostrils and made me feel cold and brittle.

"I wouldn't want to disappoint Matt," I said. "I guess I'll go. I'll just put on some long underwear."

Lucy turned to Deirdre, who was boiling water on her hot plate. When the water came to a boil she poured a little into a willow-patterned teapot and swished it around. Then she dumped the water out onto the window ledge. Because she had been doing this all winter unusual ice structures had formed.

"Oh well, we wouldn't want to disappoint Mattie." Deirdre knew Lucy hated it when she called him Mattie. "But I suggest we all have some tea before we go." Deirdre opened several of her tins and put a pinch from each one into the teapot.

"Someday she's going to poison us," Lucy said to me.

"Or herself," I suggested.

Deirdre smiled and filled the teapot with steaming water. "Only if I meant to," she said. She tapped the lid of a small, red lacquer box. "I have some stuff that would put a person to sleep for a long winter's nap."

Deirdre poured out the tea into three china cups. She handed one to me and one to Lucy.

"But I would never do that to you guys," she said. "I mean, you guys are the best friends I've ever had. One for all and all for one, right? *E Pluribus unum.*"

Deirdre held up her steaming teacup and we all clinked cups together.

The tea actually made me feel better. It coursed through my veins like the warm currents that you sometimes swam through in the lake. I could imagine the glow in my blood staving off the winter chill. We waited that night until after the last bed check and then pulled jeans and sweaters over our long underwear. The hard part was holding on to the drainpipe when we climbed out the bathroom window. I had to take off my mittens to get a good grip and the metal was so cold that my clammy hands nearly stuck to it. Even after I put my mittens back on my skin felt raw. And not just the skin on my hands. The fire Deirdre's tea had lit in my blood had turned into an icy trickle. My whole body felt flayed by the cold.

We followed the path around the west side of the lake. A few inches of new snow had fallen that evening so the path looked clean and bright in the moonlight; I felt like I could see each individual crystal. The path had narrowed between two low walls of snow so we couldn't walk three abreast. Sometimes I walked behind Lucy and Deirdre and sometimes Deirdre would run forward on the path and Lucy and I were next to each other. I thought to myself that my mother really was wrong about threesomes, that the balance between us was always shifting, not set in stone. Sometimes, though, I missed how it was when it was still Lucy and Matt and I.

Just before we reached the end of the lake I heard a movement in the woods. I stopped to peer into the maze of pine trunks and the long shadows they cast on the white snow. I watched the shadow of a branch swaying in the wind and then realized that there was no wind. The branched shape suddenly detached itself from the shadows and moved away from me, flitting over the white surface of the snow.

I turned back to the path to find Deirdre and Lucy but they had walked on without me. They must have rounded the end of the lake because they were nowhere in sight along the path. When I turned back to the woods the branched shape had vanished. I figured it must have been a deer. Nothing else could move so swiftly and silently.

Or else Deirdre really had added something to the tea and I was hallucinating.

The thought was terrifying. Had Deirdre drugged me and then somehow gotten Lucy to go along with abandoning me in the woods? What might I see next? I turned around quickly and my eyes caught a movement in the trees—a glitter like fireflies drifting through the pine needles. Only it was the dead of winter; there were no fireflies.

When I rounded the end of the lake I thought that must be it— I was hallucinating—because standing on the path with Deirdre and Lucy were three hooded figures.

Deirdre detached herself from the group and came skipping toward me. She grabbed my hand and pulled me over to one of the hooded figures. She was babbling something in my ear that I found difficult to make out. There were too many things wrong here for me to sort out: too many people and it should have been Lucy, not Deirdre, taking my hand and making sure I was included.

One of the hooded boys—they were just boys, I realized now, all three of them wearing hooded sweatshirts beneath their down parkas—nodded gruffly to me and I realized I had missed hearing his name. I noticed, though, that he had the same square jaw and ruddy complexion as Matt, even the same height and build, and it occurred to me that he must be the cousin from downstate I was always hearing about. I understood then why Deirdre was so anxious to pair me up with him. Deirdre the matchmaker. He wouldn't do for Lucy because he was Lucy's cousin.

I turned to the other three on the path: Lucy, Matt, and Ward Castle. Jesus, I thought, whatever possessed Matt to bring Ward Castle? Lucy had barely endured his insults throughout ninth-grade Latin. His favorite epithet for her was "Loose Toe-Hair." She called him "Wart."

"Hey, hey, hey, my darling Clementine," he warbled to me. "How's it hanging?"

Behind Ward I saw Matt wince. "You remember Ward Castle," Matt said to me. "Ward's my lab partner this year. He said he wanted to see the lake freeze."

"Yeah, I'm here for the chemistry lesson," Ward said.

Had Matt really believed Ward was interested in seeing the lake freeze? For the first time it occurred to me that Matt could be too trusting.

"Oh, we'll be experimenting with an assortment of chemicals." Deirdre had somehow worked her way around Matt's cousin and Ward and repositioned herself next to Matt. She lit a joint and passed it to Matt. "Shall we start with some cannabis before the sacred rites begin?"

"Sacred rites?" Ward asked. "Like sacrificing a virgin?" Ward put his arm around Lucy and pulled her to him. The night was so still I could hear the rustle their down coats made rubbing against each other. Lucy's head barely reached his armpit. She smiled up at him sweetly.

"Yes," she said, "we're going to sacrifice a virgin. A boy virgin. Any volunteers?"

I could see in the bright moonlight Ward turn as white as the snow.

"Hey, it's a little cold out here for that stuff," he said. "I thought you said you had a place."

Matt jerked his chin in the direction the path led. "Yeah, it's up here. We just have to cross the stream." He turned and we followed.

We walked in twos now: Matt and Deirdre, Lucy and Ward, me and the nameless cousin, who seemed mute as well as nameless. He's probably mortified to be paired with me, I thought. No doubt he had been taken with Deirdre before I showed up on the path. That was why Deirdre had been so anxious to pair us off, because if she got stuck with the cousin, I'd get Matt. And I knew that was the last thing she wanted.

The Schwanenkill was nearly frozen, but when I was halfway across it my foot broke through the ice. I would have fallen if the cousin hadn't grabbed my elbow and steadied me. It was tricky, too, getting up the opposite side. He scrambled up the bank deftly, with more grace than you'd expect from a boy his size.

He's probably terrified of ending up alone with me, I thought, as I struggled up the slippery bank. I'd taken my mittens off so I could grab tree branches to pull myself up, but my hands were still sore from climbing down the drainpipe and I couldn't get a grip. My throat felt raw, whether from cold or holding back tears I wasn't sure. I looked up, expecting the cousin to be well on his way to the ice-house, but instead he was standing at the top of the bank, his feet angled into the snowy slope for purchase, his arm stretched out toward me. I took his hand and was surprised to feel warm skin. He'd even taken his glove off to grip my hand better.

"Thanks," I said when he'd pulled me to the top of the bank.

He shrugged and mumbled something. God, he was even clumsier and shier than I, I thought, but before he let go of my hand I felt his broad thumb stroke the inside of my wrist and the movement sent a warm electrical current through the core of my body, reigniting the warmth that had started that night in Deirdre's tea.

We got to the icehouse, but the door was shut. I reached for the handle, but he stopped me.

"Uh, maybe they want some privacy," he said.

"The four of them?" I asked incredulously.

He turned his head up the path and I saw two figures just disappearing over a rise. From the disparity in their heights I guessed it was Lucy and Ward. That left Matt and Deirdre in the icehouse. And it left me and the cousin out here in the cold.

"Where do you think they're going?" I asked.

"Lucy said something earlier about sneaking back into the dorm. You two share a room?"

I nodded. I couldn't imagine Lucy and Ward together, but then a lot of things had happened this night that I hadn't been able to imagine. The cousin rubbed his hands together and blew into them to warm his face.

"I guess you'd like to get inside," I said. "There's a supply shed on the lower school playground . . ."

"You know, I'd like to see if Mattie's right about the ice. I've lived near frozen ponds all my life, but I can't say I've ever been there when the ice formed."

I looked at the lake. It was black and still, but as far as I could tell, unfrozen.

"We could go to the swimming beach," I said. "The boathouse is locked, but there's a place in the rocks that's almost like a little cave. At least it would be sheltered, and we can see the lake from there."

"Sounds good," he said.

We walked the rest of the way in silence, but it didn't feel like an uncomfortable silence now. Once I thought I saw something moving in the woods and I was glad I wasn't alone. I was glad, too, when we got to the top of the swimming beach steps that I didn't have to warn him to be quiet so Miss Buehl wouldn't hear us from her house. I led the way down the steps and showed him the hollow in the cliff wall behind the second sister stone. Part of the cave was under water, but there was a raised ledge along the cliff wall you could follow to get inside and then there was a flat rock above the water where two people could sit. It was out of the wind, but as soon as we sat down I started to shiver.

"Do you think we could make a little fire without attracting attention?" he asked.

"We can't be seen from the mansion or the dorms here," I told him. "And Miss Buehl is probably fast asleep."

We gathered some branches and pinecones from the beach and banked them against the cliff wall. He took out a wooden match and lit it by striking his fingernail against its sulfur tip. Then we sat with our backs against the cliff and watched the lake. When he saw I was still shivering he put his arm around me and I put my head against his chest and closed my eyes.

I must have fallen asleep because when I opened my eyes the fire was out. I looked at the boy next to me and in the shadow of the cliff it could have been Matt. I slipped my hand out of my mitten and with the backs of my fingers I stroked the side of his face, along the jawbone, just under his ear. He stirred at my touch and moved into the light that angled into the cave. In the dim gray light of dawn I saw that this wasn't Matt, and wouldn't ever be.

I became aware of a numbness spreading through my legs and I got up to get my blood moving. From the east, where the sun was rising, a flock of Canada geese were moving through the sky. I watched them land on the lake and, instead of skidding into the water, stand on its surface. I moved closer to the edge of the cave and saw that a thin layer of ice covered the water. I hugged myself against the cold and against the sense that I had missed something.

Chapter Eighteen

●

AFTER CHRISTMAS BREAK MATT AND LUCY'S COUSIN WENT back home. The three of them had come looking for me on New Year's Day to take me skating, but my mother had turned them away at the door, saying I had chores to attend to, so I never did see the cousin again. I was disappointed, at first, that I didn't get a chance to say good-bye to him, but then, remembering that moment at dawn when I'd touched his face, I was relieved. I knew I'd be embarassed every time I saw him, even if he had been asleep.

By the time school started again the lake ice measured a good three inches. By all rights, we should have disbanded the first ice club. But we didn't. When the ice was thick enough Matt suggested we turn the first ice club into a skating club. Deirdre was none too happy about this development because she didn't know how to skate.

"You don't have to come," I told her, sharpening my blades. I still had the skates Lucy had given me. I'd changed from thick socks to thin in order to get into them this year. I hoped that my feet had stopped growing.

"Oh, is that right, Clementine? You'd like that, wouldn't you?"

I'd noticed that Deirdre was a little on edge since Christmas break. She'd spent it with an aunt in Philadelphia because her parents hadn't been able to leave their new post in Kuala Lumpur. Her aunt had told her, though, that she'd have to spend spring break on campus and she'd been enrolled in a boarding school in Massachusetts for the summer. I think that the sense of being shuttled between institutions and apathetic relatives was beginning to get to her. The only person she seemed sympathetic to those days was, oddly, "Lucy's little shadow" as she called Albie, the lower school girl who still dogged our steps around the campus.

"I thought she gave you the creeps," I whispered to Deirdre one day when I came back to our room and found her helping Albie with her Latin homework. I didn't think she could hear me—the girl was in Deirdre's single; Deirdre had come out to borrow Lucy's Latin dictionary—but she looked up at the two of us and I realized it probably was obvious that we were talking about her.

"Hey, Albie," I called. "So, you're in Latin now. *Salve!*" The girl looked at me for a long moment and then looked down at her book without answering. There was something about her appearance that struck me as strange, stranger even than usual, and then I realized what it was: She was dressed all in white, a white blouse and a white pleated tennis skirt.

"Why is she wearing all white?" I scribbled on a page in my journal, which I showed to Deirdre.

"It's Miss Macintosh's influence," Deirdre wrote back. "She told the girls about Emily Dickinson always wearing white."

"Don't you think that's weird?" I wrote.

Deirdre shrugged and went back to Albie, shutting the door of the single behind her. Later, Deirdre complained to Lucy that I'd made Albie feel uncomfortable.

"Uncomfortable? How do you think she makes me feel—she looks like a ghost and won't even talk to me?"

"I wish you girls would quit bitching at each other," Lucy snapped. Deirdre and I both looked up in surprise, more at Lucy's choice of words than her tone.

"Lucy, dear," Deirdre cooed, "what have you been picking up from Ward Castle? Nothing contagious, I hope."

Lucy flung her skate down on the floor. The serrated tip of the blade gouged a deep scratch into the wood floor.

"We don't all give out on the first date, Deir." Lucy grabbed her parka and stormed out of the room. I grabbed mine and followed her without looking back at Deirdre.

I found her on the path in front of the dorm, stalled in the crossroads between three paths. There was the path that led to the lower school, the one that led to the mansion, and the one that led to the lake. They had each grown a good foot narrower since Christmas break. It was hard now to walk even two abreast.

Lucy kicked at the thigh-high wall of snow. I put my hand on her arm, but she shook it off and suddenly, like a deer bolting from cover, she vaulted the snow mound into the woods. Half her leg disappeared into the snow but, miraculously, she kept on moving, surging out of each deep hole like a swimmer doing the butterfly stroke.

I clambered over the snow wall and tried to follow her, staying in her deep footsteps. I couldn't keep up with her though. By the time her trail led me to the lake she was gone—I couldn't tell which way. I looked out over the lake, looking for breaks in the ice, but there were none. I stood at the shore, listening to the sounds the ice made. The new ice made a skittering noise, as if a thousand mice were scurrying just below its surface. It made me nervous. I felt like something was crawling up my legs. I spun around and caught a glimpse of the girl Albie just ducking behind a tree.

"Hey," I called, "have you seen Lucy out here?"

I saw half a face appear from behind a pine tree. One icy blue eye stared at me.

I took a step toward her, slowly, the way you'd approach a wild animal.

"Hey," I said again. It was the way I'd talk to a scared animal. "You know me; I'm Lucy's roommate. I'm looking for her."

The girl didn't move, but I had the sense she'd spring away if I moved an inch closer.

"You like Lucy, don't you?" I said. "I like her, too. I'm just trying to help her."

The blue eye narrowed, the w
about to pounce.

"No, you're not." Her voice wa
the cold air. It sounded like the sc
me. "You just like her brother."

"I think you're confusing r
Deirdre."

Albie smiled. "Yes, she likes hir

"You certainly notice a lot." I
said about her, how she'd grown up
real family. Although I had a fami
Since I'd come to Heart Lake my
strangers. My father, I think, was sh
acquired here; my mother, who I'd
was moving up in society, seemed
friends other than Lucy and Deirdr
and I had something in common. S
be reaching out to, the way that Lucy
ninth grade.

"I bet you know a lot of stuff ab
meant to draw her out, but I saw ri
wrong way.

"Yes," she said, "but I'm not telli
last word.

"Hey." I moved a step forward, "I

I heard a crack behind me and t
moment I thought I saw a hole in the
and I saw it was only a shadow. When
She'd disappeared as quickly as the sl
night of the solstice, and I wondere
then. But the girl was only eleven or
ning around the campus alone at night

I made my way back to the dorm,
When I got back to the room I foun
pot of tea and trying on skates.

"Hey
skates fit

AS THE
from a
in my re
and Luc
woman
Crevecc
been o
been n
groans
gion of
De
free to
them,
thick c
knew
Deirdr
the rou
again
them t
T
ter cla
the m
area.
bear
Miss
then
and t
were
ing p
arms
dry a

Jane," Lucy said as I came in. "What do you know, my old
Deirdre, too."

ICE THICKENED THE SOUNDS IT MADE CHANGED,
rvous skittering to a low-pitched moan I could hear even
om. I listened to it, alone, on the nights Deirdre and Matt
and Ward went skating on the lake. It sounded to me like a
eening and for some reason it made me think of India
ur and the daughter she had lost. I knew by then that it had
y the one daughter—Iris, for whom my scholarship had
ned—who died in the influenza epidemic, but still the
d wails the lake made could have been the sound of a le-
others grieving for a legion of daughters.

re was only interested in using the skates at night, so I was
ke them during the day. I felt squeamish sliding my feet into
e way I felt putting on bowling shoes or stepping into the
ton swimsuits issued by the school. I'd never minded when I
cy had worn them first. Now, though, I could feel how
wide ankles had stretched out the uppers and I imagined
n leather liner was darker with her sweat. I wore heavy socks
l pulled the laces so tight I broke two pairs and had to knot
gether again.

whole school, practically, was on the ice in the afternoon af-
s. We were only allowed to skate in the shallow cove below
sion lawn. Miss Pike set up orange cones to mark off the safe
e wore heavy black hockey skates and moved like a polar
oss the ice. Some of the teachers, like Miss Macintosh and
orth, teetered nervously around the marked-off circle and
ickly found their way to the log benches on the shore
iron cauldron of apple cider set on a small bonfire. Others
prisingly graceful. Miss Buehl, for instance, performed dar-
uettes and traced figure eights around the cones with her
sped behind her back. Her short, dark hair crinkled in the
with electricity. Once, when she passed me, I felt a spray of

ice hit my face and I could see a glittering trail of ice crystals following her like the tail of a comet.

Domina Chambers had a more modest style, but was equally proficient on the ice. She was certainly the most stylish of the skaters. She wore a sky blue Nordic sweater that brought out the blue in her eyes and trim black ski pants. Her skates were gleaming white with alpine flowers stitched into the leather. I'd never seen skates like them and once I overhead her tell Miss Buehl that they had been a gift from a family whose son she'd tutored in Geneva. She and Miss Buehl often skated together, their arms crossed and linked. They took turns teaching the younger girls and I noticed that Miss Chambers made a special effort with Albie. I thought at first that Albie was an odd choice for *Domina* Chambers to choose as a favorite, but then I learned that Lucy and Deirdre's tutoring had paid off.

"Albie is our star Latin scholar," I overheard *Domina* Chambers telling Miss Buehl as she helped the girl to her feet after yet another fall. When she got to her feet the poor girl wobbled pathetically at first, her ankles caving painfully in, but by the end of that winter she could make it around the skating circle with a serviceable choppy stroke that made up in speed what it lacked in grace.

Domina Chambers asked me, almost every day, why Lucy wasn't skating with me and every day I gave her the same answer.

"She sleeps after class because she's up so late studying."

It wasn't difficult to believe. *Domina* Chambers surely noticed the dark rings under Lucy's eyes and her tendency to drop off in class.

"She's so very dedicated." *Domina* Chambers made a clucking noise. "Tell her she mustn't work so hard." She said it as if it were my fault. I noticed Albie, behind her, listening.

"Oh you know Lucy," I said, "she wants to do well. All your students do, *Domina*." I could see a little smile on Albie's face. Did she know, as I did, that Lucy spent her nights in the woods and on the lake?

"But she's not like you, Jane. Let's face it, you'll have to slave to achieve even a tenth of what Lucy's capable of." With that remark, my teacher spun on the ice and stroked away, the spray from her skates shimmering in the still, cold air.

Albie stood on the ice looking up at me, a small feline smile stealing over her usually dull features.

"You'd better get in, Jane," she said. It was the first time I'd ever heard her use my name. "I think you've got windburn. Your face is all red."

ONE NIGHT IN FEBRUARY I RETURNED TO OUR ROOM AFTER working in the dining room and found a corniculum tacked to the door. I knew it was a sign from Lucy to Deirdre that the boys would meet them at the lake. I knew the sign wasn't for me, but I decided to treat it as if it were. I decided to follow them. I pretended to be asleep when Deirdre and Lucy left the room. I waited until after the last bed check and then went to the window and listened for them climbing down the drainpipe. I put on long underwear and my heaviest jeans—the only ones without holes in their knees—and two sweaters, an old turtleneck and a blue Fair Isle cardigan *Domina* Chambers had given Lucy for Christmas.

I went around the east side of the lake so I wouldn't meet them on the trail. It meant climbing over the rocks on the Point to avoid Miss Buehl's house. Ice had filled the glacial cracks in the rock, making the footing precarious. It would be easy, I thought, for a person to fall to her death here.

I made it down to the swimming beach and looked across the lake to where the icehouse would be on the other side. I thought I saw a glimmer of light coming from the opposite shore. Maybe they had made a bonfire. I imagined Deirdre, Lucy, Matt, and Ward toasting marshmallows over a small fire and drinking hot cocoa. I amended the picture to beer and joints. Still, it was a homey scene in my mind. Why couldn't I be a part of it? If I cut across the ice I'd be there in minutes. But then, I thought it might be dangerous to cross the whole lake.

I followed the path around the east side of the lake. As I walked I became warm under the two sweaters and parka. I took off the cardigan and wrapped it around my waist, but then I felt hot and itchy. I decided to leave the sweater on the side of the path and get it on my way back. I realized the temperature must be rising. I looked out over the lake and noticed that a white fog was hovering above the ice. I was glad I hadn't tried to cross it.

By the time I reached the icehouse the fog from the ice had crept into the woods and I had trouble seeing the path ahead of me. Twice I walked right into an overhanging branch and scratched my face. The second time something metal brushed against my face. I reached up and retrieved from the tree branch a bundle of hairpins—a corniculum. From the palm of my hand the horned face seemed to leer up at me. I stopped to get my bearings and listen for my friends' voices.

I heard voices, then, coming from the lake. It was a boy and girl, but I couldn't tell if it were Deirdre and Matt, or Ward and Lucy. I could hear the scrape of ice skates on the ice and someone laughing. I stepped off the path into the deep snow to get closer to the lake. The snow gave way slushily under my feet and soaked my jeans. I couldn't tell, in the fog, when the snow gave way to ice, but suddenly my feet slid out from under me and I skidded out onto the lake.

I tried to get up but slipped again. The ice felt greasy under my gloves. I crouched there and looked around me.

The ice fog had grown so thick I couldn't even make out the bank, which I knew must be only a few feet behind me. But which direction was that? I'd lost my bearings when I fell and couldn't be sure which direction was the bank and which led out farther onto the lake. What was clear to me, though, was that the ice was beginning to melt.

I listened again for the voices of the skaters, but heard instead a low moan. I felt the sweat under my long underwear turn icy. The sound seemed to be coming from everywhere at once, but mostly from beneath me. From under the ice. I thought of the stories the senior girls told at the bonfires. That the faces of the Crevecoeur sisters had been seen peering up from beneath the lake ice.

I looked down half expecting to see the upturned face of a long dead girl trapped beneath the ice, but all I could see was a white void of fog. I heard, though, another moan accompanied by a rhythmic thumping that seemed to reverberate deep inside my body. This time, though, I was almost sure it came from a spot ahead of me on the ice.

I crawled toward it. As I moved through the fog on my hands and knees I imagined what was out there. I imagined wraithlike shapes emerging from under the ice to pull me down—girls with jagged icicles hanging from their tangled hair and malice in their drowned eyes. Once I heard something on the ice behind me and when I turned thought I saw a shape, a thickening in the white fog like a clot in cream, moving away from me, but then it was gone and the only sounds on the lake came from the opposite direction. I turned and crawled toward the sounds and bumped into something wooden.

It was the icehouse door, hanging partially open over the ice. I'd made it back to the shore. The moans had led me back.

I pulled myself up, using the door for balance, and looked into the icehouse.

The only light came from a candle on one of the ledges. It cast into shadow on the opposite wall the hull of the boat rocking rhythmically as if buffeted by an invisible current.

I couldn't make out the shape of the girl lying in the hull of the boat. The boy above her was clearly outlined in the shadow on the wall, but I couldn't tell who he was either. He wore something over his head and shoulders, a hood or mask that fell in shapeless folds. The shapes springing from his head were clear. They were horns, stiff and branching like a stag's.

Chapter Nineteen

●

"We ought to do something for May Day," Deirdre said.

She was sitting on the windowsill blowing smoke rings out the open window. It was raining hard and each time the wind blew a spray of rain sifted across the room over Lucy, who lay on the floor reading *The Crystal Cave*, and over the desk where I sat. The pages of my journal were damp and smeared. "April is the cruelest month," I wrote in peacock-blue ink that bled through the paper and stained the scratched, wooden desk. The glue in the binding of my Wheelock's Latin Grammar had melted in the damp and the pages had all sprung free.

After the night I had gone out onto the lake the spring rains had begun, pitting the ice and turning the paths into small rivers of snowmelt. The skating season was over.

Now it was April, but the only sign of spring was the mud that seeped into everything.

Lucy rolled over onto her back and stretched her legs up, pointing and flexing her bare toes. "There's the Founder's Day picnic," she said, yawning lazily. "And the Maypole dance."

India Crevecoeur's birthday fell on May 4, but Founder's Day was always celebrated on May Day. This year India Crevecoeur herself was coming to celebrate her ninetieth birthday and the school's fiftieth anniversary. To celebrate there would be a traditional May-pole dance. In the Music Room, next to the family portrait of the Crevecoeurs, there hung a sepia-toned picture of girls in starched, high-necked white dresses standing in two neat circles around a Maypole. They each held the end of a ribbon attached to the top of the Maypole. The girls in the outer circle faced one way, the girls in the inner circle faced the opposite way. There was a girl in the right corner of the picture whose dress hem was blurred, as if she were swaying, impatient for the dance to begin. Otherwise, it was hard to imagine these girls frolicking around the Maypole. The picture looked more like a military procession.

"They'll sanitize the whole damned thing," Deirdre said, tossing her cigarette carelessly out the window.

"Hey, someone might see that," I complained.

Deirdre rolled her eyes and hopped off the window ledge. "There's a foot of mud under our window, Janie. You'd have to be an archaeologist to excavate that cigarette butt."

"What do you mean *sanitized*?" Lucy asked, her brow wrinkled.

"A May Day dance should be performed at dawn. Naked. Or at least in flimsy nightgowns. It's a pagan fertility rite," Deirdre explained.

"Everything's a pagan fertility rite with you . . . ," I began, but Lucy shushed me, so I wrote in my journal, "Deirdre is such a slut."

"We should go out at dawn in white robes and bare feet," Deirdre said, "and wash our faces in the dew. It's said if you wash your face in the dew at dawn on May Day you'll be granted eternal beauty. Think about it, Jane, it's cheaper than Clearasil."

I felt my skin go itchy where scabs had formed over old blem-ishes. My skin had erupted in the fetid spring air.

"They also say that if a girl goes out on May Day dawn to gather flowers, the first boy she meets on the way back to the village will be her heart's true love."

It was on the tip of my tongue to ask who "they" were, but I didn't. I liked this story. It had a nice element of chance to it. Who was to say I wouldn't run into Matt first?

"We'd need a Maypole," Lucy said.

"There's one in the drama department closet," Deirdre said. "They used it last year for *The Maypole of Merry Mount.*"

"And a May Queen," Lucy said.

"I think it should be Lucy," I said, anxious to be included in this outing.

"Of course we still need a stag-king," Deirdre said, nudging Lucy's leg with her foot. "He was part of the May Day rite."

"We'll let the boys decide who it'll be. He'll be masked, so no one will know," Lucy said. Then she turned to me. "We'll have three to choose from because our cousin'll be in town that weekend."

IN THE END ALL THREE BOYS AGREED TO WEAR THE STAG MASK. Deirdre made the extra masks in art class. When Miss Beade complimented Deirdre on her stitching (Deirdre was good at precise things like sewing and rolling joints), Deirdre told her the masks were for an extra credit assignment in Latin class. That was how *Domina* Chambers got word of our plans.

She asked us to her rooms in the mansion for tea. We'd been there before, but usually with several other girls from the class. This was the first time we'd been singled out as a group. We spent a lot of time discussing what we should wear. Lucy insisted that Deirdre wear a bra and she told me to wear my hair up. She herself wore an old plaid skirt, which I think had belonged to her mother, and a pale yellow cashmere sweater that I had never seen before.

When we got to *Domina* Chambers's room I was glad we had spruced up a bit. *Domina* Chambers had put out her good china tea set (Deirdre reported later that the pattern was "Marlow" by Minton—she'd turned her teacup over when *Domina* Chambers wasn't looking) and Mrs. Ames had sent up a tray of tea sandwiches and freshly baked scones. When we'd come with the other girls it had been paper plates and store-bought cookies.

"I got into the habit of afternoon tea when I was at Oxford,"

Domina Chambers said when we'd all been poured a cup of tea. "The habits we form when young may last a lifetime. You girls have a good start studying Latin. Learning one form of discipline teaches one to be disciplined in other areas of life. Like diet for instance . . ." *Domina* Chambers glanced at Deirdre who was heaping clotted cream on her second scone. "And telling the truth."

Lucy took a sip of tea and set her teacup in its saucer, which she balanced on her knee. "Miss Beade told you about the masks," she said.

"Yes. I was rather surprised to hear about an extra credit assignment, seeing as I don't believe in extra credit."

Deirdre opened her mouth to say something, but *Domina* Chambers was looking at Lucy now and I think we all realized that she was waiting for her to explain. I was sorry it had fallen to her and amazed at how calm she seemed.

"We're planning a May Day rite," Lucy told our teacher. "For dawn. Of course, we're not allowed out of our dorm rooms at dawn, so we had to keep it a secret."

"A May Day rite?" *Domina* Chambers took a sip of tea and smiled. "How lovely. We did the same thing in our time. In fact, your mother and I used to slip out of the dorm in nothing but our nighties and swim across the lake on May Day morning."

"You must have frozen your asses . . ."

I kicked Deirdre so hard she spilled her tea on her blouse. Thank goodness Lucy had talked her into that bra.

"Yes, it was most bracing," *Domina* Chambers said, still addressing Lucy as if she were the only one in the room. "Do you have a Maypole?"

"We do. We . . . borrowed it from the drama department."

"That gaudy thing? I would have thought a freshly cut birch sapling would have been more suitable, but I suppose it will do." *Domina* Chambers sighed and for a moment I thought she was planning to actually join us for our May Day festivities. I wondered what she would make of our stag-king.

"Ah, to be young again," she said. "Well, I understand now why you had to tell a fib to Miss Beade. Of course, she would never understand."

"So you're not going to turn us in?" Deirdre asked.

Domina Chambers turned to Deirdre, looking surprised that she was still in the room.

"I mean it is against the rules," Deirdre said.

"Weren't you paying attention when we read *Antigone*, Miss Hall? The same rules do not apply to everyone. When Antigone performed the burial rite for her brother, even though she was breaking Creon's decree, was she wrong?"

"No," Lucy answered, "because she owed that to her brother."

"Exactly. *Which of us can say what the gods hold wicked?* The true tragic heroine is above the commonplace laws of the masses."

"I always figured Antigone didn't have a chance," Deirdre said. I could tell she was anxious to show *Domina* Chambers that she had gotten something from the play. "I mean, what with her mother being her grandmother and her father being her half-brother . . ."

Domina Chambers waved her hand dismissively. "There's far too much attention paid nowadays to the incest theme in the plays. The Greeks weren't as squeamish about such matters as we are. After all, Antigone is betrothed to her first cousin, Haemon, and no one mentions that."

"Yeah, but Oedipus did put his eyes out when he realized he'd married his own mother."

"And killed his own father. The Greeks were very clear on what a child owed a parent. But incest . . . well, Zeus and Hera are, after all, brother and sister. And Sir James Frazer tells us in *The Golden Bough* that in countries where the royal blood was traced through women, the prince often married his sister to keep the crown from going to an outsider. Of course, when wrongful incest did occur it was sometimes necessary to sacrifice to the goddess Diana."

"Why Diana?" Lucy asked.

"Because incest is supposed to cause a dearth . . . droughts and famine . . . so it makes sense to make atonement to the goddess of fertility."

"But I thought Diana was a virgin," Deirdre interrupted. "How can a virgin be a goddess of fertility?"

Domina Chambers waved her hand again as if Deirdre were an annoying insect. "You persist in thinking in black-and-white terms, Miss Hall. It's a very simplistic way of seeing things. Diana is a goddess of nature, and hence, fertility. It was believed she shared the grove of Nemi with Virbius, the King of the Wood. Their sacred nuptials were celebrated each year to promote the fruitfulness of the earth. There's your May Day rite. Not some silly circle dance around a gilded pole."

"So this King of the Wood," Deirdre asked, "is he kind of like the stag-king? I mean, he wore horns?"

"Yes," *Domina* Chambers answered. "Diana Nemesis is associated with the deer. It's likely that the stag-mummers of medieval May Day rites derived from this tradition."

I saw Deirdre and Lucy exchange a knowing look. *Domina* Chambers had just confirmed the way they had chosen to celebrate May Day. I wondered what our teacher would think if she knew just how literally her students were taking her lesson. But then, I wasn't sure anymore if what Deirdre and Matt, and Lucy and Ward, had been doing in the icehouse and planned to do in the woods on May Day dawn would shock *Domina* Chambers. *Which of us can say what the gods hold wicked?* I had a pretty good idea of the things *Domina* Chambers would disapprove of: sloppy Latin translations, Lipton tea, synthetic fabrics. But sex with a masked stranger in the woods? I couldn't tell.

We finished our tea and sandwiches and scones. *Domina* Chambers played for us a recording of Stravinski's *Rite of Spring* to get us in the mood, she said, for our May Day rite. She promised she wouldn't breathe a word to anyone of our plans.

"But if you're caught," she told us at the door as we were going, "you're on your own. You must always accept responsibility for your actions, girls."

We all laughed and said we were ready to do just that.

•   •   •

IT WAS ONLY FIFTY-FIVE DEGREES AT DAWN ON MAY DAY (according to the thermometer nailed to a tree outside Miss Buehl's cottage), but at least the rain had stopped. The ground was still muddy, though, and the woods were damp and misty, so we decided that the best place to set up the Maypole was the swimming beach.

"Otherwise it'll be more like mud wrestling than Maypole dancing," Deirdre said. "Not that I'm adverse to a little rolling in the mud."

"You're welcome to it," Lucy told her. "We'll have to split up after the Maypole dance."

The plan was for the three of us to carry the Maypole down to the swimming beach and perform the ceremonial circle dance around the Maypole in the middle of which we would be "surprised" by the three boys dressed as stag-mummers. We would then flee, being careful to go in three different directions. Since the boys would be masked, we decided it was only fair that we be disguised as well, so Deirdre attached hoods to the simple white shifts she had sewn for us.

"Of course it will be obvious which one is Lucy," Deirdre said, holding up the shift she had sewn for her. "She's so small. Ward'll pick her out in a minute, which is a good thing. We wouldn't want Lucy ending up with her cousin after all."

"It's a symbolic rite, Deir. You don't have to really do anything. You're scaring Jane."

Deirdre smiled at me. "Oh, I don't think Jane's scared. After all, since she and I are the same height, she might end up with Matt and I'll end up with the cousin . . ."

"He has a name—Roy."

"Roy," Deirdre repeated. "Roy from Troy."

"Cold Spring," Lucy corrected. "Our aunt Doris lives in Cold Spring."

"Whatever. He looked pretty cute, the little I saw of him. But maybe Jane has her eye on him after the night they spent together. . . ."

"I told you: We just sat on the beach and watched the sun rise. Actually, I watched the sun rise. He slept."

"Wore him out, eh, Janie?"

I blushed. Not because of Deirdre's teasing, something I was well used to by then, but because I was remembering stroking the boy's cheek . . . pretending he was Matt.

IT WASN'T EASY CARRYING THE MAYPOLE DOWN THE STEPS TO the swimming beach. Deirdre went first, then Lucy, and I brought up the rear, which meant I had the part of the pole decorated with flowers. They were cheap plastic flowers, spray-painted silver and gold by the drama department, and they scratched against my bare arms and blocked my view of the steps.

"Take it easy," I heard Deirdre hiss from below. "You're going to skewer me with this damned pole and that's not how I planned to spend the morning."

It was hard to believe it would be morning soon. We'd left the dorm at 4:30 so it must have been close to 5:00, but the sky was still pitch dark. Below us I could hear water lapping against the rocks, but not even a glint gave the lake away. Deirdre had looked up the phase of the moon and found it was a new moon.

"I think that's supposed to be bad luck," she said, "but who knows?"

I only knew I had reached the beach when moss-covered rock gave way to wet sand, and even then my bare feet were so numb I could hardly tell the difference.

"Heave ho!" Deirdre called. "Raise high the roof beam, carpenter!"

I heard Lucy's small voice inquire if that were from Sappho while I pushed the pole into an upright position and felt it sink into the sand. Deirdre pushed it deeper into the sand and Lucy knelt at the base and mounded more sand around the pole.

"We don't want it to fall over," Lucy said.

"No, a wilting Maypole would definitely be unpropitious," Deirdre agreed. "Plague and barrenness would certainly follow."

"Why do we want fertility anyway?" I asked. "I mean, it's not like any of us want to get pregnant."

"Well, I'm on the Pill so it's not bloody likely," Deirdre said.

"Really?" I asked. I wondered where Deirdre had managed to get a prescription for birth control pills.

"She forgets to take them half the time," Lucy said. "So she's just messing up her hormones for nothing."

Usually I would have been more disconcerted to realize that Lucy and Deirdre had such a store of confidences than at the news that Deirdre had access to birth control. But the subject had been bothering me lately.

"I guess it's not likely you'd get pregnant the first time . . ."

"Jesus, Janie, I don't think you'll have to worry about it. Look at you, you're shaking like a leaf. Here, take a swig of this."

Deirdre had brought a wine flask made out of goatskin that she had bought at the army/navy store in Corinth.

"What's in it?" I asked, eyeing the greasy-looking sack suspiciously.

"I pinched some cooking sherry from Mrs. Ames and added a few herbs."

I put my mouth around the grooved metal screwtop and tasted, first, copper, then sweet almond–flavored wine, and finally, as an aftertaste at the back of my throat, something bitter and grassy.

"As Horace says: *Nunc est bibendum,*" Deirdre said, passing the flask to Lucy. "Now is the time for drinking."

Lucy tilted her head back and took a long, deep swallow. Her hood fell back and in the dim light I could just make out her pale forehead and see that she had painted some kind of design there. But then her hood fell forward as she lowered the flask and the design was hidden in shadow before I could make it out.

"*Nunc pede libero pulsanda tellus,*" Lucy said in a husky voice I barely recognized. "Now is the time to beat the earth with a liberal foot."

"In other words: Now is the time for dancing."

Deirdre released the crepe paper ribbons that had been wrapped around the pole. They hung limply in the still, damp air. Although the sun still hadn't appeared across the lake, the darkness had paled to a pearly gray. Looking out over the lake I still couldn't tell where water and air met.

Deirdre held up a limp ribbon and stomped the ground with one foot.

"Nunc pede libero pulsanda tellus!" she commanded, and Lucy, stomping her feet, took up the chant. We hadn't rehearsed what to say as we danced around the Maypole. I also searched my head for some appropriate Latin and came up with nothing but the first declension.

"Puella, puellae, puellae," I shouted. I thought Lucy and Deirdre would make fun of my choice, but they took up the declension with me.

"Puellam, puella, puella."

It sounded oddly right. *Girl, girl, girl,* we chanted as we half-skipped, half-danced around the pole, *girl* in all its grammatical permutations.

Then, suddenly, Deirdre skidded to a stop, spraying sand up my legs. She held her hand up for silence. I listened, and heard, above the thud of my heart and the lap of the lake water, footsteps on the rocks. I thought they came from the steps, but when I peered into the gray mist in that direction I heard another sound behind me; again, footsteps on the rocks, but this time they came from the lake. Someone was on one of the sister rocks.

Deirdre passed the flask around and we each took a long drink. I tasted, this time, the bitter grassy taste first and then the sweet and then the metal.

Deirdre tossed the flask into the darkness outside our circle. *"Puer, pueri, puero,"* she whispered.

"Puerum, puero, puer," Lucy chanted.

Boy, boy, boy.

We began to dance again, but in the opposite direction, so that the ribbons we had wrapped around the pole now came undone. The damp crepe paper clung to my arms and brushed against my face, clammy as seaweed. Pieces came off and clung to my shift. I felt the wet strands tangling between my legs and when I tried to kick them away I lost my balance and fell.

When I got to my hands and knees I was looking toward the lake. I saw, through the lightening mist, a figure balanced on the second stone. A figure with the head of a stag. I took a deep breath and told myself it was just a boy in a deer mask, but then the figure leaped off the rock and with one bound landed in the shallow water and I saw that he wasn't wearing the brown felt mask Deirdre had sewn in art class. He was wearing the bleached skull of a ten-point buck.

I screamed and somehow scrambled to my feet.

I heard Deirdre and Lucy scream, but their screams were theatrical.

"*Aiaiai,*" Deirdre keened somewhere off to my left. To my right, Lucy made a whooping sound like a crane calling to its mate. I felt sure they hadn't seen the boy with the skull. Still, that was all he was, surely, a boy with a skull mask. I was running up the steps, though, away from him. Only when I reached the top did I look back to see if he was still following me.

He was four steps below me, his head bent down, watching his footing on the slippery rock. I saw that beneath the white skull he wore the brown felt mask, but at the nape of his neck I could see his hair: sandy brown hair that just then turned fiery red in a ray of light that skidded across the lake from the eastern shore. I noticed, too, his shirt, a hockey jersey with the name "Corinth Lions" emblazoned on the back. Matt's team. Behind him I saw Deirdre run left into the woods, pursued by one of the masked boys. Lucy stood facing her masked partner and then she turned and walked into the water and started swimming. I didn't stay to watch if Ward would swim after her. It was hard to imagine him braving that cold water, but maybe that was what she was counting on. By taking to the water, she'd issued him a challenge.

I turned and ran across the path and into the woods. I skirted behind the lower school and the dorm and then headed west. I knew that once I got past the road there was a large tract of pathless woods, an old grove of giant hemlocks that Matt had once told me was one of the few patches of virgin forest in the area. I felt sure he would know I was heading there and that he'd know why. It was one of the few places where we were sure to be alone and, I knew, one of his favorite places. I wanted him to know that I knew it was him under the deer skull.

The sun was up now, streaming through the morning mist from behind me. I saw the first young hemlocks appear. As I ran, the hemlocks grew taller and the undergrowth thinned. The trees were spread out and evenly spaced like a colonnade. I was running through a wide avenue between the towering trees and their shadows, stretched out in front of me like a black pattern laid out on the gold forest floor. Echoing my own footsteps and the sound of my heart were the footsteps and ragged breath of the boy following me.

I came to a clearing and slipped on the hemlock needles. I lay on my stomach panting until I felt a hand on my shoulder turning me over.

We were both breathing so hard neither of us could talk. The deer skull mask was gone, but he still wore the brown felt mask Deirdre had made. My hood had fallen back.

He stroked my arm and took my hand as if to pull me up, but I pulled him down. He half fell on me, but he moved one leg in between mine to keep his full weight off me. I moved underneath him and felt the heat of his skin beneath his clothes. I touched, with the back of my fingers, a strip of bare skin above the waistband of his jeans, stroking the red-gold hairs, and he moaned. He lowered himself on me and I moved down so that my shift bunched up underneath the small of my back. I could feel the small, flat needles against my bare skin and see the slanting sun streaming over his back as he came inside me.

When we were done the sun was just above his shoulder and shining in my eyes, blinding me. I burrowed my face into his collarbone and felt the damp felt of the mask brush against my cheek. I could see the green thread Deirdre had used to stitch the seam and the small green heart she'd embroidered at the edge of the fabric. She'd used a different color for each mask. "So you'll know your heart's true love," she had said. I was just about to ask him to take off his mask when I heard voices. I felt him stiffen. He got to his knees and snapped his jeans closed. I pulled my shift down and raised myself on my elbows to listen.

"As you can see the undergrowth has become progressively thinner. This is because the fallen needles of the hemlock make a thick, acid mulch in which the seeds of most plants cannot germinate."

"Miss Buehl," I whispered. "You have to get out of here." He got to his feet and held his hand out for me, but I waved him away. "Go!" I hissed. "I'll distract them."

He seemed confused, for a second, about which way to go. The voices were approaching us from the north. I pointed south and said, "You can get back to the icehouse that way. Just make sure you make it off campus before they catch you."

Again he seemed to hesitate. It occurred to me he didn't like leaving me so abruptly after what we had just done.

"It's all right, Matt," I said, "we'll talk later."

He must have been reassured, because he turned and left instantly. I watched him running through the woods and then lost sight of him behind one of the hemlock trunks just as a troop of lower school girls burst into the clearing. As soon as they saw me the girls began screaming. Miss Buehl rushed to my side and knelt down beside me.

"My God, who did this to you? You've been butchered."

For a minute she really frightened me. What I had done with Matt had been painful and I knew there might be blood, but when I looked down at my shift I was shocked to see that it was bright red. My hands and arms, too, were stained and lurid in the morning sun. I felt faint and for a moment I think I did lose consciousness, but then I heard a familiar voice.

"Die," she said. I looked up and standing over me was Albie. She was holding a long strand of red crepe paper that she rubbed between her thumb and forefinger. "Look," she said holding a crimson hand up in the sunlight, "Dye. It's just dye."

Chapter Twenty

●

M ATT WAS CAUGHT JUST OUTSIDE THE ICEHOUSE BY THE extension agent who had come to use her boat. So, Lucy explained to me, it wasn't really my fault because even if Miss Buehl hadn't come upon us in the hemlock grove he still might have run into the extension agent on his way home.

It was kind of her to try to make me feel better, but we both knew she was lying. That first sight of me, in my torn and "bloody" shift, had sparked a hysteria not easily quelled even when the "blood" turned out to be crepe paper dye. Three of the lower school girls on Miss Buehl's nature walk were so traumatized at the sight of me they had to be sent home. Not Albie though, because she had no home to go to. She sturdily related the whole story to anyone who would listen. To give her credit, she always ended by explaining I hadn't been covered by blood after all, but somehow, the way she told it, the fact that I was covered with red dye came to sound even more *lurid*.

It didn't help, either, that Miss Pike found Deirdre's wine flask on the swimming beach and correctly assessed the contents as a mixture of cooking sherry and opium.

Still the scandal might have remained localized if it hadn't been for the Founder's Day picnic. I imagine that the dean and her staff debated long and hard that morning over whether to cancel the picnic or not. The problem was that this year India Crevecoeur had been invited to the Maypole dance. How to explain to our ninety-year-old founder that because a boy had been caught wandering the campus in a deer mask and bloodied shirt (the crepe paper dye again), and several girls were found half-naked and reeking of alcohol and opium, Heart Lake's traditional Maypole dance might suddenly look like a pagan rite? By noon that day there was already talk in town that there was a campus cult that lured innocent boys into drugged sex orgies.

Deirdre laughed when she heard the rumor. "Oh, like they need to be lured into *that*." We were sitting outside the Music Room, waiting to be called in to see the dean. Hurriedly we had agreed to say there'd only been Lucy's brother (since Ward and Roy had gotten away unseen) and we'd asked him to play a part in a May Day pageant that we planned to perform later at the Founder's Day picnic.

"What about the wine flask?" Deirdre hissed as Miss North came out of the Music Room and signaled for Deirdre to come in alone.

"Just say you bought it used and it must have had the opium in it already," Lucy told her. "I mean, how much trouble can you get in for stealing some cooking sherry?"

Lucy shook her head as Deirdre followed Miss Buehl into the Music Room. "God knows what she'll say."

A few minutes after Deirdre went in, the door to the Music Room opened and Albie came out. She must have been called in to relate her story about finding me covered with dye again. She came over to us and I actually thought she might be about to apologize for causing such a stir. Instead she spoke to Lucy.

"You won't get kicked out, will you?"

"Nah, I don't think so. Besides, I live just down the road. Even if they kicked me out of the school I could come back to visit."

Albie shook her head. "You wouldn't though. Girls always say they'll stay in touch when they switch schools, but they don't."

"Yeah, but this school's different. It's in our motto."

Albie looked confused. I didn't blame her; I didn't know what Lucy was talking about either and I wondered if she was still high from the opium. But Lucy got to her feet quite steadily and led Albie to the front door. She pointed to the fanlight above the door where the morning sun was shining through the colored glass. The words of the motto glowed like molten gold, but you couldn't read them of course—they were backwards from this side of the door.

"You know what that says?" Lucy asked.

Albie shook her head.

"Cor te reducit," Lucy said. "It means 'The heart leads you back.' It means no matter where you go after you leave this place your heart will always bring you back here. It means there's always a place for you here. And it means I'll always be here for you, too—me and Deirdre and *Domina* Chambers and Jane . . .'"

I saw Albie frown and look over her shoulder at the mention of my name. I tried to smile encouragingly. Truthfully, Lucy's speech had touched me, too.

"Go on now," Lucy said, pulling open the heavy door and holding it for Albie. "Go back to your room and don't worry. And don't ever forget what I told you."

The girl nodded and left. Lucy came back to the bench and slumped down beside me. I could tell her little speech had worn her out. I noticed that her hair was still damp from her morning swim in the lake. We'd been allowed to change our clothes, but there hadn't been time to shower. Lucy had told me to wear my nicest outfit and when she wasn't happy with what I'd picked gave me something of hers to wear. The plaid skirt she'd given me was a little too short and I kept pulling on its hem to cover more of my bare legs, which still had streaks of red dye from the crepe paper streamers. Lucy, in a dark blue jumper and turtleneck looked proper as always, except for a piece of grass caught in her damp hair. I picked it out of her hair and noticed that there was a light film of sawdust on the back of her neck.

When the front door opened I sniffed at the spring air like a prisoner who may only have a few hours of sunlight left to her.

What I smelled, though, was something like talcum powder and moth balls—a distinctly old-ladyish smell. Outlined against the bright gleam of lake, a small, bent figure stood in the doorway making little clucking sounds with her tongue. As she moved into the foyer her pale blue eyes wandered over the pictures on the wall above our heads and then settled on me and Lucy. As old as the woman was there was something unnervingly steady in her gaze. I had been scared about being questioned by the dean, but suddenly I wished it were my turn to go into the Music Room.

The front door opened again and Miss Macintosh and Miss Beade rushed in—I'd never seen either teacher move so fast. Miss Macintosh's hair was coming undone from its chignon and Miss Beade's face was bright pink.

"Mrs. Crevecoeur," they both exclaimed. "We thought you were waiting for us to escort you to tea."

"This was my home for forty years. What makes you think I'd need escorting," the old woman answered without turning to look at the two flustered teachers. "Who are these girls and why aren't they in the Maypole dance?" She waved her cane at us and came closer. "In trouble, are you?"

Lucy and I looked at each other and then at our teachers who hovered behind India Crevecoeur.

"Actually," Miss Macintosh said, moving to Lucy's side, "these girls are our two Iris Scholarship recipients. They expressed a desire to meet you and um . . ." I could see Miss Macintosh, who had begun so well and so boldly, was running out of innovations. Luckily Lucy, always cool in awkward social circumstances, came to her rescue.

"To thank you for the great privilege of attending Heart Lake," she said, rising to her feet. For a second I thought she might even curtsy, but she merely held out her small hand, which Mrs. Crevecoeur, switching her cane to her left hand, took briefly and then let drop.

"This is Lucy Toller," Miss Beade said, coming to Lucy's other side and standing almost directly in front of me. "One of our finest students. Miss Chambers says she's the best Latin student she's ever had."

"Toller, eh? Your mother's Hannah Corey, isn't she?"

Lucy nodded.

"The Coreys are cousins of the Crevecoeurs, if you go back far enough. You've got the same blue eyes my girls Rose and Lily had."

I couldn't see Lucy's expression, but I imagined she was smiling modestly. I was hoping no one would notice the bits of sawdust that clung to the backs of her bare legs. I was too busy staring at Lucy's legs to notice that Mrs. Crevecoeur's attention had swerved in my direction.

"And who's this girl lurking in the shadows here? Didn't anyone ever teach you to stand in the presence of your elders, girl?"

Blushing, I got up and squeezed myself in between Miss Macintosh and Miss Beade to hold out my hand to the old woman. As I stood I saw the old woman's pale blue eyes widen, the pupils enlarge and darken. For a second I was afraid I'd missed a button on my blouse or she'd noticed the red streaks on my leg. She looked at me in a way that made me feel naked.

"Who are you?"

"Another Iris recipient, Mrs. Crevecoeur," Miss Macintosh patiently explained, clearly thinking the old woman had forgotten what she'd been told five minutes earlier. "Remember, there were two of them last year . . ."

"I'm not senile," she snapped. "What's your name, girl?"

"Jane Hudson," I answered.

The washed-out blue eyes narrowed. "Who was your mother?"

"Margaret Hudson."

"Her maiden name, child," she said impatiently.

"Oh," I said, "Poole."

For a moment a film seemed to lift from the eyes. I could see how blue her eyes must have been.

"Your grandmother worked for me," she said, "as my maid. I never thought I'd see her granddaughter here at Heart Lake."

"Oh." I didn't know what else to say. I felt like I'd been caught impersonating my betters—a serving girl found trying on her mistress's fine shawl. I guess it was a shock for the old lady to find her maid's granddaughter attending her school. But wasn't that what the Iris Scholarship was supposed to do? Give us poor town girls a chance? I looked up at Mrs. Crevecoeur, prepared to offer some explanation, an apology even, but her eyes had drifted to a spot two inches above my head where, no doubt, she'd been accustomed to focus her gaze when talking to servants such as my grandmother.

I must have been overtired, because what I said wasn't very polite. "Well, here I am. Better late than never."

That wrenched her eyes down to meet mine. She gave me a curt nod and a tight smile. "Yes," she agreed, as Miss Macintosh and Miss Beade each took a thin arm—suddenly she looked frail and very tired—and herded her off toward the Lake Lounge. I heard her as she left muttering to herself, "Better late than never. Ha!"

The door to the Music Room opened; Deirdre came out and, without looking at me or Lucy, hurried out the front door. Miss North came out of the Music Room and told Lucy that it was her turn to come in. Left by myself, I got up and paced the hall. I tried to distract myself by looking at the old photographs on the wall, but there was little in the dour faces of the Crevecoeur ancestors to hold my attention. At least not until I came to the picture directly above the chair where I had been sitting. There was India Crevecoeur again, in a smaller copy of the family portrait that hung in the Music Room. Yes, I could see the resemblance, the square jaw and haughty tilt of her chin. Both her older girls had it, too, only the youngest, Iris, skulked in the shadows. I moved closer and looked at the servant who hovered over Iris fixing her bow and for the first time recognized her. It was my grandmother, Jane Poole. That's what old Mrs. Crevecoeur had been looking at over my head—her old servant who'd unexpectedly spawned an interloper to her precious school. "Well," I thought, settling back in my chair to await my summons to the Music Room. "I might not be here long."

•   •   •

NONE OF US WERE EXPELLED THOUGH. THE HARSHEST PUN-
ishment for the May Day affair, as we later referred to it, fell on
Matt. What Lucy hadn't figured on when she'd tried to persuade her
to take the blame for the wine flask, was Deirdre's history of boarding school expulsions. Heart Lake was her third boarding school in
six years. Each successive school had been a little less prestigious, a
little shabbier, than the last. Heart Lake was, at least, still a reputable
school, but Deirdre knew that if she admitted that the flask was hers
she would be kicked out of Heart Lake. What kind of school, on
what frozen outpost, she might go to next Deirdre had no desire
to discover. She might even end up on the Canadian border at
St. Eustace's—or St. Useless, as the girls called it—known as the
school of last resort—where they sent you when no other school
would have you.

She told the dean the flask belonged to Matt.

"After all," Deirdre explained later to an enraged Lucy, "he
doesn't go here. What can they do to him?"

Heart Lake, of course, couldn't do anything to Matt Toller, but
Domina Chambers, as his mother's old friend, could. True to her
word, *Domina* Chambers had let us take the consequences of our
actions without intervention from her. But when she heard that
Lucy's brother had brought drugs onto the campus, she stepped in.
She went to Hannah Toller and told her, in no uncertain terms, that
Matt mustn't be allowed to compromise Lucy's chances of making
something of herself. Obviously, Heart Lake wasn't far enough away
to protect Lucy from her brother's bad influence. And since Lucy
couldn't be sent farther away, there was only one solution. Matt must
be sent away.

When Lucy told me what she had overheard in her house, I reassured her that nothing would happen right away. After all, there were
only six weeks left to the school year. Surely they wouldn't send
Matt away until the fall. And by then the whole incident would have
died down and the Tollers might relent.

But *Domina* Chambers was adamant. On May 4, Matt took the
train south along the Hudson to Cold Spring, where he was to

attend the Manlius Military Academy for Boys. I didn't even get to see him before he left.

As miserable as I was at Matt's expulsion from Corinth, Lucy was inconsolable. In fact, the aftermath of May Day seemed to leave her physically sick. She lost her appetite entirely and grew thin. Mrs. Ames, frantic to "put some meat on those twigs of bone" as she put it, stuffed Lucy's book bag with freshly baked biscuits, which Lucy promptly tossed into the lake.

"An offering to the Lake Goddess?" I asked her one afternoon when I found her standing on the Point lobbing biscuits into the water.

She turned to me and I saw that besides how thin she had grown, there were dark blue circles under her eyes and her skin had a greenish, sickly pallor. Her hair, once bright and shiny, hung lank and tangled around her face. She looked like someone three feet underwater, like a drowned person.

"Don't you think we're getting a little old for that stuff, Jane?" she asked me. Then she turned and walked into the woods.

Even though she said she no longer believed in the Lake Goddess, I heard her praying to someone in the night. The first time it happened I thought I was dreaming. I awoke to an incessant whispering and when I opened my eyes I saw something crouched at the foot of Lucy's bed. The figure was so small and compact I imagined for a minute it was a succubus, like the demon in Fuseli's "Nightmare," which Miss Beade had shown us in art class. No wonder, I thought groggily, Lucy has looked so worn out: that thing is sucking the life blood out of her.

That thing, though, *was* Lucy. With her knees drawn up to her chest and Matt's old hockey jersey pulled down to her ankles, she was rocking back and forth, muttering something I couldn't make out.

I wondered if I should go to her, but there was something so private, so naked, about her grief, I felt I would be intruding.

I didn't know whom to go to.

Deirdre and Lucy weren't on speaking terms since the wine flask incident. Nor did Deirdre seem upset by what had happened on May

Day. She ate heartily and had put on weight in the last few weeks. She'd thrown herself into her schoolwork, anxious to redeem herself after the threat of getting thrown out. When I tried to talk to her about Lucy she answered brusquely, "Miss prima donna should get over it. She's just pissed I took her boyfriend on May Day."

"What do you mean?"

"Didn't you know? I was with Ward, which means she ended up with Roy. I'll tell you this: Ward wasn't sorry. He told me Miss Ice Princess—that's what he called her—would hardly let him touch her all those nights we were taking turns in the icehouse."

I thought about the scene I had witnessed in the icehouse. I'd always hoped the masked boy had been Ward. I told myself that it didn't matter. What mattered was that Matt and I had been together on May Day.

I even tried talking to my mother about Lucy when I went home for Memorial Day weekend.

"If I were you I'd quit worrying about that Toller girl," she told me. "She'll land on her feet. You ought to be thinking of how you can help out around here. Charity begins at home."

I expected the lecture to go on, but it ended abruptly with a coughing fit. My mother had been running the carpet sweeper over the threadbare living room rug while we talked. She kicked at its unraveling hem and muttered through her coughing, "Damned sawdust."

I looked at the rug. I couldn't see any sawdust, but my mother's hand on the sweeper's handle did look yellow. I looked at her and noticed for the first time how sallow and worn-out she looked, as if after a lifetime of living in the paper mill's shadow the sawdust had crept under her skin.

"Are you feeling all right, Mom?"

She put her hand on the back of her hip and leaned back. "I could use a little help around here."

My mother had told me what to do my whole life, but this was the first time I'd ever heard her asking for help.

"School will be over in two weeks," I said. "I'll be able to help out then."

I waited to see if she'd mention any summer job. For the last three years she'd gotten me a baby-sitting job with one of the West Corinth families.

"I think your father could use you around the house this summer," she said, and then resumed sweeping up the invisible sawdust.

I FINALLY WENT TO THE ONE PERSON WHO, I WAS SURE, WOULD share my concern over Lucy— *Domina* Chambers.

I waited for her after her last class and walked back with her to the mansion.

"Yes, I've noticed she's lost weight fretting over Matthew. She's got a sensitive nature, not unlike myself. I can never eat in times of sorrow. Not like your other roommate, eh? Nothing seems to interfere with Miss Hall's appetite."

I smiled nervously, unsure of how I was supposed to respond to comments about a fellow student's eating habits. It seemed, somehow, inappropriate. I steered the conversation back to Lucy.

"She doesn't sleep either. I'm worried about her."

"Yes, I am, too. I have a plan, though. Don't worry, Clementia, I'll take care of Lucy."

We'd gotten to the mansion steps. Sitting on the bottom step, hugging her books to her chest, was Albie.

"Ah, Alba, I'd nearly forgotten it was your tutoring day."

Albie glared at me as if *Domina* Chambers's forgetfulness was my fault. *Domina* Chambers turned back to me. "Is there anything else you wanted to tell me about Miss Toller?"

I saw Albie curl her lip back and I realized it sounded as if I had been telling on Lucy. I blushed, not only because I looked like a snitch, but because I had a sudden, unbidden image of all that there was to tell: Specifically, the picture that came to mind was of the masked and horned figure in the icehouse.

I shook the picture away. Why had I thought of it? But then I realized what had reminded me of that night. It was Albie's sweater, a blue Fair Isle cardigan several sizes too big for her. It looked just like the one I'd borrowed from Lucy; the one I'd left hanging from a branch on the side of the path.

"Miss Hudson?" *Domina* Chambers repeated my name. "Are you satisfied?"

I tried to think of something to say that would make it clear to Albie that I was only looking out for Lucy. "Well, school's almost over and Matt will be home for the summer," I said. "I'm sure she'll feel better then."

"Oh, no." *Domina* Chambers shook her head so hard some strands of silver hair came loose from her chignon. "The military academy has had such an excellent effect on Matthew his parents have enrolled him for the summer program. As for Lucy, I have other plans for her summer."

IT TURNED OUT THAT *DOMINA* CHAMBERS'S PLANS FOR LUCY involved taking her to Italy for the entire summer break, where she had a grant to study at the American Academy in Rome. Lucy would accompany her and have the opportunity to see the art and architecture of ancient Rome firsthand.

"She says it will be excellent for my classical studies when I go on to college. Of course, I'll major in classics. I'm also supposed to study Italian. On the weekends we're going to Florence and I'm supposed to memorize like every painting in the Uffizi." Lucy was packing her suitcase. I was sitting on her bed looking out the window at the lake. We'd started swimming classes these last few weeks of school and I'd thought about coming back out to the lake over the summer and swimming, but now I wondered if I would do it alone, without Matt or Lucy.

"Do you have to go?" I asked. "I mean, wouldn't your parents let you stay if you asked to?"

Lucy shrugged. "What difference does it make? Matt's not here anyway."

I'm still here, I thought, but I didn't say it. Lucy did rouse herself enough to realize she might have hurt my feelings.

"And you're always so busy over the summer anyway, Jane. Hasn't your mother hired you out as an indentured servant?"

I shook my head. "No. She seems to want me to stick around this summer."

"Gee, that's a change. Well, think of it this way, at least you're not being shipped off to some other boarding school, like Deirdre or Albie. Your summer can't possibly be as bad as theirs is going to be."

But Lucy was wrong. When I came home after the last day of school I found my father home from work in the middle of the day. He sat me down in the living room and told me that my mother had been diagnosed with stomach cancer and had six to eight months to live.

Chapter Twenty-one

●

OVER THE SUMMER I WATCHED AS MY MOTHER LOST thirty pounds and most of her strength. By August she was barely able to get out of bed to use the bathroom. She lay, sunken and yellow, waiting for me to bring her meals she couldn't eat and complaining about the way I prepared them or how long it took me to bring them. She never complained about the cancer or the pain, which I knew about from the way she sometimes drew her lips back from her teeth, but if I had hoped that sickness would put an end to my mother's endless complaining about me, I would have been sorely disappointed.

She complained about the way I dressed and the way I wore my hair. "You look like a deranged old maid," she told me one day. My hair was pulled back in a sloppy bun, which was as close an imitation of *Domina* Chambers's chignon as I could manage, and I was wearing a plaid gym kilt and a salmon-colored button-down shirt that Matt had given to Lucy and Lucy had given to me. "Is this why I sent you to that fancy private school, so you can look like a freak?"

I could have pointed out that she hadn't *sent* me anywhere; I had earned the scholarship for Heart Lake on my own. But then I looked at her. She had lost most of her hair to chemo by then and her arms had grown so thin that they fell back from her shoulder bones and disappeared under the covers, making her look like a double amputee. Her legs, on the other hand, had swollen to twice their normal size. Ballooning under the covers they looked like one bloated appendage. A mermaid's tail. That's what she looked like: a bald, yellow, armless mermaid. This was the person calling me a freak.

So I told her that this was the way the girls dressed at Heart Lake and, Lucy had told me, at college. I tried to distract her by reading to her my college application essays. I showed her my SAT scores and explained how good they were. I told her that Miss Buehl thought I had a very good chance of getting a scholarship to Vassar.

"Another scholarship," she said, looking out at me through her yellowing eyes. "That's all they'll see you as: the charity student. It'll never make any difference. You'll always be the housekeeper's granddaughter. Mill folk. That's what my mother tried to explain to me, but I wouldn't listen. Now look at me, I can't even die without the sound of that infernal mill pounding in my ears."

The sound of the logs being processed into lumber and paper had always been a low hum in the background of our lives that I'd long ago stopped hearing. I tried to close the windows so she wouldn't hear it, but it made the house insufferably hot, and the hum of the mill seemed to vibrate though the windows. Each time a lumber truck passed our house it made her old iron bed shake and she would wince in pain from the motion. Sometimes, when I heard the sound of gears shifting on the hill beneath our house, I would try to hold the headboard to keep it from shaking, but then she accused me of shaking the bed myself.

My father found me one day sitting on the floor outside her room.

"Try not to mind the things she says," he told me. "It's the cancer talking, not her."

I tried not to listen to her, but by the end of the summer I felt as if everything in my world had shrunken and wasted away.

So accustomed was I to the look of sickness that it was something of a shock, then, to see Lucy on the first day of school. Apparently *Domina* Chambers had been right about the salutary effects of Italy: Lucy had bloomed over the summer. She'd put on weight, especially in the hips and chest, her skin was golden and her hair, pulled back in a new elegant twist, shone like the Mediterranean sun.

"All that pasta and olive oil," she said unpacking silk shirts from Bellagio and sweaters from Harrods (they'd stopped in England for two weeks on the way back) and beautiful leather shoes.

"My God, you've got tits," Deirdre announced the minute she saw her. "Why does everything *I* eat go to my ass?"

I expected Lucy to make a snide comment—Deirdre had gained even more weight over the summer—but instead she smiled benignly and said, "Helen says if we all ate like the Mediterraneans we'd be much healthier. She's going to start a Mediterranean cooking club. Do you want to join with me, Deirdre?"

And so, along with all the other surprises, I found that Lucy had apparently forgiven Deirdre over the summer and wanted to be friends again.

"Matt's doing fine at military school," Lucy told us. "He spends the weekends at Aunt Doris's house. He says Roy asks about you, Jane."

"Oh?" I said, feigning nonchalance. I would have been happier to hear that Matt himself was asking for me, but perhaps this was just his oblique way of communicating.

"He'll be back for Christmas break," she said. And that was all. As if seeing her brother twice a year was suddenly just fine with her. "Oh, and he says he was sorry to hear about your mom," she added. "We both are."

"Yeah," Deirdre chimed in, "tough break." And then they were back to making plans for the year. Cooking class and a cross-country ski club—"Helen says it's chicer than downhill skiing"—and a play.

"Helen says that when she was here they did Aristophanes's *The Frogs* in the lake," Lucy told us.

"*In* the lake?" Deirdre asked. "What a hoot! We've got to do it."

Lucy and Deirdre kept busy that fall, pursuing extracurricular activities with a near frenetic zeal. I couldn't participate in most of the activities because I was expected to spend my afternoons and weekends at home. I was most disappointed about not being in the class play. They'd decided, instead of *The Frogs*, to do their own version of *Iphigenia* based on Euripides's two plays, *Iphigenia in Aulis* and *Iphigenia in Tauris*. They called it *Iphigenia on the Beach*.

It came about because when our Greek tragedy class, which *Domina* Chambers and Miss Macintosh taught together, read *Iphigenia in Aulis*, Deirdre was furious that the play ended with the girl's death.

"It just sucks," Deirdre blurted out, "It's so . . . so patriarchal. They kill this innocent girl so these men can go off and fight their stupid war, which they're fighting all because some impotent jerk couldn't satisfy his wife in the first place."

"Well, you'll be happy to know, Miss Hall, that Euripides apparently agreed with you. Although I doubt he would have phrased it in quite the same words." The class giggled and I noticed Miss Macintosh furiously scribbling notes in her lesson plan book. Someone wondered aloud what the Greek for "sucks" was. I'd noticed that even *Domina* Chambers seemed more tolerant of Deirdre since Lucy had warmed to her.

"How do we know that Euripides felt that way, Miss Chambers?" Miss Macintosh asked. I noticed that Miss Macintosh eschewed the title *Domina*.

"Euripides wrote a second play called *Iphigenia in Tauris* in which Iphigenia reappears and tells us that just before the priest would have slit her throat she was spirited away by Artemis to the island of Tauris and a deer was sacrificed in her place."

"Cool," said Deirdre.

"Why don't we read that one next?" asked Lucy.

I saw Miss Macintosh stabbing her finger at her carefully prepared syllabus (I believe we were scheduled to read *Medea* next), but *Domina* Chambers answered without a glance in her direction.

"Excellent idea, Miss Toller. We shall."

And so we read *Iphigenia in Tauris*. Deirdre was disappointed that Iphigenia's stay in Tauris wasn't the goddess/commune she'd thought it would be. Instead, Iphigenia, as a priestess of Artemis, is forced to sacrifice any shipwrecked sailors who are unlucky enough to wash up on the Taurian shore. But Lucy loved the play. Iphigenia's brother, Orestes, and his friend Pylades, come to the island, but because Iphigenia doesn't recognize him she prepares to sacrifice him at the altar of Artemis. Lucy loved the scene where Iphigenia and Orestes talk about how they've lost, respectively, a brother and a sister without knowing that they've already found each other.

"A perfect example of dramatic irony, wouldn't you say, Esther?" *Domina* Chambers asked Miss Macintosh, who sullenly agreed. Since having her syllabus preempted she'd retreated into an incommunicative funk at the back of the room where she kept copious notes in her lesson plan book. I knew, too, that she hated when *Domina* Chambers ignored school protocol and referred to her colleagues by their first names in the presence of students.

"I know it's corny, but it gives me the chills," Lucy said. "She almost kills her own brother."

Their identities are revealed only when Iphigenia recites a letter for Pylades to bring home to Greece. "A greeting comes from one you think is dead. Your sister is not dead at Aulis." Lucy begged *Domina* Chamber to let the class do the play.

"We can do it on the swimming beach," she said. "We can use one of the rocks as the altar at Aulis and Artemis can appear on a boat to take her to Tauris. One of the rocks can be Tauris . . ."

I noticed Miss Macintosh lift her head from her lesson plan book and raise her hand to object. "We couldn't possibly. Think of the insurance problems. Girls falling in the lake . . ." As she spoke I imagined it: stola-clad girls getting tangled in their sheets and sinking to the bottom of the lake. But *Domina* Chambers was not one to be swayed by conventional concerns. She waved a hand in Miss Macintosh's direction as if she were batting away an annoying insect. I noticed Miss Macintosh turn pink above her white high-necked collar. *Domina* Chambers admitted that the plays were not her favorites and she thought the addition of a happy ending for Iphigenia was pure soap opera melodrama; however, she thought the material lent itself to reinterpretation.

"We should always recall," she lectured, "that the Greek

playwrights felt free to bend the mythic material to their purposes—as Shakespeare did—" here she shot a meaningful look at Miss Macintosh. "And so, why shouldn't we?"

Of course, Lucy was chosen to play Iphigenia. Deirdre played Orestes. They wanted me for Pylades, but I couldn't make enough rehearsals, so they got another girl. All the speaking parts were taken by seniors. The swim team played the chorus. They stood in a lifeboat, led by Miss Pike, who looked splendid in a Greek stola. She insisted on holding a lifesaving float in case any of the girls went overboard, but she managed to hold it in such a way that it looked like some kind of heraldic icon.

We all wanted *Domina* Chambers to play Artemis. She demurred at first, recommending Miss Macintosh, as a sop, I think, to her wounded feelings, but when Miss Macintosh stoutly refused, she agreed.

Although I couldn't be in the play I helped Deirdre with the costumes. We made a gold helmet embossed with an owl for Miss North, who'd agreed to play Athena, and a silver helmet with a moon and deer etched in tin foil for *Domina* Chambers. We already had a deer mask for the deer who takes Iphigenia's place at the altar. We used one from May Day. I noticed it was the one with the green heart embroidered on it.

The problem, as I heard Deirdre and Lucy discuss day after day, was how to make the switch—the deer for Iphigenia—dramatically. Deirdre suggested the priest could fling a sheet over Lucy and then she could slip under it and get in the boat with *Domina* Chambers.

"But everyone will see me wading up to the boat. It ruins the effect. And where's the deer going to be before she slips under the sheet? There's no backstage, you know."

"Hey, you're the one who was so hot to do it on the swimming beach!"

I had to admit I almost enjoyed hearing them bicker. But then Deirdre came up with a brilliant solution.

"If we use the second stone as the altar the deer can wait in the cave behind it. When I throw up the sheet you can slip in the water and swim underwater to the boat. The deer can swim underwater to the rock and pop up under the sheet."

Lucy liked it. The only problem was getting someone small and agile enough to play the deer. Someone who was also a good swimmer and wouldn't mind sitting still in the cave throughout the whole play.

"I know just the right girl," Deirdre woke us both in the middle of the night to announce. "Albie. She's small and she can move without making a sound. And she'd do anything for Lucy."

On the day of the performance my father agreed to come home early from work to take over watching my mother. The play was timed to end at sunset and so I found myself sitting by my mother's sickbed anxiously watching the sun sink over the lumber mill smokestacks.

"You think by staring at it you'll stop the sun in the sky," I heard my mother's voice from the bed behind me. I had thought she was asleep.

"They're doing a play on the swimming beach," I told her.

"On the beach? What nonsense. It was no lucky day you won that scholarship. You should be learning practical things not wasting your time with rich girls. You'll never be more than a servant to them, that's what my mother always told me . . ."

"Lucy's not rich." I was only able to interrupt my mother's tirade because she had run out of breath. She started to wheeze now, impatient to answer me. I helped her sit up and gave her a drink through a straw.

"You wait," she said when she'd regained her breath. "Lucy'll come into her share of wealth some day and then see how much you're worth to her."

I'd have asked her where Lucy was going to get this money, but my father came home and I could tell by the angle of the sun that I'd already missed most of the play. I ran all the way up River Street and then cut behind the Tollers' house and followed the Schwanenkill to the south end of the lake. I could see when I got to the icehouse that the play was still going on. I started out along the eastern side of the lake, but I realized I would miss the whole thing by the time I got to the swimming beach. I knew where there was a rock on the east shore where I could sit and watch at least the end of the play. I wanted to see how they managed that last scene.

As it turned out, I had a perfect view of the stones. I could see, as I settled myself on the rock, that the second sister stone was covered with a white sheet that glowed a fiery red in the light of the setting sun. It looked exactly like the bloodred altar it was supposed to represent.

From where I sat I could see things the audience was not supposed to see. It didn't ruin the effect, though, when a hand reached out from the cave and tugged the sheet away, revealing the prone shape of a naked girl tied to the rock. I could hear, over the still water, the gasp of the audience on the swimming beach.

"Jesus," I thought, "*Domina* Chambers really is fearless!" But then I realized, as the rest of the audience must have soon discovered, that Lucy was wearing a pale pink swimsuit that clung to her newly ample figure like a second skin.

The chorus's dinghy swayed erratically as a figure in a robe with a gold foil mask disembarked and waded through the thigh-deep water over to the rock. The players had been lucky that the warm weather had lasted this long, but still I didn't envy the actress playing the priestess who had to stand in this water. I stretched out on my rock and dangled my hand in the water. It felt icy.

The robed figure lifted a dagger and held it above Lucy's white arched throat. Just as the blade came down toward her throat, the priestess lifted her left arm and her long trailing sleeve hid the victim from the audience. There was a scream that echoed off the wall of the Point and rippled over the still water and a bright spray of blood splashed the priestess's robe. Even from where I sat it looked so real that I stood up and tried to see Lucy sneaking into the cave behind the stone. But the setting sun was in my eyes, turning the water such a lurid red I could almost believe it was Lucy's blood flowing into the lake. Barely a minute passed, but it felt like an eternity. I looked toward the beach and could see that many in the audience had also gotten to their feet and were craning to see what was behind the priestess's robe. And then the priestess swept away her arm again and we saw, in Lucy's place, a slaughtered deer, blood dripping from its torn neck. At almost the same moment a small boat rounded the Point and we saw Lucy at the prow, swathed in scarves the color of the sunset. Behind her stood Artemis holding a chaplet of gold above Lucy's head. The boat was rowed by Miss Buehl in a short toga.

Just then there was a loud crack. I was so taken up in the play that for a moment I thought it was a sound effect, but then I looked behind me and saw the eastern sky split by a lightning bolt. On the lake, the masked figure of Artemis held her hands up to the sky and in a voice magisterial enough to carry across the water to my rock proclaimed, "So speaks Zeus! Instead of taking this girl to Tauris I will take her to Olympus where she will live among the gods."

At a nod from Artemis, Miss Buehl turned the boat around and headed back around the Point. I was marveling at *Domina* Chamber's adept improvisation when I realized that the rest of the actors were not coping quite so well with this unplanned finale. Rain came down like a curtain falling over the last act. The audience fled shrieking up the steps of the swimming beach while the chorus beached their dingy and took shelter in the boathouse. Only the priestess remained standing in the water next to the slain deer. Under the priestess's soaked robe I could see the outline of two familiar breasts. It was Deirdre. She started wading toward the beach.

She was halfway to the beach, her back to the stone, when the figure in the deer costume sat up and started struggling with the ropes that tied her to the rock. I could see her mouth was open, but her cries were drowned out by the roar of the rain. Through the curtain of rain I thought I saw her looking toward me. She lifted an arm as if to signal me, but it only made her lose her balance. The top half of her body slipped off the rock and into the water. I stood for what must have been only seconds knowing the fastest way to reach her would be through the water, but I remembered how cold the water was. I turned, instead, into the woods and ran along the trail to the beach. It took longer than I thought it would because of the rain and the mud. I was sure that when I got there I'd find the girl drowned.

I ran down the steps so quickly I slipped and missed the last five or six steps. I landed flat on my stomach on the beach, my face ground into the wet sand. When I got up I saw Lucy and Deirdre dragging a wet brown figure out of the water.

They dropped her next to me and I reached out and took off the mask. "You," Albie spat at me. "You ran away into the woods to let me drown."

Lucy and Deirdre both looked from Albie to me. I tried to explain what happened, but my mouth was full of sand.

Lucy put her arm around Albie. "Jane would never run away from someone who needed help," she told Albie as she helped her to her feet. I was grateful for Lucy's defense of me, but as Albie slumped against Lucy and let herself be led from the beach, she gave me a look over her shoulder that I understood to mean she didn't believe a word of it.

Chapter Twenty-two

●

THE STORM THAT CLOSED THE FINAL ACT OF *IPHIGENIA ON the Beach* also brought an end to the warm weather. Lucy's good mood vanished with the advent of the Canadian cold fronts and the first snows. The first thing I noticed was that she stopped wearing the beautiful clothes *Domina* Chambers had bought for her in Europe. She wore, instead, an oversized sweatsuit Matt had sent her from military school.

"It keeps me warm," she told me.

Another piece of odd behavior was that when the heavy snows began in November she refused to stay on the paths.

"I feel like a rat in a maze," she said. "I'm going to make my own tracks." And she'd leap over the banked snow at the woods' edge and take off, leaving me and Deirdre on the path.

"What we need," Deirdre said one night as we were working on our Tacitus translations, "are cross-country skis. Then we could go anywhere."

Lucy looked up from her Tacitus. I saw Deirdre's face light up at even the prospect that she had recaptured Lucy's attention. "She's even more desperate for her friendship than I am," I wrote in my journal. "I feel sorry for her."

"Yeah, but where will we get the skis?" I asked.

"We'll have a bake sale," Deirdre said, "and raise money for a cross-country ski club."

The bake sale was a financial success but it failed to revive Lucy's flagging spirits. Where before she had given up food and sleep when she was depressed, now she did little except eat and sleep.

When the cross-country skis were delivered, she mustered some interest, but instead of practicing with the club, she took off through the woods by herself.

"What do you think is wrong with her?" I asked Deirdre one day in early December. We were skiing through the woods on the west side of the lake. Miss Buehl and *Domina* Chambers were leading the group. As soon as the teachers were out of sight, Lucy had taken off south without a word to me or Deirdre. Deirdre and I had paused on top of a rise and watched her go.

"Didn't you know?" Deirdre said. "Matt's not coming home for Christmas."

"You mean their parents won't even let him come home for Christmas?"

Deirdre shook her head impatiently. "He's going on a skiing trip with his cousin. I think Lucy's really hurt that he's *chosen* not to come home. It's like he's avoiding her."

Or me, I thought. Wasn't it more likely that it was me he was avoiding? We were skiing through a part of the woods with little underbrush. I looked up at the sky, which was white and swollen with impending snow, through a green feathering of branches. We were in the hemlock grove through which Matt had chased me on May Day. I looked ahead and saw that the narrow grooves the skiers had made before us led to the clearing where Matt and I had made love. *Made love?* Could I really go on calling it that? He hadn't even bothered to call or write me or get a single word through to me since May Day. For all he knew, I could have gotten pregnant that morning.

"She's so upset about it she says she's going to spend the break here on campus."

"Alone?" I asked.

"I said I'd stay with her."

"Oh," I said. I couldn't think of anything else to say. My eyes were stinging and I suddenly felt unbearably cold. I dug my poles into the snow and swung my left ski out at a forty-five-degree angle to the tracks. Deirdre moved out of my way.

"What are you doing?" she asked.

"I'm going back," I told her. "My feet are cold." She didn't say a word as I stomped out a semicircle in the snow. When I'd repositioned my skis in the tracks I pushed off down the hill, my skis moving easily in the tracks we'd already laid.

I WAS HURT THAT LUCY HADN'T ASKED ME TO STAY ON CAMPUS that Christmas. We'd stayed on campus Christmas break sophomore and junior year earning extra money by helping Mrs. Ames clean the dorms. But Lucy hadn't said anything to me about staying this year. As it turned out, I wouldn't have been able to stay even if she had asked. The day before Christmas break my mother was admitted to a hospital in Albany and my father picked me up after my last final to drive down there. He'd been to the dorm already and gotten my suitcase.

"Your friend said to wish you a Merry Christmas," he said. "If you want, I can wait while you go say good-bye." I shook my head no. I didn't even ask which *friend* he meant.

It was snowing hard on the Northway and my father responded to my questions about my mother with monosyllabic grunts. I finally gave up and let him concentrate on the slippery road. When we pulled into his sister's house on the outskirts of Albany he turned to me. I thought that now he would tell me how long—how little—my mother had to live, but instead he said, "You mustn't mind the things she says to you. It's the cancer talking."

He'd said this before and I knew he meant it to be a comfort, but I just couldn't believe it anymore.

"But she's always said these things to me," I complained, ashamed at how whiny my voice sounded. "Why does she hate me so much?"

My father looked away from me. "If it seems like she's never gone out of her way to make you feel wanted, it's because she's always wanted you to get out. Not end up like she did—trapped."

"Then why didn't she ever leave?"

"She tried. She tried all her life. When she was in high school she studied for that scholarship that you got, but then her mother wouldn't let her take it."

"Why not?"

My father sighed. "When they turned the old Crevecoeur place into a school your grandma lost her job there. She must've parted on bad terms with the people up at Heart Lake, because she'd never have mention of them, or the school, in her house. Your mother still managed to get a scholarship for the state teacher's college, but by then your grandmother was sick and she had to stay and take care of her. Then she met me . . . and we had you . . ."

As my father's voice trailed off I realized for the first time that I was the reason my mother had gotten trapped in the little mill town she hated so much.

"I know it's hard for you, the way she talks to you, Janie. But you gotta try not to take it to heart. It's the way her mother talked to her. You just try not to listen. I mean, listen with your ears, but don't take it in here." He tapped my sternum with his blunt, stubby finger. "And remember that underneath it all your mother's always wanted the best for you, she just doesn't know how to go about getting it for you."

I tried in the next days, while I sat in a chair by my mother's bed, lulled to sleepiness by the watery gurgle of the pump that drained her lungs, to feel some sense of gratitude toward her. But all I could think was that I would have traded everything—Matt and Lucy and Heart Lake and Vassar and whatever shimmering mirage of a future I'd imagined—for one good word from her. "Dear God," I wrote in

my journal, "I'll give up everything for one good word from her. I'll
drop out of Heart Lake and go back to Corinth High. I'll enroll in
community college and take a secretarial course. I'll get a job in the
mill and maybe, if I'm lucky, marry someone like Ward Castle." I
reread what I'd written and then crossed out "someone like" and
promised God I'd marry Ward Castle himself.

But although my mother remained lucid and conscious to the
end she said nothing to me. Finally, on the day before New Year's,
she took her last breath and closed her eyes on me forever.

Because the ground was frozen, my mother's remains would be
stored until spring when she could be buried. There was a short memorial service held on New Year's day at the Presbyterian church my
aunt's family attended. Afterward we went back to my aunt's house
and I nodded politely while my father told relatives I didn't recognize how proud my mother had been of me.

Later that night he took me aside and told me that he'd be staying at his sister's house for a while. He might even look into a job at
the glove factory where my uncle worked. If I didn't mind that. I
could still come down to Albany on weekends if I liked.

"To tell you the truth, Janie, I'm sick to death of that sawdust. I
thought gloves might make a nice change."

I told him I thought it was a fine idea, and not to worry about
how I spent my weekends. I'd be busy studying for finals and college
entrance exams. In fact, I was a little anxious to get back.

"Of course you are," he said with such obvious relief that I had
to remind myself he was only happy I had something to take my
mind off my mother's death. It wasn't as if he were trying to get rid
of me. "You can go back tomorrow. If you're not afraid of taking
the train back yourself," he told me. It occurred to me that with all
the stress he had been under my father probably didn't remember
that it was still Christmas break, school didn't start until the second
week in January. It seemed unlikely to me that he would have so
blithely sent me back to a deserted campus.

I didn't tell him his mistake. I took the fifty-dollar bill he removed from the pocket of his ill-fitting dark suit and told him I wasn't afraid at all. After all, it was the same train I'd be taking to college next year.

I thought of that, the next day, riding the train north along the Hudson, the river a dark gray ribbon rimmed with pale green ice under a pearly sky. Because we shared the same name I'd always thought of the river as a blood relative, and it seemed right, somehow, that my future lay along its banks. Matt's school was just an hour or so south. In a matter of months I'd follow the river to Vassar and then, who knew? Perhaps I'd follow the river farther south to New York City. There my imagination reached its limit; I'd never been to New York City. But as I watched the chunks of pale green ice float downriver, even as the train took me in the opposite direction, I thought of a description from a fairy tale I'd read once of a palace formed of the drifting snow, its windows and doors cut by the wind, its hundred halls all blown together by the snow. The Snow Queen's palace with a frozen lake at its center. And even though I was moving in the opposite direction, I felt like I was traveling toward my future.

When I reached Corinth I took a taxi to the school. The taxi driver said there was a Nor'easter on the way that was expected to drop several feet of snow on the southern Adirondacks. He jabbed his finger at the windshield, at a bank of clouds massing in the north. The sky had an ominous green tinge to it. When we got to the school he helped me get my suitcases into the lobby of the dorm but he didn't ask if I wanted help getting them upstairs. He must have had a moment's compunction about leaving me, though.

"Are you sure you're all right here?" he asked me, eyeing the empty desk where the dorm matron usually sat. "Is there anyone here?"

"Oh, my friends are here. They'll help me with my bags once I let them know I'm back," I told him. I'd pictured myself lugging my suitcases up the two flights of stairs, but suddenly I knew I was far too anxious for that. A great sense of urgency had overtaken me. Maybe it was just the weather: the drop in air pressure, those strange green clouds, that expectant sense of snow coming. I left my suitcases in the lobby and ran up the stairs.

On the second landing I paused and listened. I had thought I heard someone crying. But when I listened, all I heard was the hiss of the steam radiators. I remembered then that the maintenance crew always turned the heat on full blast over vacation to keep the pipes from freezing. Last year, Deirdre had left three pillar candles in her room and they had all melted. The funny thing had been that they had all melted differently. The red one had sunken into itself so that it looked like a Hershey's kiss. The purple one had keeled over sideways like the leaning tower of Pisa. The blue one looked at first like nothing had happened to it at all, but then we realized that while the outside shape had stayed the same, the wax had dripped out from the inside and pooled on the floor, leaving behind a hollow column.

As I walked along our hall I stripped off my coat and scarf. How had Deirdre and Lucy been able to stand it? It was like a sauna in here. When I put my hand on our doorknob it was warm to the touch.

I heard, again, the sound of crying as I opened the door. On the bed under the window—Lucy's bed—someone was lying under the covers with her back to the door. I thought it was Lucy and that she must have been the one who was crying, but as I crossed the room I heard the sound again, and another sound, like metal scraping metal. I turned in that direction just as the door to the single opened and saw in the doorway, not Deirdre as I expected, but Lucy.

She was wearing a red flannel shirt—Matt's, I thought—that was so big on her that when she held up her arms and put a hand on either side of the doorjamb, the shirt covered the whole doorway. If she hadn't been so short she would have blocked my view of the single. I could see, though, over her head, but I couldn't see why she was trying to block my view. Then we both took a step forward at the same time and nearly collided.

"Jane," she said, "what are you doing back?"

"My mother died," I said, as if that explained everything. I was looking at Deirdre's single, trying to figure out what was different about it, but the only thing I could see that was different was that she had gotten a new bedspread. A red bedspread. I didn't even notice that Lucy wasn't saying the things she should have been saying, like "I'm so sorry" or "How terrible." I took another step toward the room so that I was on the threshold and realized that what I was looking at wasn't a red bedspread. It was a sheet soaked in blood.

I looked at Lucy and then at the body under the covers on Lucy's bed.

"She's asleep," Lucy whispered. She took my hand in her small hand and pulled me into the single. She had to pull quite hard because I didn't want to go in there. I'd forgotten what a strong grip she had.

She closed the door behind us.

I stood over the bed and noticed that the blood had soaked through the mattress.

"She tried to kill herself?" I asked.

Lucy looked up at me for a moment and then shook her head. "Yes, it's Deirdre's blood," she said, "but she didn't try to kill herself. She was pregnant. She had a baby."

"Deirdre was pregnant? How could that be?"

"You remember last year, the nights we spent out at the lake, and May Day. I think it was May Day because she didn't go out all those weeks it rained and I think the baby was early, it was so small . . ."

I grabbed her arm and shook it. I noticed how thin her arm felt under the big shirt. "She had the baby *here*?" I said, her words finally sinking in. *"Alone?"*

Lucy looked offended. "I was here," she said, "I stayed with her all night."

"Why didn't you go to the infirmary?"

"She begged me not to. She said they would definitely throw her out and put her in a reform school this time. What could I do, Jane? And then it came so quick. I think because it was so small . . ."

It was the second time she had mentioned the baby's size, but small or not it surely wasn't invisible.

"Where . . . ?"

Lucy looked over at Deirdre's bureau and I followed her gaze to the large metal tea tin, the one decorated with golden mountains that Deirdre used to store her pot.

"It wasn't breathing," she said. "It was born dead."

My knees felt suddenly watery as if the tendons holding them together had just melted. I brushed my hand against my face and it came back wet. The one window in the single was opaque with water condensation. I walked over to the window and wrenched it open. I leaned out the window and threw up onto the ledge.

Lucy came up behind me and put a cool hand on my forehead. She held my hair back until I had finished throwing up and then sat me down on the inside ledge. She held me by the shoulders until I stopped shaking.

"Fuck, Lucy, we've got to tell someone."

She shook her head. "They'll throw her out for sure. What good will it do?"

"But what if she's still bleeding." I looked at Deirdre's bed. Could a person lose that much blood and be all right?

"I gave her a sanitary napkin and it seemed like most of the bleeding stopped an hour ago. I think she'll be all right."

"But what are we going to do about that?" I pointed at the tea tin. "We can't just leave it there."

"Of course not," Lucy said reasonably. "I've been thinking about it all morning. The ground's too frozen to bury it . . ." For some reason I thought of my mother's body lying in a funeral home's refrigerator in Albany, waiting for the spring thaw. I tasted bile in my throat and would have thrown up again if Lucy hadn't placed two cool hands on either side of my face. Looking into those blue eyes of hers I suddenly felt calmer.

"You understand why we have to take care of this, Jane? It's not just for Deirdre, it's for Matt, too."

"But he wasn't with her on May Day," I said.

"He was the only one caught that morning and Deirdre will say it was him. Remember how she caved in on the wine flask. It will ruin Matt's life forever."

"But if the ground's frozen . . ."

"But the lake's not," she said, "we can sink it in the lake."

Chapter Twenty-three

●

"W E'LL HAVE TO TAKE THE BOAT," LUCY SAID AS WE were leaving the dorm. "It's the only way we can be sure it sinks deep enough."

"It" was the way Lucy referred to the thing in the tea tin. She had placed the tin in her gym bag and carried it, not by the handles, but cradled upright in her arms—the way a person would carry a cake in a box.

Before we left the room I checked on Deirdre. She was sleeping soundly, her lips moist and parted, her cheeks pink in the overheated room. She didn't look like a person bleeding to death, but like someone drugged.

"I gave her some of that tea she's always saying is such a good sleep potion," Lucy told me. I noticed the red lacquer box lying empty beside the bed. "She'll be OK."

When we left the dorm I turned onto the path but Lucy steered me into the woods. "We can't risk taking the path," she said. "We might run into someone."

The campus felt deserted. I knew that some teachers stayed on over break. Miss Buehl, for instance, tended her lab experiments and followed animal tracks in the snowy woods. There was a groundskeeper and Mrs. Ames, but I imagined that the workers from the town, like my taxi driver, would have gone home by now rather than risk getting caught out here in the storm.

Lucy's footpath through the woods was so narrow we had to walk single file. At first I kept my eyes on her back, on her pale blue snow parka, but my gaze kept drifting to the navy blue gym bag that she cradled over her right hip. Although I couldn't see it in the bag I kept picturing the tin. The gold mountains under a blue sky. A green lake in the foreground.

I turned my eyes to the path. It had been trod into the snow over many weeks and then frozen into a knee-deep crevasse—a miniature of the ones in the film strip on glaciers Miss Buehl showed us. I thought of the weeks it took Lucy to make the path and wondered if it would be filled in by the approaching storm.

We came out at the south tip of lake, not far from the Schwanenkill. When I looked up I noticed for the first time that there was a thin sheet of ice covering the lake.

"Damn, it must have frozen just last night," Lucy said, more to herself than to me. She shifted the gym bag to her left hip and eased herself down the bank. She swayed in the deep, untrodden snow and I thought that I should offer to hold the gym bag, but I didn't.

Lucy stretched one leg down to the lake's surface and tapped it with her booted toe. A splintering sound echoed across the lake.

"How thick is it?" I called and heard my words echo hollowly. I looked up at the sky and saw that the ominous green clouds hung low over the lake like a shallow dome. I felt as if Lucy and I were being pressed between the sky and snow-covered ground, like autumn leaves ironed between two sheets of waxed paper.

"Not very," Lucy said coming back up the bank. "It's thinnest where the Schwanenkill flows out of the lake. I think we can break the ice with the boat oars."

First we had to cross the stream, which was only partially frozen. Lucy, usually so surefooted, seemed unbalanced by the weight she was carrying on her hip. I pictured her falling and dropping the bag and the tin snapping open.

"Here," I said, crossing the stream ahead of her, "take my hand." I planted one foot in the middle of the stream and felt the icy water creeping through the soles of my boots. I noticed when I took her hand that Lucy was shaking.

We made it to the icehouse only to find that the door was locked.

"The extension agent must have locked it after she saw Matt here on May Day," Lucy said. We hadn't used the icehouse this winter. "But I doubt she could have locked the doors on the lake side because they don't close completely. We'll have to go around."

I looked at Lucy and noticed how pale she was; her skin had a greenish cast to it, as green as the snow-laden sky. After all, she had been up all night with Deirdre and the shock of witnessing that birth—a stillbirth, no less—was no doubt beginning to tell on her. I was suddenly filled with hatred for Deirdre. Why should we have to clean up her mess? But then I remembered that we were doing it for Matt, too.

"I'll go," I said. "You stay here and rest on this rock."

Lucy nodded and sat down on a large flat rock. She hugged the gym bag to her chest and closed her eyes.

I went down to the edge of the lake and studied the narrow ledge of mud and ice that ran in back of the icehouse. I noticed that one of the doors was wedged partially open—just as it had been on the night I'd approached it from the ice.

I came back around and called to Lucy. "This door is open." I heard "open" echo across the lake. "But the front door is probably padlocked so I'll have to get the boat out onto the water and bring it to shore."

I half expected Lucy to object. I wasn't really sure I'd be able to get the boat out by myself. But she only nodded and lay back on the rock, one hand resting on the gym bag by her side.

I made my way along the icy edge of the lake, one hand on the wall of the icehouse. Both my feet were soaked by the time I reached the open door and pulled myself into the small hut. I was relieved to see that the rowboat was still there, with both its oars lying in the shallow hull. The prow of the boat was facing the lake.

I opened both doors and then went to the rear of the boat, took a deep breath, and pushed. At first nothing happened, but then I heard a scraping noise as the boat inched forward on the wooden floor. I crouched down and put my shoulder to the stern and pushed again. The scraping sound changed to a crash that was so loud in the echoing silence of the lake that I was sure someone from the school must have heard it. I looked across the lake toward the cliff wall of the Point and for a moment thought I saw a figure standing on the rock. I thought of Miss Buehl in her cottage just beyond the Point. But then the figure vanished and I couldn't be sure if I'd imagined it or not.

I looked down and saw that the boat was drifting out into the lake.

I lunged after it, caught the rear, and pulled it back to the shore. My jeans were now soaked up to my knees, so I figured I might as well wade through the water, guiding the boat with me until I'd gotten it past the icehouse. By the time I'd pulled it halfway up onto the shore I couldn't feel my toes anymore. I trudged up the bank, the wet sucking sound my boots made somehow familiar. I paused and saw in my mind my mother's hospital room and heard the wet gurgle of the pump that cleared her lungs of fluid. I felt suddenly, of all things, immeasurably sleepy and I think that if I had been alone I would have lain down in the soft snow and taken a nap under that pillowy green-gray sky.

But from where I was I could see Lucy lying on the rock and the navy blue gym bag lying beside her. I shook myself awake and approached her. She didn't move at my approach even though the sound my boots made scraping through the crusted snow seemed unbearably loud to me. I looked down at her and saw that she had fallen asleep. Again I was startled by how pale she looked, her eyelids and lips blue in the cold, shimmering air. I shook her arm and her eyes snapped open.

"I've got the boat," I said.

She looked at me as if she didn't know what I was talking about, but then she noticed the gym bag and nodded her head. She got up slowly, swayed unsteadily, and sat back on the rock.

"We need some rocks," she said.

It was my turn to look at her uncomprehendingly.

"To weigh it down," she explained, gesturing toward the bag.

I looked around but of course any rocks that might have been there were two feet under the snow.

"In the stream," she said. "There are always rocks at the bottom of the Schwanenkill."

I turned back to the stream, expecting her to follow me, but she stayed seated on the rock. At the stream's edge I knelt in the snow and took my gloves off. I reached into the middle of the stream, I was into it up to my elbow before my fingers grazed the bottom. I felt frozen mud and something hard and round. I pulled up a smooth, round rock about the size of my fist and laid it on the stream bank. When I'd found about a dozen rocks I stuffed them into my pockets and went back to Lucy.

I emptied the rocks onto the flat rock next to where she sat and she nodded.

"That'll do it," she said. Then she slid the tea tin out of the gym bag and opened the lid.

Inside there was a tiny white baby about the size of a small cat. Its skin was nearly translucent, gleaming blue and pink like an opal. Its eyelashes and the light hair on its scalp were sandy red. Lucy picked up a rock and wiped the mud off on her jeans. Clean and dry the rocks were a beautiful greenish bluish gray—the color hazel eyes were sometimes. Lucy arranged them around the baby as if she were packing eggshells in tissue paper. Then she took out a white cloth from her pocket, shook it out, and smoothed it over the baby. It was one of the linen napkins from the dining room, stitched with a heart and the school's motto: *Cor te reducit.* The heart takes you back. Not a bad requiem for the little thing about to be buried in the lake. Then she closed the lid and fastened the metal catch.

"We ought to wrap something around it to make sure it doesn't open. Do you have any string?"

I shook my head. String? What the hell was she thinking? She opened her coat and felt the top of her jeans. "I'm not wearing a belt," she said. "Are you?"

I opened my coat and unthreaded my belt through the belt loops of my jeans. It was made of thick, webbed cotton—I'd bought it at the army/navy store in town—with an adjustable brass buckle.

"Perfect," Lucy said, tightening the belt around the tin and fastening the buckle. "That should hold. Let's go."

I had to help Lucy into the boat while she held the tin. This time I did offer to take it from her but she shook her head and held on to it more tightly.

I pushed the boat into the water and then hopped in and grabbed the oars. I turned the boat around so the prow faced the lake and I faced the shore rowing. Lucy sat behind me. When the boat grazed thicker ice she directed me.

"There's a path of thinner ice that goes all the way through the lake," she told me, "it must follow the underground spring." I remembered the day we had skated here and she had gone through the ice. The place she had gone in must have been over the spring.

Twice we had to stop and I had to pass her one of the oars to chop the ice. I was afraid, each time, that she'd drop the oar into the lake and we'd be stranded out here.

"It must be deep enough here," I said after we were stopped by the ice for the third time, but she shook her head and battered the ice with the oar. The chopping sounds reverberated against the layer of heavy clouds and the rock wall of the Point. The jutting prow of the Point seemed close now and I could see, a little to the east, one of the three sister stones emerging from the ice, standing like a silent witness to our deed.

"We're more than halfway across the lake," I said. "We're getting too close to the other shore."

Lucy stopped hammering with the oar and looked behind her. Her hair was so damp with sweat that it had frozen together in clumps and when she swung her head back to face me I could hear the sound her frozen hair made brushing against her nylon parka.

"OK," she said, "here."

We both looked down at the tea tin sitting in the bottom of the boat. The blue sky over golden mountains looked to me like a dream of summer during winter. I looked up at the lowering black-green sky above us and tried to remember what such a sky looked like. Lucy knelt down in the bottom of the boat and picked up the tin. She tried to hold it in one hand while using one hand to brace herself against the rim of the boat to get up. The boat careened toward the east shore and then swung back to the west, sluicing us with icy water.

"Jesus," I said taking the tin from her, "let me have that." I heard the stones knock together inside the tin. The whole thing felt lighter than I expected and I wondered if it would really sink to the bottom. "Let's get this over with," I said. I balanced the tin on the edge of the boat and looked at her. She nodded.

I leaned over, holding the tin parallel to the water's surface in a patch Lucy had cleared of ice. I didn't like to think of it flipping over and sinking to the bottom upside down. When it was a few inches from the surface I let it go. I watched it sink below the water and saw the blue sky and gold mountains turn pale green and then vanish into the green-black depths of the lake. I stared for a moment at the shards of white ice floating on the black water until I noticed that white crystals were beginning to fill in the black spaces. I thought the water was freezing again in front of my eyes and I was afraid that when I looked back at how we had come the path across the lake would be sealed with ice. But when I looked up I saw that the path back to the icehouse hadn't closed. It was the green sky above that had opened up to disgorge its burden of snow, a stream of snow so thick it felt as if the sky were falling down upon us.

PART THREE

•

The Ice Harvest

Chapter Twenty-four

●

EVEN THE AIR HERE IS TAINTED, DYED A CITRINOUS GREEN that shimmers under the frosted dome like green Jell-O. We spend the day splashing in murky water the same color and temperature as the air. Or Olivia swims and I lie in a plastic lawn chair staring up at the pale green bubble of sky. We play putt-putt on spiky green plastic grass. We eat our meals at a restaurant next to the pool and so even our food tastes like chlorine. Our room's only window looks onto the interior dome. By the third day I've lost all sense of night and day; it seems like we've been here for years, not days. When I turn out the light for bedtime, the green light from the dome seeps through the cracks in the curtains. Even Olivia is restless and spends the night clinging to me in the oversized bed. I awake, tangled in her damp hair, breathing in its comforting smell of bleach and salt.

I thought it made sense to stay in a hotel with an indoor pool, so I spent the last of my savings on two weeks at the Westchester Aquadome. When I gave Dean Buehl the phone number she asked how long I planned to stay and I realized that I might not have a job anymore. When I told her I didn't know she said to call her in two weeks and we'd talk it over.

"Take some time to think about what you really want to do,

Jane." The words sounded familiar and I realized it was the same thing she had said to me the day I graduated from Heart Lake. She'd come down to the train station to see some of the younger girls off. She did this every year and usually she was a cheerful sight, calling a hearty "see you next year" and waving her handkerchief at the departing trains. But that year a lot of girls wouldn't be coming back. Two students and a town boy had drowned in the lake and a teacher had been let go because she had somehow been involved. Parents reacted by pulling out their children and their money. I saw Miss Buehl first on the opposite side of the tracks, the northbound side, fussing nervously over Albie, trying, unsuccessfully, to slick back her pale wisps of hair into a large bow pinned to the back of her head. When she saw me she hurried over the bridge leaving Albie looking small and lost beside a tower of matching monogrammed suitcases.

"I wanted to wish you luck at Vassar, Jane," Miss Buehl said when she had crossed to the southbound side. "You don't know how lucky you are to be getting out now."

"Have that many girls been pulled out?" I asked.

"About half," she said, lowering her voice. "Of course, we'll get more girls, but not of the same sort."

"Albie's been pulled out?" I asked in a low voice even though the girl couldn't possibly hear us from across the track.

"I'm afraid Albie's been kicked out," Miss Buehl said in a quaking whisper, leaning her head close to mine. I thought I smelled liquor on her breath and I noticed for the first time how haggard she looked. "We discovered it was she who broke the fanlight over the doors to the mansion. She threw half a dozen rocks through it."

"Really? Albie did that?" It was hard for me to imagine frail little Albie having the strength to throw even one rock that high.

"Yes, I tried to argue in her behalf, but then there were other infractions, curfew breaking, erratic behavior . . ."

"Where is she going?" I asked, trying to keep from stealing a look across the tracks. I felt sure she was watching us and that she guessed she was the topic of our whispered conversation.

"St. Eustace," Miss Buehl answered.

"Oh." *St. Useless.* The school Deirdre'd been so afraid she'd end up at. I did look at Albie then, but she had turned away from us and set her small, pinched face into an expression of bland indifference, as if she were on her way to a tedious but necessary luncheon, and not to the Siberia of girls' boarding schools. Then the northbound train pulled in and blocked my view of her.

"So you see how lucky you are, Jane," Miss Buehl had said to me. "You can put this whole thing behind you and take some time to think about what you really want to do. You've got your whole life ahead of you." She said it like she almost envied me. That she wished she were getting out, too. But then I might have imagined that. After all, Heart Lake was her whole life.

THIS TIME SHE DIDN'T TELL ME I HAD MY WHOLE LIFE ahead of me. We both knew my options were limited, they had narrowed to . . . what? Did I even have more than one option? "Maybe it's not too late to work things out with your husband," she had added instead.

I suppose she would feel better firing me if she knew I had somewhere to go.

The idea of working things out with Mitch was the furthest thing from my mind when I came here, but he has been unexpectedly kind.

He joins us for dinner almost every night and has even offered to pay part of my hotel bill. When I told him, on the first day while we both watched Olivia swimming in the pool, about what the police had found in the lake along with Aphrodite's body, he thought I meant, at first, that the baby in the tea tin had been Aphrodite's. I had to explain, for what seemed like the hundredth time since the diver had emerged from the lake with that tin, that the baby belonged to my old roommate Deirdre Hall. I told him, as I told the police and Dean Buehl, that Lucy and I had helped her by sinking the tin in the lake.

"Are they charging you with anything?" he asked.

"Not that I know of."

"Good," he said. "You were a minor and you were only an accomplice in disposing of the body. The baby was dead at birth, right?"

I nodded. "That's what Lucy told me."

He paused for a moment, perhaps seeing my uncertainty. Even as I assured him, I realized I was no longer so sure. Maybe it's being in this place—the warm humid air and the way voices echo under the dome. Since I've been here I've remembered standing in that damp, overheated dorm corridor listening to a thin wail of crying. "Well, if it was a lie, it was Lucy's lie. You should be OK. I'll call Herb Stanley in the morning." Herb Stanley was Mitch's lawyer. He'd drawn up our separation agreement. "Don't talk to anyone without consulting him first. You say you knew this police officer back in school?"

"He was Matt and Lucy's cousin. I met him once or twice."

Mitchell smiled at me. "An old boyfriend?"

I was surprised to detect a note of jealousy in his tone.

I shrugged my shoulders. I remembered holding hands with Roy Corey on the swimming beach, stroking my hand along his face. "Not exactly," I said.

"Not exactly no either. Maybe he still likes you." I thought of the way Roy Corey flinched when I touched his arm. No, I didn't think he liked me, but I wasn't obliged to tell Mitchell that.

"You're looking good by the way. That north country air must agree with you."

I saw his eyes moving up and down my body and I felt, suddenly, self-conscious in my bathing suit. It was true I had lost weight over the fall semester, finally shedding the pounds I'd gained having Olivia. I knew Mitch had minded how I'd changed after Olivia was born. And I had minded how he minded.

"I'm sure Roy Corey is busy with his job right now. Aphrodite's . . . I mean Melissa's death will probably be declared a suicide, but now he's got this other body . . ."

I stopped myself, appalled at how the word "body" echoed in the watery air. I lowered my voice and went on. "They're going to exhume Deirdre Hall's body—she was buried in Philadelphia—and Matt Toller's body."

I stopped again, remembering the day they found Matt and Lucy. Although it had felt like spring the night I went to meet Matt at the icehouse, it had been a false spring. One of those premature February thaws we get in the Adirondacks. Overnight the temperature had plunged and the lake froze over again. They tried sawing holes in the ice the way they used to for the ice harvest. It turned out that the extension agent had all the equipment and had been thinking of doing an ice harvest for a history demonstration. When they couldn't find the bodies, though, they brought in a small ice cutter from the Hudson and tore the whole lake apart.

I was in the woods behind the icehouse on the day they found them. The divers carried the bodies into the icehouse while they sent for the family to identify them. It must have been hard on the divers, pulling that tangle of limbs up from the lake bottom. They stood on the shore afterward, smoking cigarettes, their backs to the icehouse. One skipped a stone over the water, but stopped because there was too much broken ice. They didn't notice me when I came down from the woods and stood in the doorway.

They had laid the bodies on one of the ledges where they used to store the slabs of ice. At first I thought they'd only found Matt, but then I saw, tangled in his hair, the small hand and, nestled below his ribs on the side farthest from me, in the shadow of the ledge, her face, pressed against his chest.

They had been bleached clean by the lake, their flesh the same marble white. It was hard to tell where his body stopped and hers began.

"I THOUGHT YOU SAID IT COULDN'T BE MATT'S BABY." Mitchell's voice broke into the memory of those twisted limbs.

I took a deep breath of the warm chlorinated air.

"I may have gotten it wrong," I told Mitchell. "Roy Corey seems to have some other idea."

When I told Roy Corey what had happened—from the day I came back to the school early to the last argument between Matt and Lucy—he didn't seem completely surprised. "I thought something was wrong that night Matt left to hitch back to Corinth. He said he'd gotten a letter from Lucy and he was afraid he'd 'really messed something up.' He wouldn't tell me what. I was afraid . . . well, never mind what I was afraid of. We'll have our answers in two weeks."

That's how long it would take to get the results of the DNA tests. They'd found an aunt of Deirdre's who agreed to the exhumation. As for Matt, Cliff and Hannah Toller had both died in a car accident four years after their children's deaths. Ironically, Matt's next of kin was now Roy Corey. I asked if he'd call me when he got the results.

"Oh, you'll be hearing from me, Jane," he said.

"At least he didn't tell you to stay in Corinth," Mitchell said. "That's a good sign."

"Yeah, but he told me not to leave this hotel without telling him where I could be reached."

Mitchell nodded. "Why don't you call and say you're staying at the house."

I thought I had misheard him in the weird acoustics of the Aquadome, but when I looked at him I thought I saw tears in his eyes. But then it might have been the way the air here stings your eyes.

"What are you saying, Mitch?"

He shrugged. "I never understood what went wrong, Janie. I never understood why you left. Was it that bad . . . living with me? I know I could be preoccupied."

I looked down at Olivia paddling in the pale green water. With her purple and pink bathing suit and orange water wings she looks like one of those paper flowers they float in exotic cocktails. The truth was I didn't understand completely why I left either.

"It wasn't your fault, Mitch," I said. Yes, he had been preoccupied, but hadn't that been what I was looking for—someone who wouldn't pay too much attention, someone who wouldn't look at me too closely?

"Maybe it's not too late for us." He reached out across the space between us and laid a damp hand on my bare knee.

I felt an odd mixture of hope and nausea. I hoped that any look of queasiness was covered by the green tint that lay on everything around us, because it had occurred to me that I shouldn't be too quick to turn down Mitch's offer.

"I have to think it over, Mitch."

"Of course, Janie, take all the time you need."

TIME IS SOMETHING I HAVE AN ABUNDANCE OF HERE AT THE Aquadome, but when I try to attend to the question at hand my thoughts slither around like slippery fish in the green air. I try to go back, in my mind, to when I met Mitch and decided to marry him. I think that if I can remember loving him I can salvage some of that feeling now and it will be enough to build a new future on, the way a seed crystal teaches the other molecules to make ice. All I need is a seed, but I can't really remember ever *deciding* anything. When I met Mitchell, a few years out of college working in the city, I was nearly drowning.

Take some time to think about what you really want to do. That's what Miss Buehl had told me that day at the train station. But I didn't have to think about it. My path had already been laid out for me the day I listened to Helen Chambers's plan for Lucy. *I see her as a Vassar girl and then she'll go to the city and work in some arts-related field—publishing, I think.* I had rejected, that day, Helen Chambers's plan for me to go to the State Teacher's College and teach Latin, and decided instead to do what she meant for Lucy.

I worked hard at Vassar and got reasonably good grades. My Latin professor urged me to apply to graduate school, but I was tired of treading the same pattern of paths that meandered around the pretty campus. Wouldn't graduate school just be another set of paths around another campus? I felt something like Lucy's impatience with the snowbound paths of Heart Lake and decided to do what I thought she would have done.

After graduation I moved to New York City and got a job as an editorial assistant at a publishing house. I shared an apartment with two other girls—both from good colleges—who worked at the same company. I wore the same kind of clothes as they did: short black skirts and silk blouses, a simple strand of graduated pearls. So what if my blouses were polyester instead of silk, my pearls paste instead of real? I stayed up late reading the manuscripts the company asked us to read on our own time. I packed my own lunch and walked to work because it was hard to make my share of the rent on the little money I made.

I turned down invitations to drinks and dinners after work because I couldn't pay my way. Besides, I told myself, it was better to spend the evenings reading manuscripts while my roommates went out. Sometimes one of the boys—they still seemed like boys to me, in their sloppily ironed Oxford shirts and slim khaki pants—would ask me out, but I always declined. I told myself it was better not to get involved with anyone just yet. But really, it was the way they all reminded me of Matt, of what Matt might have become. I'd look at one of these nice, clean-cut boys in his prep-school tie and button-down shirt and think: Matt would be his age now, twenty-two, twenty-three, twenty-four.

One day, when I was twenty-five, I was sitting in an editorial board meeting looking at a young man who worked in copy editing and always passed my desk on his way to the Xerox machine even though it wasn't really on his way. As I looked at him a shaft of weak sunlight came in through the dirty, sixteenth-floor windows and touched his mousy brown hair, turning it a bright and shining red. I felt a chill move through me as if I had just swum through a cold current and the air around me seemed to shimmer. I was seized with an unreasoning panic that the next breath I took would choke me. I left the meeting and told my boss that I'd suddenly felt ill.

"A late night?" she asked, nodding with complicity. She, I knew, stayed out to all hours in the clubs and spent the morning hours nursing hangovers with V-8 juice and Tylenol. I hated to think she attributed my illness to the same cause, but it was easier to nod and agree to her sympathetic smile.

When it happened again, that same rush of cold followed by a fear that I couldn't breathe—this time in a conference with an author and his agent, she was less sympathetic. When I emerged from the ladies' room, still trembling and sweating, she asked if there was anything I wanted to tell her. What could I tell her? That I had begun to be afraid of drowning on dry land? That I could no longer go to movie theaters, supermarkets, subway stations, or any other place where I had once had that sensation of drowning for fear of it happening there again?

I quit the job. I took another job as a secretary at a temp agency. That way, I reasoned, if I had an attack in a particular setting I wouldn't have to go back. My roommates had decided to move to a bigger apartment in Brooklyn. Since the subway was on my list of places I couldn't go anymore, I moved into a women's hotel near Gramercy Park. I could walk to most of the places the temp agency sent me. It was on one of these jobs, filling in for the receptionist at a building contractor's office, that I met Mitchell. He was older than I, his hair already thinning, his build a little thicker than a boy's. When he asked me to lunch, I accepted. When I told him I liked to take the stairs instead of the elevator for the exercise he not only believed me, but he approved. He told me he admired what good shape I was in. It was true that I had gotten very thin, mostly because I had so little money to spend on food and I walked everywhere.

He was impressed that I had gone to a private girls' school and Vassar, but he didn't ask me many questions about either place. We mostly talked, on our dates, about his job and his plans for the future. He wanted to go out on his own—build houses in the suburbs. He said the city wasn't a good place to raise children. He seemed to me, above all else, cautious and polite. When he asked me to marry him I didn't ask myself if I loved him. I had assumed that my chances of loving anyone had vanished into the black water of Heart Lake the night Matt and Lucy drowned below the ice.

Those first years of my marriage to Mitchell were peaceful. He built us a house north of the city and I helped out in the office. Mitch did seem disappointed that I didn't get pregnant right away, but when I did conceive I thought everything would be all right.

What I hadn't counted on was how much I would love Olivia. When I first saw her, her body glistening with blood, I was over-come by violent shivering. The labor nurse explained that the con-vulsions were caused by my body's inability to adjust to the change in mass. But to me it felt like something was breaking up inside of me, setting something free that had been frozen all these years. I wanted to hold her, but Mitch said I was shaking too hard to be trusted with her.

In an unguarded moment I had told Mitchell about my panic at-tacks. He had seemed, at first, unconcerned, but after Olivia was born he wanted me to see a psychiatrist to make sure I wouldn't have an attack while I was watching Olivia. "You might drop her," he said, "or hurt her during an episode." He spoke as if I had epilepsy. The psychiatrist prescribed an antianxiety drug that made my mouth dry and prevented me from breast-feeding Olivia. Still, Mitchell worried. He made me promise not to drive with Olivia. Our new house was in a housing development far from anything. I spent my days wheeling Olivia in her carriage around the winding streets that always seemed to dead-end in a cul-de-sac.

I thought, because he was so worried about me watching Olivia, he would come home right after work, but instead he stayed at the office later and later. After I got Olivia fed and bathed and put to bed I would go through my old books, which were stored in boxes in the basement. One night I took out my Wheelock's Latin grammar and started at the beginning, memorizing the declensions and conjugations all over again. I was reciting the third declension to Olivia in her high chair one night when Mitchell came home unexpectedly early.

"What the hell are you teaching her, Jane, that mumbo-jumbo witchcraft you practiced in high school?"

I stared at him, pureed yellow squash dripping from the spoon I held out to Olivia. My journals, all of them except the fourth one which had disappeared, were in the same box in which I had found my Wheelock. I'd left the box, opened, in the basement.

Olivia, impatient for the proffered spoon, slammed her small fist on the high-chair tray. Startled, I dropped the spoon and Olivia began to cry.

Mitchell pulled her out of the high chair. "That's OK, Livvie, Daddy'll take care of you."

I knew that in five minutes Mitchell would give her back to me to do the bath and bedtime, but in that instant I felt, as he intended, his power to take her from me. There were things in those journals that made me sound like an unfit mother. There were things in the psychiatrist's files that made me sound insane. I didn't know when Mitchell had started to hate me, but I suspected it was when he discovered I had never loved him. And in a way, I couldn't blame him. I had thought it was all right to marry someone I didn't love, but what I hadn't counted on was how it felt to share someone I loved with someone I didn't.

And so I decided to make the first move. For the next few weeks, while I wheeled Olivia around the endless maze of suburban streets, my mind moved around in the same dead-end circles, trying to find a way out. When I told Mitch I wanted a divorce he laughed at me. "Where will you go? How will you live? When I met you, you couldn't even hold a secretarial job for more than a week."

I knew he had me. If I went to work in the city I'd have to put Olivia in day care ten hours a day. A lot of Mitch's business was off the books, which meant the child support he'd be obliged to pay me wouldn't amount to more than a few hundred dollars a month. I had no family or friends to turn to. I read ads for jobs I could do from home, but anyone could see that I'd never make enough to support myself, let alone Olivia. I had no skills to speak of.

"For God's sake, Jane, you majored in Latin," Mitch was fond of saying to me. "How impractical can you get?"

One day, though, I read in the newspaper that Latin was making a comeback. I knew that Mitch would never pay for the classes I'd need to get certified to teach in the public schools, but maybe I could get a job in a private school. I'd already started relearning my Latin. Now I set myself a passage of Latin to memorize each night. I found it oddly soothing. As I picked away at case endings and declensions, alone at the kitchen table, the tangled words unraveled into flowing strands of lucid meaning.

When I had memorized most of Catullus and Ovid, I called Heart Lake and asked to whom should I write about a teaching position. The secretary told me that all hiring decisions were made by the dean, Celeste Buehl. I hung up the phone. I realized then that I had been lying to myself. I didn't want a Latin teaching job at some private school. I wanted to go back to Heart Lake. But how could I ask for a job from Celeste Buehl, who knew everything.

It wasn't until Olivia was three and a half and I overheard Mitchell telling her, along with her bedtime story, that she should tell Daddy if Mommy ever acted funny, that I called Heart Lake again. I asked to speak to Dean Buehl. When the secretary asked who was calling I gave my maiden name, Jane Hudson, but I didn't say I was an alumna.

"Jane Hudson, class of seventy-seven!" Dean Buehl sounded as if she were greeting a celebrity.

"Yes, Miss Buehl, I mean Dean Buehl, I didn't know if you'd remember me."

"Of course I remember you, Jane. Tell me what you've been doing with yourself."

When I told her that I was looking for a job teaching Latin the line went quiet and I steeled myself for the inevitable disappointment.

"You know we've never really been able to replace Helen Chambers."

My heart sank. I hadn't thought that by applying for the Latin position I was trying to take Helen Chambers's place. How could I ever?

"But then," she went on, "we've never gotten an old girl in the position." It had taken me a moment to realize that by "old girl" she meant me. I vaguely heard her bemoaning my generation's lack of interest in teaching. My attention came back when I heard her say that she couldn't think of anyone better to take the place than one of Helen Chambers's girls.

When I finally got off the phone, having arranged to come up to see the new preschool and the cottage where Olivia and I would live ("It's the one I lived in when I taught science. It's not much, but, as you might recall, it has a lovely view of the lake"), I felt so warm I felt my forehead to see if I had a fever. It wasn't, I realized as that warm feeling stayed with me instead of fading over the next difficult months of arguing with Mitchell, just that I had been offered a job. It was what Dean Buehl had called me. *One of Helen Chambers's girls.* That was what my problem had been all these years. I had forgotten who I was. I had forgotten where I belonged.

NOW I WONDER, AS I JOIN OLIVIA IN THE WARM GREEN pool, how I could ever have thought that that was what I wanted. *One of Helen Chambers's girls.* I had been lured by that old attraction, the old game that we had played—Lucy and Deirdre and me—to be like her. Look what had become of them. Deirdre and Lucy were dead. And me? I had taken Helen Chambers's place at Heart Lake and one of my own students had died just as hers had. I have nothing to offer those girls. My place is here with Olivia. So what if I'm not in love with my husband? How many wives are?

I swim several laps with Olivia paddling behind me. I do dolphin dives under her and spring up in unexpected places making her squeal with delight. Her screams echo off the opaque surface of the dome. I dive deep, all the way to the bottom, and as I begin to come up for air I see, on the other side of the water, a familiar face. The green water seems, suddenly, thick and heavy, pressing me down to the bottom of the pool. I can feel its weight pressing against my mouth, waiting to fill my lungs. I struggle to the top, but even when I break the surface I'm afraid to take a breath. Afraid that breathing in this shimmering air will drown me.

The man at the edge of the pool reaches out his hand for me and helps me up the ladder. It's only Roy Corey. I take a breath, gasping in the chlorinated air. I'm so relieved it's him that for a second I don't even question what he's doing here—two hundred miles from his police district—but then he tells me.

"I went to talk to my old forensics professor at John Jay," he says, "and now I'm heading up to Cold Spring to visit my mother. You were on the way, so . . . here," he says handing me a towel, "you look cold. And pale. Don't tell me you've been in this fish bowl for the whole two weeks."

"Has it really been two weeks already?" I ask, toweling myself down and then wrapping the towel around my waist.

"Yeah. Time flies. Isn't there a saying in Latin for that?"

"Tempus fugit," I say.

"Yeah, that's it. Mattie used to say that." He motions for me to sit down on one of the plastic picnic chairs that surround a glass table. I have the feeling as he settles himself down on the creaking, insubstantial plastic that what he has to tell me about the DNA results requires sitting.

"The baby was Matt's." I say it so he won't have to.

He nods. "Yeah, it was Matt's all right." He's looking at me to see how I'm taking the news.

"I guess I knew all along," I tell him. He looks so pained to be giving me this information that I find myself wanting to reassure him. "That's what they argued about the night they drowned. Matt kept asking Lucy whose baby it was. He must have realized it was his." Roy Corey puffs up his cheeks and blows air out. He reminds me of those drawings of the wind. "But it was Deirdre he should have been mad at," I add.

Roy shakes his head. I notice the way the flesh around his mouth shakes a little. Matt would never have turned out like this, I think.

"No, Deirdre had nothing to do with it."

I feel myself smiling a tight, polite smile that makes my skin, dry from so much chlorine, crease. "What do you mean?" I ask.

"Deirdre Hall wasn't the baby's mother," he says. "The baby was Matt and Lucy's."

Chapter Twenty-five

●

"BUT HOW?"

Roy Corey holds up one hand, palm out like a traffic cop. It reminds me that he is a cop and I had promised Mitchell not to talk to him without consulting a lawyer first.

"I gotta tell you something before you say anything else," he says.

I think he is going to read me my Miranda rights, but instead he tells me that he's read my journal.

"You did what?" My voice is so loud that everyone under the Aquadome—Olivia in the pool, a family playing putt-putt, the waiters in the poolside restaurant—stop what they are doing to look at us.

"I'm sorry, Jane, I didn't mean to invade your privacy, but it's evidence. We found it with Melissa Randall's effects."

"So she's the one who had it."

Corey nods. "Dean Buehl and Dr. Lockhart agree that she must have found the journal hidden in your old room, under the floorboards, maybe?"

I nod to indicate that this is not outside the realm of possibility. Lucy must have hidden it that night she followed me to the icehouse. Maybe she was afraid that something in it would reveal that the baby was hers. But what? If I hadn't guessed her secret, how could my journal reveal it? Could I have written something that revealed the truth without even knowing the truth? The idea that my journal contains secrets even I do not know makes the fact that it has been in the possession of one of my students even more alarming. Even if the student is dead.

". . . and in acting out her paranoid fantasies of persecution . . ." I catch a shred of what Roy Corey is saying, mostly because the language he is using no longer sounds like his own.

"Dr. Lockhart's diagnosis?" I ask

He nods and grins. "Yeah. Basically she thinks Melissa decided to reenact the events of your senior year and torture you along the way."

"But what about Ellen's suicide attempt?"

"Melissa had a prescription for Demerol—for cramps, her mother said, can you believe that, letting your daughter take a jar full of Demerol away to school—which she could have used to drug Ellen and then cut her wrists."

I wince. "Then Athena was telling the truth. She didn't try to kill herself."

"It was a fake suicide attempt—just like Lucy's was a fake."

"But then why take her own life? Shouldn't Vesta have been the next target?"

"Dr. Lockhart says the guilt was probably too much for her. I think she was afraid of being caught. Same difference, I guess. I've seen guilt and fear unhinge tougher characters than that poor kid."

I look up and see that he is looking at me hard. I feel, like I did with Mitchell, an awareness of being exposed, only I know that Roy Corey is not scanning my body the way Mitch had. He leans closer to me, his hands on his broad thighs, and I can hear the plastic chair creak under his weight.

"You've had a lot to carry all these years," he says. His voice is husky. When I answer my own throat feels tight.

"I guess I should have told someone about the baby."

"Yeah, you should've. But then, who did you have to tell?"

I think that this is an unconventional line for a policeman to take, especially this policeman who had lectured me about personal accountability, but then I remember that he has read my journal. He knows just how alone I was.

I pull myself up and adjust the towel around my legs. "Am I being charged with anything?" I ask. "Because if I am—"

"You'll want to call your lawyer? What would we be charging you with, Jane? Keeping a journal? Trying to help your best friend? *Believing* your best friend? I know it's embarrassing for you that I read your diary, but the one thing it does is establish your innocence. You had no idea what was really going on."

I almost laugh at the bluntness of his last comment, but instead the sound that comes out is more like a sob. I think of the night Matt and Lucy drowned, of those last moments on the ice when he kept asking her whose baby it was. He wasn't asking if it was his; he was asking if it was hers. *Matt and Lucy were lovers.* How many other things had I missed? Roy Corey is right. I had no idea what had really been going on.

Corey moves his hand as if he's going to pat me on the knee, but then thinks better of it. He is so scrupulous in avoiding physical contact with me that I wonder if he has attended some workshop on how to avoid a sexual harassment suit. "Don't feel bad. No one knew the full story. I suspected there was something *different* about Matt and Lucy . . ."

"But my God . . . it was incest."

Roy puffs up his cheeks and blows out air again, but now he looks less like a jovial wind cloud than a very tired middle-aged man. "Well, that's the other thing. When we got the DNA results we noticed that Matt's and Lucy's were entirely different. . . ."

"They didn't have the same father," I say. "Everybody knew that."

"Yeah, everybody knew Cliff Toller wasn't Lucy's father. But what no one knew was that Hannah Toller wasn't Lucy's mother. Matt and Lucy weren't brother and sister. Apparently, they weren't related at all."

• • •

THE DAY AFTER ROY COREY'S VISIT I DECIDE TO GO BACK to Heart Lake. I tell Mitchell that I owe it to Dean Buehl, who has generously forgiven me all my lapses of judgment, to finish out the year. We arrange that I will come to visit Olivia every other weekend and I will stay, whether at his house or the Aquadome we don't say, for spring break. Mitchell says he is disappointed, but I think I see some relief as well. I'm not sure how that makes me feel. I have been trying, these last two weeks, to understand my marriage by review-ing the past, but now I see that I have to go back even farther. I don't think that I can come to any decision without understanding what happened at Heart Lake all those years ago.

Olivia cries when I tell her I am going. I tell her I will see her every other weekend and talk to her every night but she keeps shak-ing her head at whatever I say. I say, "Don't you believe that Mommy will come see you?" and she answers, "But what if the Wilis don't let you?"

"Oh honey," I say, "no Wili will ever keep me away from you. I promise."

"But what if they drag you down into the lake and hold you un-der the water until your face turns blue and the fish come and eat out your eyes?"

It is such a horrible, vivid image that I am sure it comes from someone else. "Olivia, the day I found you on the sister rock and you told me the Wili lady took you there, did she tell you that would happen to you?"

Olivia shakes her head. I am relieved, but then she says, "No, she said that's what would happen to you if I told anyone about her."

DRIVING NORTH ON THE TACONIC PARKWAY I TRY TO SORT out all the new information I've received. My parting with Olivia is uppermost in mind for the first part of the drive. I am horrified by the idea that she has been living with that threat against me all these months. It's the sort of thing that a child molester would say to intimidate his victim. Not *his*, I correct myself, *her*. Child molesters can be female, too. I have to wonder now if anything else happened to Olivia out on that rock. When I asked Olivia to describe the Wili all she would tell me was that she was a "white lady." But I couldn't get out of her whether she was referring to race, hair color, or clothing. Melissa Randall's hair had been bleached. Can I assume that since it was Melissa who had my journal, Melissa who staged Athena's suicide, and Melissa who fell from the rowboat at the sisters rock, that Melissa was the Wili? I'm not sure if I can assume it, but I do hope it. Then, at least, the whole thing would be over.

Still, when I try to imagine Melissa Randall threatening Olivia, or drugging Athena and cutting her wrists, my imagination balks. She simply didn't seem the type to do such awful things. But then, how good have I been at judging types? I bring to mind another young, blond girl: Lucy Toller, my best friend. I replay in my mind that whole last year. The way Lucy looked when she came back from Italy, rounder and curvier, but also happy and *smug*. Had she known she was pregnant? With her own brother's child? Did she know he wasn't her brother? And did that make any difference? After all they had grown up together as brother and sister.

I remember the morning I came back from Albany, how Lucy met me at the door to the single while Deirdre slept. How fast she had thought it through! Deirdre was asleep, so she could tell whatever story she wanted. How had she made Deirdre agree to the deception? But I also remember how Deirdre had adored Lucy, how anxious she had been to please her. She had been almost as devoted to Lucy as I had been. I remember all the times I blamed Deirdre for being ungrateful. *We cleaned up her mess,* I said, again and again, to Lucy. How cool Lucy had been! And that whole trip to the lake and back. She had just given birth. All that blood on the bed—it was hers.

When I think of the blood on the bed I nearly swerve off the curving road and I see that I am clutching the steering wheel so tightly my knuckles are white. I get off at the next exit and pull to the side of the road. When I pry my hands off the steering wheel they are cold and damp and I feel nauseous. I open the car door and throw up on the grassy verge. All that blood. I don't know why it is worse that it was Lucy's not Deirdre's. I guess it's something like the difference between seeing someone else's blood and seeing your own. It explains, I realize, how weak she had been when we'd walked back from the lake.

BY THE TIME WE GOT BACK TO THE DORM IT WAS SNOWING SO *hard we could barely see two feet ahead of us. I begged Lucy to take the path—what would it matter, now, if we met someone?—and she agreed placidly. Halfway back she took my arm and leaned her whole weight on it so I had to struggle to keep us both upright in the driving snow. I didn't know how I'd get her up the stairs to our room, but she held on to the banister and hauled herself up the two flights of stairs.*

When I opened the door to our room Deirdre was sitting up on the edge of Lucy's bed facing the door.

"You got rid of it?" she asked.

"Yes," Lucy answered.

"What are you going to do about that?" Deirdre pointed toward the single and the bloody bed. I was amazed at Deirdre's tone—as if we were her servants and this was our problem instead of hers. But Lucy seemed unfazed.

"I've got an idea about that." Lucy went over to Deirdre and sat next to her on the bed. They both looked at me and I think that Deirdre finally took in that I was back.

"She knows?" Deirdre asked Lucy.

Lucy took Deirdre's hand. "She won't tell anyone," she said to Deirdre, and then to me, "Jane, your suitcases are still in the lobby. Someone might notice and come up here. Could you bring them up please?" Lucy seemed calm and steady now, and in control. As I turned to leave the room I saw Lucy and Deirdre leaning their heads together, whispering.

I walked back downstairs. Five steps from the bottom I lost my footing and fell the rest of the way down, landing painfully on the base of my spine. I clutched the newel post at the foot of the stairs, leaned my head against the

soft wood, and wept noisily for I don't know how long. I kept thinking someone would come—a cleaning lady, the night watchman, Miss Buehl—and
I'd have to tell them everything. From my mother dying to the thing we'd put
in the lake. I'd tell them everything. It was ridiculous, I realized now, to have
gone along with Lucy's plan. We would never be able to explain all that
blood. Deirdre would just have to fend for herself. What did I care what happened to her? I'd tell everyone I had been with Matt so the baby couldn't be
his. I'd sacrifice my name for him.

When I finally realized that no one was going to come I pulled myself
up and lugged my suitcases back upstairs. The room was empty and the door
to the single was closed. Putting my suitcases down next to my bed, I went to
the door and put my hand on the knob. Like the outside knob when I first
came back, it was warm to the touch. I turned it but something was blocking it.

"Who is it?" Deirdre's voice came to me from behind the closed door.
From the direction it came I guessed she was sitting on the floor, her back
against the door.

"It's Jane," I called. "Let me in."

I heard something shift along the floor and the door opened as if of its
own volition. Deirdre was sitting on the floor, facing the bloody bed. Lucy
wasn't in the room. Then I heard her voice behind me.

"OK," she said, brushing past me. Something silver glinted in her
hands. "I know what to do, but you both have to promise me not to freak
out. Jane'll take me to the infirmary and Deirdre should stay behind and
bundle the sheets up. They won't be able to tell exactly how much blood there
was."

I looked at Deirdre to see if she understood what Lucy was talking
about, but for once she was as much in the dark as I was.

Then we both looked up just as Lucy, sitting in the middle of the bloodied sheets, took a razor to her left wrist and slashed her wrist.

WHEN I HAVE STOPPED SHAKING I DRINK A LITTLE WATER
from the bottle I bought at the last rest stop. I look at the road I have

pulled off of and notice a green-and-white sign with a stylized drawing of a figure in a cap and gown. It points to a local college, and even without reading the words beneath the generic picture I realize that I've gotten off at the Poughkeepsie exit and the sign is pointing to Vassar. It's funny, I think, that the sign shows a male figure for what has been, for most of its history, a women's college. Then I think of another picture: the yearbook picture of Hannah Toller and Helen Chambers at the Freshman Formal with the mysterious man off to the side. Hannah Toller had come back from her freshman year at Vassar with a baby. Although she would never tell who the father was, everyone assumed she was the mother. But if she wasn't the mother, who was?

I have been thinking, on the road to Heart Lake, that the answers lie there, because that is where my story began. But now it occurs to me that the story started elsewhere.

I pull onto the road and drive, not back toward the Taconic, but west, toward the river and Vassar.

THE CAMPUS, AS I PASS THROUGH THE ARCHED GATEWAY AND drive toward Main Hall, looks even prettier than I remember it. There is a light dusting of snow on the ground and icicles hang from the row of pines flanking the drive. The winter sun warms the bricks of Main and sets fire to the green patina of the mansard roof. There is a certain clarity of light here that I instantly remember even though it has been over fifteen years since I saw the campus. I have not been back since I graduated, not for my fifth reunion, not for my tenth or fifteenth. It had always seemed pointless; I had made no friends at Vassar. And when I thought of the questions people asked at reunions, I knew I did not have the kind of life that would translate easily into polite cocktail banter at the reunion banquet.

I park my car in front of Main and get out. I notice instantly how still and quiet everything is—it is still winter break here. I am glad, as I walk toward the library, that I am unlikely to meet any of my old teachers. It occurs to me, though, that for the first time since I graduated it might not be so hard to answer the inevitable questions. True, teaching Latin at a private girls' school is no one's pinnacle of success and Heart Lake isn't exactly Exeter or Choate, still, it used to be considered rather good, and not everyone would know of its slow slide into second-rate.

I pass under the giant London plane tree that spreads its dappled boughs before the library's gothic facade. I remember the feeling of peace I had, each evening after dinner, walking beneath the ancient tree and through the arched doorway of the library. After the tumult of high school, the years I spent behind these gray stone walls, toiling away at Latin translations like some medieval monk, had seemed like a cool balm applied to a feverish forehead.

The girl behind the main desk is young, probably a financial aid student working over the break to make her tuition. It's what I used to do. I almost think to tell her that, but I am enjoying the silence of the library too much. I ask her, briefly, where I can find the old yearbooks and she directs me to a room that contains not only yearbooks but the college's archives.

I take down the 1963 yearbook and slowly leaf through the pages. I look for Helen Chambers's picture in the seniors' photographs, but I can't find it. It seems unlike *Domina* Chambers, with her love of tradition and adherence to form, not to have posed for her yearbook picture. I have to go through the book twice to find the picture of the Freshman Formal. Then I find it toward the end of the book, between the lacrosse team and a candid picture of the bridge club. "Freshman Formal," the caption reads, "Helen Liddell Chambers '63 and Hannah Corey Toller." There is no year following Hannah Toller's name. In this book where every name is followed by those two digits, the final mark of belonging, their absence seems like a brand. The girl who dropped out after freshman year because she had a baby out of wedlock. That's how her classmates would have remembered her. But that wasn't what happened. She had taken the blame for someone else.

I look closely at the picture. I remember thinking that the handsome blond boy on the edge of the picture smiling at the girls—why had I thought he was smiling at Hannah?—looked like Lucy. How blind had I been not to notice the resemblance? It's Helen Chambers, young, her pale swept-up hair shining like a swan's wing, who looks like Lucy. Like mother like daughter, I think. Just as Lucy pretended that Deirdre had been the one to give birth to that baby, so Helen Chambers had let her friend assume the shame of an out-of-wedlock baby. It explains, of course, all the extra attention Helen Chambers had lavished on Lucy. No wonder *Domina* Chambers had been so horrified the night Lucy cut her wrists.

I PRACTICALLY HAD TO CARRY LUCY TO THE INFIRMARY. EVEN though Deirdre had wrapped her wrist in a thick linen napkin, blood splattered the snow at our feet. When I looked behind us, though, I saw that the drops of blood were already covered by the fast-falling snow.

When we reached the infirmary we found the door locked and a 3 x 5 card taped to the window. "HOLIDAY HOURS: 9 A.M. TO 4 P.M. FOR EMERGENCY CALL THE CORINTH FIRE DEPARTMENT."

Lucy was leaning against the wall of the building while I read the card to her. When I finished she slid down the wall and wrapped her arms around her knees. Her jeans were already damp from the snow, but I thought I saw a new stain spread over her left knee where her wrist lay against the cloth.

"We'll have to go back and call an ambulance," I told her.

"I can't walk anymore," she said. "I'm too tired. You go back and call. I'll wait here."

"I can't leave you here, Lucy, you'll freeze to death."

She didn't answer me. Her eyes were closed and she seemed to have fallen asleep. I looked out into the snow, spinning in a cone of light from the porch lamp. At least Lucy was out of the snow here. Maybe I should go back to the dorm and call from there.

I took off my coat and laid it over Lucy. When I stepped off the covered porch and out of the lamplight I was immediately enveloped in a world of spinning snow. I could barely make out where the path split off to go back to the dorm. I couldn't even tell if I was on a path, let alone if I was on the right one. I walked for several minutes when I realized I was no longer walking on a dirt path covered by snow, but over rocks sheeted with ice. I stopped and slowly turned in a circle and realized I had lost all sense of direction. I must have missed the path leading back to the dorm, but then where was I? Under the sounds of wind and snow falling I heard another sound—a creaking noise, like a door opening. I moved toward it and lost my footing on the ice.

When I stopped sliding headlong down the curved surface of the rock I was looking down into a void of swirling snow. The creaking sound was directly below me now, but still far away. I stared into the glittering whirlpool below me and it was like looking into deep water when you opened your eyes and looked into the deepest part of the lake and saw the drifting silt lit up by the sun shining through the water. I was on the Point hanging over the edge of the cliff. The creaking sound I'd heard was new ice cracking in the wind.

I tried crawling backwards from the edge but when I lifted myself to my knees I slid forward a few more inches. I took off my mittens and felt around me for the deep cracks in the rock I knew were there. Chattermarks, Miss Buehl had called them, left by a retreating glacier. When I found one deep enough I dug my fingers into it and pulled myself around so I was facing away from the lake. I only moved forward when I found a crack deep enough to use as a handhold. By the time I'd worked my way up to level rock, my fingernails were broken and bloody and I'd realized I'd left my mittens behind. I crawled over the rock face, not daring to stand until I'd gotten to the woods.

I stood up and realized that I still had no idea how to get back to the dorm or how long it had been since I'd left Lucy. She could have bled to death by now. Even if I found the dorm it would take too long for an ambulance to get here. I stood in the falling snow and thought about the icy plunge from the Point to the lake.

Then I noticed a light shining through the woods. At first I thought it was the infirmary porch light and I was amazed at how little distance I had traveled, but then I remembered the nights we had sneaked over the Point to avoid Miss Buehl's cottage. Could it be Miss Buehl's light? And was it possible she was in her cottage? I knew she stayed for part of the break. Also, I remembered that before she'd become a science teacher she'd been a nurse. She helped out, sometimes, when the infirmary was understaffed. She'd know what to do for Lucy.

I headed straight for the light even though it meant walking through the deeper snow in the woods. I didn't take my eyes off the light until I reached the cottage and started beating the door with my frozen, bloody hands. When the door opened I couldn't see who opened it because burning spots blurred my vision.

Someone pulled me inside and rubbed my hands. I was pushed into a chair and wrapped in a blanket. I closed my eyes and tried to get rid of the light spots dancing in front of my eyes. I was sure the afterimage of Miss Buehl's porch light would be seared into my retinas forever.

When I opened my eyes, though, I could see perfectly. Miss Buehl was holding a towel around my hands and behind her Domina Chambers was offering me a steaming tea cup.

"Drink this before you try to talk," Miss Buehl said, taking the cup from Domina Chambers.

I looked around the room and took in the cozy scene I'd stumbled upon. A fire in the fireplace, a teapot and cups on a low table, classical music on the radio. Both women in sturdy corduroys and ski sweaters.

"It's no night to be out, Jane," Miss Buehl said in the same scolding tone she used when we played around with her Bunsen burners. "Miss Chambers has been over all day working on the advanced placement curriculum and we were waiting for the storm to pass so she could go back . . ."

"Lucy," I said, interrupting Miss Buehl.

"What about Lucy?" Domina Chambers knelt down next to me and hot tea from her teacup splashed my already soaked jeans.

"She's at the infirmary. Bleeding." For a moment I couldn't remember the story we'd concocted. I was confused by the other blood I'd seen that day. Birth blood.

"She slit her wrists," I finally said.

"Lucy? No, I don't believe it." Domina Chambers gave me the very same look she gave me when I mistranslated my Latin homework, but Miss Buehl took me at my word. She was already pulling on boots and a coat.

"I've got the key to the infirmary in my book bag, Helen, would you get it for me?"

"But this is absurd, Celeste," Domina *Chambers said, rising to her feet, "this child is hysterical."*

"Hysterical or not, something is obviously wrong and if Lucy Toller is out in this storm—bleeding or not—we'd better find her."

Domina *Chambers opened her mouth as if to argue, but at another look from Miss Buehl she clamped her mouth into a tight line and turned on her heel. I heard her rummaging around in the other room muttering under her breath. I'd never seen* Domina *Chambers so cowed by anyone.*

I thought I'd had enough surprises for one night, but then a small figure appeared in the doorway of the room Domina *Chambers had gone into.*

"Oh, Albie," Miss Buehl said, "I'd forgotten all about you. You'll have to come, too. Go get dressed in your warmest things." She turned to me. "Albie's grandmother dropped her off a little early from break," she said, and then, lowering her voice, "She must have gotten the dates mixed up."

I thought to tell Albie that my father made the same mistake, that we had that in common, but she'd already gone back in the other room, slamming the door behind her.

BEFORE I LEAVE, I ASK THE GIRL BEHIND THE DESK—SHE'S yawning over a copy of Dante's *Purgatorio*—if the library has a copy of the Vassar alumnae directory. She puts down her copy without bothering to save her place and slips out from behind the desk. Following her, I notice she's wearing sandals and thick white gym socks. The socks have holes at the heels. I can see her bare, unshaven calves between the hem of her skirt and the tops of her socks. I imagine how cold she'll be walking home tonight. It makes me think of my students, Athena especially, and I am, for the first time, really anxious to be back at Heart Lake.

She asks what year I'm looking for and when I tell her 1963 she gives me a scrutinizing look.

"You don't look that old," she says.

I laugh. "I certainly hope not. I was class of '81." I realize as I say it how glad I am to have those digits to name. Unlike Hannah Toller. "No, I'm looking for a friend . . . for a friend's mother."

"Oh," she says without interest. She pads back to her desk and picks up Dante at any old place and yawns into the book.

I run my finger down the list of names. Most of the names, I see, are in bold type followed by another name in lighter typeface. The names in bold are maiden names, the ones following are married names.

When I get to Helen Chambers's I see it, too, is in bold. So Helen Chambers got married after she left Heart Lake. I'm surprised but also somehow relieved. *Watch out you don't turn out like Helen Chambers,* Dr. Lockhart had said to me. Well, maybe she didn't turn out so bad after all. Maybe there was a life for her after Heart Lake.

But then I see that the record keepers have made a mistake. The name following Chambers in light typeface is Liddell. Someone must have mistaken her middle name for a married name. I pull my finger across the page to locate her address, but instead my finger comes to rest on a single word: deceased. It is followed by the date May 1, 1981. She died only four years after leaving Heart Lake. Dr. Lockhart was right after all. Helen Chambers had ended badly.

Chapter Twenty-six

●

WHILE WALKING TO MY CAR I NOTICE THE GIRL FROM the library leaving the building. She is wearing a light denim jacket and carrying a heavy backpack. I offer her a lift back to her dorm and she tells me she lives in the student housing across Raymond Avenue. I remember the complex is a good mile's walk from campus and again I urge her to take a lift from me. I see her assess me and decide I'm probably not dangerous—after all, I'm Jane Hudson '81. She is quiet, though, in the car. I ask who she's reading the Dante for and she names a medieval history professor I had junior year.

"When you do your term paper include a map of Dante's underworld and compare it to a map of Virgil's underworld," I tell her. "He loves that kind of thing—the geography of imaginary places—I think there's even some name for it . . ."

"Really? Thanks, I'll remember that."

Then she gets out of the car and runs quickly up the steps of the dilapidated housing complex. I remember that these units had been built as temporary housing five years before I came here. They were already falling apart then. I wait until she's inside and I see the lights go on, and then I drive back to the main road and, from there, to the Taconic.

I am sorry, after a few miles, that I didn't take the better lit and straighter Thruway. The road is icy, especially on the curves. Each time the back of my car fishtails on the slippery road my stomach lurches. I keep thinking about the astounding coincidence of Helen Chambers and Lucy Toller both pretending their babies belonged to someone else. Is it just coincidence though? I think of the two of them. Both beautiful with the kind of rarefied beauty of a fairy-tale princess. It was more than their beauty though; it was a certain look they each had of possessing some secret charm. They inspired, in others, not only admiration but the desire to please and emulate. I'll never know what Lucy said to Deirdre to convince her to let me think the baby was hers, but I can imagine the way Lucy looked when she asked. And I realize that if Lucy had asked me to say the baby was mine I would have. And it wasn't just me and Deirdre who idealized Lucy. There was that younger girl, Albie. I remember how mad she was at me when we went back to the infirmary and found Lucy nearly half dead on the steps.

WE FOUND LUCY CURLED IN A BALL ON THE INFIRMARY DOOR-
step, like a cat locked out in the cold. It broke my heart to think how long it had taken me to bring her help.

"I'm sorry I was so long," I told her, but she didn't wake up.

"How could you leave her here?" The voice at my ear was so low I thought it was my own conscience, but it wasn't, it was Albie.

"I had to go find help," I tried to explain, but Albie shook her head.

"You left her to die," she hissed at me, leaning close so Miss Buehl and Domina Chambers couldn't hear, so close that I felt her hot spit prick my skin.

I watched in silence as Domina Chambers picked her up while Miss Buehl unlocked the door. What could I say? Maybe Albie was right. I should have stopped Lucy from cutting herself. I should have come back sooner. I should never have left.

Inside the infirmary, Albie switched on the light and ran to get the things Miss Buehl asked for. She seemed to know her way around. Everyone seemed to have something to do but me, so I sat down on the extra bed across from where they put Lucy and watched. They went to work quickly, peeling away the cotton cloth from Lucy's wrists, getting her out of her wet clothes, taking her blood pressure.

"She's stopped bleeding," Miss Buehl reported. "Thank God she didn't sever the arteries."

"But doesn't she need stitches?" Domina Chambers asked.

"Yes, but I can do that. Don't worry, Helen, I've done it before. What I'm worried about is her blood pressure. It's quite low. Do you have any idea how much blood she lost, Jane? Had she been bleeding long when you found her?"

I shook my head. I thought of the blood on the sheets, but remembered that wasn't Lucy's blood.

"We found her right away," I said, trying to remember the story we'd agreed upon. "She went into Deirdre's single and we heard her crying so we went in." I had heard crying, I remembered, but when Lucy had opened the door her eyes had been dry.

"We?" Miss Buehl asked.

I pushed away the memory of what really happened and concentrated on what we'd agreed upon. "Yes, me and Deirdre Hall."

"Well, then, where is Miss Hall?" Domina Chambers asked.

"She stayed in the dorm." I realized now that this was a weak spot in our story. Why had Deirdre remained behind? I knew the real reason—to dispose of the bloody sheets—but what reason had we agreed upon?

"Um, she was so upset and the blood was on her bed, so she stayed behind to clean it up."

Domina Chambers clicked her tongue and shook her head. "Imagine thinking about such a thing while your roommate is bleeding to death. There's something very off about that girl. At least you had more sense, Jane."

I smiled at the rare compliment even though I knew it wasn't fair to Deirdre, and caught Albie glaring at me again. It was almost as if she knew that Lucy had told Deirdre to stay behind to get rid of the sheets.

"So there must have been quite a bit of blood," Miss Buehl said. She *was bending over Lucy, peeling back her eyelids and listening to the pulse at her throat. "I wish we could get her to the hospital for a transfusion but I'm afraid that will be impossible in this storm. The phone lines have been down and the roads closed for hours."*

"Is there anything else we can do, Celeste?" Domina Chambers asked. I noticed she was shaking and thought it was probably from the cold, and yet the room felt quite hot to me. "Will she be all right?"

"I'll give her a saline drip to get some fluids in her. That should help her blood pressure. Otherwise, we'll just have to wait. I'd feel better if she regained consciousness." Miss Buehl shook Lucy's shoulder and called her name. "Maybe you should try, Jane, you're her best friend."

I got up off the bed and walked across the room. It seemed like a long way. I noticed that the floor was slanting. I knelt down by Lucy and called her name. Amazingly, she opened her eyes.

"Jane," she said.

"It's OK. Lucy, we're in the infirmary."

"You'll stay here?" she whispered to me. "Don't go back to the dorm."

I was so touched that she wanted me to stay that my eyes filled with tears and the room went all blurry. Then it went black.

I'D BEEN TOUCHED WHEN LUCY HAD ASKED ME TO STAY AT the infirmary, but of course the real reason, I realize now, is that she didn't want me to talk to Deirdre. She had to make sure Deirdre went along with the plan to pretend that the baby was really hers.

It is one thing, though, to assume the parentage of a baby lost in childbirth, and another to drop out of college and raise someone else's baby. As I make the trip from Vassar to Corinth, less than 150 miles but worlds apart, the person I think more about is Hannah Corey Toller, class of —. Class of Nothing. Why had she agreed to take Helen's baby, return in shame to her hometown and raise a child not her own?

It's this question that plagues me as I drive slowly down River

Street looking at the big Victorian houses set back on their snow-covered lawns. Most still have their Christmas lights up and the colored bulbs spill jewel-like pools onto the sparkling snow crust. At the end of the street I pull up opposite the gatehouse on the intersection of Lake Drive and River Street and turn off the car so as not to draw attention to myself. Really, though, I needn't be so cautious; it doesn't look as if anyone is in the old Toller house. Not only are there no Christmas lights, but there are no other lights on in the house. The house has a general air of neglect—the driveway hasn't been plowed since the last snow and one of the shutters has come loose from its hinges and hangs from the window askew. I remember that I used to think the house looked like Snow White's cottage, but now I think it looks more like the witch's house in "Hansel and Gretel."

I wonder if anyone has lived in it since Cliff and Hannah Toller died in that car accident. It happened my last year in college and I read about it in an Albany newspaper. They had been driving back from Plattsburgh when a freakish May snowstorm swept across the Adirondacks. Their car was found at the bottom of a deep ravine. The newspaper made a big deal out of the fact that, like their children, the Tollers had died together. DOUBLE DISASTER STRIKES TWICE FOR ADIRONDACK COUPLE, the headline read.

I remember feeling unsurprised at the Tollers' fate. It was harder to imagine the two of them going on after losing both their children.

But only one of them was their child.

I wonder if at the end they thought of Lucy as an interloper—the changeling who dragged their own child to his death.

Just as I put my hand on the ignition key I see a light come on in the house and a figure pass behind a curtained window. It comes so hard upon my thinking of Lucy as some fiendish demon that the sight strikes me as a reproach—and indeed, there is something in the profile silhouetted in the top floor window that reminds me of Lucy. I feel that rush of cold and inability to breathe that marked the panic attacks I experienced in my twenties. I turn on the car and put the heater on high, but the cold persists and now I am sweating as well. I'm too afraid to drive like this. I look at the house again to reassure myself that the figure in the window is not Lucy, but the window is dark again. Instead, a rectangle of light appears in the doorway and a woman steps out into the deep, unshoveled snow and walks straight for my car. She taps on my window before I fully take in that it's Dr. Lockhart.

"So you decided to come back," she says when I lower the window. "Better to face your demons, eh?"

I wonder what demons she is referring to, but I am determined, for once, not to let her control the direction of the conversation.

"What are you doing in the Toller house?" I ask.

Dr. Lockhart smiles. "It's not the Toller house anymore, Jane. This is where I live."

"You live here? But . . ."

"Where did you think I lived, Jane? In one of those cozy little apartments in the mansion? I don't think so. In my profession it's very important to maintain a distance. And I like my privacy. These boarding schools can be such fishbowls. Fascinating to study as cultural microcosms, but such parochial bores to live in twenty-four hours a day. Doesn't it get to you sometimes, being *watched* all the time?"

I hadn't thought of myself as so visible, but when I think of the events of the last semester I realize that I have felt *observed*.

"From whom did you buy the house?" I ask, if only to steer the conversation away from last semester. She straightens up and glances back at the house. I can tell she is surprised by the question.

"From the estate. The house was empty for many years . . ." She trails off and I decide to pursue the subject if only because I've never seen her look this uncomfortable.

"Since the Tollers died? Maybe people thought it was an unlucky house, everyone who lived there is dead now."

"I'm not superstitious, Jane. People make their own fates. Believing this house is unlucky is like . . . like believing in the three sisters legend. It's the superstition that causes the problem. If Melissa Randall hadn't read about the three sisters legend in your journal she might still be alive today."

There is a note of triumph in her last comment. Finally, she has brought our conversation to where she wants it. I can't avoid talking about the events of last semester now.

"I told you and Dean Buehl that someone had my journal. What else was I supposed to do?" I ask.

"You should have told us what was in your journal: sex with masked strangers, sacrificial rites, a dead baby in a tea tin . . ."

"I take your point, Dr. Lockhart. Yes, I should have told someone, but it was a rather unusual circumstance. What would you think if pieces from your old journal started appearing on your desk?"

"I wouldn't know because I've never kept a journal. I would never be so foolish to commit such incriminating evidence, if I had ever done such things, to writing." I can believe it. She doesn't look like she'd give anything away.

"Well, I'll certainly be more careful in the future. Now I'd better get back to campus. I want to see if Athena and Vesta are back yet."

"If you mean Ellen and Sandy, they're both back. Perhaps you ought to consider dropping the goddess names. Didn't your old Latin teacher use Roman names like Lucia and Clementia?"

Is it just coincidence she picked my old Latin name and Lucy's? Is it something else she gleaned from my old journal?

"Yes, but I can't see what harm there is in the girls keeping their names. Doesn't it just make a bigger thing out of it?"

"Miss Hudson, one of our students is dead. How much bigger do you want it to be?"

"All right. I'll suggest they take other names. Look, can I give you a lift back to campus?" I try to make my voice conciliatory. The last thing I want is this woman for an enemy.

"No thanks, I'm going skating." She turns her right side to me so I can see a pair of worn ice skates with decorative stitching hanging over her shoulder. "There's a shortcut through the woods behind my house. I can skate straight across the lake to the school."

"Be careful," I tell her. "There's a weak spot in the ice near the mouth of the Schwanenkill."

"Don't worry, Jane," she says, smiling, "I know where all the weak spots are."

I TAKE LAKE DRIVE AROUND THE EAST SIDE OF THE LAKE. Through the pines lining the drive I catch glimpses of the frozen lake, shimmering under a full moon. Dr. Lockhart has picked a beautiful night to skate. I believe her when she says she is not superstitious. It's hard to imagine, otherwise, how she could bear to be alone on that ice at night. I don't think it's something I could do.

I turn off Lake Drive and park in the faculty parking lot. I'll have to haul my suitcase up the long path to my house without a light— of course I hadn't thought to leave any light on in the house when I left. Two weeks ago I hadn't even been sure I'd be coming back. It occurs to me it might be better to go up to the house first and turn on some lights before trying to navigate the path with a heavy suitcase.

I look in my glove compartment and find a flashlight, but the batteries are burned out. I resign myself to finding my way in the dark, the moon is full so it shouldn't be too bad, but when I get out of my car I notice the path on the opposite end of the parking lot, the one to the dorm, is ablaze with light. Dean Buehl must have had extra lighting installed after Melissa Randall's death to reassure worried parents—although how extra lighting is supposed to prevent girls from taking their own lives, I do not know.

I decide I'll go to the dorm first. It'll give me a chance to visit with Athena and Vesta before it gets too late. Maybe the dorm matron will have an extra flashlight to lend me. As I walk up the well-shoveled (Dean Buehl must have had to call in a plow to clear the paths enough to install the lights) and well-lit path I realize that all my prevarication about going up the unlit path to the cottage amounts to one thing: I'm not ready to be alone in that house yet.

The dorm matron has a plentiful supply of flashlights and she is happy to give me one as long as I sign it out. She also has me "sign in" to the dorm and leave a photo ID. I notice, as I walk up to the second floor, hand-lettered signs posted exhorting students to travel in pairs and flyers for community counseling groups. I think I recognize Gwen Marsh's handwriting. The thought that poor Gwen has spent her Christmas holiday making up flyers, with carpal tunnel syndrome no less, and planning how to help the girls cope with returning after the trauma of Melissa Randall's death, suddenly makes me feel guilty and self-absorbed. It makes my two weeks at the Aquadome seem like a luxury vacation by comparison.

The second floor is quiet except for the hissing of the steam radiators. One of the flyers advertises a "Welcome Back Sing" for tonight and I'm afraid that Athena and Vesta will be there, but when I knock on their door I hear the familiar shuffle and window shutting that tells me they are in, and they haven't given up smoking over the break.

Vesta unlocks and opens the door, but only a few inches. When she sees it's me she scrunches her eyebrows together suspiciously and reluctantly opens the door the rest of the way.

"Sandy," I say, determined to avoid the girls' classical names as per Dr. Lockhart's suggestion, "nice to see you. How was your break?"

Vesta shrugs and sits down on the bed underneath the window. Athena turns around in her chair and smiles at me. I notice right away that her face looks less drawn and, somehow, more open. I can't quite put my finger on it, but she looks healthier. The two weeks away from Heart Lake have done her good.

"*Salve, Magistra,*" she says, "*quid agis?*"

"*Bene,*" I say, "*et tu,* Ellen?"

"Ellen? Why aren't you calling me Athena?"

I shift uncomfortably from foot to foot. The room is hot and damp.

"Here," Athena says, getting up from her chair and seating herself cross-legged on the floor, "take off your coat and sit down. They keep it like a sauna in here."

I sit down at my old desk. Now that Athena is sitting beneath me I can see one thing that's different about her. She's let the dye grow out of her hair. I can see several inches of her natural color—a light mousy brown—showing at the roots. I scan her books and realize that I'm still looking for the black-and-white notebook. I see instead Wheelock's Latin grammar and a paperback copy of *Franny and Zooey*. "I read this when I was your age," I say.

"You didn't answer the question," Vesta says. "Why have you dropped our Latin class names?"

"Dr. Lockhart thinks the goddess names might not be appropriate . . ."

Vesta snorts. "The names are the best part," she says. "I always hated *Sandy*. My real name is Alexandria, which is even worse. If you stop calling me Vesta, I'll drop Latin."

"Yeah," Athena chimes in, "I've always hated 'Ellen.' "

"OK, *Athena*," I say, "and *Vesta*, I can't have you all dropping out of Latin."

Immediately I notice a change come over the girls. They seem more serious and somehow embarrassed.

"A bunch of girls have," Athena says. "Some of the parents didn't want their kids in the class after what happened to Melissa."

"Yeah, there's this rumor we were sacrificing babies and stuff."

I look at Vesta when she says "babies" but she doesn't seem to attach any significance to the example she's chosen. Dean Buehl said that no one was told what was found in the tea tin. But then if Melissa had my journal, she might have shared its contents with her roommates.

"It's our fault," Athena says. "If we hadn't started that stuff with the three sisters and making offerings to the Lake Goddess none of it would have happened."

"Who thought of that?" I ask. "Going out to the rocks and offering prayers to the Lake Goddess?"

Athena and Vesta look at each other and shrug. "I don't know. We all kind of did. I guess Melissa got into it the most because she was worried about Brian." I remember the night I watched the three girls at the stones. Melissa had asked for loyalty from her boyfriend, Vesta for good grades, but I hadn't been able to hear what Athena asked for. I find myself wondering now what it was she asked for and whether she has gotten what she wished for.

"Did you notice that Melissa had a black-and-white notebook?" I ask.

"Like this?" Athena opens a desk drawer by my feet and takes out a marbled notebook. I see that the name written on the white box on the cover is "Ellen (Athena) Craven."

"Yes," I say, "something like that."

Athena shakes her head, but Vesta is looking at me strangely.

"Why do you want to know?"

I see that I have wound myself into a trap with my own questions. If the girls really don't know that Melissa had my old journal (and Athena, at least, seems innocent) I certainly don't want to tell them.

"I just thought that if she kept a journal," I say with feigned casualness, "we'd understand more about what happened to Melissa."

Vesta looks unconvinced. "You think she wrote down why she drugged Athena and slit her wrists?" Vesta points at Athena's wrists and Athena tugs at the cuffs of her sweater even though they already reach down to her knuckles. I notice that the cuffs are frayed and unraveling, as if they'd been plucked at again and again. "Jesus," Vesta says, "who would be stupid enough to write down all that stuff?"

I MAKE AN EXCUSE TO LEAVE BEFORE VESTA CAN ASK ME ANY more questions about the journal. I realize as I leave their room that I've made a tactical error visiting the girls before talking to Dean Buehl and finding out what exactly they were told about Melissa's death. I promise myself that I'll call Dean Buehl as soon as I get into the cottage, but I see that I won't have to. Dean Buehl is waiting for me at the matron's desk.

"Ah, Jane, I saw your name in the sign-in book and thought I'd wait for you."

The matron hands me back my driver's license without looking up at me. I wonder if she called the dean to tell her I was here in the dorm. I wonder if she had been instructed to do so.

"Did you see the note I left on your door?" Dean Buehl asks. "Asking you to call as soon as you got in?"

"I haven't been back to my house yet," I tell her. "I came here first to get a flashlight." I hold up the flashlight as corroborating evidence.

"Ah," Dean Buehl says, nodding. "I remember the path up to that cottage could be tricky. Of course I've walked all these paths so many times I think I could find my way around the campus blind-folded. Let me walk you back to the parking lot and help you with your luggage. We can talk along the way."

IN ADDITION TO MY SUITCASES I'VE BROUGHT BACK SOME boxes of books from the house in Westchester. Although I tell her they can wait until the morning, Dean Buehl cheerfully hoists up two and takes off down the darkened path so quickly I am hard put keeping up with her with my one box. I am reminded of the nature hikes she used to take us on when she was the science teacher—the way she strode through the woods, leaving her students scrambling over rocks and puddles, desperately trying to stay close enough to hear her lecture. We'd be tested on every rock and flower identifica-tion, we knew, and inability to keep up was no excuse. "The race goes to the swiftest," was one of her favorite sayings and in her class it was literally true.

Twenty years haven't slowed her down a bit. When I do finally catch up with her I have to stay behind her because this path hasn't been plowed. Fresh snow covers the narrow track that had been shoveled before Christmas break and the sound of our boots crunch-ing in it makes it doubly hard to hear what Dean Buehl is saying. She is talking over her shoulder to me as if I had been right behind her all along and I realize I've already missed half of her "getting me up to date on the Melissa Randall affair" as she calls it. She is tossing out autopsy and DNA findings the way she used to rattle off the names of trees and wildflowers. I gather, though, that there's nothing I haven't learned already from Roy Corey. Then I hear her refer to "that journal you kept senior year" and I interrupt to ask how many people know about it. "Well, Dr. Lockhart was there when we found it," she tells me. We have reached the door of the cottage, so this I get to hear clearly, "but the only people who have read it are me and that nice young detective. Of course, I told Dr. Lockhart a little about the contents so she could assess their influence on Melissa. It should make an interesting chapter in the book she is writing on teenage suicide."

I am somewhat unnerved by the idea of my journal figuring in Dr. Lockhart's research, but I smile at Dean Buehl in a way that I hope is ingratiating. "Thanks for helping with my stuff. I'll make us some coffee, we can sit and talk . . ." I gesture toward the old Morris chair by the fireplace, the armrest of which still holds the teacup I drank from the night before I left. I see her follow the sweep of my hand and take in the little living room, the battered, old floral love seat under the window, the coffee table stacked with Latin books and Land's End catalogs and piles of ungraded blue books. The lines of her face, which had looked firm and rosy from the cold air and exertion of our walk, seem to settle downward and her skin pales. I think it is my untidiness, but then I remember that this was once her home. The furniture was here when I moved in and, now that I think of it, is arranged just as it was that night I stumbled out of the snowstorm and into this room. Only then there was a fire in the fireplace and classical music on the radio and the room shone with a kind of brightness that has now dulled with dust and the usage of uncaring tenants.

She walks out my door and heads in the opposite direction from the parking lot.

"Beautiful night . . ." I hear her say as she disappears down the path to the Point. "Better to talk out of doors."

I follow her to the Point where she has taken a stance—legs

spread apart and arms clasped behind her back, like a general survey-
ing her troops—on the curving rock above the frozen lake.

"Always find this a good place to think," she says as I come up
beside her.

"Yes," I say, "the view is beautiful."

She shakes her head impatiently and scuffs at the snow with the
heel of her heavy hiking boot like a horse pawing the ground. "Not
the view," she says with the weary patience of a teacher used to hearing the wrong answer, "the rock. Right where we're standing was a
mile-high glacier. This rock here is so hard it's barely eroded in ten
thousand years, but the marks the glacier left are still here. Puts
things in perspective."

"Yes," I say, although I am not exactly sure what the perspective
is. Is it that human suffering is insignificant in the face of the majesty
of nature, or that the scars of the past are still with us and always
will be?

"You're embarrassed," she says. Actually, I'm more perplexed at
the moment but I nod.

"Because I've read your old journal." Dean Buehl sighs and relaxes her stance a bit so I can see, suddenly, the slight curve in her
shoulders and the droop in her once taut figure. "Don't be, it was a
great relief to me."

I can no longer pretend to understand what she's talking about.
"My journal was a relief to you?" As the words come out I realize I
can no longer hide my anger either. First the outpourings of my
foolish young heart are appropriated by a hysterical teenage girl, then
they are co-opted as a research tool for an ambitious psychologist,
and now they are balm to my former teacher and present boss?

"Yes," she says, ignoring the outrage in my voice. She looks
down at the rock where she's kicked away the snow. "All these years
I've felt it was my fault what happened to Helen. I thought if only I
had spoken up at the hearing she might not have been fired and if
she hadn't been fired she wouldn't have killed herself . . ."

"Killed herself? *Domina* Chambers killed herself?" I picture my old Latin teacher—her proud and haughty profile, the way she lifted one eyebrow when a student mistranslated a line of Latin. She is the last person I can imagine taking her own life.

"Yes." Dean Buehl looks away from the rock as if the perspective the rock has offered has vanished and the scars of that distant calamity are fresh again. "Four years after she was let go. It was a terrible blow for her. For me, too." When she doesn't go on I turn to look at her. The lines in her face stand out starkly in the moonlight, like fault lines that have deepened after a quake and then I realize that the trembling that passes over her face is her trying to keep from crying.

"I even tried to get her a teaching position at a Catholic school up north," she says when she has regained control of her voice. Up north from here? That could only mean St. Eustace. I couldn't blame *Domina* Chambers for turning that down. "Some of the girls from here had gone there after . . . after the scandal . . . and I thought she might take an interest in keeping up with them, but she didn't. Instead she went down to Albany and got work as a substitute."

"Really? A substitute? *Domina* Chambers?" This surprises me more than the idea of her killing herself, even as it goes some way to making that idea more plausible.

"You can imagine what she thought of that." Dean Buehl tries to smile, but the effort seems to release that trembling again and she gives it up.

I remember how we treated substitute teachers at Corinth High. I have a sudden picture of *Domina* Chambers standing at a blackboard (she would have been reduced to writing on the board if only to write her name), her elegant black dress besmirched with yellow chalk, the silver hair coming undone from its intricate twist.

"When I heard she had killed herself I thought it was because of how she had come down in the world and perhaps I could have made a difference. And then, our relationship didn't help at the hearing . . ."

Dean Buehl's voice hoarsens and trails off. There's a final shudder and then her face gleams in the moonlight, her emotions so naked and exposed that I have to make an effort not to look away. "You mean you and Miss Chambers . . ." My words sound childish and prurient even to myself. I remember Deirdre Hall's salacious conjectures about Miss Buehl and *Domina* Chambers. I remember again the cottage the night of the snowstorm, the fire and the teapot and the classical music. . . . What was it she had said? That they had been working on some curriculum project together?

"*Domina* Chambers was staying at your cottage," I say.

Dean Buehl nods. "She spent every break at the cottage. It was the only time we really had to ourselves, but then that girl showed up and we had to pretend that Helen had come by to work on the AP curriculum. We had to make up a story. Do you know what it felt like? Having to pretend—like schoolgirls caught breaking curfew?"

I remember the tangle of lies I'd been caught in and nod—yes, I know what she means—but she doesn't notice; she's lost in the past.

"We had to pretend even when we knew they all knew. We knew what you girls whispered about us behind our backs and the stories our so-called colleagues carried back to the board. I knew that was why they were so hard on her at the inquest, but I was afraid that if I spoke in her defense I would be fired, too. I've been so ashamed . . . all these years . . . not for what we were but that I denied it. And it wasn't just Helen who was hurt. The girls who had to leave the school because of the scandal . . . I felt such a responsibility for them. It's why I took the dean's job even though it was like taking over a sinking ship. . . ." She breaks off and I look away while she struggles to get her voice under control. On the lake I see a black speck circling on the white ice. I think it's a bird but then realize it's a skater. Dr. Lockhart, no doubt.

"It wouldn't have made a difference," I say, "even if you had spoken at the hearing . . ."

Dean Buehl waves her hand at me impatiently. "It's not just that," she says. "You see, it was my fault Lucy found out that Helen was her mother, and I always thought that must have been what Matt and Lucy were fighting about when they went through the ice."

I look away from the skater and back at Dean Buehl. "You knew that Lucy was Helen's daughter?"

She smiles at me. Finally, I am the student with the right answer. "You guessed, too. You always were smarter than people gave you credit for, Jane."

I wonder what people.

"Of course Helen told me. We told each other everything. And it explained so much. The way Helen missed her freshman spring semester at Vassar . . . oh, I was at Smith," she fills in hurriedly when she sees my perplexed look, "but I wrote to Helen often. I remember her writing that she had to go nurse a sick relative. It sounded very odd at the time. Of course I realized later she must have had the baby then and given it to Hannah. . . ."

"Why did Hannah Toller go along with it?" I ask.

Dean Buehl stares at me as if I had interrupted her lecture on cell division to ask a question about thermodynamics.

"Well, Hannah adored her of course. From the ninth grade on. The only reason Hannah even went to Vassar was to be near Helen. . . ." I detect a note of jealousy in her voice that she shakes off like a dog shaking off cold water. "Helen said she had first planned to give the baby up for adoption and it was Hannah's idea to say the baby was hers. She wasn't really cut out for college life, and there was a boy from back home who would marry her in a heartbeat. It made so much more sense for Hannah to give up college than for Helen, who had such promise. . . ."

"Then why did she come back here?"

Dean Buehl looks down at the rock as if the answer were in the glacial inscriptions.

"She missed the girl. She wanted to be closer to her. I told her she might as well tell the girl she was her mother."

"When did she tell her?"

"In February. A week before she died."

I remember the day Lucy came back from tea with *Domina* Chambers and wrote Matt that letter. She told Matt that Helen had told her something that changed everything.

"That's why she wrote Matt and asked him to come," I said. "She was going to tell him they weren't brother and sister." *Only she had never gotten the chance.*

"Of course I had no idea what disgusting things they had been up to. All of you cavorting around the campus like a pack of wild dogs and right on my doorstep." Dean Buehl flings a hand in the direction of the cottage so abruptly she nearly hits me. I step back and, for a moment, lose my balance on the snow-covered rock. She grabs me by the arm before I can fall. We're quite a way from the edge, but still I feel that queasy sensation of vertigo, like when you stand on the beach and feel the tide sucking the sand out from under your feet. Dean Buehl must also be aware of the precipitous drop not so far away, because she does not release her grip on my arm right away. I can feel her strong fingers digging painfully into my forearm. I look at her face and see that the tears are gone and that look of naked grief I'd glimpsed a moment earlier has hardened into something else, something I find harder to read.

"But when I read your journal, Jane, I realized it wasn't all my fault. I may have been responsible for Lucy learning who her mother was, but you must have let on to Matt about the baby, didn't you? That's what happened out there on the ice, isn't it?"

I nod, amazed she has put together so much from that last journal entry. I had written, "Tonight I will go down to the lake to meet him and I'll tell him everything." I think of what I had written next and blush to think of Dean Buehl reading that very last line.

"I didn't tell him the baby was Lucy's and his. I didn't know that."

"But you told him enough so he guessed."

"Yes," I agree limply. If not for Dean Buehl's grip on my arm I might sink down to the cold rock.

"It was my fault," I say. *Mea culpa,* I say to myself, *mea culpa.* This is what Roy Corey had been talking about. Taking responsibility for the sins of the past.

"And that's what they were arguing about when Lucy ran out onto the ice." I nod weakly. "At the inquest you said they were arguing about Helen, but that wasn't it? Unless Lucy told Matt what Helen had told her . . . that she and Matt weren't brother and sister . . ."

"No," I say, "she never got the chance."

"So you lied at the inquest." I expect now that she will shake me, even hurl me from her, but instead she relaxes her grip on my arm and smiles at me. I've told her what she wanted to hear. I've cleansed her of sin. I can see the weight of it, lifting from her, the burden of all the guilt and shame she's carried with her all these years. She's shed it like the layer of dust the sculptor's chisel leaves and now her face is as smooth and firm and pale as marble in the moonlight. "Well, dear, don't be too hard on yourself. The thing to do now is put the past behind you. That's what I'm going to do. I've made what amends I could and now I'm going to put the whole thing behind me. Can you do that, Jane?"

I almost laugh. Now that she's shifted the blame from herself to me she tells me to forget. But I nod to let her know I'll try.

Then she turns on her heel and leaves abruptly, that fast stride taking her into the woods and out of sight before I realize that she is leaving.

I stand for a few moments trying to collect my thoughts, but all I hear is Dean Buehl's advice to me. Forget the past, forget the past. For the moment the words seem to block out any thought, but can I really do it? Can I forget the past? Do I even want to?

I look at the skater on the lake. It must be Dr. Lockhart, but it's hard to connect the stiff and forbidding psychologist with this ethereal figure dancing on the ice. She skates over the ice like a black swan on white water. So effortless do her movements seem I am reminded of those magnetized skaters on the ornamental ponds that decorate shop windows at Christmas time. The ones with little plastic figures that turn in the same magnetized grooves over and over again. It seems that the loops Dr. Lockhart inscribes on the lake follow some pattern, too, so that if I could see the lines her skates cut in the ice some intricate mandala would be revealed.

It reminds me of a dream I've been having lately. In the dream I am skating on the lake, as beautifully and skillfully as Dr. Lockhart is now skating. I feel, in the dream, finally free of the past, but when I look back from the shore I see I've cut a pattern in the ice and the pattern is Matt Toller's face. As I watch his face sink into the black water I can clearly read his expression. He is disappointed in me. I can't hear the words his lips are forming, but I know what he is saying. *You'd pull me out, wouldn't you, Jane?*

I suppose this is the sort of thing Dean Buehl would say is best left forgotten. Yet as painful as it is to see that look in Matt's face every night in my dreams, it's far more unbearable to think of never seeing his face again at all.

Chapter Twenty-seven

●

I FIND, IN THE NEXT FEW WEEKS, THAT IT IS EASIER TO FOL-
low Dean Buehl's injunction to forget the past than I would
have imagined. My own unpreparedness comes, blessedly, to the
rescue. Since I hadn't quite believed I'd be back at Heart Lake, I
didn't spend my break getting ready for the next semester. It was a
sort of hedge, I realize now, against the possibility of being fired.
It makes me realize how much I was afraid of being *let go* (my
predecessor's fate) and how glad, after all is said and done, I am to be
back, even though I miss Olivia so much I feel physically ill. Again,
it's a blessing of sorts to be so busy. And when I make the drive
down to Westchester she seems happy enough. Happy with her father, happy with the young college girl who watches her during
the week, happy to see me when I come down every other weekend. It's only when Sunday comes and I have to say good-bye that
she seems to fall apart a little. When I get back to the campus on
those Sunday nights I throw myself into translating to catch up on
the time I've lost.

Because even though my classes are smaller, I have to scramble to
prepare translations. Often I am only one step ahead of my students
in the reading and occasionally I have to sight read second year's Catullus and third year's Ovid. I can't take that chance with fourth

year's Virgil, though. For one thing the class is now so small (besides Athena and Vesta it's just Octavia and Flavia, who are too worried about their classics scholarships to quit the class) that I have to shoulder at least an equal load of translating or we'll never get Rome founded before the end of the year. For another thing, the Latin has gotten harder. As we approach Book Six of the *Aeneid*, I find myself dreading the visit to the underworld. I remember that even *Domina* Chambers admitted that certain passages were almost untranslatable. It was as if, she told us, the syntax becomes as twisting as the minotaur's maze that is carved on the Sibyl's gates through which Aeneas must pass before his visit to the underworld.

I tell my advanced girls they won't be tested on the really hard parts.

"Why did he make it so hard?" Vesta asks. "I mean, didn't he want people to be able to read his stuff?" There's a note of irritation in her voice that goes beyond annoyance with Virgil. It feels to me as if she's asking why I'm making it so hard *on her* and I begin to suspect we're not just talking about Latin. I think she holds me at least partly responsible for what happened to Melissa, and therefore it's my fault they have to go to all these counseling sessions and communal sings.

I tell the girls *Domina* Chambers's theory about the language being a maze. "After all, he's about to take us into the underworld . . ." I notice that the girls always perk up when I mention the underworld, the way a toddler might at the promise of a trip to Disneyland. ". . . and that's not supposed to be easy. It's like a secret he's not supposed to reveal, so he has to disguise the instructions."

"Like they use five-five-five phone numbers on television," Athena suggests.

"Exactly." Excited, I write a passage on the board and have them take turns linking up the adjectives and nouns, the nouns and verbs, the relative clauses with their antecedents. When we are done the lines we have drawn between the words do look like a maze.

"A maze with no exit," Vesta points out. "Where's Ariadne with her thread when you need her?"

"The thread is the way the words link up," Athena says, raising her hand in her excitement even though I have long dispensed with such formalities in this little class. "When you see which words go together you solve the puzzle."

I look at her with amazement. Not only because of how she has caught on, but because of how suddenly beautiful she looks. The light coming in the classroom window touches her straggly, multi-colored hair, and where the light brown is showing through the dye I see flashes of red. Her green eyes shine back at me with the pleasure of getting it right and for a moment it's as if we were alone in the classroom, teacher and student sharing that rare flash of illumination that comes after slogging through the muck. But then she notices how in raising her hand her sweater sleeve has slipped down her arm, revealing the tangle of scarred flesh. She sees Octavia staring at her wrist and whispering something to Flavia. She looks away from me and tugs the unraveling cuff down over her knuckles.

The next day Octavia is absent and Flavia explains to me, apologetically, that her sister is dropping the class because every time she looks at Ellen Craven she thinks about the suicide legend. "Our grandmother says that the ghost of a murderer is never at rest."

I ask Flavia if she shares her sister's superstitions. "Nah. Besides, Octavia has a good shot at a tennis scholarship, but my backhand sucks."

I am so concerned with preparing the girls for Book Six that I forget how Book Five ends. It's only while Athena is reading aloud the part where Aeneas's boat is approaching Italy that I remember this is where Palinurus, the helmsman, drowns.

As she reads I tell myself that it's not going to be so bad. After all, we can't ignore every reference to drowning just because Melissa Randall drowned. This is about the helmsman of a boat, not a seventeen-year-old girl. But there's something in the way the god of sleep tricks Palinurus into falling in the water that makes me uneasy. I look around my dwindling class and see it's making everyone uneasy.

"Datur hora quieti," Athena reads. "The time for rest has come?"

I nod. "Yes, you noticed the passive. *Bene.*"

"*Pone caput fessoque oculos furare labori*—put your head down and rest your eyes?"

"Basically," I say.

"Sounds like a good idea," Flavia says, putting her head down on her desk and closing her eyes. Athena reads on, alternating between Latin and English, her words barely audible above the hiss of the steam heat and the gurgling of the radiators. I can tell from Flavia's breathing that she is asleep. I'm certainly not supposed to let the girls fall asleep in class, but I don't have the heart to wake her. Before class she told me she hasn't been sleeping because of bad dreams.

"I keep thinking about Melissa Randall in the lake," she said. "I know they found her body, but I keep thinking she's still there. Octavia says she can hear her voice coming from the lake."

"It's just the ice buckling," I told her, but I know what she means. The noise has been keeping me up, too.

"*Mene huic confidere monstro?*" Athena reads. "Would you have me put faith in such a demon?"

The noise the ice makes sounds like a monster trapped under the ice.

"*Ecce deus ramum Lethaeo rore madentum vique soporatum Stygia super utraque quassat tempora . . .* Look! The god shook a branch at Lethe who was sleeping."

She has totally mangled the translation, but I say nothing. The God of Sleep coaxes Palinurus into forgetfulness as the drip of the radiators lulls my students into a drugged stupor. Forget the past, Dean Buehl said, drink deep of Lethe's water and forget.

Palinurus falls headlong (*praecipitem,* from *praecipitare,* my favorite Latin verb) into the Mediterranean Sea and Aeneas sails on to Italy, narrowly avoiding the Sirens' rocks, ". . . which once were hard to pass and whitened by the bones of many men," Athena translates. "Far out we heard the growl and roar of the stones where the salt surf beats unceasingly."

Even my eighth graders have noticed the sounds coming from

the lake. "They come from where the rocks are and isn't that where that senior fell in?" one of them blurted out in the middle of a lesson on the passive periphrastic today.

Athena finishes her translation and there is a moment of silence when we all listen to the sound of the steam hissing in the pipes and the incessant crackling that comes from the lake.

"I think it sucks that Aeneas went on without Palinurus," Vesta says. Vesta hasn't liked Aeneas since he ditched Dido in Book Four.

"Yeah, but what else was he supposed to do? Stop the boat and go back? I mean, he had to get past those Sirens and found Italy. Right, *Magistra*? It was his duty. Like you gotta go on."

I am so grateful for this reading of the *Aeneid* that it is all I can do to stop myself from hugging Athena. We've navigated another minefield, gotten through another day of Latin. Aeneas is within sight of the Italian shore. Outside the lake has quieted down. But then Vesta pipes up, "Yeah, but Palinurus's death comes back to bite him on the ass."

"Vesta!" Athena says so loudly that Flavia wakes up. They look at me to see if I'll reprimand Vesta for inappropriate language, but instead I commend her for reading ahead.

"That's right, Palinurus meets Aeneas in the underworld and tells him the truth about his death and begs him to give him a proper burial."

"The dead sure are a whiny lot," Vesta says just as the bell rings. There's not much I can do but nod my agreement, but I notice Flavia turns pale at such a cavalier dismissal of the demands the dead make upon the living, and the next day I learn that she has dropped out of the class.

Now it's only Athena and Vesta and me. I have the feeling, when the three of us convene in the drafty classroom overlooking the lake, that we are the last survivors of some monstrous ice age. Each night it snows, and although Dean Buehl has asked the board for extra money for plowing, the footpaths grow narrower and narrower between the rising walls of snow that guard the edges of the woods.

One Friday afternoon the snow accumulates so fast I'm unable to get my car out of the faculty lot and I have to call Olivia and tell her I'll be late for our weekend together. She seems unconcerned enough at first—wrapped up in some television show she's watching with Mitchell, but when I call her Saturday morning to tell her I still can't get my car out she cries. Mitchell complains that he'll have to pay the baby-sitter overtime because he has plans for the evening. I try not to wonder what plans. We haven't talked since Christmas break about the possibility of getting back together and I sense that particular window of opportunity has closed.

All weekend the snow falls and I shovel my car out only to watch the snow fill in the space I've cleared. I feel like one of those tortured souls in Hades condemned to perform some meaningless task over and over again. Beneath the soft snow the wipers are frozen onto the windshield. I spray chemical de-icer on the windshield and then reach inside to turn on the wipers. They quiver under the snow, like small animals trying to break free, and then, when they do break free, they sweep a handful of slush and de-icer into my face. The chemical burns my eyes and I have to scoop up handfuls of fresh snow to flush the de-icer out of my eyes. My vision remains blurred for the rest of the weekend, making it impossible to drive to Westchester even if the roads were cleared. When I call, Olivia is calm and tells me she understands in a voice so uncannily grown-up I am simultaneously proud and grief-stricken.

I stay in bed that Sunday and have to cancel my classes on Monday. Gwen Marsh stops by to check on me and bring me some soup and a stack of papers she's collected from my students. I'm touched by the soup, but wish she hadn't bothered with the papers. My eyes hurt too much to read or grade papers, so instead I watch the snow mounting in the window frames, depositing layer upon layer of white and gray sediment like the cross sections of mountain ranges Miss Buehl used to show us. Above these miniature ridges, large lofty flakes cling in clumps that look like cumulus clouds—a dioramic landscape to make up for the fact I can't see the real world behind the falling snow. It's the same sense of enclosure I had the January of my senior year that I spent in the infirmary.

LUCY NEEDN'T HAVE BEEN CONCERNED THAT I'D STAY IN THE *infirmary. As it turned out, I stayed longer than she did. When Miss Buehl and Domina Chambers picked me up off the floor after I lost consciousness they discovered I was burning up with fever. I guess all those hours roaming around the campus in wet clothes had done their trick. They kept me in the same room with Lucy because, Miss Buehl later informed me, Lucy insisted I stay with her.*

"She wouldn't let you out of her sight," she told me.

I remembered sometimes waking up and seeing Lucy in the bed across from me, lying on her side facing me. I tried once to talk to her about what had happened. I wanted to know if they had believed our story—if Deirdre had gotten rid of the bloody sheets, if anything had been discovered in the lake. But each time I tried to talk about it, Lucy shushed me. I heard her tell the nurse once not to bother me or try asking me questions.

"You should leave the poor kid alone," I overheard her say once to Miss Buehl. "After all, her mother just died." It seemed as if Lucy was the only one who remembered that. Even my father, who came to visit me only once, spoke about his new job at the glove factory with such enthusiasm that I thought I had dreamt up the hospital room in Albany and the funeral afterward. And if I had imagined that, maybe I had imagined everything that followed, the overheated dorm room, the baby in the tea tin . . .

But then I woke up one day to find Deirdre standing next to Lucy's bed. They seemed to be arguing about something in angry whispers and I knew then I hadn't imagined any of it.

Domina Chambers came often and I heard her questioning Lucy about what had happened, about why she had tried to take her own life.

"I don't think I really meant it," she told Domina Chambers. "I think I knew Jane would find me and save me."

I was touched by the story even though I knew it was a lie.

Then one day I woke up and found the bed next to me empty. I was so alarmed I managed to get out of bed and walk out into the hall where I found the nurse. "Where's Lucy?" I asked as I was led back to bed.

"She's been discharged, honey," the nurse told me, "and if you want to be you'd better stay in bed."

Lucy visited me that day. She brought me my Latin homework. I was amazed to think that classes had started. I'd had a feeling, in the white-washed infirmary room, its windows filled with snow, of suspended time, like in a fairy tale when the whole world goes to sleep with the heroine. But then if anyone were the heroine, I thought, it was Lucy, and she looked as if she had rejoined the world of the living. Her cheeks were pink, her hair shiny, and she was wearing one of the nice outfits she had gotten in Italy. She hadn't looked this good since October.

"I'm trying to impress them that I've regained my mental health," she said when I complimented her appearance, and then, leaning closer to whisper, "If I'd had any idea what a bother this suicide thing was going to turn out to be, I think I'd have done it for real!" She giggled. "But I don't think I hate it nearly as much as Deirdre."

"Deirdre? But she didn't try to kill herself."

"No, but they've called in this psychologist from Albany who says that suicide is contagious. And since Deirdre's my roommate and they think she acted funny about the sheets they're giving her the third degree. They'll probably start bugging you once you're well enough."

"Well it serves her right," I said. "If she'd just told someone she was pregnant in the first place . . ."

Lucy frowned. "I guess she was too scared," she said. "Anyhow, it's over now."

"I hope she doesn't tell anyone," I said, "I mean with all this psychiatric interrogation. Then it might come out that you and I got rid of . . . the thing."

Lucy turned pale and I was immediately sorry I'd reminded her of what we'd done. "She'd better not tell," Lucy said. "Get better soon, Jane, I might need your help with her."

I wasn't released until the next week. I still felt wobbly but I convinced the nurse that I was all right and pleaded that I was afraid of falling too far behind if I didn't go back to class. I walked back to the dorm on a bright, sunny day, half-blinded by the glare of the sun glancing off the frozen lake. Girls passed me on the path and greeted me, but I felt like they were all moving at a sped-up rate and I became conscious of how slowly I was walking. It made me feel apart to see them all, with their shiny hair swinging against their down vests, their pastel shetland sweaters bright in the sun. These were the girls I had admired in the town drugstore; they were the reason I had wanted to come here, but I was no closer to them—no more like them—now than I had been when I was still a townie. I hadn't made any friends at Heart Lake. I hadn't tried to. Lucy had always been enough.

When I got back to the dorm I ran into Deirdre in the hall just outside our room. "Oh good," she said when she saw me. "Maybe the shrinks can spend some time picking your brains. I'm tired of explaining that I'm not suicidal."

Lucy was coming out of the single when I came in the suite. "Did you just run into Deirdre?" she asked me. "I thought I heard you talking in the hall. What was she saying to you?"

I told her what Deirdre had said. I was a little disappointed in Lucy's greeting, but then I guessed she was preoccupied.

"She'd better hope the shrinks don't get a hold of this," Lucy said, holding up a notebook covered in red Chinese embroidered silk.

"Is that Deirdre's journal?" I asked, a little surprised that Lucy would be snooping.

"I don't think you could call it a journal," she said, "more like a book of the dead. She keeps quotes about death in it. Listen to this, 'He who saves a man against his will as good as murders him.'"

"Horace," I said. "Didn't Domina Chambers give us that quote?"

"Yes, half the quotes in here come from Helen. Honestly, I don't think it would look good for her if Deirdre did kill herself. I'll have to talk to her at dinner tonight."

I must have looked baffled. "Oh yes, since my so-called suicide attempt Helen has insisted I eat with her every night. Frankly, it's driving me batty. She keeps asking me questions about my 'outlook,' as she calls it, and giving me mimeos of poems that are supposed to cheer me up. Only they're pretty morbid, too. Here." Lucy put down Deirdre's journal and picked up a folded sheet of paper with blue printing on it. She read aloud. It was Yeats's poem "The Lake Isle of Innisfree." We'd had it in Miss Macintosh's class last term. What struck me now were the last lines: "I will arise and go now, for always night and day / I hear water lapping with low sounds by the shore; / While I stand on the roadway, or on the pavements gray, / I hear it in the deep heart's core."

"You know," I said, "those last lines remind me of the three sisters story. The way the girls are supposed to be lured to the lake to kill themselves by the sound of the water lapping against the rocks."

"How clever of you, Jane. I thought exactly the same thing." Lucy folded the sheet in two and laid it on her bed next to Deirdre's journal.

"Aren't you going to put that back?" I asked.

"Oh, I guess," Lucy said, yawning. "Would you do it for me? It was in her bureau in the top drawer. I'd better go now. Helen hates it when I'm late."

When Lucy left I went into Deirdre's single and replaced the journal in the top drawer of her bureau. I felt nervous and, I realized, not just because I was afraid of Deirdre catching me with her journal. It was the bed. I was afraid to look at it, afraid that when I looked at it the blood would somehow still be there. But when I did force myself to look at it I saw only rumpled sheets—Deirdre almost never made her bed—and a blue and gold Indian bedspread that used to hang on the ceiling over the bed. The Balinese dancers were still dancing on their tapestries as if nothing unusual had ever happened in that bed. I thought I saw a splotch of red over one of their breasts, but when I looked closer I saw it might be part of the pattern.

I went back into the room I shared with Lucy and noticed that my suitcase had been stored underneath my bed. I pulled it out and opened it. It was empty. I opened my bureau drawers and found my clothes neatly folded (more neatly than I remembered packing them that last morning in Albany) and put away. Under one stack of clothes I found my journal. I leafed through it, wondering if Lucy had read my journal, too, and what she'd have made of what I'd written. There was nothing bad about her in it, but there were embarrassing things, like how jealous I'd felt of Deirdre and Lucy's friendship and how much I missed Matt. As I read through it I was startled by how much of what I had written could be misinterpreted. So many of the things I had written could mean so many different things, depending on who the reader was. I read through parts pretending I was Lucy or Deirdre or Domina Chambers or Miss Buehl—or even myself when older—and with each new "reader" what I had written shifted in meaning as if it had been translated into another language.

I'd better put it back under the floorboards, I thought. But first I wrote about what happened the night I came back from Albany. It felt risky committing to paper that awful moment when I watched the tea tin sink into the lake, but there was something in me that needed to get it out, if only to my journal. "You're the only one I can ever tell," I wrote. And then I hid the journal under the loose floorboards beneath my desk.

I tried to do a little Latin translation, but the words swam in front of my eyes and I started seeing spots. At first they were only small glints of light, like gnats flying in front of my eyes, and then they merged into one large sun spot that spread across my vision like a hole burning through a home movie. I closed my eyes and lay down on my bed, but I could still see the burning spot on the inside of my eyelids. Even when I fell asleep I saw the light. I dreamed it was Miss Buehl's porch light and I was crossing the woods to reach it, only I went the wrong way and ended up back at the Point. I slipped on the icy rock and fell into black space flecked with white sparks. Snow, I thought in my dream, but then the darkness turned green and the flecks of light were golden silt drifting down to the bottom of the lake. I looked up at a pattern of white shards on black; I was under the broken ice, which, even as I watched, knit back together, sealing me beneath it. Drifting down beside me was a tea tin painted with golden mountains and blue skies. It turned as it sank, spinning like a leaf, and then, when it reached the bottom, its lid slowly opened.

IT'S THAT SAME FEELING—OF LYING AT THE BOTTOM OF THE lake looking up at the underside of the ice—I have lying in my room, my vision blurred, the snowscapes on the window screens like distant mountains. I think of Deirdre, of how the ice must have looked to her as she sank into the lake. In my dreams I try to tell her that I know now that the baby wasn't hers, but when I reach for her she turns away from me, just as Dido turns away from Aeneas when he meets her in the underworld. *The dead sure are a whiny lot,* Vesta had said. But she was wrong. The dead are silent.

When my vision clears, I feel curiously energized. I decide to go skating. I had been afraid that part of Dean Buehl's "forget the past" campaign might include banishing ice skating, but I had forgotten how much she liked to skate.

"Best thing for these girls," she says on an unusually mild day in late January. "Exercise. Fresh air. And just look at this ice! Best ice we've had in twenty years."

"Coldest January in twenty years," Simon Ross, the math teacher, says gliding by on hockey skates, "until today, that is. A few days like this and that'll be it for the skating season."

"It's supposed to get cold again tonight," Gwen Marsh says, backskating a circle around me.

"But first we're going to get some sleet and icy rain," Meryl North, who is skating with Tacy Beade, says. "We might have a real ice storm on our hands."

I turn to say something else to Gwen, but she's gone. I wonder if I've offended her in some way. Since I've been back she's been distant. I had thought at the beginning of the school year that we might be friends, but I realize now that I've done very little to build on the promise of that friendship. As I watch my fellow teachers skating together in pairs and small groups I realize how little I've connected to anyone here at Heart Lake. It's the same feeling I had walking back from the infirmary senior year, that I hadn't bothered making other friends because Lucy had always been enough. And, in a way, she's kept me from making friends all these years. At first, I told myself, because I was afraid of being hurt again. But later it was because when I did come close to someone I would hear Lucy's cool assessing voice, criticizing something about my new acquaintance. This one was too fat, that one was too earnest, this one a little loud, that one just plain dumb.

I tried to ignore the voice, but it put a distance between me and the girls I might have befriended. Who might have befriended me. It wasn't as if there were that many candidates.

I make an effort today to talk to everyone. I skate with Myra Todd and listen to a long drawn-out tirade against animal rights activists. I discuss a plan for a reenactment of an old-fashioned ice harvest with Dean Buehl. I catch up to Gwen, who's skating now with Dr. Lockhart, and offer to help with the literary magazine. I join Tacy Beade and Meryl North and ask Miss Beade if she'd come give a lecture on classical art to my juniors. She says she's busy right now with plans for ice sculptures to accompany the ice harvest, but will be happy to come later in the year.

"It's time to turn back, Tacy," Meryl North says. "See, we're at the Point."

"Oh," my old art teacher says, "yes, of course." That's when I realize, watching Meryl North steer Tacy Beade along the ice, that Beady can hardly see. I remember watching her set up her art room, everything in its place, and wonder how long she's been losing her sight and how long she would keep her job if the board knew. Meryl North must realize I suspect something because, as we skate back toward the mansion, she chatters enthusiastically about the coming ice harvest. I notice, though, that she keeps confusing the dates and at one point I realize she thinks it's 1977 and I'm still a student here. When Dr. Lockhart and Gwen Marsh skate by, Meryl North says, "There goes your little friend." It's sad, I think, that my two old teachers have lost the aptitudes most important to their fields: the art teacher, her sight; the history teacher, her sense of time.

My ankles have begun to hurt, but when I see Athena and Vesta I skate toward them. Vesta is wearing a fleece headband that makes her lavender-red Little Mermaid hair stick up in spiky points. Athena is wearing a Yale sweatshirt over red plaid pajama pants. Her mottled hair, which is now about half brown and half black, makes her look like an Australian sheep dog. I realize, skating toward them, that I'd far rather talk to them than to any of my colleagues.

As I skate closer, I notice someone else approaching the two girls and it gives me pause. I try to slow my forward progress by digging the serrated tips of my skate blades into the ice, but instead of slowing down I trip and sail headlong into Roy Corey, who has reached the girls just as I do. I slam hard into his chest and I'm sure we're both going down, but instead I feel his arm curve around my waist as we spin across the ice.

"All right, *Magistra!*" I hear the girls cheering me on, as if I had just completed a double axle instead of nearly crashing to the ice. And I do feel suddenly graceful, with Roy's arm around my waist, but then he takes away his arm and crosses his arms behind his back. We skate side by side, but not touching, around the western edge of the lake. I'm impressed with how well he skates and then I remember him telling me, all those years ago, that he'd grown up skating on these ponds. Just like Matt. At the thought of Matt I catch the tip of my blade on the ice and pitch forward. I see the hard white ice speeding up to my face but he catches me just in time.

"Whoa," he says, "are you OK?"

"Sorry," I say, "my eyes still aren't so good. I had a little accident with some de-icer."

"Yeah, Dean Buehl told me. I called last week to ask you a few questions." I remember suddenly that he is a police officer and that he probably isn't here just for the ice skating.

"A few questions?" I ask. "What about?"

Before answering I see him look quickly around us. We've stopped just where the Point juts into the lake, not far from where the third sister rock curves out of the ice like the back of a whale arrested mid-dive. The rest of the skaters are in the west cove. They're too far away to overhear us, but I see he still looks nervous.

"Wasn't there a cave around here," he asks, turning to face me. "You took me to a cave that morning."

It's the first reference he's made to that night we spent together and it makes me blush. But why? Nothing happened. He was asleep when I touched his face. I notice that he's blushing, too. Was he asleep?

"There are a bunch of caves in the Point," I say, "but I think the one you're talking about is over here."

I lead him to a shallow opening in the cliff wall just where the ice meets the shore. It's not even really a cave, just an indentation in the rock covered by an overhanging ledge and partially blocked by the second sister stone.

He wedges himself into the tight space and pats the rock by his side. Embarrassed, I squeeze in next to him. He takes up quite a lot more space than he did when he was boy. But then, so do I. Only the view from the cave hasn't changed. I can see the tall stone casting a long shadow on the ice, which the setting sun has turned a creamy orange. The cave itself is full of this orange light, reflecting off the ice and onto the limestone walls.

Roy is also looking at the view from the cave. When he looks back at me I guess I'm not the only one who's been thinking about the last time we were here.

"So what did you want to ask me?" I ask. I wonder if I should have asked to have a lawyer present. I almost laugh out loud imagining a lawyer crammed into this narrow space.

"What?"

"Nothing. I was just thinking this isn't your typical interrogation room. Can I assume this won't be a typical interrogation?"

He doesn't smile, neither does he confirm or deny what I've said. "I'm just trying to get a few things straight in my head," he says, "about Deirdre Hall's death."

"Oh," I say.

"I've been going over your journal . . ."

"I thought you said there was nothing to incriminate me in there. I believe your exact words were 'You had no idea what was really going on.' "

"Well, maybe I didn't give you enough credit. I read over the part about Deirdre's death and I think there was something you felt uncomfortable about. I wanted you to tell me what happened that night."

"But why? What's the point? Are you investigating Deirdre Hall's death now?"

He shrugs. "Humor me, Jane." He grins at me then with the kind of boyish grin that Matt might have given me to coax me into another fifteen minutes of Latin study. So I do what he wants. I tell him everything I remember about that night.

I HAD BEEN ASLEEP, DREAMING THAT AWFUL DREAM ABOUT sinking under the ice, the tea tin drifting down through the water beside me, when their voices woke me. They were in the single, arguing.

"I'm going to tell."

"You can't."

"There's nothing you can do to stop me. I've had enough."

Someone rushed through the room I was in. The door to the hall opened, letting in a slice of light, and then slammed shut. Someone else followed from the single and opened the door. I could see in the light that it was Lucy and I called to her.

Lucy spun around and then closed the door. She came over and sat on the bed next to me. "I didn't know you were awake," she said. There was a little light coming from the single, but I couldn't make out Lucy's face in the shadows. "Did you hear?"

"I heard you arguing with Deirdre. Where's she gone?"

"She's going to Miss Buehl. To tell."

"Tell what?"

Lucy paused before she answered. "About the baby," she said.

"Why would she tell Miss Buehl she had a baby?"

Lucy sighed. "I guess she wants to get it off her chest," she said. "Confession's good for the soul, and all that junk." I thought about my journal writing guiltily, but at least that wouldn't get anyone in trouble.

"But then everybody will know we helped get rid of it."

Lucy nodded. "She doesn't care," Lucy said. "She doesn't care about anyone but herself."

I sat up in bed. "Can we stop her?" I asked.

Lucy took my hand and squeezed it. "Good old Jane," she said, "that's an excellent idea. Come on. Maybe we can catch up with her."

We didn't bother going down the drainpipe. The dorm matron was asleep at her desk, so we just tiptoed by. Once outside I started running down the path, but Lucy stopped me. "I've got a shortcut through the woods," she said. "We might be able to catch up with her before she gets to Miss Buehl."

We followed the narrow trail that Lucy had carved out of the snow. I noticed that it was freshly trodden and was surprised that she had obviously used her trails after the last snow. The trail led directly to the Point. When I saw where we were I stopped at the edge of the woods, thinking of my dream. I didn't want to go out onto the rock.

"I think I see her," Lucy hissed, "get back."

Lucy motioned me back until we were hidden by the shadows. Only when Deirdre was directly in front of us on the path did Lucy step out from the shadows, blocking her way. Deirdre was startled when she saw Lucy and moved toward the trees, but then she must have seen me, because she moved off the path in the other direction, toward the Point. When she was on the rock Lucy started walking toward her, but not on the curved surface on top of the Point. She took a step down to the ledge on the east side of the Point and approached Deirdre slowly but steadily.

"I think we should talk this over, Deir," I heard Lucy say. Her voice sounded calm and reasonable.

"I don't want to talk about it, Lucy, just get away from me." I heard the fear in Deirdre's voice and it surprised me; Lucy was so much smaller than Deirdre. What did Deirdre have to be afraid of? It made me, suddenly, angry. I stepped out of the woods and walked carefully onto the icy rock. My anger quickly turned to fear, though, when I saw how close Deirdre and Lucy had gotten to the edge.

"Hey," I called. My voice sounded feeble. "Let's go back to the dorm and talk this over."

Deirdre snorted. "Yes, Jane, let's have a nice long talk. There's a lot you might be interested to learn."

Lucy turned toward me and in turning lost her balance. Her arms flailed wide and beat the air like the wings of some large, awkward bird. I tried to grab her, but she was too far away, below me on the ledge, and I stumbled be-

fore I could reach her. Just before I landed on the rock I saw Deirdre reach for Lucy's arm and then I heard someone scream and the sound of something cracking. I looked up and saw one figure crouched on the rock. I crept toward her and found it was Lucy. She was looking over the edge of the cliff at the frozen lake below where a long black gash had opened in the ice.

"You say Lucy was below you on the ledge and that when you stepped forward Deirdre stepped back?"

I nod. He seems lost in thought for a moment. "What?" I ask.

"Nothing," he says, "at least, I have to take a look at the Point again to tell if it's anything. Go on, tell me what you did after Deirdre went through the ice. Did you go down and try to help her?"

"There was nothing we could do."

He looks at me without saying anything. I remember that he's read my journal. "Whose decision was it to leave without trying to help her?"

"Mine," I say, and when he still stares at me, I add, "Well, first it was Lucy's and then it was mine."

I tried to pull Lucy away from the edge but it was as if she were stuck there, transfixed by that long dark opening in the ice.

"We have to go down and see if we can help her," I said.

Lucy looked at me, her eyes wide. "I saw her when she hit the ice," she said. "Trust me, she was dead before she went into the water." I saw the horror in Lucy's eyes and it frightened me.

"We can't just leave her. We have to be sure."

Lucy nodded. She let me lead the way down to the beach. When we got to the edge of the ice I stopped but Lucy walked right out onto the ice, to the edge of the hole where Deirdre had fallen through. I caught up to her and grabbed her arm and she wheeled around on me so suddenly that I almost lost my balance and fell in.

"You said you wanted to be sure," Lucy said. "One of us has to go in.

Obviously it should be me. It was my fault she fell." She spoke softly but her words chilled me. She had that look she got when she was determined to have her way. I didn't doubt that she'd be willing to plunge into the icy water to find Deirdre's body. I had the feeling she wouldn't stop until she found her, not even if it meant following Deirdre to the bottom of the lake. I realized I might lose her, too.

I stared into the black water. Already I could see a thin film of ice forming on the top. How many minutes had passed since Deirdre fell? Even if she had survived the fall wouldn't she have drowned by now? Why should Lucy risk her life if Deirdre were already dead?

I put my other hand on her arm and turned her to face me. "I don't want you to do it," I said. "It's bad enough Deirdre's gone. I don't want to lose you, too." Her eyes regarded me as if I were far away, as if that thin film of ice that was forming over the black water had gotten in between us. I couldn't tell if she even understood what I was saying and then she looked back at the water and I saw such a look of longing on her face that I immediately started pulling her back to the shore.

"But we have to tell someone," she said.

"Of course, you were right in the first place. We'll go back to Miss Buehl's cottage. . ."

"But what if she's gone out? No. It's safer to go back to the dorm and wake up the matron."

Lucy led the way because she knew a shortcut following one of her narrow footpaths. We went single file, Lucy walking so fast I could barely keep up with her. I was glad she had shaken off the trancelike lethargy that had come over her at the lake, but I was surprised that when we got to the dorm Lucy climbed up the drainpipe to the second-story bathroom. When I caught up with her inside I asked her what she was doing. "Why are we sneaking in? We've got to wake the dorm matron anyway."

"I need to check something first," she said. "Deirdre was writing in her journal before she ran out. What if she wrote about what we did, Jane? Do you want people to know you drowned a baby in the lake?"

"Drowned?"

"Not so loud." Lucy put a finger to my lips. Her hands were ice cold.

"The baby was dead," I said.

"It's our word against hers. What if she wrote it was born alive and you and I killed it? Do you want people thinking that about you? Do you think you'll get that scholarship to Vassar if that gets around?"

I shook my head and Lucy opened the bathroom door, poked her head out and then gave the all-clear sign. It wasn't until I was following her down the hall that I wondered how she knew about the scholarship. I hadn't told anyone but Miss Buehl and Miss North, who had written my recommendation letters. It didn't seem the right time to ask, though, so I followed Lucy in silence.

We crept down the hall and Lucy opened our door slowly so it wouldn't creak. We'd done the same thing countless times, but always with Deirdre. I kept looking behind me expecting to see her and then I would think of her in the lake, below the ice. I remembered my dream and hoped, for Deirdre's sake, that Lucy was right about the fall killing her.

Lucy went straight into Deirdre's single and I heard a drawer opening. When she came out she was holding Deirdre's journal. She sat down at her desk, turned on the lamp, and opened the notebook to the last written page. I stood behind her and read over her shoulder. Under the Horace quote, which had been the last thing in the journal when I'd seen it this afternoon, Deirdre had written another line: "Whatever happens now, it's all because of what Lucy did at Christmas." There was nothing about the baby being alive at birth.

"What does she mean?" I asked. "She makes it sound like it's all your fault. That's not fair."

Lucy looked up at me. "She blamed me for hiding the truth. She said it would have been better if it had all come out into the open."

"But you were only trying to help." I was getting angry at Deirdre, forgetting that she wasn't around to be angry at.

Lucy shrugged. "Apparently she didn't see it the same way."

"Well, we can't let anyone see this," I said. "We'll hide it. We'll dump it in the lake. I'll never tell."

Lucy smiled. "You're a good friend, Jane, but I don't think that will be necessary. Listen." She read the line out loud. "'Whatever happens now it's all because of what Lucy did at Christmas.' It's perfect! All that shrink from Albany has been going on about is how one suicide attempt leads to another.

Like it's catching. They expected Deirdre to do this. Especially since I had the bad manners to cut my wrists in her bed. They'll probably pat each other on the backs for seeing it coming."

"But she didn't kill herself," I said. "It was an accident. We'll just explain . . ."

"Don't be silly, Jane. It looks like a suicide. It even fits the three sisters legend because she landed right in between the second and third sister. It's what they'll want to believe. They'll lap it up like cream."

"Maybe it was a suicide," I said. "I mean, think how bad Deirdre must have felt about the baby . . ." I thought Lucy would be glad of my theory, but instead she seemed distracted. She looked around the room as if she had lost something.

"There's just one more thing needed to make it perfect." She popped up from her desk and crossed to the bed. I was a little startled at her energy. She snatched a piece of white paper from her bed and flourished it above her head.

"Voila!" she said, sitting back down at the desk. "Ecce testimonium." It was the mimeograph of Yeats's poem "The Lake Isle of Innisfree." "I think just the last stanza will do." Lucy cut out the last stanza of the poem, being careful to cut evenly. Then she taped it into Deirdre's journal, again taking time to line it up perfectly.

"Even if it was her suicide note," Lucy said, "Deirdre was so fucking precise."

"So you two made it look like a suicide. You changed her journal and then took it to the dorm matron."

"Yes. We said that I'd woken up and saw Deirdre's door open, her bed empty, and her journal lying open on the bed. I know it sounds bad, but I thought she really might have killed herself, that she felt so bad about the baby . . ."

"But it wasn't her baby."

"No."

"And what was it Deirdre said just before she fell?"

" 'Yes, Jane, let's have a nice long talk. There's a lot you might be interested to learn.' "

Roy watches me, waiting for me to take the next step.

"She would have told me it wasn't her baby, that it was Lucy's baby . . ."

"And you say Lucy flailed her arms just before Deirdre fell?"

"Yes, because she lost her balance . . ."

"But you say she was on the east ledge. You can't fall from there because there's a rock blocking the edge of the Point. But it is close enough to the edge of the Point to reach out and push someone . . ."

"I didn't see that." I've raised one hand to my mouth and I feel the wool of my mittens dampen with my breath. Roy reaches over and pulls my hand away from my face.

"Because you were trying to reach Lucy and fell. You wouldn't have seen anything."

I snatch my hand away from Roy and press both hands over my eyes as if to blot out the picture Roy is drawing. I grind the heels of my hands into my eyes until bright sunbursts bleed into the blackness, sunspots that turn into the glitter of rock and ice, a miniature landscape of glaciers from which I look up and see, against a moonlit sky, like actors performing in front of a silver scrim, Lucy's small pale hand reaching up and pulling Deirdre's foot. A swift hard yank the strength of which must have surprised Deirdre because I see her mouth form a little O before she falls back.

Roy pulls my hands away from my eyes and when I open them I am looking directly into his eyes and I read there the hope that I have remembered something.

"What does it matter?" I say, too angry at being forced to relive that night to give him the satisfaction that he's right, that maybe I did see something more. "It happened twenty years ago. Both Lucy and Deirdre are dead. So is Melissa Randall. Whatever she read in my journal, whatever it made her do, it's all over now."

"Is it?" Roy asks. "First there's a fake suicide attempt—that's like what Lucy did at Christmas—and then a girl drowns in the same spot Deirdre drowned. Two of the events from your senior year have recurred, but what about the last act? What about what happened to Matt and Lucy? We've been assuming that Melissa Randall did it all,

but why? Because we found your journal with her things. But isn't that also like what happened twenty years ago? You and Lucy tampered with Deirdre's journal so everyone thought it was a suicide. What if someone planted your journal in Melissa's things?"

I stare at him now not so much with anger as with horror. What he is suggesting is my worst fear, that the events set in motion twenty years ago would never really be over until they have swept over me, counting me a victim: the third girl. And really, why should I have been spared?

I close my eyes and see once again, sharper now, Lucy reaching up to grab Deirdre's leg and know the memory's always been there. I open my eyes again and nod. "Deirdre's death wasn't an accident," I say. "You were right. It doesn't matter that we were young; I'm responsible for what happened back then. For Deirdre's death, too . . ."

Roy puts his hand over mine. I notice the fine red hairs that catch the light reflected from the ice at the opening to the cave. "Jane," he says, "that's not what I meant . . ." I look up at him, into the green eyes that look so familiar, and then I notice the light is gone.

I turn toward the narrow entrance to the cave just in time to see the long shadow cast by the sister stone split in two and half of the broken shadow move away. It's as if the stone's shadow had come to life and skated away across the ice, but Roy disabuses me of this notion. Getting to his feet, he skates out of the cave and I stumble along clumsily behind him. I catch up to him on the other side of the Point where he stands watching the skaters in the west cove. There's Dean Buehl, Tacy Beade, Meryl North, Gwendoline Marsh, Simon Ross, Myra Todd, Dr. Lockhart, Athena, Vesta, and a dozen more teachers and students. It's impossible to say, though, which one had been listening to our conversation inside the cave.

Chapter Twenty-eight

●

I HAVE THE SKATING DREAM AGAIN THAT NIGHT, ONLY IN THIS dream I can hear the ice cracking beneath me, fissures erupting in the wake of my blades. I keep skating, though, around and around, in an ever-tightening circle, as if following a magnetic track laid below the ice. Whereas in the dreams I had before there was a feeling of lightness, now there is weight, a heaviness that pulls my blades deep into the ice. When I look behind me I see the fissure open into a crevasse: a pale green tunnel descending for miles beneath my feet. It occurs to me that I am no longer skating on the lake, but on Miss Buehl's glacier. I stare into the pale green crevasse. Its walls are bubbled, like old glass, only the bubbles are moving. I look closer and see, miles beneath me yet impossibly clear, figures suspended in the ice. Matt and Lucy and Deirdre and Aphrodite, even Iris Crevecoeur, small and brown like a sepia photograph come to life, are all there, streams of bubbles spewing from their mouths.

There's another figure in the ice, but when I move closer to see I slip into the crevasse and as I slide down, deep into the pale green ice, I can hear the ice cracking closed above me.

I awake to the sound of something cracking above my head. My room is filled with an eerie green light. The light, I realize after a moment, comes from the luminescent dial on my alarm clock, which reads 3:33. As I stare at it something crashes on the roof above my head and skitters down the walls of my house. It sounds as if the house were bursting at its seams. I swing my legs out of the bed, half expecting to feel the floor trembling beneath my feet. I am thinking earthquake, tornado, another ice age, glaciers already on the march. But the floor, though icy cold, is reassuringly solid.

I get up and shove my bare feet into felt-lined boots and pull my down parka on over my nightgown. In the living room the crashing is louder. It sounds as if an army of raccoons were bivouacking on my roof. Raccoons? Hell, it could be bears. Wishing I had a rifle, I fling open the front door and switch on the porch lamp, hoping that any nocturnal intruder will be startled by the light just long enough for me to slam the door and call Animal Control.

Instead I see, in the nimbus of light from my porch lamp, a world made out of glass, a crystal world, like the inside of a candy Easter egg. Every branch and pine needle in the woods is glazed in ice. As I step out into the clearing in front of the house I can feel a light, needle-sharp sleet falling. Tree branches, weighed down by the ice, crack and crash to the forest floor. I should go back inside but I'm enchanted. I haven't seen an ice storm like this since I was little. I know how dangerous they can be, dragging down power lines and taking down trees, but for the moment I'm enthralled by the precision of it. The way the ice turns each blade of grass and dead leaf into an artifact.

Between my house and the Point there's a giant white pine. Each feathery needle is encased in ice. I can hear, above me, the rustle of them, rubbing against each other in the wind, a sound like muted chimes or bells tolling underwater. In the light from my porch they glitter like the eyes of some woodland animal, and then I think I can actually see a face of some sort of animal in the pine needles, watching. I move closer and see that the needles have twisted themselves into an animal face—a horned animal with its bloody prey dripping from its mouth. I reach out and pull the face from the tree and feel, under the thin ice casing, metal. I am holding three interlinked hair-pins: a corniculum.

IN THE MORNING I GO OUT TO THE POINT. I SCRAPE THE ICE on the ground with my boots and shake the branches, but find not one hairpin. There's just the three in my pocket. I walk onto the Point and look out at the lake. The storm has passed, leaving clear skies. The rising sun sets the lake on fire. I look down at the three sister stones and see that they, too, have gained a mantle of ice during the night. The third stone looks like an opal set in gold, the middle stone casts a long shadow like a crooked finger pointing toward the cave where Roy Corey and I sat yesterday. I remember how we saw that shadow, pointing in the opposite direction in the setting sun, split in two.

I look down at the three hairpins in my hand. Miss Macintosh once said that the question the reader should ask the narrator of any book is, "Why are you telling me this *now*?"

I've been back at Heart Lake for four weeks and it has been, above all else, quiet. No messages from the past, no torn journal pages or totem hairpins or dead girls. I'd assumed it was over, that the messages had stopped because Aphrodite was dead. But apparently I had assumed wrong. Someone had been keeping quiet. So why send me this message now? A sign that would appear innocent to anyone else—what could I say: that someone was threatening me with hair-pins?—but which is full of menace to me.

It *is* menace I feel, and that I have felt since yesterday when I saw the shadow split away from the stone. Someone listened to the con-versation between me and Roy. Something in that conversation has awakened an avenging spirit. But what? I go over in my mind what we talked about and instantly I remember the image of Lucy toppling Deirdre into the lake. I'm standing now at just the place where I stood the night Deirdre fell. To my left is the ledge where Lucy stood. I step down to that level—it's only about three feet below the top part, and work my way to the edge of the Point. The rock is flatter here and it almost reaches to the edge, but then there's an outcropping of stone and a stunted pine tree that blocks the edge of the cliff. Was that why Lucy stepped down here? Because the footing was better than the curved surface at the edge of the Point? She'd have known this from the nights we climbed down from here to the swimming beach. From where I'm standing I could reach up and touch someone standing at the edge of the Point. Or reach up and trip someone standing there. Once again I see the scene as I saw it yesterday in the cave. I climb back up to the curved stone of the Point and, staying on my hands and knees, inch myself as close the edge of the cliff as I can before vertigo forces me to creep back.

I look down at the rock and see that I've dug my nails into the narrow crevices as if I were a rock climber ascending a vertical wall. The glacial chattermarks remind me of my dream—the pale green crevasse opening in the glacier.

Whoever listened to our conversation yesterday heard what I said about Lucy and me covering up Deirdre's death. They also heard Roy say that he didn't believe Melissa Randall killed herself, that whoever "faked" Athena's suicide attempt and killed Melissa Randall might still be alive. If he's right, if that person were still alive and listening, it would have sounded like a challenge. And the corniculum is an answer to that challenge.

THROUGHOUT MY CLASSES I AM SO DISTRACTED BY THIS QUESTION that I can hardly follow the easy faked Latin in the *Ecce Romani* textbook (today we follow our Roman family to an inn on the Via Appia) let alone the advanced girls' translations of Virgil. We have followed Aeneas into the underworld where he encounters his spurned lover Dido and tries to apologize for abandoning her in Carthage. Dido, however, will have none of it. She turns away from Aeneas and refuses to talk to him.

I remember the dream I had of Deirdre turning away from me.

"I'm glad Dido doesn't talk to Aeneas," Vesta, never a fan of the Roman founder, says.

"She should have done more than just give him the cold shoulder," Athena says, tugging her unraveling cuffs over her wrists. "People . . . people who hurt other people . . ."

Vesta starts to hum the Barbra Streisand song, "People, people who need people . . ."

"Can it, Vesta," Athena screams, clutching her *Aeneid* as if she were going to hurl it at her classmate.

"*Puellae!*" I say rising to my feet and clapping my hands. "*Tacete!*"

Both my students glare at me.

"What's up with you girls?"

"We're just tired and we've got a big chemistry exam with Moldy Todd next period."

I can't help but laugh at the sobriquet, even though I know it's the height of unprofessionalism. At least it gains me a smile from Vesta, but Athena glares all the harder at our shared mirth.

"Vesta," I say, "why don't you go out in the hall? I'll give you both some extra time to study; I just want to have a word with Athena."

Athena rolls her eyes—overdoing, I think, the role of student asked to stay after class.

"Hey," I say when Vesta is gone, "I thought we were friends. What's bothering you?"

"People . . ." remembering Vesta's jibe she amends, "some of the girls are making fun of me because of this." She holds up her arm and shakes her wrist so that the loose sweater cuff falls down to her elbow. "And it's not fair. I haven't cut myself since last year. Someone else did this."

"You mean Melissa?"

Athena shrugs and wipes her eyes with the back of her hand, giving me an even better view of the savaged skin. "Well, Dr. Lockhart keeps telling me it was Melissa, but I still find it hard to believe. I mean, we were friends . . ."

"*Keeps telling?*" I ask. "How often do you see Dr. Lockhart?"

"Twice a week, which, like, really sucks. She keeps asking me how it made me feel to have my roommate kill herself. Like what am I going to say? It makes me feel good? It makes me feel like shit—sorry—but it doesn't make me want to off myself. She acts like killing yourself is a kind of germ and maybe I've got it. The other girls act that way, too, like I've got cooties or something."

I almost laugh at the childish term, something Olivia would say, but stop myself.

"I know what you mean. When one of my roommates killed herself my other roommate and I had to go to counseling."

"Did it bother you?"

"Well, I didn't love it, but it really drove my other roommate crazy."

"Yeah, it would." Athena gives me a small, tentative smile. "People thinking you're crazy could make you go crazy."

The smile encourages me to reach out and rub her arm. "Well, you'll just have to prove them wrong." The advice comes out a little forced, a little too cheerleaderish, but Athena nods and dries her eyes and tries another smile.

"Thanks, *Magistra,*" she says gathering her books to go, "that's the best argument I've heard for not plunging through the ice and drowning myself."

DURING LUNCH I KEEP REPLAYING ATHENA'S LAST WORDS, trying to convince myself that it's a coincidence that the method of suicide she chose to cite was the way Matt and Lucy died. What I can't help thinking, though, is that if someone were playing out the events from twenty years ago, that would be the next method of death. I'm roused from these morose musings by a harsh, jangling sound in my ears. I look up and see Dr. Lockhart standing by the empty seat next to me, dangling a silver key chain in her right hand and absentmindedly shaking it while she answers a question from Gwen Marsh.

"No, Gwen, I don't think we should cancel midterms because the girls are having a tough semester," she says. When she sits down she lays the keys next to her plate. Not only doesn't this woman carry a tote bag bursting with books or papers like the rest of us, she doesn't even feel the need of a purse or pockets. No doubt the clutter would disrupt the line of her tailored suits.

I reach into the pocket of my baggy cardigan and find a pen, chalk stubs, and a note I confiscated from one of my sixth graders. I take the wadded paper out of my pocket and see that it's a "cootie catcher"—a fortune-telling device popular with prepubescent girls. There are colored dots on the outside folds and numbers on the inside, which you pick to find out which flaps to open.

Gwen Marsh reaches over and takes the cootie catcher from my hands. "Ooh, I loved those when I was a girl. Let me tell you your fortune." She slips her fingers into the folds. "Pick a color."

"Green," I tell her.

"G-r-e-e-n." Gwen opens and shuts the paper mouth for each letter. When she's done she asks me to pick a number.

"Three."

"One, two, three, open the door to your destiny."

I reach to open the flap but Gwen's already folded it back, " 'You are such a fake, go drown in the lake.' Oh my," she says. "We had stuff like, 'You will marry a millionaire.' You see, Candace, what I meant about the girls being under so much pressure. How can we give the midterms . . ."

"If you go easy on them, they'll take advantage of you," Dr. Lockhart says, rising from the table even though she has barely touched her lunch.

"I don't think my girls take advantage of me," Gwen says. "They mean everything to me . . . this school . . . it means everything. . . ." Her voice wobbling between tears and anger trails after Dr. Lockhart.

I wonder if she'll turn back, but it's Dean Buehl who calls her back to the table. "Candace, you've left your keys again, here." Dean Buehl scoops the keys up and tosses them to her. She catches them neatly in one hand and turns to go without a thank-you to Dean Buehl or a word or apology to Gwen.

Gwen sniffs noisily. "Well, I'm still going to bring up the issue at today's faculty meeting."

"We have a faculty meeting today?" I ask.

I hear Myra Todd click her tongue at my forgetfulness and what she no doubt believes to be my reluctance to attend. But she's wrong. Although I usually hate faculty meetings, it's given me an idea. I've finally hit on what's been bothering me about my talk with Athena this morning. It wasn't just the comment about plunging through the ice. When I told Athena that my high school roommate killed herself she wasn't surprised. It's something she could only know if she had read my old journal. It makes me wonder what's been going on at those twice weekly sessions with Dr. Lockhart. I remember a pale green folder with Athena's name on it in Dr. Lockhart's file cabinet and I'm quite sure that the key to that file cabinet, and to her office door, will be lying on the table at tonight's meeting.

I ARRIVE EARLY TO THE MEETING, BUT THEN LOITER AT THE door to the Music Room, pretending to read the notices on the bulletin board. Along with the usual chess club and suicide intervention group notices there's a new flyer with a black-and-white photocopy of an old Currier and Ives print. The print is of a frozen pond. A horse stands in the middle of the pond, harnessed to a wagon filled with what look like giant sugar cubes. In the right foreground stooped figures stand around a hole in the ice. One of the figures holds a long, spear-tipped rod which he uses to prod a square of ice. In the left foreground a slant-roofed shed, which looks exactly like the Schwanenkill icehouse, stands at the edge of the ice. In the background, tiny figures skate on the ice.

"ICE HARVEST MEETING TONIGHT," it says under the picture. "8:00 P.M. IN THE MUSIC ROOM. SLIDE SHOW AND LECTURE BY MAIA THORNBURY, COUNTY EXTENSION AGENT." Under the typed print someone has hand-drawn, in jagged print intended to look like icicles, but which look more like daggers, a promise of ice pops for refreshments. The notice is dated yesterday. It's just the type of thing I should be attending to get back in Dean Buehl's good graces.

"Jane," I hear from behind me, "are you interested in the ice harvest?"

I turn to Dean Buehl. "Yes," I say, "I'm sorry I missed this, I was busy sewing stolas for our Lupercalia Festival." The lie comes so easily to me that I blush with shame at myself.

"Well, then you're in luck," Myra Todd, coming up behind Dean Buehl, informs me. "The meeting was postponed till tonight right after the faculty meeting. I could use some help bringing the ice pops up from the basement freezer."

Before I can think up an excuse, some classical garment I need to sew, like Penelope's shroud perhaps, Myra Todd passes me and goes into the Music Room. I can see the table is filling up. If Dr. Lockhart doesn't get here soon I won't get a seat next to her.

I see her then, descending the main stairs unhurriedly, the silver key chain dangling from her right forefinger. I try not to look at the keys as she comes up to me in the doorway.

"Dr. Lockhart!" I say cheerily. "Are you going to the Ice Harvest meeting later?"

She looks at me as if I've taken leave of my senses, but at least it makes her slow her pace enough so we walk into the room together. "I think it's appalling," she says, as she makes for a solitary seat at the near end of the table. "It'll ruin the lake for skating."

"Why, you're right," I say, enthusiastically grabbing her elbow and steering her toward two seats at the far end of the table. "I hadn't thought of that. Let's sit together and oppose the project." I feel her arm flinch away from my touch, but she allows herself to be herded into the chair next to mine. I watch to see if she'll lay the key chain on the table, but instead she folds her hands in her lap, keeping the key chain between them. At lunch she needed her hands to eat, but here she could keep her hands in her lap the whole time.

Dean Buehl is calling the meeting to order. I notice that most of my colleagues have produced paper and pens for note taking. I scramble in my tote bag and find a Xeroxed handout I'd prepared for the senior class. It's a maze I drew of Aeneas's route to the underworld that can only be solved by following a word trail. You have to connect an adjective to the noun it modifies and then find a verb to match the noun, and so on and so on. I am quite proud of it and I admire it for a moment before turning it over and scribbling the date and "faculty meeting" on the reverse side. Dr. Lockhart apparently feels no compulsion to take notes.

The first order of business is reviewing the costs of snowplowing the main paths and installing the new lighting system.

Myra Todd, who serves as secretary to the Board of Trustees, reports that the costs were approved by the board, but that the board expressed concern over any further expenditure, "especially considering that the school's lease is coming up this spring."

I scribble "What lease?" on the back of my handout and slide the paper over to Dr. Lockhart's place at the table. She scowls at me and waves her right hand, which, I notice, no longer holds the keys, dismissively.

When the financial business is concluded, Dean Buehl asks Dr. Lockhart to report on the status of the suicide intervention program.

"We haven't lost any more students, have we?" Simon Ross says loudly. "So I guess it's going pretty well."

Dr. Lockhart gives Ross a withering look as she rises from the table. I notice that, in rising, Dr. Lockhart has placed the key chain on the table.

"I've had three girls come to me complaining of nightmares about Melissa Randall's death. Curiously, the common thread in these nightmares seems to be a conviction that somehow Melissa is still in the lake, below the ice."

I think of my dream of the figures trapped in the crevasse. I feel suddenly cold. I reach into my bag for my sweater, but instead of pulling it out I haul the bag onto the table with a loud thump. Myra Todd purses her lips at me and makes a shushing sound. I smile apologetically.

"Several girls have also reported that the noises from the lake keep them up at night. They think that the noises are the moans of the dead girl." Dr. Lockhart raises her voice to be heard over the commotion I am making with my tote bag, but otherwise she doesn't in any way acknowledge the disruption I'm causing during her speech. In pulling out my sweater, my Cassell's *Latin-English Dictionary* and *Oxford History of the Classical World* thud noisily to the table and slide onto the floor.

"Such ignorance!" Myra Todd exclaims.

I lift my head, thinking she's talking about my behavior, but I see that even my rudeness at a faculty meeting can't compete with attributing superstitious beliefs to a natural phenomenon.

"I've explained again and again," Myra says, thumping her hand on the table with each "again," "about contraction and expansion of the ice, but they just don't get it!"

"You're the one who doesn't get it."

Everyone at the table stares at Gwen Marsh. Two red spots have appeared on her face. I've never seen her this angry. I'm so taken aback that I forget my plans to get the key for a moment.

"Don't you see what a shock Melissa Randall's death has been to them? They haven't just lost a friend, they've lost their faith in Heart Lake. It's supposed to be a haven for them, a safe place to come back to, a place where everybody knows them . . ."

Someone, I can't tell who, starts humming the theme song to "Cheers."

"You can mock if you like, but unless we go easier on them there will be another death."

"If we go easier on them," Dr. Lockhart says in slow, measured tones, "we're enabling their helplessness."

"I am not an enabler!" she says so shrilly that I wonder if she's been accused of this before. I reach over to touch her arm and she shrieks.

"That's my bad arm, Jane. You know that." She stands up and leaves the room. Everyone watches her go. Except me. I use the moment to sweep my books, along with Dr. Lockhart's keys, into my tote bag. As soon as I've got them, I rise from my seat.

"I'll go after her," I say, and I'm out the door before anyone else can offer to help.

I sprint up the main stairs to the second floor and head, not to the Lake Lounge, but to Dr. Lockhart's office. At the door to her office I have to dig in my bag to find the keys, and when I do find them the metal slips greasily through my sweaty fingers. The first key I try doesn't fit. The second does, but it won't turn. I remember that in my old dorm room you had to pull the door toward you to make the key turn. I pull the knob toward me and the door bangs against its frame so loudly the sound echoes down the hallway. I stop to look down toward the stairs, but then feel the key turn and the door, taken by a draft in the hall, pulls me into the dark office.

I have to push the door against the draft to close it and again the sound it makes is horribly loud. I'm afraid to risk turning on the light, but fortunately, Dr. Lockhart has left her drapes open and the moon reflecting off the lake fills the room with silvery light. The varnished wood of her desk, which is empty except for some stone paperweights, gleams in the moonlight like a pool of still water. The round stones cast elliptical shadows on the smooth surface. I pick up one and immediately feel that I've disrupted some pattern that Dr. Lockhart will notice has been disturbed.

I place the stone back again, aligning it with the other two in what I hope is the same spot, and cross to the file cabinet. The middle drawer, I remember. The little key opens the drawer, which slides silently forward on its metal casters. I walk my fingers along the tops of the files, which are neatly labeled in an elegant, sloping script. They're arranged alphabetically within class years, so I find "Craven, Ellen" about two thirds through the drawer. I pull out the pale green folder and move into the moonlight to read its contents.

The first few pages are the standard forms everyone at the school fills out. I notice that Athena's parents are divorced and that the emergency contact number is an aunt in Connecticut. I flip through the pink insurance forms and Athena's transcripts from previous schools. She started at Dalton, transferred to Miss Trimingham's in Connecticut, and then went to some place called the Village School in southern Vermont. Her grades had gone from A's and B's at the good schools to C's and D's at the worse schools. While she worked her way up the northern seaboard, she'd been steadily sliding down the academic scale.

Until this semester at Heart Lake. In the first quarter she'd still gotten mostly C's except for the B I'd given her in Latin. In the second quarter she'd gotten an A in Latin and Bs in the rest of her subjects. It looked like she was trying to turn herself around. So why did she seem so out of sorts? And why was she seeing Dr. Lockhart twice a week?

I turn next to a sheaf of handwritten notes on unlined paper. The date of each session is entered in a beautiful flowing script in the right-hand margin. The notes are in the same precise and elegant hand, written apparently with a fountain pen. I've never seen notes taken from a psychiatric session, but I would have imagined that there would be cross-outs, abbreviations, additions in the margins. There are none. Dr. Lockhart wrote from one margin to the other in a steady, slanting script. The sentences could have been exercises from a calligraphy workbook.

The story they tell flows smoothly from one session to the next. If not for the dates in the margins I would think I was reading from a novel. What stands out the most, though, is the compassion Dr. Lockhart feels for her patient.

"Ellen has been shuttled from one institution to the next with little concern for her emotional well-being," I read. "Such displacement readily explains her tendencies toward depression and self-loathing. No wonder she inflicts harm on herself when the adults closest to her take so little responsibility for her."

Farther down the same page I read, "Ellen claims to have made several friends here at Heart Lake. It is obvious, though, that she has become emotionally dependent on these girls to an unhealthy degree. She would do anything to keep their friendship. Clearly she is using these friendships as a replacement for the affection she's failed to receive from her mother." This interpretation has never occurred to me and I'm ashamed at myself for having had so little insight into my student—a student whom I thought I was close to. It's even more chastening to see here Dr. Lockhart's empathy for Athena's situation. In fact her notes read not so much like a transcription from oral conversation as a direct channeling from Athena's mind onto the page—as if Dr. Lockhart had access not only to her mind but to her heart and soul.

I notice, too, that as I page through the stack of notes, the handwriting changes. It becomes not exactly messier so much as tighter, as if Dr. Lockhart were trying to cram more into each line, as if the story she were getting from Athena threatened to swell beyond the confines of the written words. I have to move closer to the window to make it out.

"While it is probably true that the suicide attempt in October was faked, it is unlikely that Ellen had no complicity in it. It is more likely that she agreed to fake the suicide attempt to assist her friends in their persecution of Jane Hudson. Clearly their attempt is to discredit their teacher and get her fired."

I am so startled by the appearance of my name that for a moment the words in front of me blur. Has Athena truly revealed some calculated plot to torture me? Or is this Dr. Lockhart's interpretation? The notes are maddeningly obtuse, and now, nearly illegible. I take another step closer to the window and realize, finally, that the reason I can't see is that the moonlight is gone.

I look up at the window, expecting, I think, to find it blocked by some hovering figure outside the glass. But that's ridiculous. Dr. Lockhart's office is on the second floor. It's only a cloud passing over the moon that has blocked the light. As I watch, the moon reemerges and its white light pours down on the curved rock face of the Point so that I can see, directly across from me at roughly the same level as this second-floor window, a figure standing close to the edge of the cliff. The figure lifts its arm to its forehead so that for a moment I have the absurd notion it's waving at me. But then I see a glint of moonlight on glass and realize it's worse; the figure on the Point—whoever it is—is watching me through binoculars.

Chapter Twenty-nine

●

I LOWER THE FOLDER TO THE DESK AND THE FIGURE ON THE Point eerily mirrors the motion by lowering its own arm. For a moment I feel as if I'm looking into a mirror and I briefly wonder which would be worse, for the figure on the Point to be a figment of my imagination or a real observer who's caught me ransacking school property? But then the figure turns and disappears into the woods. A moment later it reappears on the path leading toward the mansion.

"OK," I whisper under my breath, "better it's real and I'm not going crazy, but still, that's a real person heading this way."

I know I should leave right away, but I'm compelled to read to the end of Athena's file. I scan through the remaining pages looking for my name, searching for some explanation of why my students would want to persecute me. Instead I find something finally in Athena's own words.

"When asked how she feels about her teachers, Ellen replied, 'Miss Hudson acts like she really cares.' I asked her why she used the word 'acts.' Did she think Miss Hudson was faking her concern? She said that she'd had a lot of teachers who had seemed to care about her, but in the end they'd never go out of their way to help her. In the end they were too wrapped up in their own problems. 'It's not like I'm her kid or anything,' Ellen told me. 'She has a daughter.' I asked if she felt jealous of Miss Hudson's daughter and she claimed she did not, but . . ."

Here the handwriting becomes so cramped I can't make it out. I flip to the last entry. It's dated today. I read the last line and then hurriedly reorder the papers and place them back in the green folder. I check the path again before putting the folder back in the file drawer. Both the path and the Point are empty.

I lock the file cabinet and let myself out of the office, holding the door carefully so it won't bang again in its frame. As I head down the stairs I find myself repeating the last lines of Dr. Lockhart's notes on Athena.

"A person who has been shut out from love her whole life may form unhealthily close attachments. When someone (a teacher or an older girl) finally seems to care about her she may become obsessed with that person. If that person fails her, betrayal may be shattering. There's no telling what the betrayed one might do."

DOWNSTAIRS I FIND THAT THE FACULTY MEETING HAS BROKEN up and students are filing in for the Ice Harvest slide show. There are quite a few students. Either they are really bored or some teacher has offered extra credit for attendance.

Myra Todd, who is rearranging chairs for the slide show, scowls when she sees me. "There you are. Did you find Gwendoline?"

"No," I say. "I looked all over the building for her, but she must have gone outside."

"That's just great. She was supposed to get the ice pops and run the slide projector. How am I supposed to get this meeting started on my own?"

"Where are Dean Buehl and Dr. Lockhart?"

"Dr. Lockhart misplaced her keys, so she went to her car for her extra set. Dean Buehl and the extension agent went out to look at the lake and decide where to cut the ice."

"I see. Well, I guess I can get the ice pops."

"Do you know where the freezer is in the basement?"

"Sure, the cook used to send us down for stuff all the time."

"Well, it would be a help . . . ," Myra says, "but you won't be able to carry them all—I've had my girls making them for a week now."

"I'll take a student," I suggest. I notice Athena and Vesta milling around the front of the room near the slide carousel. Octavia and Flavia are skulking at the back of the room, embarrassed, I think, to be seen by me after defecting from the class. Several of my eighth graders are clustered at the door, their heads bent together over something. As I approach them I see one girl is holding another cootie catcher. Her fingers open and close the folded paper so quickly it's like watching a speeded up film of a flower opening and closing. When the girls see me approaching they whisper to the girl holding the cootie catcher and the white flower disappears in a blur into a pocket.

I change my mind and head over to Athena and Vesta. "Would one of you like to help me bring up ice pops from the basement?"

Vesta stares at me blankly as if I were speaking a foreign language.

"I'll do it, *Magistra,*" Athena says, rolling her eyes at Vesta. "Miss Pruneface is in a bad mood. She failed her chemistry exam and had to show up here for the extra credit."

"Shut up, *Ellen*. I wouldn't have failed the exam if you hadn't kept me up half the night with your light on. Baby's afraid of the dark," Vesta says sneeringly to me. "She's afraid the lake monster's gonna get her. Afraid the curse of the Crevecoeurs is gonna make her off herself."

I see Athena's already pale skin go a shade paler. "Cunt-sucking dyke," she says very quietly, and then turns on her heel and heads out the door. I follow her.

I catch up to Athena on the stairs leading down to the basement. "Why are you and Vesta fighting?"

"She's such a bitch, *Magistra* Hudson. She's acting like I really tried to kill myself in October. She says she doesn't believe it was Melissa who cut my wrists . . ." Athena's voice cracks and trails off.

She turns from me and puts her head against the wall at the bottom of the stairs. The only light down here is a naked bulb hanging from a wire at the foot of the stairs. The walls of the basement are bare, damp, moss-covered rock that swallow up the faint light and smell like dead fish. The Crevecoeur family carved the cellar out of the living rock and used the natural springs to keep their food cold down here. I shiver and wonder what the hell they needed to cut up ice from the lake for. It's cold as the grave down here.

"There's nothing to be ashamed about," I tell Athena. I'm thinking about Dr. Lockhart's notes. What she said about Athena being in on the faked suicide. I touch her arm and she turns on me. I see such fury in her eyes that I instinctively step away from her and back up against the cold stone wall.

"You don't believe me either," she says. "I thought you were different."

When someone finally seems to care about her she may become obsessed with that person.

"Athena, I do want to help you, but I can't do that unless I understand what's been going on." Because of the cold my voice shakes and it makes my words sound to my own ears nervous and false. Athena wraps her arms around her chest and glares at me. The lightbulb hanging above us makes her eyes glitter feverishly. The shadows make her multicolored, jaggedly cut hair look even wilder than usual.

But if that person fails her, the betrayal may be shattering.

Athena looks like someone who has been shattered. In fact, Athena looks like the madwoman in the attic from *Jane Eyre*. Only we're in the basement not the attic. I can feel icy water dripping down between my shoulder blades. I would far prefer an attic to this basement.

"You know what's going on," she says. I start to shake my head, but I see she's not looking at me any more. "It's the Crevecoeur curse," she says.

"Athena, that's just a story . . ."

"It's what made those girls drown themselves in the lake. You should know—it happened to your friends and now it's happening to us. It's because you came back. The lake wants the third girl. That's what the motto means: *Cor te reducit.* The heart—meaning Heart Lake—pulls you in."

I am about to correct her translation, but then I realize she's right. Leads back, pulls in, both are acceptable translations for *reducit.*

"How do you know about my friends?"

Athena shrugs and wipes her eyes. The gesture makes her look like a tired child. It reminds me of Olivia. I want to tell her that—that she reminds me of my own daughter—but I remember what Athena said to Dr. Lockhart. *It's not like I'm her kid or anything.* I picture Olivia standing on the rock. Could it have been Athena who lured her there? Out of some obsessive jealousy?

Athena sees, I think, the look of suspicion on my face.

"Someone told me," she says. "I don't remember who. I bet you've felt bad about it all this time—about your friends dying."

How can I deny it? I nod.

"It feels pretty shitty when you let someone down, doesn't it?"

I nod again. *There's no telling what the betrayed one might do.*

"Don't worry," Athena says, almost kindly. "It's not half as bad as being the person who's let down."

BY THE TIME WE GET UPSTAIRS WITH THE ICE POPS, THE lecture is already in progress. There aren't two seats together, so Athena takes a seat at the end of a middle row. A few rows behind her, Octavia and Flavia reluctantly make room for me to sit between them. I look around for Vesta, but don't see her. Dr. Lockhart is sitting in the first row. If it's possible for good posture to convey disapproval her ramrod-straight spine is speaking volumes of contempt for the proceedings.

I notice that Gwen is back and that she's manning the slide projector. I try to catch her eye, but she stares resolutely ahead at the screen.

Meryl North presents a short lecture on the history of ice harvesting in the Northeast. She tells us that giant ice blocks could be preserved in sawdust so well that blocks were shipped as far as India. Tacy Beade presents her idea for using the harvested ice for ice sculptures. She shows some slides of Michelangelo's series of unfinished statues called "The Captives." "Michelangelo believed the figures were in the stone waiting for the sculptor to free them," she concludes. "Who knows what figures we'll find hiding in the ice."

There's a smattering of embarrassed applause as Miss Beade goes back to her seat. "Figures hiding in the ice," I hear Simon Ross whisper. "Where has she been all year? Does she even know there's been a death on campus?"

Maia Thornbury takes the floor to present a history of ice harvesting on the Crevecoeur estate. She is a small, middle-aged gnome with a cap of graying hair cut in a style that I think used to be called a Prince Valiant. Her round eyeglasses reflect the mote-filled light from the slide projector and make her face appear even rounder. After all these years hearing about the county extension agent this is the first time I've actually seen her. I remember how we worried she would catch us using the boat and that she was the one who found Matt on May Day. I had always pictured her as some imposing, Girl Scout Valkyrie. She is all of four feet five. More wood sprite than Valkyrie.

"The Crevecoeur family were descended from the Huguenots who fled religious persecution in their native France in the seventeenth century," she lectures. I can hear several girls yawning. They must really want those popsicles or else they really need that extra credit. "Unlike most of the Huguenots, who settled in communities farther south along the Hudson or in New York City, the Crevecoeurs preferred solitude and self-sufficiency."

The screen darkens and then resolves into muted tones of brown and white. A row of men with old-fashioned sideburns and tall, sturdy women with strong, square jaws stand in front of a small slant-roofed hut. The women are carrying tin milk pails.

"Like most Frenchmen, the Crevecoeurs loved their homemade cheeses and butter, but they needed ice to keep them fresh in the humid Adirondack summers."

The sideburned men and square-jawed women fade and a family portrait of the Crevecoeurs, in full skating regalia posed on the ice, appears. I've seen the picture before—it's the same one that hangs in this room right behind where the slide projector screen hangs now—so I recognize India Crevecoeur as the stately matron in the foreground, her head tilted coquettishly under a fur cloche. Although it is hard to connect the woman in the picture to the desiccated old woman who accosted me on May Day junior year, I do recognize the arrogant glint in her eyes that I saw in the old woman when she realized that her former maid's granddaughter was attending her school. I remember that the way she looked at me made me feel like an impostor, and that's just how I feel now. The caring teacher. *One of Helen Chambers's girls.*

The two blond amazons on either side of India must be her older daughters, Rose and Lily. A little to the right, a smaller girl stands unsteadily on the ice, her arms held akimbo for balance. I recognize the plain sepia face from my dream of the night before; it's Iris Crevecoeur, who died in the flu epidemic of 1918. I wonder if Maia Thornbury will mention her, maybe this would be a good opportunity to point out that one girl died, not three, and so dispel the legend. Looking at the skinny, sallow girl next to her fair, hearty sisters it's not surprising that she was the one to fall victim to illness. The way the servant hovers anxiously over her—my grandmother— also says something about her frailty. But Maia Thornbury doesn't bring up Iris Crevecoeur's fate; she has another ax to grind.

"India Crevecoeur and her daughters loved to skate on the lake, but their favorite activity was attending the annual ice harvest."

If Dr. Lockhart's spine could get any straighter it does so now. I've always wondered why she seems to dislike me and now I think I know. Twice a week she listens to Athena talk about me, about how I pretend to care but really don't. No wonder she seems to see right through me.

The next slide shows the icehouse from the lake. A long narrow channel has been cut out of the ice leading to the open doors. On one side of the channel a muffled figure leans over the ice with what looks like a large saw. Another figure holds a long pole up toward the camera. He looks like an angry Eskimo shaking his spear at an intruder.

"After the snow was scraped off the ice, saws were used to cut out a 'header'—a channel through which the ice could be moved through the water to the icehouse. Then a plow marked out cakes of ice. Pike poles were used to push the cakes of ice down the channel and onto a conveyer belt into the icehouse. Would someone turn on the lights for a moment?"

I close my eyes against the sudden light and when I open them I see Maia Thornbury wielding a spear-tipped pole nearly twice her height. She shakes the pole with both hands. Perhaps my original idea of her as Valkyrie wasn't so far off.

"This is one of the original poles used on the Crevecoeur estate for ice harvesting. It's eight feet long."

"Oooh," someone coos, "what a long pole you have there."

The girls giggle while the teachers make shushing noises.

"Is that point sharp?" someone else asks.

"Oh yes," Maia Thornbury says, hefting the pole up and angling it so we can all see the six-inch-long steel tip. "It had to be to grip the ice. Would you like to touch it?"

More hysterical giggling as the girl who spoke rises from her chair. I'm surprised to see it's Athena. I wouldn't have expected her to express such an interest in ice harvesting after our scene in the basement, but here she is, walking up to the front of the room where the extension agent holds the pole parallel to the floor. As Athena walks toward the spear I have the disturbing thought that this is how Roman senators killed themselves: by falling on their own swords. I am poised to rush toward Athena, but she only lifts her arm and touches the point of the spear with the tip of her index finger.

"Sharp, isn't it?" Maia Thornbury asks like a magician testing the veracity of some trick with a volunteer from the audience.

Athena nods without taking her eyes off the spear point. Then she turns and walks back to her seat. Before the lights go out I see her look down at her finger, to a drop of blood poised there. Then she puts the finger in her mouth and sucks.

"To celebrate the ice harvest, the villagers carved decorative statues out of the ice," Maia Thornbury says as the lights go out. I am still looking at Athena when the next slide appears, so when I hear the rest of the audience gasp I have the awful thought that there's been some accident with the ice pole. But when I look up I see it's the slide that has made everyone gasp. This picture is in color. It shows a girl, nearly naked except for some flimsy white drapery, stretched out on the second sister stone. The girl and stone are so pale they could be almost mistaken for some particularly skillful ice sculpture. Except for the gash of bright red blood across her throat. I immediately recognize the girl as Lucy, but it takes me a few moments to recollect where the picture is from. As the lights go on and Dean Buehl tries to calm the now hysterical girls I try in vain to explain to someone that what the picture portrays isn't real. It's just Lucy Toller playing Agamemnon's daughter in our senior year production of *Iphigenia on the Beach*.

By the time I make my way to the front of the room I can see that my explanation won't help. Dr. Lockhart is arguing with Myra Todd about the wisdom of going on with the ice harvest given the inevitable connotations the girls will now have. Maia Thornbury is going over her numbered slides with Dean Buehl to prove to her that the picture of the slaughtered girl was not part of her original demonstration. The slide itself has been passed from Maia Thornbury to Meryl North to Gwen Marsh to Dr. Lockhart to Myra Todd, and, finally, to Dean Buehl, so any fingerprints that might have been found on it are probably now obscured. I surprise myself by thinking of fingerprints. Could I, perhaps, take this slide to Roy Corey and ask for it to be fingerprinted? Maybe, but now it's too late. I promise myself, though, that if any other relic from my past shows up I'm taking it straight to him. I pick up the slide now and look at it. Lucy as Iphigenia. I remember watching the play from the eastern shore of the lake. This picture shows the reflection of the setting sun on the side of the rock nearest to the camera, so it must have been taken from the opposite side.

Someone plucks the slide from my fingers. "Like a scene from a Greek tragedy, don't you think, Miss Hudson?" Dr. Lockhart smiles at me as she slips the slide into a plastic bag. I'm not sure if she means the slide itself, or the furor its appearance has caused.

"I was thinking we could have it fingerprinted," I say, even though I had already rejected that idea.

"How convenient then that there will be an explanation for your prints on it," Dr. Lockhart replies as she hands the bag to Dean Buehl.

"I guess the same goes for you," I say. "Since you handled the slide as well." I hadn't really planned to insinuate that Dr. Lockhart could have been responsible for planting the slide, but as I see her already pale skin go a shade paler it occurs to me that it could have been her as well as anyone else. I wonder, though, how she could have come by it in the first place.

IT'S AFTER ELEVEN BY THE TIME I LEAVE THE MANSION AND walk back to my cottage. I take the same path that the person I saw on the Point would have taken. I look at the packed snow underfoot for some clue, but dozens of people have traversed the path since the last snow. I pause on the Point and look back toward the mansion. I can see Dr. Lockhart's window. Although the office is unlit I can see now how the light from the hall filters in and makes the interior room faintly visible. A person standing in there would only appear as a vague outline, though, like the shadowy shape her desk and filing cabinet make now. I turn from the Point and follow the path to my cottage, which is less trodden than the path from the Point to the mansion. Still I can tell that someone else has been walking there since the last snow.

When I get to my house I see that the porch light has burned out again. It takes me a moment to fit the key in the lock, and when I do my hand is trembling so hard I can't make the lock turn. And why shouldn't I be afraid? I ask myself. Someone obviously bears me some grudge.

"Then why not just come out and knock me over the head or something," I say aloud to my own door. "Get it over with. Why so coy?" My voice, I notice, sounds more angry than afraid. Good, I think. I'm tired of this game of signs.

As I enter the house I feel sure that someone has been there in my absence. I am not afraid, though, that the intruder is still there. Whoever it was would have gone back to the slide show. Why miss out on the fun? I go through the rooms, flicking on the lights, scanning the walls and tabletops for something missing, or something new. I'm expecting, I don't know what. Some bloody scrawl on the walls? For the first time it occurs to me that whoever is sending these signs is as frightened of me as I am of her. Whoever she is, and I'm certain it is a she, was silent until I talked to Roy Corey in the cave. Then she sent the corniculum. Tonight, when she saw me in Dr. Lockhart's office, she retaliated by dropping that slide in Maia Thornbury's carousel. It's as if we are playing tug-of-war with the past, you look into my past, she is telling me, then I'll fling your past back at you.

"Well, what have you got for me tonight," I call into the empty rooms. When I get to my bedroom and see the lump under the bed-clothes and what's seeping from that lump my bravado fades.

"Oh, fuck," I cry as I fling the blankets off the bloody deer's head. "Fuck, fuck, fuck," I say maybe a dozen times over until I real-ize it's only a felt mask of a deer's head, with red paint dripping from its felt neck.

Chapter Thirty

●

"Do you recognize this?" I ask, flinging the mask on Roy Corey's desk. It nearly topples a Styrofoam cup half-filled with grayish coffee, but I am not sorry. I have been wanting, since eleven o'clock last night, to fling the mask at *someone*. After a sleepless night I called Dean Buehl to cancel my classes.

"I was up all night with a toothache," I lied, "I've got to go into town and have this thing out."

She seemed neither suspicious nor interested in my excuse. "I'll have your girls help Maia Thornbury with the ice harvest," she told me.

"It's still on?" I asked.

"I will not let some saboteur change my plans," Dean Buehl replied. "That would be like giving in to the demands of terrorists."

Apparently I was not the only one tired of this game of cat and mouse.

"Hey watch . . . ," Roy Corey says looking up from the mask to me, but when he sees my expression he stops the complaint he'd been forming. He looks back down at the mask, picks it up, sniffs at the dried red paint and inspects the stitching along its seams.

"Look familiar?" I ask.

To my surprise, Roy Corey turns white.

"It's not real blood," I say, my anger deflected by his reaction.

"Why don't you have a seat, Jane?"

"You recognize it, don't you?"

Roy picks away some of the red paint, revealing a green embroidered heart. "Where did you find it?"

"In my bed, a là *The Godfather*," I tell him. "Did you hear about the little surprise at our slide show?"

Roy nods. "Your dean called me last night. I went out there and took the carousel and slide. We're having both dusted for prints, but both were handled by so many people we don't expect much. This happened afterward?"

"When I went home. Which was around eleven."

"Must've given you quite a start."

I shrug. "I'm getting used to it." I tell him about the corniculum in the tree the night of the ice storm. "It was right after our conversation in the cave. Someone overheard us and then the signs started again."

He nods. "I thought they might."

"You bastard! You knew someone would eavesdrop on us in the cave."

"I couldn't be sure, but what with the whole school there on the ice, I thought it was possible someone might take advantage of the situation."

"You took advantage of me," I say rising to my feet. I wish I still had something to throw at him, but then I see the effect my words have had on him. It's as if I have thrown something at him. He's looking down at the mask, still fingering that green heart, as if he can't bear to look me in the eyes.

"It was only a matter of time before this person surfaced again. We're talking about a murderer—someone who drowned one teen-aged girl and drugged another and slit her wrists with a steak knife."

"Unless it was Athena who slit her own wrists."

"You mean a real suicide attempt?"

"I mean she faked her own 'suicide' and then killed Melissa." I tell Roy about the conversation I had with Athena in the basement.

I don't tell him about Dr. Lockhart's file because I'd rather not admit to breaking and entering, but I manage to filter some of the information I gleaned there into my observations. "I hate to think Athena's the one," I conclude, "I've always liked her and I thought she liked me, but now she feels I've let her down and she's gotten it into her head that I've started the whole Crevecoeur curse again since it was my roommates who died."

"How does she know about that?"

"I don't know. She'd know from the journal . . ." I pause, remembering something Athena said to me in the basement. "She said she knew I felt responsible for my friends' deaths. That's what I said to you in the cave, that I knew Deirdre's death wasn't an accident. So it might have been her listening to us in the cave." I sink back into my chair, exhausted and disheartened. I hadn't realized how much I'd wanted not to believe it was Athena who was trying to hurt me. I look at Roy, hoping he'll contradict my theory. He's still peeling the red paint away from the mask and smoothing the brown felt.

"Did she say anything else?"

"She said it felt pretty shitty to know you had let someone down, but worse to be the one who's let down."

Roy looks up from the mask. "I don't know about that," he says. "I think it's a draw. I think the guilt of hurting someone you care about can last a long time, maybe even longer than the love itself."

He whisks the red paint flakes off his desk with the side of his hand and crumples the mask in a ball.

"You mean Matt, don't you? You think he'd still be alive if you hadn't let him come back to Heart Lake that night?"

He nods. I try to think of something I could say to relieve his burden, one I understand only too well, but anything I say would only mean taking more of the burden on myself, and I don't feel up to that. Instead I throw him a crumb, a relic of the person we both miss. "You know," I say, "that's the mask Matt wore that morning. His was the one embroidered with the green heart. He must have dropped it in the woods and someone found it."

Roy looks at me through narrow, tired eyes and sighs. He gets up and passes behind me to close the office door. When he comes back he doesn't sit down behind his desk, but instead sits on its edge, so close to me the stiff cloth of his uniform brushes my leg and I can see the fine red hairs on his arms where he's rolled up his sleeves. He's still holding the mask. His thumb brushes the last of the red paint off the green embroidered heart. *By this sign you'll know your heart's true love,* Deirdre had said, embroidering a different color heart, green, blue and yellow, on each mask.

"You're right that it was dropped in the woods, Jane. And I suppose someone must have found it there. But this isn't the mask Matt wore, Jane."

"But I saw that green heart . . ." I stop and look up at him, into familiar green eyes.

"This is the mask I wore."

I AM STILL LIGHT-HEADED DRIVING BACK TO HEART LAKE. Exhaustion, I tell myself, fear and aggravation and frustration. All natural emotions considering what I've been through. But I know it's something else. Since that moment in Roy Corey's office when I realized who it was I was with that May Day morning all those years ago I have felt something vibrating through my core, like a hot wire snaking up from the base of my spine. When I touch the cold metal handle of my car door I'm surprised I don't set off sparks in the dry air. I feel electric.

"So what," I had said over and over again to the hard glitter coming off the Hudson, "So what. So what." I had parked my car across from the old Toller house, facing the river, and waited for the hot, wobbly feeling to go away. "So it was Roy Corey I had sex with on May Day morning and not Matt Toller. What earthly difference does it make?"

By this sign you'll know your heart's true love.

Crap. It was just a stupid superstition Deirdre'd made up. Only I had believed it and believed, for all these years, that my heart's true love had drowned in the lake under the ice.

"Crap," I told myself, pulling into the faculty parking lot at Heart Lake. "Stupider than believing in the three sisters story and the curse of the Crevecoeurs. And it doesn't solve anything. Doesn't tell you who's sending these signs from the past or who killed Melissa Randall."

In the end Roy was unconvinced that it was Athena. But maybe that was because I didn't really want to convince him because I don't want to believe it's Athena either.

He thought it had to be someone connected with what happened to Matt and Lucy and Deirdre twenty years ago. Who else would know so much about what happened then? Who else could have found that mask, which Roy said he abandoned somewhere in the woods that morning. Helen Chambers was dead. Dean Buehl had been there, but why would she deliberately wreak havoc on her own school now? Didn't she have more to lose? I told Roy my suspicions about Dr. Lockhart—"She certainly wants to stop the ice harvest"—but neither of us could come up with a motive for the other events. What could she possibly have to do with what happened twenty years ago?

"Whoever it is obviously has some grudge against you, Jane. I'm not sure it's safe for you to stay in that isolated cottage all by yourself."

"Where do you suggest I stay?" I asked, half-shocking myself with the provocative tone of my own voice. I hadn't meant it to sound like that, had I? But I was disappointed when he only shrugged and suggested I stay in the mansion.

I shuddered, thinking about what Dr. Lockhart said about living in a fishbowl.

"The dorm then?"

I thought of the hothouse atmosphere of the dorm, the hissing steam radiators, all those girls in flannel nightgowns damp from just-washed hair. The rancid smell of burnt popcorn and face creams.

"No," I told Roy. "Like Dean Buehl says, that's like giving into the demands of terrorists. I'll be OK."

He'd looked at me in silence for a few moments and then leaned down to search for something in his drawer. A lock of hair fell over his forehead and, catching the light from the grimy window, briefly flamed red. When he lifted his head, his hair fell back, extinguishing the bright color so that I could see the ashy gray at his temples. "Here," he said, holding out something in a clear plastic bag. "I've been meaning to give this back to you. We don't need it for evidence anymore."

I look through the thick plastic and recognize my old journal. "Thanks," I say, trying not to sound too disappointed. I'd thought he was going to give me his phone number.

I GET OUT OF MY CAR AND WALK TOWARD MY HOUSE, BUT halfway there I hear shouts coming from the lake, so I cut through the woods and head out onto the Point. At first, when I see the black gash in the ice and the figures with poles I think the worst: Someone has fallen through a crack in the ice and they're trying to save her with long, lifesaving poles. I look for someone thrashing in the icy water, but instead I see a neat rectangle of ice floating down the dark channel toward the icehouse and I realize it's only the Ice Harvest.

They've made remarkable progress in such little time. Or else I've been gone longer than I realized. I look at my watch and see it's already four o'clock. I hadn't realized I'd spent so long in Roy's office—or sitting in my car looking at the river. While I've been gone, Maia Thornbury and the girls have cut out a long narrow channel, perhaps four feet across, from the icehouse at the southern tip of the lake to halfway to the Point. Some of the girls are wearing skates and others, under Gwen Marsh's direction, are wielding the long ice poles, pushing cakes of ice up onto a ramp into the icehouse. The scene is as cheerful and bucolic as the Currier and Ives print I'd seen on the flyer last night. In fact, it seems more populous than I would have thought possible. Everyone must be out.

Then I look again and see that some of the figures on the ice aren't people.

What I'd taken for stationary children dressed in white are actually statues carved out of ice. As I watch I see two girls carry a cake of ice from the icehouse and stack it on top of three or four more. Other girls are chipping away at stacks of ice to form rudimentary bodies. Tacy Beade is using a pick and hammer to shave the ice away. Even from here I can hear the steady thwack of metal hitting metal with a force that's alarming considering Beady's half blind. Chips of ice fly under her hands like sparks from a forge. The shape emerging, though crude, already has the feel and motion of the human form, something trying to break free of the encasing ice.

There are about a dozen of these figures standing on the lake. I can see now that they are half-formed and incomplete, but as the last rays of the sun catch each one they seem to gain a spark of life. I look directly below the Point and for an instant the whole lake seems to spin before my eyes. The sky on the eastern shore is black with storm cloud, so that the ice, lit by the low-lying sun, burns with a fierce, white light. Beside each of the sister stones stands an ice statue. Or rather the first one, the one closest to shore, stands. The second kneels, and the last one lies, supine on the white ice, only half of its body visible above the surface, so it's as if the girl is half in, half out of the lake, one arm lifted and crooked as if suspended in midstroke. But what really unnerves me is the impression made by the dark backdrop of storm cloud. It's as if the black water is rising from the ice and the pale figures are shapes seen underwater.

What I feel is a kind of seasickness. A vertigo of reversal. I tilt my chin up and focus on the horizon, a trick to avert motion sickness Miss Pike taught us when we went canoeing. At the horizon line of deep green pines I see a figure standing still as the trees. At first I think it's another ice statue, she's standing so still, but then I realize it's Dr. Lockhart. She's wearing her skates, but she isn't moving. When she sees me looking at her, though, she lifts out her arms and flexes her wrists, like a ballerina getting ready for a pirouette, and begins to spin, effortlessly, on her skates. She spins in a small tight circle, her skates sending up sprays of ice into the darkening air, like a whirlpool spiraling through dark water.

. . .

I GO BACK TO MY HOUSE AND EAT ALONE. I TELL MYSELF I don't want to get caught out in the approaching storm, but it's a weak excuse. Although the clouds in the east appear menacing and a wind has come up since the sun set, there's no snow in the forecast. Just wind and cold. On the television I tune into an Albany station just long enough to hear that electrical storms, rare for this time of year, have been reported in the southern Adirondacks, and then the broadcaster's face dissolves in a blizzard of static. I turn on the radio, but I can't even get the country-western station in Corinth.

The truth is that I don't want to talk to anyone. I can't imagine what Dean Buehl was thinking by going ahead with the Ice Harvest. And old Beady really must be senile as well as blind to have the girls make those macabre statues. I know it's all anyone will be talking about in the dining hall and I can't bear right now to field innocent questions about the three sisters legend. Even my cold, rattling cottage—shack, I think to myself tonight, it's really a shack—is more appealing than that.

So I turn up the heat as high as it goes and fry eggs over a gas burner that spits blue flames at the frying pan. Outside the wind seems to be moving in circles around the house, like an animal trying to get in. I put on wool socks and pad around on the worn rag rugs, pulling curtains shut and double-checking window locks. Twice I check the phone to make sure I've got a dial tone. The third time I pick up the phone I get such an electric shock I drop the heavy old-fashioned receiver on my toe. All that padding around in wool socks, I tell myself. Still, it keeps me away from the phone for the rest of the night, even though I'd been planning to call Olivia to remind her I'm coming this weekend. "I'll see her tomorrow," I tell myself, but I have to admit that part of the reason I don't call is that I've begun to detect a distance in her voice, a guardedness that I might cancel on her again.

I get in bed early. My old journal, that Roy gave me today, sits on my nightstand. I flip through it, not really reading, and notice that the pages flop loosely between their covers, like a person who's lost weight wearing old baggy pants. I remember that pages have been ripped out. I flip to the end and see that the very last page is missing. Yet that's not one of the pages that was sent to me.

I put the journal back on my nightstand and decide to read *The Aeneid*. Nothing like a little classical literature to calm the nerves, I think. Unfortunately, I'm at the part in Book Seven where Juno sends a fury to goad the Trojans and Latins into war. The description of the fury is so gruesome—*a shape-shifting monster writhing with snakes*—that I'm unable to read on. I remember that Helen Chambers told us that the Furies were sent out to avenge unavenged deaths. Curses personified, she said, the flip side of the three graces so beloved of Renaissance painters. I turn out the lights and burrow deep under the heavy wool blankets, covering my ears so that I won't hear the wind and imagine some grotesque avenging monster hovering above Heart Lake, sowing dissent and suspicion among us.

But I can't drown out the sound of the wind. And under the high-pitched keening of the wind I hear a lower sound, a deep basso profundo moan that makes my hair stand on end. I slowly lift the blankets away from me and a shower of sparks cascades through the charged air. As I get out of bed, my hair lifts off my back like a fan. I walk to the front door and open it. Outside the trees are thrashing and fine ice particles spiral up from the ground like miniature tornadoes. I listen to all the tumult of the wind, but deep and steady, under the fitful tossing of the wind I can hear the moan, like a background theme that's always there beneath the flightier variations.

I know it's got to be the lake, the ice contracting and expanding, a natural process that I've heard described a dozen times by Dean Buehl and Myra Todd. But I've got to see for myself. I walk into the woods in my thick socks and flannel nightgown and I hardly feel the cold at all. It's as if all the electricity I've stored during the day is burning inside me now, keeping me warm. The lake is shrieking like a creature that's been ripped in half and of course it has, hacked down the middle with saws and poked at with steel-tipped spears. I feel now it's calling me and who can resist the call of something so wounded?

It's only when I reach the Point that I see the danger. The wind is all around me, pushing like a hand at my back, tugging at my nightgown with tiny icy fingers. It lifts my hair and nightgown up and I feel myself being borne light and charged as ionized electrons toward the brink. Then I feel another grip, hard and warm, and something pulls me back into the sheltering woods.

"Jane, are you crazy? What are you doing out in this?"

It's Roy Corey who's pulling me out of the wind and holding me by both arms, my back brushing against the rough bark of a white pine. My flannel nightgown rubs against his flannel shirt and the little shocks of electricity bring me back to my senses.

"I could ask you the same thing," I say, surprised at the calmness of my voice.

"There was something I wanted to see." He points to the ledge on the west side of the Point. "I wanted to see if someone could hide there. You didn't see me when you came out onto the Point, did you?" I shake my head. His hand is still on my arm and it feels warm. The wind is kicking the hem of my nightgown up, baring my legs.

"But I saw you. I saw you moving toward the Point just as you did that night Deirdre died. If someone was hiding on the west ledge that night she would have seen you come out of the woods and approach the Point. She would have seen Deirdre back away and fall. What she wouldn't have seen is Lucy on the east ledge reaching up to grab Deirdre's ankle."

"So it would have looked like it was my fault?"

He nods. Suddenly I feel the cold and I start to shiver. Roy takes off his jacket and wraps it around my shoulders. He has to pull me away from the tree to get it around me and as he does my flannel nightgown catches a charge from his shirt and clings to him.

"So you decided to conduct this experiment in the middle of an electrical storm?" I ask through chattering teeth. He releases his grip on my arms, but I don't move away. I can't move back, anyway, because of the tree.

"I also wanted to keep an eye on your house," he tells me. "I didn't feel you were safe."

I lay my palm flat on his chest, expecting another shock, but instead his shirt feels damp and warm and I can feel his heart beating wildly. "Maybe you ought to come inside then."

He nods, but neither of us move. I hear the moan again, only now I realize it's not coming from the lake. It's in my throat and his. I lightly touch the back of my hand to his face and he slides his fingers under the collar of my nightgown and strokes my collarbone. I feel the cold air brush against my breasts and I start to shake. He moves up against me so that I'm wedged between his body and the tree and I can feel he's shaking, too. When he ducks his head to my throat my head arches back and I can see the pine boughs above us, moving like bodies in a dance, moving the way we start to move. I lead him back to my house. We get under the blankets and, wordlessly, he makes love to me, slowly, never taking his eyes away from my eyes. I understand. This is not a fluke, he's telling me, we know each other this time.

When I have breath enough to speak I turn to him and say, "How you must have hated me."

He touches my forehead, strokes the damp hair back. "I didn't hate you, Jane. I hated myself for not telling you there and then who I was."

"We had Miss Buehl and her Girl Scouts shrieking and pointing at us. Hardly the moment to unmask."

He lifts himself on one elbow and runs the back of his hand down the length of my arm. I feel his breath cooling the sweat in the hollow of my collarbone. "But that's not why I didn't show you who I was. I didn't want to see the look of disappointment when you saw I wasn't Matt."

I look at him hard so that I don't, by looking away, admit the truth of what he's saying. I want to tell him he's wrong, but I can't. I would have been disappointed—more than disappointed, *crushed*—to have seen any face but Matt's beneath that mask. And for a moment, I do see Matt's face, rising in Roy's features, as if the seventeen-year-old boy is looking out of his cousin's eyes. I see him so clearly I feel as if every minutest hair on my body were sheathed in ice. And then he's gone. Matt's face fades from Roy's, just as in my dream it sinks into the black water, only I suspect that this is the last time I will see that face.

I can't lie to Roy, so I tell him the next best thing. "I'm glad it's you. Here. Now."

Chapter Thirty-one

●

IT'S STILL DARK WHEN THE PHONE WAKES US. I SEE FROM THE glowing green numbers on the digital alarm clock that it's 5:33. The phone is on Roy's side of the bed and he answers it by saying his name. I'm surprised by how unsurprised I am at this. As if I'd been with him for years and known how a cop always knows the call in the middle of the night is for him.

He listens without saying anything and then says, "I'll be right there." He swings his legs over his side of the bed and finds his jeans and shirt on the floor. When he stands up he sees me propped on one elbow, watching him, and he sinks back onto the bed and cups my face with his hand.

"I'm afraid this time it's worse than getting interrupted by the Girl Scouts."

ROY DOESN'T HAVE FAR TO GO. I FOLLOW HIM DOWN THE steps to the swimming beach where a little group is huddled in a circle of flashlights. I recognize three seniors, none of whom take Latin. The only one whose name I know is Mallory Martin, the girl whom my girls call Maleficent. She doesn't look too maleficent right now, crying and shaking under a trooper's heavy leather coat.

"We came out to watch the sun rise," she's telling someone. I get the feeling she no longer needs an audience to tell this story. She'll be telling it for the rest of her life. "We thought it would look cool—with all the statues? A bunch of girls talked about doing it yesterday at the Ice Harvest. At first we thought it *was* a statue." She points a wobbly finger in the direction of the stones. On the lake, police officers bundled in heavy coats are moving slow-footed over the ice, their arms held out to their sides for balance. Their posture reminds me of something—it's how Miss Pike told us to move through water looking for drowning victims, toes feeling the bottom, arms held out to feel for dead limbs. It reminds me of the morning they found Melissa Randall's body.

I walk past Mallory Martin and her circle. I'm going to follow Roy onto the ice, but at the edge of the lake a police officer holds up his hand to stop me.

"I'm sorry, miss, we don't want any civilians on the ice."

Roy turns and sees the look on my face.

"It's OK, Lloyd, she's with me."

I don't even think about the slipperiness of the ice, but stride out to where Roy is. We pass the first stone and the ice statue standing next to it. I look at its face and am startled to see the detail there. Someone went to a lot of trouble. The surface of the ice is smooth and glowing, as if the wind last night had polished it.

At the second stone the kneeling ice figure has been whittled down by the wind, so that it looks more like a lump on the ice than a statue. I look from it to where the third statue should lie, but although the first light has reached that part of the lake there is nothing there. It's as if the supine figure had sunk beneath the ice.

I turn to Roy to ask if this is what all the fuss is about and see the fourth statue. It's stretched out on the second stone, a girl's smooth marble-white body arched up as if in some terrible throes of pain or pleasure to meet the eight-foot ice pole thrust through its middle. It's only when the light creeps over her and touches her mermaid-red hair that I recognize Vesta.

．　　．　　．

"SHE SAID SHE COULDN'T SLEEP AND WAS GOING TO GO skating on the lake," Athena is telling us for perhaps the third time. "She thought it would be cool to skate around the statues. Some other girls had talked about doing it at the Ice Harvest. I offered to go with her but she was still mad at me about keeping the light on. She said if I was going to go she'd just as soon stay and turn out the light."

Athena looks up from the low chair in front of Dean Buehl's desk and we can all see the deep shadows under her eyes. A lock of stringy, multicolored hair falls over her left eye and the hand she lifts to push it back is trembling so hard she quickly returns it to her lap and clasps both hands together. I can see from my seat on the couch along the side wall that her cuticles are ragged and bloody. She squints in the glare from the early morning light on the ice outside Dean Buehl's window. I look away from her to the frozen lake. Mercifully, the view of the east cove is blocked by the Point. I wonder if they have removed Vesta by now or will they still be taking pictures of the body? I notice two police officers standing on the Point looking down into the east cove. One has set up a tripod and is taking aerial shots of the crime scene.

"And *you* heard nothing, Jane?"

I flinch at the sound of my name and look up at Dean Buehl, but it's Dr. Lockhart, who is standing at the large plate-glass window behind Dean Buehl's desk, who has asked the question. For a moment I don't understand what she thinks I would have heard, then I remember the shrieks and moans coming from the ice last night. Could they have been Vesta's cries for help and not the ice?

"There was a storm," I say. "I heard wind and the ice buckling."

"The ice buckling?" Dr. Lockhart repeats. I look up at her, but the glare from the lake ice surrounds her like a harsh aura and I have to shade my eyes to look in her direction. Even so, I can't read her expression.

"Yes," I say, "cracks and pops and . . ."

"Moans?" she asks. "Shrieks? That's what the ice sounds like. Did you go out and look?"

"I did go out," I say, "I went to the Point, but I never looked over."

Even Athena swivels her head and stares at me.

"I ran into Officer Corey—he was . . . um . . . patrolling the area."

There's a moment of silence during which I vividly remember what happened on the Point after I ran into Roy Corey. I look down at my hands and see they are bright pink and for a moment I'm sure I must be blushing, but then I realize it's only the morning light from the window.

"So did you both look over the Point to see where the sounds were coming from?" Dean Buehl finally asks. I think we're both surprised that Dr. Lockhart isn't the one to ask, but she has turned back to the window, her attention drawn to the two men taking pictures on the Point.

"I was going to, but Officer Corey led me back from the Point— I guess he was afraid it was too dangerous out there . . ." I'm mercifully interrupted by a soft knock on the door, which opens to admit Roy Corey. For a moment I'm so happy just to see his face that I don't think about the fact he's a police officer.

"What's going on here? Why is this student here?" he directs the question to Dean Buehl, but it's Dr. Lockhart who answers.

"It's her roommate you've been peeling off the rocks out there. We thought she might know something about it."

At the word "peeling" I see Athena's face crumple. She turns to look at me. "What does she mean? I thought she was stabbed to death."

"Why did you think that, Ellen?" Dr. Lockhart steps away from the window, walks around Dean Buehl's desk and perches on its edge. She crosses one long, gray-stockinged leg over another and waits for Athena to answer. I notice there's a small pull in her pantyhose, just where her skirt rides up, and for some reason it makes me absurdly happy to see some tiny flaw in Dr. Lockhart's usually perfect ensemble. Otherwise, she is as calm and cool as ever. I wish I could say the same for Athena.

"S-s-someone told me," Athena says. I remember that's what she said to me when I asked her how she knew about my roommates' deaths twenty years ago. I've never heard her lisp before. "Didn't someone say she was stabbed? I mean, I thought with all those big ice poles lying all over the place . . ."

"Which you took such an interest in during the slide show . . ."

"Dr. Lockhart, if you have some theory to share with the police, perhaps you'd like to come down to the station . . ."

"Yes, I'd like that, Officer Corey. I'd like to know why a police officer was on the Point last night, preventing one of our teachers from looking over to see where all those awful sounds were coming from?"

Roy looks at me.

"I didn't say he prevented me . . . ," I start to explain, but then I think about what happened on the Point last night and it occurs to me that, effectively, that's what he did. I falter and look up at Roy and he sees my hesitation.

"It was windy and the rocks were icy," he offers the explanation to me instead of Dr. Lockhart, but it's she who replies.

"So did you look over the Point to see where those noises were coming from?"

"I assumed it was the ice," Roy answers.

"Then you're either even stupider than the average cop or you're trying to cover up something you did see," she says calmly.

I can see a muscle in Roy's jaw flinch, but it's Athena who loses her composure. She springs out of her chair so abruptly it topples, hitting Roy in the kneecap and forcing him to step back.

"Why are you so mean?" she screams, lunging at Dr. Lockhart. The impact of Athena's collision with Dr. Lockhart knocks the desk back a good six inches, sending Dean Buehl's swivel chair careening backward into the window. I hear glass shatter, and for a sickening moment I imagine Dean Buehl propelled out into the air, but it's

Athena I'm moving toward. I throw my arm over her head in a shoulder hold that I learned from Miss Pike's lifesaving class and pull her back, her arms flailing as though she really were a drowning victim. Apparently she's a victim who doesn't want to be saved, because as soon as she gets her balance she sinks, sidesteps, and drives her elbow into my solar plexus. While I crumple over in pain, she runs from the room. When I can lift my head, I look for Dean Buehl, afraid of what I'll see, but she's all right, visibly shaken but untouched by the glass of the shattered window behind her, every inch of which is veined by an intricate maze, somehow magically suspended, as if held in place by the bright morning sun streaming in now through the cracks.

ROY HELPS ME TO A SEAT ON THE COUCH. DEAN BUEHL moves gingerly away from the shattered window and sits down next to me on my other side.

"Are you all right, Jane?" Dean Buehl asks. "I had no idea that girl was capable of such violence."

"I'm fine," I say. "It wasn't Athena's fault. She was . . ." I falter, unable to come up with a plausible explanation for my student's behavior. The word "provoked" comes to mind. "Upset," I say instead, which sounds weak in view of the destruction left in Athena's wake. "I should go talk to her."

"I think it's better if I go," Dr. Lockhart says. "I've been working with her. I think I understand her issues."

"She seemed pretty angry with you," Roy says.

"That's all part of the therapeutic process," Dr. Lockhart says, putting on her coat. I look to Dean Buehl and she nods to me.

"Candace is right, she should go."

Dr. Lockhart smiles at me like a child who's won at some squabble mediated by grown-ups. When she's gone Dean Buehl adds, "Candace has a special empathy with these girls—she had the same sort of upbringing. Over the years I've seen so many girls like Ellen and Candace, girls whose parents have too little time for them and leave their care to us."

"Abandon them to you," Roy says.

"Don't be too harsh, Detective Corey. It's what they know; it's how they were brought up. I'm sure they think they're doing what's best for their children. Maybe it's the best they can do for them."

I have a sudden vision of Olivia, left with Mitch for safekeeping, that reawakens the pain in my stomach where Athena jabbed me with her elbow. I'm supposed to go see her this weekend.

As if reading my intention, Roy stands up, reassuming an official air. He addresses Dean Buehl, but I understand the message is for me. "You understand that now that this is an official murder investigation no one should leave the campus." Dean Buehl nods and, when he looks in my direction, so do I.

I CAN TELL ROY WANTS TO COME WITH ME WHEN I LEAVE Dean Buehl's office, but there's the phone call to be made to Vesta's parents and Dean Buehl asks him to stay. I stand in front of the mansion for a moment wondering where Athena and Dr. Lockhart have gone, but there's no sign of them. I'm stalled here trying to think of the words I'll use to explain to Olivia that I have to cancel again. I canceled the last weekend I was supposed to visit because of the snow. How can I disappoint her again?

I head back to my cottage to pick up my purse and the overnight bag I'd packed yesterday with clothes and papers to grade. I cut through the woods to avoid the police officers on the Point. I find, to my surprise, a narrow trail carved through the snow that leads me right back to my house. I find another one that gets me to the faculty parking lot. Someone's grown tired of staying on the regular footpaths and made their own, just as Lucy used to.

It's only when I'm in the car, waiting for my windows to defrost (I still have the chemical de-icer in my glove compartment, but I've avoided using it since almost blinding myself with it) and the heat to thaw my hands so I can drive, that I realize the seriousness of what I'm doing. It will look as though I'm fleeing a crime scene. But Roy will know I couldn't have anything to do with Vesta's death. He was with me after all.

But can I say the same about him? Do I really know what he was doing up on the Point? I think about what he said. Whoever was behind these events had something to do with what happened twenty years ago. Matt was Roy's cousin. For twenty years he's felt responsible for his death. What if he suddenly had someone else to blame for it? The thought is so monstrous that all I want to do is get away from Heart Lake. And even though I still can't see through my rearview window, I back up blindly and drive as fast as I can to the Northway.

Chapter Thirty-two

●

SOUTH OF ALBANY I GET OFF THE THRUWAY TO TAKE the Taconic the rest of the way south. Driving south on the Taconic I watch the Hudson Valley unscrolling toward the Catskill Mountains. It's a familiar, gentle landscape and for a while it takes my mind off Athena and Roy Corey and Heart Lake. I think instead of how so much of my life has been played out along this corridor. I remember taking the train from Albany to Corinth after my mother died, of how I felt I was moving into my future even as I was traveling back to Heart Lake. Now, even as I'm fleeing Heart Lake as fast as I can, I feel as though I'm traveling into my past.

I think about Matt and Lucy. I've shied away from thinking about them since I learned the baby was theirs, but now I force myself to imagine them together. It would have been May Day. The same morning I was with Roy Corey. I remember how Lucy and the masked boy faced each other on the beach and how Lucy calmly walked into the water, daring the boy to follow. When I'd thought it was Ward Castle, I thought he wouldn't brave the cold water. I didn't have time to wait and see; I thought it was Matt, below me on the steps, waiting for me to flee so he could follow.

Now I imagine what happened after I turned my back on them. Lucy slipped into the mist rising from the water and started swimming for the icehouse and Matt followed her. He would have had to take off his mask. They were strong swimmers, used to swimming side by side in the lap lanes at the local pool. I picture them, cleaving the lake, their arms curving over the green water like two wings of the same bird. They would have been cold by the time they got to the icehouse. I picture Lucy, her lips blue and trembling, and Matt wrapping his arms around her to keep her warm. Maybe it wasn't the first time. I remember the way they danced through the falling leaves on the first day I walked home with them, and how Matt spun Lucy on the ice when we skated on the lake. Maybe it was the first time.

I imagine they told each other it wouldn't ever happen again. But then Lucy found out from Helen Chambers that Matt wasn't really her brother. She thought that changed everything. People still might have talked—after all, they grew up *like* brother and sister— but Lucy wouldn't have cared and she could always talk Matt into doing what she wanted. It might have worked out for them, if I hadn't let slip to Matt about the baby.

I think about the night they died. Matt would have hitchhiked up this same road to get to Heart Lake after he got the letter from Lucy. He probably didn't know what to make of it. Neither had I, when I read it.

It was an afternoon at the end of February. She had just come back from dinner with Domina *Chambers. She said she'd learned some things that were going to change her life and she had to write and tell Matt. I assumed that* Domina *Chambers had outlined some plan for where Lucy would go to college and what she would do afterward.*

"Also, I want to make sure he's not worried about me with all this non-sense about my so-called suicide attempt," she told me. "D'you want me to put in a message from you?" she asked. "Like . . . oh, I don't know . . . Come, my Matthew, come, let's go a-Maying?"

I stared at her but she kept on writing with her head resolutely bent over the pale blue stationery that Domina *Chambers had given her. After May*

Day I had copied over Robert Herrick's poem "Corinna's Maying" into my journal. In the last line I had substituted Matthew's name for Corinna's. Had Lucy read my journal? Or had she just made up the line herself? After all, we had both read it in English last year. Either way, I was surprised at her for referring to what happened on May Day so casually.

She must have finally noticed me staring at her, because she looked up at me. "Jane, you're blushing. I'll just write the line at the end of the letter without mentioning your name. He'll know what it means, right?" She winked at me and bent back over the page. "How do the lines go again? 'And sin no more, as we have done, by staying, but, my Matthew, come, let's go a-Maying?'"

"Those come earlier in the poem," I said.

"Doesn't matter," she said, happily folding the letter and stuffing it in an envelope. "One more thing, have you got any more hairpins?"

I had a broken teacup on my desk in which I kept paper clips and hairpins. I handed it to her. She took out two U-shaped hairpins and one bobby pin. I watched as she fashioned a corniculum and put it in the envelope, carefully slipping it between the folds of her letter.

"Why are you sending him that?" I asked.

"So he'll meet me at the icehouse."

"But he's away at school," I said. "How can he meet you anywhere?"

Lucy smiled. "I have a feeling that once he gets this letter he'll find a way to come."

I pass a sign for Beacon and realize I'm not far from the military school Matt had gone to. It's been more than two hours since I left Heart Lake. I wonder how long it took Matt to make the trip. He must have come as soon as he got the letter. It was only a few days after she'd written that I came back to the room after dinner and found, thumbtacked to our door, a corniculum.

Lucy was at dinner with Domina Chambers and the only other person who knew about the corniculum was Deirdre. I shivered for a moment, imagining it was somehow a sign from her, but then chided myself for being so melodramatic. Obviously it was from Matt. He must have sneaked up to the room and left it as a message for Lucy to meet him at the icehouse. She'd be so happy when she saw it.

I left it on the door and went into the room. I tried to start my Latin translation for the next day, but I couldn't concentrate. It was lonely doing the work by myself. I had always studied in a group, first with Matt and Lucy, and then with Deirdre and Lucy. I remembered that first day, in ninth grade, walking home with Matt and Lucy chanting declensions and how Matt had taught me what they meant, and how he had presented me with a red maple leaf. I still had the leaf, pressed in my Tales from the Ballet. I took the book down from the shelf above my desk and turned to where the red leaf lay, pressed in between the pages of Giselle.

And then something occurred to me. What if the corniculum wasn't a sign for Lucy, but was, instead, meant for me? After all, Lucy had put that line about going a-Maying at the end of her letter. Wouldn't Matt know it had come from me?

I got up and opened the window. A gust of wet air blew into the room, but it wasn't cold. It wasn't exactly warm either, but there was something in it—the smell of snowmelt maybe—that made me think of spring. I stuck my head out the window and took deep breaths. A fine white mist rose from the melting snow as if all the snow that had fallen that winter was rising back to the sky. I could hear water dripping from my window ledge and from the pine trees and, farther away, the sound of water moving in the lake where the ice had broken.

I felt, suddenly, as if something were breaking up inside of me. When I closed the window I felt restless. I took out my journal and wrote, "Tonight I will go down to the lake to meet him and I'll tell him everything," before I knew that was what I meant to do. I paused with the peacock blue pen hovering over the page, waiting to see what I'd write next. I wrote, "I know I shouldn't go, but I can't seem to stop myself." Was that true? Could I stop myself? Would I even try? I wrote, "It's like the lake is calling me," and I thought, yes, that's what it is, that restless sound of water moving through the night, not just in the lake, but rising from the snow and dripping from the trees, a whole watery world out there calling to me. I wrote, "Sometimes I *wonder if what they say about the three sisters is true. It's like they're making me go down to the lake when I know I shouldn't." I'd come to the end of a page. I turned it and saw I'd come to the last page of the notebook. I wrote one more line and then closed the book and went out.*

THAT'S HOW DESPERATE I'D BEEN TO SEE MATT; I BLAMED MY going on the three sisters legend. It's almost funny. I notice, though, that I'm not laughing. I'm crying so hard it's difficult to see the road. It doesn't help that the sky has darkened and a sharp wind is buffeting the car. I take a curve too fast and feel my tires skitter on the gravel on the shoulder. Shaken, I pull into a scenic overview and stare at rain clouds massing over the Catskills while waiting for my crying jag to stop.

What had Matt thought of the May Day reference in Lucy's letter? Did he suspect that Lucy had gotten pregnant on May Day? Is that why he rushed up to Heart Lake? I shake my head. How will I ever know? Matt's dead. Lucy's dead. Everyone who could tell me is gone.

I stare at the soft folds of the Hudson Valley as if the landscape could answer my questions, but even this familiar vista fails me as the clouds from the west move across the valley, darkening the land and obscuring my view. But not everybody from back then is dead. Roy's alive. He was with Matt when Matt got Lucy's letter, with him at his parents' house in Cold Spring when he decided to leave for Heart Lake. Hadn't Roy said, when he met me at the Aquadome, that he'd just been visiting his mother in Cold Spring? (*Our aunt Doris in Cold Spring,* I hear Lucy's voice, as if she were there beside me in the car, whispering in my ear.)

I wipe my eyes and look at the car clock. It's only one o'clock in the afternoon. Olivia will still be at school. I have time, I think, to make one quick stop.

As I pull back on the road I know I'm being foolish. What can I possibly expect to find in Roy's mother's house? If Matt hadn't told Roy why he was he leaving for Heart Lake, he certainly wouldn't have told his aunt. But even as I tell myself all the reasons I shouldn't be going I'm getting off the exit for Cold Spring and looking for a gas station so I can look up the address. If it's not listed, I tell myself, I'll take it as a sign that I'm on a fool's errand and drive straight to Mitchell's house.

Not only is Doris Corey listed, she lives right on the main street of town. The road into town slopes steeply down toward the river. I can see, on a bluff overlooking the river, a low dark building with crenellated towers. The Manlius Military Academy for Boys. Matt's old school. I look away from it and concentrate on looking for the Coreys' house. It's almost the last house on the street, a small yellow Victorian just before the train tracks and a stone's throw from the river.

The woman who answers the door looks so much like Hannah Toller that for a moment I think the report that I'd heard all those years ago of her death in a car accident must have been a mistake. When she smiles at me, though, me a stranger standing at her door-step in the pouring rain, I see she's softer than Hannah Toller ever was. I realize how guarded and strained Lucy and Matt's mother had always been—bowed down, no doubt, by all the secrets she had borne.

This woman, Doris Corey, has me into her house before I can even explain that I live in Corinth and know her son. "Is it Roy?" she asks, her hands arrested in reaching to help me off with my down parka. "Are you with the police, dear? Have you come to tell me something's happened to Roy?"

For all the panic in her eyes she's still polite. If I were to tell her that something had happened to Roy she wouldn't scream and make a scene; she'd know I was only the blameless messenger of bad news. I think of all the sadness she's lived through. Her niece and nephew drowning in a lake, her sister and brother-in-law dying in a car acci-dent. She holds herself like someone braced for tragedy.

"Oh no, Mrs. Corey. Roy's fine. You see . . ." I try to think how to explain to her why I'm here and can think of nothing better than to tell her my name.

"Jane Hudson," the hand that was tugging at my wet coat comes to rest on my forearm and squeezes, "weren't you Mattie's girl?"

The noise I make must sound as if I'm choking. *Mattie's girl.* It's all I ever wanted to be. But I can't lie to this woman. "I was a friend of Lucy and Matt's, Mrs. Corey, but that's all."

She waves a dismissive hand at my disclaimer.

"Oh, he talked about you all the time, dear. He told me about the time Lucy fell through the ice and you pulled her out. He said you were the bravest person he knew."

You'd pull me out, wouldn't you, Jane?

My tears are falling again, mixing with the rainwater dripping from my hair, before I can do anything to stop them. Mrs. Corey makes a soft sound at the back of her throat, something between a tisk and an ahh, and pulls me down next to her on the couch. She pulls a brightly colored afghan from the back of the couch and tucks it around my shoulders, but the scratchy wool only sets me to shivering.

"I know, I know," she says, over and over. "It still comes to me some days, the thought of those two drowning. I confess it's Mattie I think of most often. I guess because we'd come to feel he was like our own all those weekends he stayed here. Lucy . . . well, she was always a quiet one—not one to let you get too close. Even when she was a baby she'd struggle in your arms . . ."

"Did you know she wasn't Hannah's?"

Mrs. Corey sighs and smoothes the afghan over my shoulders. "Hannah was my little sister," she says. "When she came home with that baby everyone else believed her when she said it was hers, but I could tell. She didn't nurse her—when Mattie was born she nursed him. It's not that she didn't treat Lucy good—she took extra pains with her. She seemed . . . I don't know . . . almost in awe of her. And then she didn't look a bit like her or any of us . . ."

"Did you confront her?"

"Only once. When she let Matt and Lucy start school together. I asked her if she thought it a good idea, encouraging the two of them to be so close. She asked me what I meant, weren't they brother and sister? When I didn't say anything to that she looked away and told me to mind my own business. We never spoke of it again, but when she asked me to keep Mattie here . . . well . . . she said she was sorry she hadn't listened to me before."

She sits back and folds her hands in her lap. She looks away from me to the mantel. I follow her gaze and see there the picture of Matt. It's a posed portrait with a flag in the background. His school picture for his senior year at Manlius. His hair looks darker than I remember it and longer, the seventies haircut looks dated. I look away from the picture to Mrs. Corey. I want to ask her what else Matt said about me. What else did he say to give the impression that I was his girlfriend. But I realize suddenly how little it matters anymore.

"Did you know who Lucy's real mother was?" I ask instead.

"I guessed it was that friend of hers, Helen Chambers. That's who the girl looked like, after all. And then after Hannah died I found out that Helen Chambers had owned the house on River Street. She'd left it to Cliff and Hannah when she . . . when she passed on." She unfolds her hands and plucks on the tufts on the upholstery. She doesn't want to say "killed herself." I look down at the worn chintz pattern on the couch and realize I've seen it before.

"And then you inherited the house from Hannah."

"I was the only one left," she says, "but I couldn't hardly bear to be in that house for five minutes. Roy helped me move some of the furniture—Hannah'd always had better than what we could afford—but neither of us could bear to clear out the attic rooms. We figured whoever bought the house would clear it away, but then the house never would sell. People must've thought it was unlucky."

I remember that it's what I suggested to Dr. Lockhart, but then, how had she come to live there?

"But you sold it eventually?" I ask.

"Only last year. I'd been renting it out summers, and then I got this letter from someone at Heart Lake . . ."

"From someone at Heart Lake?"

Doris Corey frowns. "I don't remember. Let me see, I think I still have the letter. It had something nice in it about Lucy, so I saved it." Doris Corey gets up and pushes open the top of a rolltop desk—a desk I suddenly remember as standing in the Tollers' front hall. I look around me and recognize other pieces of furniture from the Toller household—a highboy carved of some dark wood, a wing-back chair, a grandfather clock. They crowd around the couch, these relics from the past, like the dead heroes clamored around Aeneas in the underworld.

"Something nice about Lucy?" I repeat. "But how . . ."

Doris Corey comes back to the couch and hands me a letter written on pale gray stationery in blue-green ink. "Dear Mrs. Corey," I read. "I'd like to inquire about purchasing the house on River Street. I know it's been vacant for many years and I understand how you might be reluctant to part with your sister's old house."

Doris Corey points to the first paragraph. "I thought this girl must be either very naive or very rich. Or both. Imagine keeping a piece of real estate for sentimental value!"

I continue reading.

"I'd like to assure you that the house would be in very good hands. You see, I, too, have sentimental reasons for wanting to live in the house on River Street. I attended Heart Lake for three years in the late seventies (because of circumstances outside my control I had to leave) and that was how I came to know your niece, Lucy. Although she was several classes ahead of me, she was kind enough to take an interest in me. I had a very lonely childhood and I've never forgotten the kindness she showed me, almost as if she were an older sister. When she died I felt as if I had lost a part of my family, almost, indeed, a part of myself. Now that I've returned to Heart Lake (I often think that my decision to work with troubled adolescent girls is a way of repaying my debt to Lucy) I would cherish the opportunity to live in her old house."

There followed a generous cash offer for the house.

"Can I use your phone?" I ask, handing the letter back to Doris Corey.

I dial Dean Buehl's office. She answers on the first ring and at the sound of my voice nearly shouts at me. "My God, Jane, we've been looking everywhere for you. Where are you? Are Athena and Dr. Lockhart there with you?"

Doris Corey must see how pale I get because she wraps the afghan around my shoulders.

"No. How long have they been missing?"

"Since Athena stormed out of my office this morning. We're afraid she's done something to Dr. Lockhart—"

"Dean Buehl," I interrupt. "Was Dr. Lockhart a student at Heart Lake?"

"Well, yes, for a few years, but she didn't like people to know because she was expelled. But you know all about that, Jane, I told you . . ."

I remember standing at the train station looking across the tracks at the small girl posed rigidly beside her luggage, her face set in a frozen glare, while Miss Buehl told me that she had been expelled for breaking the fanlight above the front door of Main.

"She's Albie. You hired Albie, didn't you? You felt sorry for her and you hired her."

"Well, yes. That poor girl had been through so much. All she wanted was to come back to Heart Lake. But I didn't lie, she wasn't an old girl because she didn't graduate . . ."

"But you should have told me."

"But Jane, I thought you knew. After all it's what her name means in Latin: white. That's why she was called Albie."

Candace. It means fire-white. That's what I feel now—a mix of fire and ice that tingles in my veins and gets me to my feet, Doris Corey's afghan falling to the floor like a pile of brightly colored leaves.

"Listen," I say to Dean Buehl, "explain all of this to Roy Corey. Tell him that Dr. Lockhart is Albie and tell him I'm on my way back."

BEFORE I GET BACK ON THE TACONIC I STOP AT A PAY PHONE and make another call. I could have used Doris Corey's phone but I'd been ashamed to make this call in front of anybody. I'm out of change so I call collect.

Mitch accepts the charges and without a word to me hands the receiver over to Olivia.

"Mommy? Are you almost here? I'm waiting up for you so you can read me my bedtime story."

"Honey," I say, and then pause, letting my head rest on the cold, grimy metal pay phone booth, "Mommy's going to be a little late, but I'll try to be there when you get up."

There's a silence so long that I think the connection's been broken, then I hear a small voice, which sounds in the rushing static as though it were underwater. "But you promised."

There's just nothing I can say to that. I tell her I'm sorry and that I'll try to make it up to her and I get off the phone before she can ask me just how I think I'm going to do that. Then I get in the car and drive north and try not to think about Olivia. I think, instead, about another little girl: Albie.

I try to remember what Deirdre and Lucy told me about her, but the truth is I was never that interested. She was a homely little kid who tagged along following us all over campus. Lucy seemed to accept her adulation as her due. Deirdre felt sorry for her, because, like herself, she was shuttled from school to school, unwanted. Even *Domina* Chambers had taken an interest in her. I had tried to talk to her once or twice, but she never seemed to like me. Maybe she saw me as a rival to Lucy's affections.

As I drive farther north, the rain turns into icy sleet. My windows frost up and my car slithers and fishtails on the upgrades. I drive fast, though, wiping the frost away from the windshield with the heel of my hand like a child pushes tears away.

Or was it the other way around? Had I seen her as a rival? After all, how many poor scraggly "orphan" girls could Lucy befriend? I think of all the times I caught her spying on us in the woods. How many times had she watched us without me knowing? I remember the figure I thought I saw on the Point when Lucy and I sank the tin in the lake, the sense I had of being watched the night Deirdre died. . . . What was it Roy had said? If someone was hiding on the west ledge it would have looked like I was the one who made Deirdre fall to her death.

When I reach the Northway I expect better road conditions, but instead I hit fog. The sleet, which I expected to turn to snow as I got farther north, turns back to rain. Most of the traffic stays in the right lane and crawls slowly through the dense white shroud. I get in the left lane and do eighty.

And that last night . . . the night I'd gone down to the icehouse to meet Matt. I had that same sense of being followed through the woods. What would she have made of that final scene on the ice? I close my eyes against the picture and nearly run into the guardrail. She would blame me for Lucy's death. Had I even thought, twenty years ago, of looking for her after Lucy died? To comfort her? No, I was too busy with my own grief. The next thing I knew about her was that she'd been expelled for smashing the stained-glass fanlight. The one inscribed with the school's motto. I remember the day Lucy explained to Albie what the motto meant. "It means there's always a place for you here. And it means I will always be here for you, too . . ."

But Lucy hadn't been able to keep that promise. In her rage, Albie had thrown rocks through the window—through the broken promise of those words. Then she had been sent to St. Eustace. *St. Useless.* Where they sent you when you were no use to anyone.

I spot the Corinth exit with barely enough time to cut across two lanes of slow-moving traffic and skid onto the exit ramp. The fog is even worse now that I'm off the highway. I can barely see the side of the road. I roll my windows down and fix on the little reflective bumps that mark the median to gauge the two-lane road that climbs up to Corinth. About halfway, I come up against a slow-moving lumber truck that is crawling up to the mill. There's no way to pass it, so I put my car in low gear and tail so close behind that I can smell the sickly sweet smell of fresh-cut pine.

I can tell I've reached town by the yellow tinge to the fog as I pass the mill. I sniff at the familiar scent of pulp. I used to think when I was little that the yellow smoke that rose from the mill was the ghosts of trees, and the white paper the mill produced their earthly remains—the bleached white bones of northern forests.

Finally, the truck pulls off and I accelerate through the rest of the village, crossing the bridge so fast my teeth vibrate. I'm on River Road, passing the old Victorians, which loom out of the fog like prehistoric monsters. At the end of the road, just before the turn off to Heart Lake, is the little house that always seemed to me like something out of a fairy tale. The only thing I hadn't realized was that as far as the woman living in it is concerned, I'm the bad witch. I made Deirdre fall off the Point. I let Lucy drown under the ice. I lied at the inquest and got her favorite teacher fired. I sent her into Siberian exile.

I turn the engine off, wishing I'd thought to park farther down the road or at least turned my headlights off. When I do that now I see that the house is not completely dark. Like the first night I found Dr. Lockhart here, there's a light in the attic.

What I should do is find a phone and call the police—see if they can reach Roy. What I do instead is reach deep into my book bag until my fingers graze cold metal. Dr. Lockhart's keys. I still have them. That I should use them seems the next logical step. I open my glove compartment and look for something I can use as a weapon. There's the flashlight, but its batteries are still dead and it's made of cheap, light plastic. The only other thing in the glove compartment is the small aerosol can of de-icer. I slip it into my pocket, figuring I can use it like mace. Then I get out of the car as quietly as I can and walk through the unshoveled snow to the front door. By the time I make it there my jeans are soaked to the knees and I'm sweating under my down parka. The snow, I notice, is slushy and steaming, exuding a thick white fog like some pestilential vapor. When I touch the doorknob I find it's warm.

There are only three keys on the chain and I already know that two of them are for Dr. Lockhart's office and filing cabinet. I put the third key in the lock and it turns easily. I push open the door into a darkness that feels smoky, as if the fog from the melting snow had somehow gotten inside and turned black. I look around the living room, trying to make out the shape of furniture, but after a moment I realize that the room is completely empty. There isn't a single stick of furniture on the first floor.

But the light I saw was coming from the attic. As I go up the stairs the darkness pales and turns pink. When I get to the head of the stairs I see why. There's a night-light in the shape of a pink poodle plugged into an outlet. The only other source of light comes from the room on the left. Matt's room. I go in and see that the light comes from a green-shaded banker's lamp on one of the desks by the window.

Lucy's desk. There's no other word for it. Even before I walk across the room and reach it I know it will be exactly as I saw it the last time I was in this room twenty years ago. The same lumpy pottery cup that Matt made for her in second grade holding the same collection of peacock-blue fountain pens. A brass eternal calendar in the shape of a globe, the day marked February 28, 1977. There's a blue Fair Isle cardigan hung across the back of the chair, which, when I lift, holds the shape of the chair in its shoulders. I see by its faded label it's from Harrods. It's the sweater I borrowed from Lucy and left in the woods.

When I drop the sweater back to the chair a moth flutters out of its folds and beats itself against the lamp. I slowly turn in a circle, taking in the whole room. Matt's hockey stick is propped against the bookshelf where Wheelock's Latin leans against Peterson's *Field Guide to Birds*. Matt's collection of Hardy Boys on the top shelf. Lucy's Nancy Drews on the middle. Over Matt's bed hangs a pennant for Dartmouth College. I'd forgotten that's where Matt wanted to go to college. He said he liked that it was founded by an Indian.

I look back at the desk and notice a few sheets of stationery with "Exeter" printed on top. The letters from Brian. There, too, are a supply of hairpins. A piece of lined paper, its edges ragged where it was ripped out of its stitched binding, lies under a smooth gray-green rock. I lift the rock and see there's only one line written on the top of the page. It's the last page from my journal. The last line I wrote before going down to the lake to find Matt. *I won't let anyone stand in my way,* I'd written, *not even Lucy.*

As I put the stone down I hear a sound from the back of the house. There's no window facing the back in the attic, so I run down the stairs, through the dark house, thankful there's no furniture to bump into. I unlatch the back door and step into the fog. I can't see more than a few feet in front of me and when I try to listen all I can hear is the drip of melting snow and the rush of moving water somewhere in the woods. It must be the Schwanenkill, thawed out, flowing out of Heart Lake. Then I look down at my feet and see that I'm standing in a narrow groove, a footpath carved out of the snow, just wide enough for one. And something gleaming in the wet snow. I bend down and pick it up. It's a tiny silver skull earring. A macabre thing, but I recognize it as Athena's. It's impossible, in this fog, to see where the path goes, but I'm already following it into the woods.

Chapter Thirty-three

●

A T FIRST THE PATH RUNS PARALLEL TO THE SCHWANEN-
kill. I know, not because I can see the stream but because I can
hear it—a faint watery whisper like the murmuring of an unseen
companion passing through the woods beside me. Then it veers
abruptly left and plunges into the deep, fog-white woods.

It's like entering a white tunnel. On either side the snow rises
steeply and where the snow leaves off the white fog rises, like a curtain being lifted from the ground to shield . . . shield what? I'm reminded of a slide Tacy Beade showed us in her ancient art lecture of
two handmaidens holding up a draped cloth to shield the goddess at
her bath. The face I see staring out behind the curtain now is the
wide-eyed frightened face of a lost child. The awkward little girl we
called Albie who used to follow us through the woods. The little girl
who's turned the game around and become the leader instead of the
follower.

The path loops around tree trunks and meanders through the
forest. When I come to the first branch I don't know which way to
go and stare hopelessly into the white mist. Then in the stillness of
the woods I hear a faint chiming. At first I think I'm imagining it—a
tinny bell that might be the ringing of my own blood in my ears—
but when I follow the sound to the left branch of the trail I catch the

faint glimmer of metal swinging from an overhanging branch. Three hairpins linked in the shape of a horned animal dangling among the pine needles. I take that trail and from then on, at every divergence, I look for the corniculum like a trail blaze and follow it. I've soon lost any sense of direction or time. The convolutions of the trail seem to grow tighter and more erratic, folding back on themselves like a Mobius strip, until I feel as though I am no longer following a path through the woods but a train of thought in some addled brain. But whose addled brain? Because even though I know it's Albie's path I'm following, I feel as if I'm traveling into my own past, taking the same path I took that night twenty years ago when I went down to the lake to meet Matt at the icehouse.

WHEN I LEFT THE DORM I GRABBED A JACKET ONLY HALF NOTICing that it was Lucy's pale blue parka instead of mine. I was halfway down the hall before I remembered that I had left the corniculum on the door. Should I go back and take it down? If I left it on the door, Lucy would no doubt come along to the icehouse when she got back. Then I wouldn't be alone with Matt. I thought of going back, but I felt too impatient, too anxious to be out, breathing the wet, sweet air. I was already past the matron's desk (I told her I'd left a book in the dining hall); I was already on the path heading around the west side of the lake.

Outside the night was even more stirring than it had promised to be. The wind moved through the trees spraying pine-scented water across my face. The lake was still coated with a white layer of ice but its surface was dull and I could hear the water moving restlessly beneath the surface as if trying to break free. Patches of ice, gritty and opaque, still littered the path. When I stepped on them pale air bubbles raced beneath my feet. All around me, the melting snow rose in a pure white mist, like a linen cloth pulled away to reveal some magical transformation: paper flowers, the flutter of pale wings. I kept looking into the woods, expecting something to show itself behind the shredded wisps of fog, but although I heard, once or twice, the snap of a branch or a watery sigh, I saw no one and I dismissed my sense of being followed to my imagination. I thought about Matt waiting at the icehouse and the thought that I was going to be with him soon moved through my body like the wind moving through the pine trees.

SHE MUST HAVE BEEN WATCHING ME THAT NIGHT, JUST AS SHE'S watching me now. When I have wandered in enough circles to wear myself out will she pounce on me from behind the white fog? Or will she merely leave me in the woods to freeze to death while she makes away with Athena? The thought of Athena sharpens my wits for a moment. What does she have in mind for her? I am beginning to understand why Dr. Lockhart hates me. As she sees it, I killed her two best friends and caused her favorite teacher to lose her job and ultimately kill herself. She spent the rest of her school days in a rigid, loveless place. She must have felt she was in exile. How Heart Lake and the memory of Lucy and *Domina* Chambers must have grown in her mind. It must have infuriated her to see me come back here and take *Domina* Chambers's place. *Think of Helen Chambers when you're dealing with your students,* she said to me at that first meeting. And from that moment on my life has been a replica of what happened to Helen Chambers. That is the punishment she devised for me.

I stop for a moment on the path and stare into the impenetrable fog. I hear, again, the whisper of water on the wind and together with the fog it reminds me of that last night I went down to the icehouse to meet Matt. I think about that last meeting and try to see it through Albie's eyes.

AS I ROUNDED THE END OF THE LAKE, I SAW THAT THERE WAS A light coming from the icehouse. I crossed the Schwanenkill carelessly, crashing through the thin ice in the middle. He must have heard me, because as I struggled up the bank I saw him above me, reaching out his arm to give me a hand up. I took off my mitten so I could feel the warmth of his flesh right away.

"I knew you'd come," he said, pulling me up the bank. His voice sounded hoarser and deeper than I remembered. He pushed back the hood of my parka and touched my face.

"Jane!" he said. I couldn't tell if it were surprise or excitement that I heard in his voice. And then I saw the unmistakable look of disappointment in his face and I knew.

"Where's Lucy?" he said. "Why didn't she come?"

I stared at him and tried to keep the tears from coming. After all, just because he'd expected his sister didn't mean he didn't want to see me as well.

"She was with Domina Chambers so I came first. I left the corniculum on the door, though, so she'll be here soon." I was glad, now, that I had left it. "I thought . . . well, I thought, you might want to see me, too."

Matthew sighed and put his arm around my shoulder. "Of course I want to see you, too. Good old Jane. It's just that I'm worried about Lucy. I heard about what happened at Christmas and then about what happened to poor Deirdre. And then Lucy sent me a very confusing letter . . ."

"She told you about what happened at Christmas?"

"Well, I heard from my parents that she tried to kill herself. At first I just couldn't believe it, and then I thought I might understand why . . ."

"But didn't she write and say she didn't really mean to kill herself?"

"Yes, but don't people always say that after they've tried and failed? That they didn't really mean it? She did cut herself, didn't she? I can't stand the idea of her hurting herself especially when it's probably all my fault."

I saw the look of pain on his face and I thought to myself, well, at least I have the power to do something for him. "She didn't try to kill herself at all, Mattie, it was all a sham."

"A sham?"

"Yes, it was a cover-up. For Deirdre. Not that she appreciated it, although I guess I shouldn't speak ill of the dead."

"What are you talking about, Jane?"

"Look, let's go inside the icehouse and sit down. I'll explain everything."

THE PATH, I NOTICE, IS BEGINNING TO SLOPE DOWNWARD. At one point it becomes so steep I have to hold on to branches to keep from sliding down the icy chute. I hear a soft moaning sound and I strain to hear if it's Athena. *It's me you want,* I say to myself, over and over. And then I call it out. "Albie, it's me you want for letting Lucy die, not Athena."

My own words come back in an echo as if they've bounced off a rock wall. And then I see why. I've come to the end of the path and it ends in sheer ice. I'm at the edge of the lake, on the southern tip, not far from the icehouse. Directly across from the rock wall of the Point. I could have gotten here in fifteen minutes from the Toller house if I'd followed the Schwanenkill instead of following the crazy meandering of Albie's path. She's worn me out and given herself more time and gotten me just where she wants me.

I hear again the sound of bells, louder than the tinny chime of the cornicula, and when I look up I see, hanging like Damocles' sword, twin silver blades. I step out from under them and see that they're skates hanging from a branch by their knotted laces. An index card has been threaded through the laces and on it, in childish scrawl, is written "Lucy's Skates," only the name Lucy has been exxed out and under it there's my name, crossed out as well, then Deirdre's name, crossed out, and then, finally, my name again. Jane's skates, it is then. I take them down and, as I'm meant to, put them on.

They're a little tight (it's a good thing I'm wearing thin stockings), but otherwise they fit well, and, I notice as I stroke out over the slick ice, the blades have recently been sharpened. As tired as I am I seem to be skimming over the surface of the lake effortlessly. I even do a little spin and land looking back at the icehouse, at the doors left open from the recent ice harvest, creaking in the wash from the channel that's been carved out of the ice. Is that where Albie hid that night, behind the doors? If she had, she would have heard everything I said to Matt.

HE'D LEFT HIS FLASHLIGHT ON THE LEDGE; THAT WAS THE LIGHT I'd seen coming from the icehouse. We sat down in the boat and leaned against the stern, next to each other so we could both look at the lake. I remembered the last time I had looked out these doors onto the lake. It was when Lucy and I were putting back the boat. The blizzard had started and the air was so full of snow it had blotted out the lake. Now the air was white from that same snow evaporating back into the sky. I liked the idea of the snow returning to the sky; it was the past rewritten with all its mistakes rubbed clean.

While I talked Matt bowed his head so that I couldn't see his face. I told him everything that had happened the day I came back from Albany, from the moment I walked into the dorm room to the last glimpse I had of the tea tin sinking into the black water. When I finished he asked one question.

"Whose baby was it?"

"Lucy thought it was Ward's because that's who Deirdre was with on May Day."

Matt lifted his head, but he didn't look at me. His eyes were on the lake, as if drawn there by some kind of magnetism.

"Why did she think the baby was conceived on May Day?"

"Because Deirdre hadn't been with . . . anyone . . . for weeks before. Because of the rain, remember? And the time before that, well, that would have been too long. Lucy said the baby was small so it was probably early and the time worked with May Day." I was beginning to realize what Matt was afraid of.

"Did you see it?"

I nodded and then realized he still wasn't looking at me. I decided then to say no, but he must have seen me out of the corner of his eye.

"Who did it look like?" he asked.

"Oh Matt, it hardly looked like a person. It was tiny." I remembered the way the skin had glowed like opals and the pale red hair like fire.

Matt turned to me and took me by the shoulders. "Did it look like me, Jane? Tell me the truth."

"Matt," I cried, surprised at how hard he was gripping me. "It couldn't be yours because you weren't with Deirdre on May Day."

"Shut up, Jane."

The words startled me more than the way Matt was hurting me. They came from behind us. Matt got up and stepped out of the boat, which rocked so hard I slid and knocked my head on the stern. When I scrambled to my *feet and got out at the front of the boat I saw Matt facing his sister, his hands balled into tight fists. I'd never seen him look so angry. Actually, I couldn't re-member ever seeing him angry at all.*

"Whose baby was it, Lucy?" he asked his sister.

"It was Deirdre's baby, Mattie. Isn't that what Jane told you?" Lucy looked toward me and the coldness of her look shocked me. "She promised not to tell anyone, but that doesn't matter now. Don't you believe her, Matt? You know Jane would never lie."

"I also know she'd believe anything you told her." Matt came around the boat toward me. He looked so unlike himself that I took a step away from him, but when he took my hand he was gentle.

"You saw it, Lucy. Tell me, what color hair did it have?"

"Babies don't always have hair," Lucy said. I heard an unfamiliar note of panic in Lucy's voice. She came around the other side of the boat and stood next to me. We were all three standing in the doorway facing the lake.

"Did it have hair, Jane?"

I looked from Matt to Lucy. Lucy shook her head and, seeing her move-ment, Matt dropped my hand and whirled around on her. "Was it red like mine, Lucy?" He took a step toward her and Lucy backed up to the edge of the doorway.

"Your cousin has red hair, too, Matt," I called over his shoulder. "Maybe Deirdre was with Roy on May Day."

Matt looked back at me and laughed. "Oh, Janie . . . ," he began, but before he could finish what he was going to say he was silenced by a sound that made my whole body go cold. It was a high keening moan, like no sound I'd ever heard a human being make, and yet there was something like human emotion in the sound. We both turned to the lake and saw that Lucy had run onto the ice. The moan was coming from the ice itself, buckling under her weight.

I STAND ON THE ICE NOW, PICTURING LUCY COMING OUT of the icehouse onto the melting ice. She'd run in a straight line from the icehouse out into the middle of the lake, the ice shuddering and moaning at every step, leaving black water in her wake. The path she took is now marked by the channel. When Matt tried to follow her he had to stay on the east side of the lake. That's how I go now, making toward the east cove and the sister stones. I look down at the ice to see if I can see the mark of skate blades, but the fog is so thick I can't even see my own feet. It makes me feel queasy, as if I've become invisible.

Then I see a figure up ahead, standing still in the fog. I skate toward it, trying to glide on each skate as long as I can so as not to make too much noise. The figure seems not to hear me and I'm afraid I'll find that it's Athena, frozen and dead on the ice, but when I reach it I see it's only one of the statues left over from the ice harvest. I look around and realize they're everywhere, standing on the ice like sentinels before a tomb. I skate from one to another, looking for some sign that Albie and Athena have passed this way. I stare into each face as if it might speak and tell me where they have gone, and so animate are they it seems they might at any moment gain voice. The crudely hewn features have softened, the caverns of their chisel gouged eyes deepening, rough-cut lips separating as if about to speak. I wonder for a moment how these hastily crafted sculptures have become so lifelike, and then I realize what it is. They're melting.

I think of the rain I'd encountered on the Northway. The temperature's been rising steadily since the electrical storm last night. That's why there's so much fog. How long, I wonder, before the lake ice melts and cracks? I listen to the low moan of the ice as if it could tell me, and then I realize the moan I'm hearing isn't coming from the ice, it's coming from the sister stones, which, I now see, are directly in front of me. I skate toward them, stilling inside myself the terrifying impression that the stones themselves are calling out to me. It's just another trick of the ice, I tell myself, and then, when that doesn't work I recite a little Latin to calm myself down.

"Tum rauca adsiduo longe sale saxa sonabat," I whisper to myself, choosing the Virgil passage Athena translated only last week in class,

which describes how Aeneas's ship navigates around the Sirens' stones and makes its way to the Italian shore and the sibyl's cave safely.

I've reached the second sister stone where the sound seems to be the loudest and, I can no longer deny, human. But this cry of human anguish is not coming from the sister stone, but from the rock face of the Point. Someone is in the cave. I shuffle forward on my skates as I approach the entrance to the cave, sure that at any moment Dr. Lockhart will pop out and impale me with one of those horrible ice pikes. I take out my can of de-icer and hold my finger over the spray top. But when I peer into the dark cavern I see only Athena, kneeling gagged and tied on the narrow ledge above the ice.

I take off the gag first.

"Dr. Lockhart," she gasps, "she's crazy."

I nod and put a finger to my mouth to shush her.

"Tace," I say, "I know. Let me untie you and get you out of here."

The ropes around Athena's wrists and ankles are too tightly bound to come undone. The more I pluck at the wet, frozen cords the tighter they seem to grow. Her trembling makes it all the harder to undo the knots.

"I need to cut them," I tell her, as if she could go into the next classroom to borrow a pair of scissors.

"Don't leave me," she cries, swinging her head toward me so that I feel the wet ends of her hair brush my cheek. I look up and see the wild fear in her eyes and the tears that streak her muddy face. "She wants to kill me. First she called me Deirdre, then Lucy, then Jane. She didn't seem to be able to keep straight who I was."

Athena sobs and I pat her shoulder clumsily. I tell her I won't leave, but she's got to help me think of a way of getting these ropes off her. I sit back on my heels to consider our predicament and sit down hard on the ends of my skates.

I've got the left skate unlaced and off before I can think through how vulnerable this leaves me if Dr. Lockhart should show up at this moment. What difference does it make though? I'm not leaving here without Athena. I hold the skate by the boot toe, place the blade over the ropes on Athena's ankles, and start to saw. My travels over the ice have dulled the blades slightly, but they still cut through the ropes, one thread at a time. Or so it seems, so slowly does the rope finally unravel and give way under the metal.

I go to work on her wrists next, twice slipping and nicking her skin in the dark of the cave, but Athena doesn't call out or complain. When I've got the ropes off I help her to her feet, but she ends up having to hold me up. My legs have cramped and I'm off balance with one skate on, one skate off.

"I better put the other one on," I say. I stuff my left foot into the skate. It feels like I'm forcing my foot into an iron vise. My feet have swollen and blistered and my stocking has torn, so it's like I'm cramming my bare foot into the stiff leather. I pull the laces tight and try to ignore the searing pain.

"OK," I say, straightening up, "let's try to get across the ice to the mansion." We step out onto the ice and for a moment, after the dark of the cave, I'm blinded by the white glare of the moonlit fog. I can barely make out the black mass of the second sister standing guard at the mouth of the cave. The looming shape seems to quiver before me and then to split in two as if I'd started seeing double. But then that second shape comes into focus and sprouts a horrible horn.

It's Candace Lockhart, crouched and wielding an eight-foot ice pike like a javelin, its steel tip quivering only a few feet from our throats.

"You run for the shore," I whisper without looking in Athena's direction, "she'll follow me."

"But *Magistra* . . ."

"Do what I say." I say it in my strictest, no-more-fooling-around-I'm-the-teacher voice and not only does it silence Athena but I see from a slight narrowing in her blue eyes that it momentarily unnerves Dr. Lockhart. I think I know why. For a moment, I sounded just like *Domina* Chambers.

I decide to take advantage of the resemblance. "Alba," I say sternly as I start to back skate along the edge of the Point, heading out onto the lake, "What do you think you are doing with that thing?"

I see out of the corner of my eye Athena making her unsteady way over the ice to the shore and then she disappears in the fog. Dr. Lockhart appears not to notice, she is staring at me. Then she blinks and laughs.

"As if you could ever take *her* place."

"I have taken her place," I say, putting a few more feet between us. I've never been much good at skating backwards, but I remember Matt showing me how to do it. *In and out, little figure eights with your feet, it's all in the inner thighs.* The insides of my thighs feel like melting ice and I can't even feel my feet, but I widen the distance between us while keeping my eyes locked on hers. I'm afraid that when she notices she'll throw the pike or rush me, but instead she starts skating toward me, slowly, as if maintaining a polite conversational distance.

"That's what you wanted to do with Lucy," she says. "You wanted to take her place. First you took her scholarship away, then you wanted Matt."

I lift my shoulders in an attempt at a casual shrug, but it feels more like cringing. "Lucy wanted me to try for the scholarship," I say.

She laughs. I'm surprised at the high-pitched nervousness of it, like a child caught stealing. Something about this conversation is getting to her, unraveling some carefully preserved veil she keeps in place. I have to keep her engaged—entertained, so to speak—or she'll tire of it and I'll end up impaled on that ice pike just like Vesta.

It's a mistake thinking of Vesta. She sees, I think, the fear in my eyes, but instead of attacking me with the pike, she digs in another way. "Poor stupid Jane," she says in a voice that's suddenly not her own. "Thought we were competing for the Iris, as if I wanted it. As if I wanted to be separated from Matt. We picked you that first day as the best one to win it so I wouldn't have to leave Mattie. Didn't realize what a slow study you were, though. Didn't even know what a declension was! Mattie thought that was hilarious."

The mimicry is so precise it almost stops me on the ice. But of course that's what she wants. I keep my feet moving. In and out, little figure eights. Press my thighs together until tears sting my eyes.

"God, what an idiot you were, Janie. You actually thought we were skating those nights we went to the icehouse," the voice has changed, now it's Deirdre's voice. "But we saw you come creeping out on the lake to spy on us, me and Mattie. That's why you wanted to get rid of me, isn't it? So you could have Mattie to yourself?"

"I didn't want to get rid of Deirdre, it was Lucy—"

"Who drove her out onto the Point? You were glad to see her die. Why else didn't you go and pull her out? You let her die there, clinging to the ice."

"That's not how it happened," I say, although I know I can't win an argument with a crazy woman; all I can hope is that as long as I keep her talking she won't throw that spear. "We went down to the hole in the ice where she went in. She wasn't there. She didn't cling to the ice."

Dr. Lockhart shakes her head. "I saw it all." Her voice is small now, the voice of a small, frightened child. "I hid behind the sister stones and watched her until she couldn't hold on any longer. She said your name over and over again. 'Jane,' she called, 'Jane, you promised.'"

This time her mimicry does stop me dead on the ice. Because it's not Deirdre's voice she's imitating. It's Lucy's.

"You mean Lucy," I say. "You watched Lucy clinging to the ice."

She has stopped, too. She lifts the back of her right wrist, the hand still gripping the lower end of the shaft, to wipe her eyes. The point of the ice pike tilts up and I realize, a moment too late, that it's my best opportunity to rush her, but she sees me coming and lowers the pole again so that I nearly impale myself on it. The metal tip slices through my down parka as I backskate away from it.

"You killed her," she cries, moving forward again. "You left her to die even though you promised you'd come back for her."

• • •

MATT FOLLOWED LUCY ONTO THE ICE AND I FOLLOWED HIM. I saw cracks shooting out in all directions from his footsteps and the ice seemed to scream as if it were human flesh being torn. The black water crept between the cracks. But still Matt walked forward as if he didn't notice the ice breaking all around him For every step he took forward Lucy took one backwards. It was like a dance along an invisible tightrope and I realized they were walking over the same ice that Lucy and I had broken through with the boat. It was where the underground spring fed into the Schwanenkill and the ice was always the thinnest.

I called to them but they paid no attention to me.

"Matt," I called, desperate to get his attention, "I'll tell you. I did see the baby and his hair was red."

Matt turned to me and in that instant a crack opened up in the ice just behind Lucy. She staggered for a moment, beating the air with her arms. For a moment I thought she had caught her balance. Matt turned back to her. He was so close to her that all he'd have to do is reach out his hand and grab her and she'd be safe. But when he turned to her I saw something change in Lucy's face. It was the first time, I think, that I'd ever seen her truly frightened. She took a step back and fell into the black water.

"It was because you told him," Dr. Lockhart says in a whisper so low I can barely hear it over the scrape of her skates moving steadily toward me. "You should have seen the look on his face when he knew it was his baby. It killed her."

"But how did you see . . ." and then I understand. She wasn't hiding behind the door of the icehouse. She'd been hiding behind the sister stone. The only part of the argument she'd heard that night was when I told Matt that the baby was his. "But Dr. Lockhart," I say, "*Albie,* I tried to save her. I loved her, too."

She lowers the ice pike and for a moment I think I've gained some ground. I think she's going to drop the pole to the ice, but instead she lifts one knee and, drawing her lips back like a snarling cat, snaps the pole neatly in two. The crack it makes echoes over the ice. "Liar," she hisses, "I saw everything," and then, holding the lighter weapon like a hockey stick, comes at me.

I turn and tear into the ice with my skates. I feel cold metal graze my neck and I fall headlong to the ice, splaying out on the slippery ice. She's on me at once. Her knee digs into the small of my back and she pulls my head up off the ice by yanking my hair back. I can feel the serrated tips of her skate blades grinding into my legs.

"You left her to die," she hisses into my ear. "You promised to save her and you left her on the ice to die." She wraps her hand once in my hair and slams my face to the ice. I hear a loud crack and I think it must be my skull. Before my eyes darkness spreads like a cool green blanket waiting to envelop me. *OK*, I think, *OK*. Somewhere far above me I hear a child crying.

"She said she'd never leave me. She promised, she promised." With every *promise* my head slams into the ice and the darkness spreads, like blood pooling. It is blood pooling. My blood. It's seeping between the cracks in the ice. Dripping into the black water. Through the red-stained blackness I see Lucy's face. Her lips are forming a word but I can't hear what she's saying because all around us the ice is cracking.

When he saw Lucy step back into the water, Matt froze. I thought he'd go to her, but he stood on the ice as if he'd become a part of it. When I passed him I brushed against his arm and I felt that he was trembling. I saw why. Between him and Lucy the ice had broken into three pieces. The piece that Lucy clung to was loose. When she tried to move her elbow forward on it, the slab tilted toward her. I got down on my hands and knees and held down the other end of the ice.

"Look," I said to Matt. "If you hold this still, maybe I can help her back up." I looked back over my shoulder to see if he had heard me. His eyes were fixed past me, on Lucy's face, just as her eyes were fixed on his. It was like I wasn't even there.

I tugged on his pant leg and pulled him down to his knees. "Just hold this," I yelled. He didn't move his eyes off Lucy, but he did what I told him to. He crouched on the edge of the unbroken ice and held the slab of ice that lay between us and Lucy. I crawled onto the slab of loose ice and felt it rock in the water, but I also felt Matt adjust his grip to steady it. I got on my belly and crept forward. When I got to Lucy I could see that ice was clinging to her hair and her lips were blue. She was trying to say something, but her teeth were chattering too hard for me to understand her. I tried to move closer, but just as I touched her hand the ice beneath me rocked free and I saw Lucy's eyes widen in fear. I looked over my shoulder and saw Matt crouched on the edge of the ice. He was still looking at Lucy, but he'd let go of the ice and stretched his arms over his head, his two hands coming together as if in prayer. I tried to remember where I'd seen him in this pose before and then remembered. At the swim club.

He only looked away from Lucy at the last moment to tuck in his chin. He went into the water without a splash. His form perfect.

"Jane," Lucy said, "Jane." I could see she was struggling to control the shaking so that she could speak. "You have to save him."

"I can't," I told her. "He's below the ice. Let me help you." But as I spoke we both saw him surface a few feet away. He got one arm onto the ice, but made no effort to pull himself up. He looked around and when he saw us—or saw Lucy, I should say, because he seemed to look right through me— he shook his head.

I took Lucy's hand and tried to pull her up but she pulled her hand out of mine. "No," she said, "I won't come out until he's safe. Go help him and then me. Promise, Jane. Promise you'll save him first."

I could see it was no good arguing with her. I turned on the ice and crawled toward Matt. I could hear Lucy behind me. Every time I stopped she called my name. "Jane," she said, over and over, "you promised." And so I kept going away from her.

When I was a few inches from Matt I think he finally saw me. He smiled. Like a boy playing keep away. Then he took a deep breath and sank back under the water. I saw his face, like a pale green star under the black water, grow smaller and smaller and then disappear. I turned back to Lucy, and saw that she'd sunk lower in the water, her lips touching the surface. She was going under. There wasn't time to crawl to her. I threw myself down on the *ice and reached for her hand. I felt her fingers under mine—felt them pull away from me and saw her slip into the darkness.*

THE ICE FEELS COOL AGAINST MY CHEEK NOW THAT DR. LOCK-hart has stopped slamming my head into it. At some point, *she promised* became *you promised*. I picture her—I picture Albie—hiding behind the sister stone and listening to Lucy saying these words to me as I crawled away from her. I can't blame her for thinking I left her to die. Even if I could explain that the promise I made was to save Matt, the truth would be the same. I let her convince me. She knew how I felt about Matt. Knew I would go. And when I reached for Lucy's hand what Albie saw was not Lucy pulling her hand away but me prying her fingers off the ice and sending her to her death.

"You promised, you promised," she whimpers. She sounds like a child and I know she isn't just repeating Lucy's last words. I wonder how long Albie stayed there that night, hiding on the ice because there was no one to come for her. Not even Lucy who had promised always to come for her. When she finally left she stole into our room and found my journal. She'd read the last line I'd written that night. *I won't let anyone stand in my way. Not even Lucy.*

When they tore up the ice on the lake Albie smashed the fan-light above the doors to Main Hall. She smashed the heart and the words of Lucy's broken promise. I picture shattered glass, like the window in Dean Buehl's office this morning, only instead of light pouring through the cracks there's black water—a blackness that's swallowing me, making it hard to think.

You promised, I hear, and there is something about the childish refrain—*you promised, you promised*—that I think I should remember.

I feel the weight lift off my back and something sharp and metal gnaws into my side. I remember who said that last. Olivia. But you promised, she said on the phone.

The knife in my side is Dr. Lockhart's skate. She's kicking me over, rolling me like a log. I roll once, and feel something dig into my side. It's not Dr. Lockhart's skate though. It's the can of de-icer in my coat pocket. I open my eyes and through a blur of blood see where I'm being rolled. We're inches from the open black water of the ice canal. She only has to roll me once more and I'll be in the water, my heavy skates pulling me to the bottom.

And then I won't see Olivia tomorrow. She'll wait and wait for me and think she wasn't worth coming for. After all, I've already abandoned her once.

I wait for the sharp metal to mash into my skin again and when the searing pain blooms there, I wrap my left arm around her ankles and pull her down. When her face is close enough I pull out the de-icer and spray it directly into her eyes. She screams and tumbles over me, almost gracefully, and would, I later think, have neatly regained her balance if she'd landed on ice and not the edge of the canal. She teeters for a moment and then slips into the black water.

I lie on the ice for a moment, trying to hear above the sound of my own ragged breath sounds of struggle in the water. But there's nothing. She's dropped as silently as a stone into the lake. After a minute, I turn myself painfully onto my stomach and creep along the ice to the edge of the canal. I'm only an inch or two from the edge when I see the fingernails embedded in the ice. I try to push back, but my hair trails in front of me and she grabs a handful and pulls herself up by it. I see her blue eyes, like painted eyes on a marble statue, just above the surface of the ice, fixed on mine. But then I realize that the chemical spray has blinded her. She can't see me.

I reach out my hand along the ice, and lay it over her other hand, the one not holding onto my hair. She tries to pull away, but I talk softly. "It's OK, Albie," I say, "It's Lucy. I've come to get you. Let me help you." I see her trying to dig her nails out of the ice to take my hand, but she can't. So I move forward another inch and take her hand, prying each finger out of the ice until I've got a good grip. I've never noticed how small and slender her hands are. Just like Lucy's.

And like Lucy she has a grip like a vise. She snakes her hand around my wrist and pulls. I slide forward on the ice and would slide in, except now I feel another pull, someone pulling on my feet. I begin to slide away from the canal, but she won't let go of my hand and she won't try to help herself up onto the ice. A clump of my hair tears away in her hand and she slips down under the water, but still she holds on to my wrist.

"Let go!" I hear someone shout behind me. It's Roy. "You can't save her. The ice is cracking."

I turn my head a little to one side and see dark cracks, like fine veins in marble, radiating out all around me.

"She won't let go of me," I say, so faintly I'm sure he won't hear me, but he does. I feel him creeping up beside me, careful to keep one arm around me so I won't slip into the canal. He must see the dark veins widening under his weight, but he doesn't stop until his face is near mine and we are both looking over the canal's edge into the water. Candace Lockhart's face is a few inches below the water, the whites of her open eyes tinged green by the lake. Roy reaches over me to where she's got my wrist and tries to unpry her fingers from my hand.

"No," I breathe.

"She's gone, Jane. Look at her."

I look back into the water. Her eyes are open, her lips slightly parted, but there are no air bubbles coming from her mouth. Still, I can feel those eyes watching me, some will rising up toward me through the filter of cold green water, and then I see her, just as I saw Matt's features rise up in Roy's, I see Lucy, her eyes looking out of Albie's blue eyes.

I reach forward with my other hand, but just as I do I feel her fingers, one by one, lifting off my wrist and her small, white hand, relaxed and open, slips below the water, the fingers slightly curled. She sinks, straight and slow, her white hair fanning up around her face, her blue eyes burning like twin stars until they're extinguished by the darkness.

Chapter Thirty-four

•

"WHATEVER MADE THEM PICK MAY DAY FOR THE Founder's day Picnic?" Hespera, the eighth grader whose stola I am fixing, complains. "It's too cold up here to frolic half naked around a Maypole."

I try to smile but my mouth is full of hairpins.

Athena answers for me. "It's the founder's birthday, or close to it."

I nod, taking the pins out of my mouth. "Yep, India Crevecoeur was born on May 4, 1886. So this would be her one hundred and tenth birthday and it's the seventieth anniversary of the school's founding. I actually met her once."

"Really, *Magistra*? You couldn't possibly be that old," Octavia, who's sewing up a seam on Flavia's stola, asks wide-eyed. Flavia rolls her eyes at her sister. When the sisters came back to Latin they demanded a Latin club. To revive our classical spirit, they said. Now they vie with one another to see who has the most classical spirit and who can be nicest to their teacher who valiantly saved the life of one of their classmates. It was their idea to stage a Procession of Floralia for the Founder's Day Maypole dance.

"*Prima*," I say, "I am that old, and *secunda*, she was ancient. Ninety, I guess, because it was my junior year and the fiftieth anniversary of the school's founding."

"Wow, was she like all senile?" Mallory Martin, although not a Latin student, has volunteered to join in the Procession of Floralia. Mostly because, Athena asserts, she thinks she looks good in a sheet.

"No, actually she was sharp as a tack. She recognized me as the granddaughter of her maid, who'd worked for her fifty years before."

"Your grandmother was a maid here?" Athena asks, pushing her hair, recently dyed sea-green, out of her eyes. I'd been looking forward to seeing its natural shade grow out, but she'd gone to the city last weekend and "caved in to peer pressure" at some East Village clip joint. I was disappointed at first, but now that I've gotten used to the color I have to admit that with her green eyes and pale skin it's kind of arresting. Especially today. For her role as goddess of the lake for the Procession of Floralia she's robed in a green satin sheet, a sheet volunteered by, of all people, Gwen Marsh. *Satin* sheets, Gwen? I say every time I see her now. It's just one of the surprising things I've learned about Gwen Marsh in the last few weeks as I've tried to get to know her better. The other is that under those ace bandages are old scars.

"Uh huh," I say absently as I notice the time. "But we're going to be late for our meeting. Hadn't you better change?"

Athena shrugs and pulls on a denim jacket over her sea-green stola. "Why? Is it a formal thing?"

"I don't know what kind of thing it is. Dean Buehl just said it was Heart Lake business and she wants both of us in the Music Room at noon."

"I think they will give you a medal for saving Athena's life," Octavia says.

"And for defeating the evil Dr. Lockhart," Flavia adds.

I could say for the hundredth time that I tried to save Dr. Lockhart and failed, but even I am getting tired of hearing myself say it.

"Well, if that's the occasion," Athena says, "I definitely think I should go as Goddess of the Lake." Athena strikes a pose—one finger to her left temple, her right hand curled in the air as if holding a scepter—much like a figure of a Greek goddess I once saw on an

Attic vase. For not the first time I think there is something regal in Athena's bearing. Maybe that's why her name seems to suit her so well.

"All right," I say. *"Deo parere libertas est."* Before Octavia can get out her book of Latin quotations I provide the source and translation. "Seneca," I say, "To obey a god—or in this case, a goddess—is freedom. OK, then, Octavia and Flavia, I leave it to you to organize the procession. You've got the wreaths and garlands."

"Check."

"Athena and I will meet you outside the mansion at one o'clock then. *Bona fortuna, puellae.*"

We have to stop twice on the path to the mansion to pin closed the seams on Athena's stola which keeps blowing open in the wind. Most of the girls have opted to wear clothes under their stola, but Athena, always a purist, is not even wearing underwear. Luckily I have a pocketful of safety pins. I remember that *Domina* Chambers always kept a supply of pins on hand for errant toga and stola seams. When we get to the foot of the mansion steps she stops and walks a few feet away to the edge of the lake. I think there must be a problem with her outfit again, but when I catch up to her I see that she's started to cry. I sit down on a rock by the edge of water and pat the stone for her to sit next to me.

"We're already late," she says tucking the folds of the sheet up around her knees so she can sit down on the rock. I'm glad that the stone has been warmed in the sun. Even though Hespera is right about it being too cold to frolic half naked around a Maypole, it is an extraordinarily beautiful day. The lake, under a cloudless blue sky, is so bright it's hard to look at it.

"They'll wait," I tell Athena. "After all, how can they start without the Goddess of the Lake?"

"Maybe that wasn't such a good idea, considering . . ." Her voice trails off as she stares into the hard glitter of the lake. We both know how much there is to consider. I wonder if Athena will ever look at this lake without remembering the two friends she lost to it. I know I can't.

"It wasn't your fault," I say, something I've said, and had said to me, countless times in the last two months. Still we go on blaming ourselves. Roy and I have gone around and around it. He suspected, as soon as I found the deer's mask, that it must be Albie because she was there on May Day and could have found the mask after he left it in the woods. But he hadn't guessed that Albie was Dr. Lockhart.

The only one who knew that for sure was Dean Buehl and she holds herself accountable for hiring Dr. Lockhart in the first place.

"I felt so awful when the girl was expelled. I told her she'd always have a home here at Heart Lake and she took me at my word. How could I turn her away again? Then she asked me not to tell anyone she'd gone here and been thrown out. You see, she wasn't really an old girl."

"She took advantage of you," I've said many times to Dean Buehl. "You couldn't have known she was crazy. Maybe she would have been all right if I had never shown up here."

"Well, that certainly isn't your fault." And so it goes—the two of us absolving each other of our sins. Sometimes I wonder if there's any end to this cycle of guilt and retribution. Even Athena has been sucked into the whirlpool of blame.

"But she couldn't have done it without me," she says now. "I told her we'd taken the boat out from the icehouse . . ."

"You certainly couldn't know she'd use it to take Olivia out to the rock that day," I say trying to keep my voice from shaking. It's still unbearable for me to think of Olivia and Dr. Lockhart in that boat. Or to think of Dr. Lockhart lurking around the preschool, seeding the ground with corniculi.

"I also told her you left your homework folder on your desk." Athena sighs. She's determined, I see, to confess all. Maybe she needs to finally get it all out.

I nod. "That's how she sent me that first journal page, but she would have found another way."

"I told her about Melissa's crush on Brian and she sent her those awful letters from Exeter pretending to be a girl who knew Brian."

"Yes," I say, remembering the Exeter stationery I saw in the attic bedroom, "and then she must have called Melissa and pretended that she was that girl, to lure her down to the lake." I remember how well she was able to change her voice. A natural mimic.

"And I told her I was mad at Vesta for planning to go skating alone that night and she waited for her out there and killed her."

"Athena, you thought you were talking to a psychologist. You were supposed to tell her things. You couldn't have known what she would do with the information. She used you," I say, "but it was to get at me. She wanted me to relive that whole awful year only, this time, not to survive it."

"But it wasn't your fault what happened twenty years ago."

"From where she stood it was." And she may have been right, I add to myself. Some part of me wanted Deirdre gone so I could have Lucy to myself and some part of me was willing to save Matt at the risk of losing Lucy. The part of me that didn't want to be left out again. In many ways, I was a lot like Albie.

"So why didn't she kill me, too?" Athena asks, shading her eyes from the glare off the lake so she can see my eyes when I answer.

I tuck a strand of sea green hair behind her ear. "I think you re-minded her of herself. Her notes on your sessions, she wasn't talking about you anymore, she was telling her own story through you. A girl who had been shuttled from school to school . . ." Athena looks away and I wonder if I should go on. "Whose parents don't seem to care . . ." I stop. How many of these girls, I wonder, have a little Al-bie inside of them?

I shiver at the thought and Athena, as if reading my thoughts, sets me straight. "I'm not that girl," she says. "And neither are you."

THEY'RE WAITING FOR US IN THE MUSIC ROOM. LUNCH TO-day is a barbecue on the swimming beach, so we've got the room to ourselves. Sitting on one side of the long table, their backs to the long windows facing the lake, are Dean Buehl, Meryl North, Tacy Beade, Myra Todd, Gwendoline Marsh, and one man in a dark suit whom I don't recognize. Roy Corey sits next to two empty chairs on the other side. The long expanse of polished mahogany is bare except for a pitcher of water and some glasses and a manila folder in front of the man, who rises as we come in to introduce himself as the lawyer in charge of the Crevecoeurs' estate. I shake his hand and sit down next to Roy. Athena is still standing.

"And you must be Miss Craven. I know your aunt. She wanted to be here today . . ."

"But she's got something, somewhere, I know." Athena ignores the lawyer's outstretched hand and plops down in the chair next to me. Two of the pins in her stola pop open, but, much to my relief, the folds of Gwen Marsh's satin sheets stay in place. I notice Myra Todd staring at Athena's outfit, pursing her lips to comment, but before she can the lawyer slaps his hand down on the manila folder.

"Well, since all the principals involved are present," he says, "let's begin."

"I don't see why Jane Hudson is here," Myra says. "She isn't on the board and she isn't a principal."

"A principal in what?" I ask, more confused than insulted. "Would someone please say what this is about."

"India Crevecoeur's bequest," Miss North, the historian answers. "When she turned the property over to be made into a school her relatives were furious. She agreed that she'd give the family a chance to reclaim the property."

"But not until the seventieth anniversary of the founding," Tacy Beade finishes.

"When most of them would be long dead," Dean Buehl adds. "It was her idea of a little joke."

We all instinctively look up at the family portrait that hangs at the end of the room from which India Crevecoeur, dour as Queen Victoria, looks down on us.

"She doesn't look like she would have much of a sense of humor," Roy says.

I'd be inclined to agree, but then I look at Tacy Beade and remember that May Day morning twenty years ago when the old woman escaped from her and Miss Macintosh and found her way into the mansion.

"So, the school could go back into private hands?" Across the table seven heads nod in agreement.

I am surprised at how bereft I feel at the thought of Heart Lake closing. After Dr. Lockhart's death I told Dean Buehl I'd stay to the end of the term but I just couldn't say for sure what I would do after that. She said she understood the place must have bad memories for me and promised that she would write me a good reference. But now, at the thought of Heart Lake closing its doors forever, I am suddenly enraged.

"That bitch," I say so loudly even Athena looks shocked. "How could she do it? What about all the girls here? Where are they supposed to go?" I imagine all of us—teachers and students—in a procession north to St. Eustace's. I wonder if it still exists. Or has Heart Lake become the last stop, the school of last resort? And if it has, what refuge is left if Heart Lake closes?

"Jane," Dean Buehl says, "I know how you feel. But the school won't close if the Crevecoeur descendants don't want it to." Her eyes slide from me to Roy and Athena. Roy shifts nervously in his chair and Athena slides a little lower down in hers and bites a cuticle.

"Oh, yeah," she says, "my aunt said we were related to those people. That's why she sent me here, because she got a break on tuition or something. Well, if it's up to me, I say, sure, the school should, like, go on."

"Wait a second," I say, "Athena's only just turned eighteen. Shouldn't she have a lawyer present? She doesn't have to decide right now, does she?"

"Now you're worried about Miss Craven's rights?" Myra Todd asks. "A minute ago you were all upset about the school closing."

"It doesn't matter," Roy says. "I'm the only other descendant, right?"

I look over at him incredulously and he shrugs. I remember then, that May Day, old Mrs. Crevecoeur telling Lucy that the Coreys were related to the Crevecoeurs if you went back far enough. Then it hits me, what any good Latin teacher should have noticed long ago. Craven and Corey. They each derive from one half on the name Crevecoeur.

Myra Todd shifts uneasily in her chair, releasing a whiff of mold into the room. "That settles it then, the bequest becomes permanent and the board now has access to the whole estate—"

"With Mr. Corey and Miss Craven installed as lifetime board members for which they will be paid a stipend . . ." Dean Buehl is already rising from her seat. All the women on that side of the table are following suit when the lawyer stops them.

"Well, that would be the case," he says, "if not for the codicil."

"The codicil?" Dean Buehl echoes, falling back to her seat. One by one the rest of the women sink down, like sails in a regatta becalmed by a lull in the wind.

"Yes, India Crevecoeur added a codicil to her bequest on May 4, 1976. It was, I understand, prompted by her visit to the school on the fiftieth anniversary of the Founder's Day. If you will all listen patiently now, I will read to you the terms of the codicil." He looks at each of us in turn to see if any one of us will object, but when we all remain silent, he extracts a thick sheet of cream-colored writing paper from a folder and reads, at first in a hurried monotone as he dutifully repeats the legal formulas, and then slowly when he comes to the substance of India Crevecoeur's missive.

"It was my intent, after the death of my youngest daughter, Iris, to transform a scene of grief to one of communal productivity and improvement for young girls. I had some qualms, though, that in providing for strangers I might be impoverishing the children of my children, and so I made my bequest provisional. I confess I was afraid, as well, that a school founded so on grief might founder, and I wanted to give my descendants an opportunity to reclaim their inheritance if such were the case.

"It is not surprising, though, that in my grief-stricken state I overlooked one thing. I'd meant the school to honor the memory of my lost daughter, Iris, and so I should have provided especially for her relations instead of just my own."

Myra Todd clucks her tongue. "She must have been senile. The girl died at twelve! She wasn't old enough to marry. How could she have relations that weren't Crevecoeur descendants?"

The lawyer glares at Myra and resumes. "My daughter Iris was adopted." He pauses a moment for us to take in this piece of information. We all look again at the family portrait at the end of the room. There's little Iris standing off to one side of the group, closer to her nursemaid than the rest of the family. She's small and dark, where everyone else in the family is large and fair.

"She was the natural child of an unfortunate girl who worked in our mill. I'd long wanted a third daughter, but the good Lord had chosen not to bless me with that boon. When I was made aware of the mill girl's predicament I proposed to give the innocent baby a good home—and offered the mill girl a position in my own household. When our little Iris left us, her natural mother chose to leave as well. I could understand her reluctance to remain on the scene of such a tragedy. I tried to make what amends I could, but I'm afraid her daughter's death left the poor woman distracted with a grief that turned to bitter gall in her heart. She even blamed my own two daughters, Rose and Lily, for the death of her child."

I look up at the portrait. Rose and Lily, smiling smugly at the camera. What use would they have had for this strange dark interloper? I remember the story of how the two older girls had taken the youngest out in a boat and she'd fallen in. She'd been saved, but she'd gotten a chill and fallen ill with the flu that was ravaging the country. When I look away from the picture, I notice that Dean Buehl and Roy are both staring at me.

"When it recently came to my attention that my former servant—Iris's mother—had subsequently married and borne a child of her own, who in turn had her own child, I realized that the chance to make amends had finally arrived. Better late than never, as the girl herself said to me."

It's that phrase, so out of tune with the rest of India Crevecoeur's language, that finally wakes me up. I remember the way the old woman looked at me when I said it. I thought she was appalled at my cheek. Appalled to find her servant's granddaughter attending her school.

Although the lawyer is still reading I get up and walk over to the picture. I look, not at poor, spindly legged Iris, but at the nursemaid, my grandmother, who bends down to fix her charge's ribbon. At least, that's what I always assumed she was doing. Now that I look more closely I see she's giving the girl a little push, trying to send her closer to her sisters so that she'll be part of the family group. Why didn't I ever wonder how the maid got in the family portrait? Was it because Iris would never have been far from her? I look at the maid's face; her brow, dark and plain, is pinched with worry, but under that anxiety, that her child will never really fit in with her adopted family, I think I can read, in the plain brown eyes, familiar to me as my own, something like love.

"And so, Miss Hudson," the lawyer is saying, as I turn back to face the table where everyone is now looking toward me, "Mrs. Crevecoeur left the deciding vote to you. The granddaughter of Iris's mother."

"Well, then I say make the bequest permanent."

"As you told Miss Craven," the lawyer says, "you don't have to decide right now. Certainly you'll want to consider the amount of money you'd be giving up."

Dean Buehl claps her hand to her breast and begins to weep as if she'd been holding back this uncharacteristic flood of emotions the whole time. Athena looks at her and starts to giggle, but stops herself by biting her thumb. Roy gets up and puts his arm around me.

"Are you sure?" he asks.

"Why? Would you like me better if I were an heiress?"

The smile he gives me comes slowly but reaches into someplace deep, someplace that feels as if it's never been touched until now, like the cold bottom of the lake that the sun has never warmed before this moment. "You forget," he says, "you're my heart's true love."

"Oh yeah," I say.

Then the others are around us, all talking at once, but it's Athena I hear.

"You're going to be late, *Magistra*."

"Yikes, you're right." I look down at my watch.

"The procession?" Roy asks.

"Something else," I tell him, giving him a quick, hard kiss on the mouth. "A surprise."

I RUN DOWN THE STEPS OF THE MANSION. MY GIRLS ARE gathered there, the flowers in their hair trembling in the light breeze coming off the lake. I wave to them and tell them that Athena will lead the procession and I'll join them at the Maypole. Beyond them I see the car parked down by the lake. As I step off the path, the car door opens and she gets out. For a moment, she is only a dark figure silhouetted against the bright fire of the lake; a small girl standing alone in an enormous swirl of atoms. Then she sees me and comes running, arms open wide.

The Lake of Dead Languages

CAROL GOODMAN

A Reader's Guide

Writing in a Dead Language

The question I'm most often asked by readers is, "What part of this book comes from your life?" I know I'm not the only author to get this question. Sue Miller writes that she prepared for her last book tour by memorizing a quote from John Cheever that begins "It seems to me that any confusion between autobiography and fiction debases fiction." She also says that reciting this quote wasn't enough to deter her audience. They still wanted to know the parts that came from real life. Truthfully, even though I know that the journey from fact to fiction is not a straightforward one, it's what I always want to know, too. Since I have a pretty good idea what events in my life gave birth to Jane Hudson—and where her story breaks off from mine and becomes her own—I can't see any real reason not to tell. Sorry, Mr. Cheever!

Jane's circumstances at the beginning of the book are similar to the situation I found myself in the fall of 1994. I had moved back into my parents' house with my two-year-old daughter after separating from my husband. I was thirty-five, soon to be divorced, broke, and unemployed. Not the high point in my life! But as bad as things were, I knew my situation would have been worse if I hadn't had generous and supportive parents to come home to. What would I have done, I wondered, without them? What did women do?

I imagined finding a job as a Latin teacher at a private school that would provide on-site child care for my daughter and a place where we could live. Out of that imagined scenario I wrote a short story called "Girl, Declined." Even in that early story my female protagonist, Jane, seemed largely defined by the things she lacked. Why didn't she have family or friends to turn to? Why had she married so badly? I began to sense connections between her deprivation and the teenage girls she might encounter in a second-rate girls' school. Their shared preoccupation with a dead language became both a distraction and a metaphor for being emotionally shut down.

I finished that story and moved on to other things. I wrote other stories, got an MFA, started teaching again when my daughter was older and, eventually, remarried. I never forgot, though, how close I was to having nothing. And that woman, alone with a young child at a girls' school, stayed in my mind. Every once in a while I'd return to her. I imagined that she'd have a hard time remembering her Latin after years of disuse, just as I had when I went back to school in my midtwenties to get my teaching certification. I pictured her studying her declensions and practicing the oral Latin they use nowadays in the classroom. The story didn't really come alive, though, until I settled on the right location for the school. In the summer of 1999, while vacationing at Mohonk Mountain House, it occurred to me that the lake there would make a good location for the girls' school. Once I chose that setting other pieces of the story started falling into place: Someone Jane loved had drowned, leaving her as closed and frozen as the lake in winter. No wonder she had married the wrong guy!

Choosing that setting introduced a dimension to the book which I couldn't have planned. I spent as much time at Mohonk as I could, taking nature hikes and speaking to Mohonk's amazing naturalist, Ann Guenther about the geology of the rock formations around the lake and the eerie moaning noises the lake made when it froze. She also recommended some books that described the process a lake goes through when it freezes (who knew there even was a process! I thought it just froze). When I read about "overturn" I couldn't help seeing it as a metaphor for how the past sometimes rises to the surface and how our lives seem to move in cycles.

By that fall, as I started working on the book, my own life moved into a new cycle. Some of the new things in my life were wonderful and they fed into the book I was writing in unexpected ways. My daughter's creativity and confidence were (and still are) a source of inspiration. It was Maggie who invented the corniculum by linking a few hairpins together into an animal shape. She asked a million questions about the book I was writing and, minus its most disturbing elements, I told her the basic plot. The part she liked the most were the legends surrounding Heart Lake. She helped me draw a map of the school and she wrote a poem inspired by the legend of "The Lady of the Lake" which won a Scholastic award. I couldn't help wondering, though, if she'd always be this confident. I'd read a lot of books about how teenage girls often suffered a falloff of confidence when they reached puberty. Looking back on my own adolescence (and reading the journals I'd religiously kept through my teens), I relived all the agonizing self-doubts of that era. Writing about the troubled teens in *The Lake of Dead Languages* was, perhaps, my way of exorcising those spirits—or an attempt to come to grips with my own adolescence before Maggie began hers.

The hardest part of my life that fall, though, was that my father had been diagnosed with stomach cancer. He died that October. Once again my life felt precarious, balanced on the edge of some precipice. It was difficult to keep working on the novel, but my husband kept urging me to work on that

"Latin teacher story." At first I worked on it so I could tell him I'd written that day. Eventually, as the days got colder, the story seemed to take on its own life and I found that working on it gave me some respite from the pain I was feeling. Just as Jane found comfort in returning to her Latin studies, I found writing about an imaginary Latin teacher in the frozen north country a distraction from my own grief. I thought, though, that in this particular instance, Jane's life and mine had little to do with each other. Jane's father is one of the most absent characters in the book. I wouldn't try to write about my father until my next novel—and in many ways, I'm still not ready to write about him. By that spring, though, I saw that I had written about grief and dying in a way that I wouldn't have been able to before my father's death. I don't think we really know what our books are "about" until they're done and maybe we never know for sure, but I think *The Lake of Dead Languages* is about how we talk to the dead. And I don't mean by using a Ouija board or attending a seance. Jane says at one point that Matt's death left her feeling "like I'd been talking to someone on the phone when the lines went down." How do you keep that conversation going? What's the language for speaking to the dead? Only after I finished the book did it occur to me that a "dead language" might also be the means by which we speak with the dead.

There are other snippets of my life lurking in Jane's. She goes to my alma mater (but is much more studious there); she has the same troubles getting her papers graded as I do; and we own the same copy of *Tales from the Ballet*. She's a much better ice-skater, though, and, I suspect, ultimately braver than me. She's someone very much like me *minus* some of my advantages, like good parents. And so, the book ends up being about deprivation and loss, but also how we traverse that terrain of grief—something as tricky and perilous as making your way across broken ice.

Reading Group Questions and Topics for Discussion

1. Given the trauma she endured there, why does Jane return to the Heart Lake School for Girls? Do you judge her options to be as limited as she does? Are there other factors at work in her decision?

2. Jane acknowledges: "I had thought it was all right to marry someone I didn't love, but what I hadn't counted on was how it felt to share someone I loved with someone I didn't." Discuss the nature of Jane and Mitch's marriage and the impact Olivia's birth had on it.

3. How does motherhood change Jane's life?

4. Discuss Jane's socioeconomic background and its impact on her. Would you agree or disagree that class mobility in the United States takes a toll that is not always acknowledged or discussed?

5. How does Jane's image of herself correspond (or not) with how others perceive her?

6. Lucy's aunt has a very different perspective on Lucy that contrasts sharply with Jane's worshipful remembrance. Do you think Jane is finally able to see Lucy in a more complicated light by the end of the novel? Why or why not?

7. How would you describe Lucy and how do you understand her actions?

8. Lucy had a magnetism that drew people to her, inspiring conflict and jealousy within her circle. Have you ever had such a friend or been such a friend?

9. Discuss the particular intensity of adolescent friendships and the havoc they can wreak as well as the benefits.

10. Do you think tragedy might have been averted if Lucy had been able to tell Matt the "something that changes everything," which Helen Chambers shared with her?

11. Matt's aunt refers to Jane as "Mattie's girl." What do you think was the true nature of Matt's feelings toward Jane?

12. Discuss the merits and drawbacks of the popular theories, ascribed to by school psychologist Candace Lockhart in this novel, about the crisis of confidence experienced by adolescent girls and its effects.

13. Discuss the strengths and weaknesses of single-sex versus coed schools. Which educational setting do you prefer and why?

14. Why do Jane's students decide to "go easy on her"? What does she think? What do you think?

15. Do you consider Jane a good teacher? What qualities constitute a good teacher?

16. What do you think of Helen Chambers's behavior toward

her students, particularly her attitude toward and decisions regarding Lucy? Was the school's decision to fire Chambers justified? Do you think this decision was based solely on her sexual orientation?

17. Discuss the many secrets finally brought to light in this novel and the corrosive and destructive impact secrets can have on those keeping them and those from whom information is withheld.

18. Jane has lived under a cloud of guilt and remorse since her senior year at Heart Lake. She wonders "if there's any end to this cycle of guilt and retribution." Do you think the truth will set her free?

19. Jane is haunted by a past that has severely compromised her ability to live in the present. Discuss how people can become trapped by the past and how to make peace with it.

20. What shape do you imagine Jane's life will take after the end of this novel? Do you think she will leave Heart Lake? Should she?

21. Do you think the Heart Lake School will survive its most recent scandal?

22. There are many mysteries to be solved over the course of this novel. How do you read mysteries? Are you content to go along for the ride or determined to unravel the

mysteries before the author reveals them? If you are the latter kind of reader, did the author stump you or did you figure out what was going on in advance?

23. Discuss the structure of this novel as it shifts between the present and the past. Did you find it satisfying? Were there characters you wanted to hear more from?

24. Choose a character other than Jane and discuss how the story would have unfolded from their perspective. What would change and what would remain the same? How would Jane be depicted?

25. If you could invite this author to your book club, what would you like to ask her? What would you want to know about the creation of this novel?

26. Why did your group choose this novel? Did it live up to your expectations? How does it compare with other works you have read?

From the author of *The Lake of Dead Languages* . . .

THE SEDUCTION OF WATER

by

CAROL GOODMAN

Available in hardcover from
Ballantine Books

For an exciting sneak preview of *The Seduction of Water*,
please turn the page . . .

My favorite story when I was small, the one I begged for night after night, was "The Selkie."

"That old story," my mother would say. She'd say it in exactly the same tone of voice as when my father complimented her dress. *Oh, this old thing,* she'd say, her pale green eyes giving away her pleasure. "Wouldn't you rather something new?" And she'd hold up a shiny book my aunt Sophie, my father's sister, had bought for me. *The Bobbsey Twins* or, when I was older, *Nancy Drew.* American stories with an improving message and plucky, intrepid heroines.

"No, I want your story," I would say. It was her story because she knew it by heart, had heard it from her mother, who had heard it from hers . . . a line of mothers and daughters that I imagined like the image of myself and her when I stood by her side in front of the mirrors in the lobby.

"Well, if it will help you sleep . . ."

And I would nod, burrowing deeper into the blankets. It was one of the few requests I stuck to, perhaps because my mother's initial hesitation came to be part of the ritual—part of the telling. A game we played because I knew she liked that I wanted her story, not some store-bought one. Even when she was dressed to go out and she had only come up to say a quick good night she would sit down on the edge of my bed and shrug her coat off her shoulders so that its black fur collar settled down around her waist and I would nestle into its dark, perfumed plush, and she, getting ready to tell her story, would touch the long strands of pearls at her neck, the beads making a soft clicking sound, and close her eyes. I imagined that she closed her eyes because the story was somewhere inside her, on an invisible scroll unfurling behind her eyelids from which she read night after night, every word the same as the night before.

"In a time before the rivers were drowned by the sea, in a land between the sun and the moon . . ."

Here she would open her eyes and touch the knobs of my headboard, which had been carved into the shapes of a crescent moon and a sun by Joseph, the hotel gardener, to replace its original broken knobs. We used the bedding and furniture too worn out for guest use—blankets with hems coming unstitched, dressers with rattling drawers, and tables with ring marks where careless city ladies had put down hot teacups without a saucer. The rooms we lived in were leftovers themselves, the attic rooms where the maids lived before the new servants' quarters were built in the North Wing. It's where my mother had stayed when she'd come to the hotel to work as a maid. Even after she'd married my father, the hotel manager, she told him she liked being up high. From the attic rooms you had the best view of the river flowing south towards New York City and then to the sea.

"In this land, where our people came from, the fishermen told a story about a man who fell in love with one of the seal woman, selkies the people called them, seals that once a year could shed their skin and become women . . ."

"So were they women pretending to be seals or seals pretending to be women?"

This interruption my mother would take in stride because I always asked the same question and she had incorporated the answer into the story.

". . . and no one ever knew which they had been first, seal or woman, which is part of their mystery. When you looked into the seal's eyes you could see the human being looking out, but when you heard the woman singing you could hear the sound of the sea in her voice."

Still unsatisfied as to whether the selkies were mainly seal or human, I would indicate to my mother that I was ready for her to go on by burrowing deeper into the covers and closing my eyes. I knew my mother had some-place to be and the story could detain her only so long. If she didn't think I was falling asleep, I risked losing the story altogether.

". . . and so it happened that on that one day a farmer went down to the sea . . ."

"Did he go to collect seashells for his garden paths?" I would ask. "The way Joseph said they did in France." Joseph had worked at all the finest hotels in Europe after the war. On his right forearm, just visible when he rolled up the cuffs of his faded blue workshirts, were faint numbers, the same color as the shirts he wore.

"Yes, a path of seashells sounds nice," she would say, smiling. She liked it when I thought up new details for her stories. "He wanted the path to his house to glow in the moonlight like broken pearls. That's what he was thinking about when he looked up and saw, sunning herself on a rock, a girl with skin like crushed pearls and hair as dark as coal."

Black hair. Like my mother. Like me. Recently, I found my mother's old book of Irish folktales that contained "The Selkie." The selkie in it is blond. My mother must have decided to make the heroine of her story dark-haired like us.

"The dark-haired girl with pearl skin sang like something you might hear in a dream, sweeter than anything you'd hear in a theater or Carnegie Hall even . . ." Here, if I peeked, I'd see that my mother, her eyes still closed, wore the expression of someone listening to music. She'd be quiet for a moment and for once I wouldn't fill the silence with a question because, I thought, if I listened carefully enough I would hear what she heard too. All I did hear, though, was the muffled footsteps and hushed whispers of the night maids and the groan of the old elevator taking late diners back up to their rooms. If there was singing it would be one of the retired music teachers who rented attic rooms for the summer. As soon as my mother opened her eyes I'd snap mine shut.

". . . and so the farmer fell in love with the dark-haired girl and decided he wanted her for a wife, but when he tried to get closer to the rock where she sat, she heard him and dived into the water. The farmer stood on the shore watching for the girl, sure that she couldn't stay in the water for long. Then he saw, out beyond the breakers, a sleek dark head appear. But she wasn't a girl anymore, she was a—"

"Seal!" I would say, forgetting in my excitement to make my voice sound sleepy.

"Yes. The farmer stood for a long time looking at the ocean thinking over what he had seen, or what he thought he had seen, but at last he remembered he had cows to milk and chickens to feed and so he turned his back to the ocean and went on home."

"But he couldn't forget the dark-haired girl and her beautiful voice."

"No. He couldn't. Could you?"

My mother always asked me the same question, but no matter how many times she asked it, I was always unprepared. Not that I doubted that I, too, like the farmer, would have been smitten by the dark-haired singer; but there was something in the way my mother asked the question that made me think I should answer differently, that I should have been able to resist the selkie's song. After all, look what happened to that poor farmer . . .

He was so lovesick for the selkie girl that he was unable to sleep and the sound of the ocean, which he'd heard since the day he was born, began to grate on his nerves. It seemed there was always sand in his bed no matter how many times he'd shake out his sheets and even with all the windows open he'd feel as if he were suffocating inside his cottage.

(I could always hear, in this part of the story, an edge in my mother's voice. When I was little I thought it had to do with the sand in the sheets. My mother had been a hotel maid, after all, and she would often tell me how rude it was when guests left cracker crumbs or *worse* in their beds. But later I guessed the edge in her voice had more to do with her own trouble sleeping.)

Things went on like this until the farmer began to neglect his fields. His cows went unmilked and his hens wandered into his neighbors' yards looking for food. In desperation, he sought out the help of an old wise woman who lived in a cottage on a cliff above the sea. The minute she laid eyes on the farmer she knew by his shrunken pupils and the way his ribs stood out under his threadbare shirt like the hull of a staved-in boat, and how his hair was tangled like a mass of seaweed, what his problem was.

"How long has it been since you saw the selkie?" she asked him, sitting him down by the fire and giving him a cup of bitter-tasting tea.

"It'll be a year tomorrow," he told her, "to the day. I remember because it was the first day of spring."

The old woman smiled. "As if you needed that to remember," she scolded, but she didn't tell him to forget the selkie. Instead she told him to finish his tea, which would make him sleep through the night. "Then tomorrow, go back to the rock where you saw her. You must swim out to the rock, being careful she doesn't hear you. By her side you'll see a rolled-up skin that you must snatch away from her. Once you have her skin she'll have no choice but to follow you home."

"And she'll stay and be my wife?"

"She'll stay and be your wife."

"And bear my children?"

"She will bear your children."

"And she might, one day, grow to love me?"

The old woman shrugged, but whether to say she didn't know or that he asked too much, the farmer never knew. Already the tea was dragging his eyelids down and making his arms and legs heavy. He staggered from the old woman's hut and only made it home because it was all downhill from where she lived to his front door. He didn't even bother finding his bed but fell asleep on a rug in front of the fire.

When he awoke he saw by the angle of the light coming through the window that he'd nearly overslept the day—he felt as if he'd been asleep for a year—but then he heard above the roar of the ocean a voice singing. Her voice.

He ran toward the sea, remembering at the last minute to creep quietly down to the edge and slip into the water making as little noise as possible. Fortunately, the slap of the waves of the encroaching tide masked his clumsy thrashing in the water as he approached the rock. He saw the dark-haired girl and there beside her a bundle—her skin—sleek and shiny in the light of the setting sun, like a coal burning slowly from within. As soon as he laid his hand on the skin the dark-haired girl turned and gave him a look that froze his blood. Her eyes, fringed by coal-dark lashes, were the pale green of sea foam. He opened his mouth and swallowed so much sea-water he would have sunk to the bottom of the ocean right then if he hadn't clutched the skin to his chest. It acted like a life preserver; it was that buoyant. He turned and swam back to shore trying to forget the look the girl had given him. She'd change her mind about him, he thought, once she got used to him.

It was harder getting to shore than he'd figured. A sudden wind had risen that whipped the waves into a frenzy. Although the skin kept him afloat it also seemed to be pulling him out to sea. The current that wrapped around his legs seemed to have muscle to it, like a giant eel squeezing the life breath out of him. By the time he dragged himself out onto the sand, he was too weak to stand. He'd imagined himself holding the skin up before the girl like a proud conqueror, but instead he clutched the soft fur to his face like a baby mouthing his blanket for comfort. The skin still felt warm to the touch—as if it had absorbed the sun into its very fiber. When he looked up he saw the dark-haired girl sitting a few feet above him where the sand rose to a crest above the shoreline. Her knees were drawn up to her chest and her long hair fell around her legs like a curtain to hide her nakedness. Her sea-green eyes watched him impassively. Waiting to see if I'm drowned or not, he thought. When she saw that he wasn't dead, she got up and walked away from the ocean toward his house. It was he, after all, who followed her home.

At this point in the story my mother would pause to see if I was asleep yet. I had to gauge my reaction carefully. If I seemed too awake she'd decide the story wasn't working and tell me sternly to go to sleep. If she believed I was almost asleep she'd slip out without a word, turning the light off and closing the door behind her. Then I'd be left in the dark with the unfinished story churning in my brain, keeping me awake just as the selkie's song had kept the farmer awake. It was that feeling you get when you put down an unfinished sandwich and you forget where you've put it; you keep hungering for that last bite. I would be alone in the dark, the sounds of the hotel slowly winding down like a music box playing out. I knew my mother shared that same horror of sleeplessness and if I asked, in just the right sleepy voice, for just a little more she would sigh and pull the fur-trimmed coat a little tighter around her arms, as if she were cold, and go on . . .

For a time things seemed all right with the farmer and his selkie bride. She bore him five children: a girl first, and then four sons, all with dark hair and pale green eyes. She learned to cook and clean and tend the farmer's animals and garden. Everything she touched became beautiful. She hung shells and pieces of sea glass in the windows in such a way that they made music when the wind blew. Her voice could calm a mare in foal and coax the sheep to stand still for shearing.

The only thing she couldn't learn to do was to knit or tat lace or mend the fishing nets. No matter how hard the village women tried to teach her she couldn't make a single knot. She couldn't even learn to braid her daughter's hair or tie the ribbon on her own dress. In fact, the women noticed that when she came into the knitting circle they all dropped their stitches and the sweaters they were working on unraveled at the hems. Soon the women made up errands to send her on to keep her out of the circle and since the knitting circle was the time the women shared their stories and gossip she was, in the course of things, excluded.

She didn't seem to mind.

She could be heard singing to herself over her chores. Her singing was so beautiful that strangers would stand on the road to listen to her. Sometimes, though, the songs would grow so sad that people in the village would find themselves weeping for no reason and they would be unable to sleep at night. This was especially true on two days of the year: the vernal and the autumnal equinox. On those days her song—and it seemed indeed to be one song, which she started at the break of day and left off only when the sun had sunk into the sea—was so achingly sad no one was able to get any work done at all. Porridge was burned, fishing nets were lost, thumbs were hammered, cheese spoiled, ink spilled, and sweaters unraveled into heaps of greasy wool.

After a few years of this the villagers asked the farmer to prohibit his wife from singing on those days.

"I might as well ask the earth not to turn," he told them. "For spring not to follow winter and winter not to follow fall."

This is the answer he gave year after year, but when their oldest child was ten years old, he grew tired of the looks the women gave him and the things the men said behind his back about not knowing how to control his womenfolk.

"It's for your own good," he told his wife. "Your singing only makes you sadder. And then you don't sleep. Think about the children. Do you want them infected with your sadness?"

The look she gave him then was the same look she gave him from the rock that day he took her skin from her. He hadn't seen that look from her since and when he did it was as if his mouth filled up with seawater and he felt himself sinking. But she did as he said and never said a word. On that first day of spring she stayed inside the house and never so much as opened her mouth. She took the chimes from the windows and closed the flue in the chimney so she couldn't hear the wind whistling through it. She scolded her daughter for chanting a rhyme while skipping rope. She'd never scolded her for anything before.

The day after the equinox the farmer thought that things would go back to normal, but they didn't. She went about her chores like a thing made of stone. She made the porridge, but she burned it. The animals shied away at her touch. When she looked at her children it was as if she were looking through clear water.

Things went on like this through the summer. The farmer hoped at first that she would change, but when she didn't he hardened his heart against her. It was the girl who followed her mother when she left the house at night. She'd find her mother curled in a ball between the cows in the barn or wedged between the rocks on the shore, trying to find a place where she could cheat the sleeplessness that seemed to be always upon her now. As the nights grew cooler she saw her mother shivering in her thin night-dress out in the open and she thought that if things went on like this her mother would freeze to death.

It was a night in September—the night before the autumnal equinox—that the temperature, as if in anticipation of the planet's tilt away from the sun, dropped so low that the girl could see her mother's breath turn into ice on the rocks around her. The heavy mist from the sea was turning to crystals in her mother's hair, so heavy that she could hear the strands chiming in the cold sea breeze. If she didn't do something her mother would be frozen solid by the morning.

She ran back to the house and opened the blanket chest but the farmer had already heaped the extra quilts on his sons' beds. Her hands scraped against the bottom of the trunk, scrabbling over the rough wood until her fingers bled from the splinters. She dug her nails into the wood just to feel the pain and then, to her surprise, the bottom pried loose and her hands sunk into something warm and silky soft.

She thought it was something alive.

Even when she lifted the heavy fur up and saw that it was an animal skin she still couldn't believe it was a dead thing. The skin pulsed with warmth and glowed like a burning coal. She held it to her cheek and smelled the ocean in it. She heard the ocean in it trapped in each bristling hair, the way a shell holds the sound of the ocean deep in its whorls.

She wrapped the fur around her shoulders and ran to where her mother lay between the rocks above the beach. Instead of weighing her down, the shawl of fur seemed to float on the wind behind her back and buoy up her steps.

When she found her mother she thought she was too late; that her mother had already frozen to death. A fog was rolling in from the sea and as it touched her mother's skin it froze in a fine skein of ice so that her mother seemed to be caught in a net strung out of crystal beads. But then she noticed that her mother's breath was crystallizing too and she knew her mother was still alive. She lay the fur over her mother and crawled in under it, wedging herself between her mother and the rocks. Instantly she felt her mother's skin grow warm; the net of ice melted and soaked into the soft, heavy fur.

The mother and daughter slept together on the beach beneath the cloak of fur, but even as they slept, the girl could feel her mother's fingers in her hair, stroking away her fear.

I sometimes fell asleep at this point too. There was a corner of my blanket that had unraveled and then matted back together like a piece of wool that's been felted. After my mother had gone, I liked to tuck this under my cheek and pretend it was the selkie's skin or the fur collar of my mother's coat, the one she wore if she was going someplace special: a party the local college was throwing for her, dinner with her editor across the river in Rhinebeck, or a reading in the city. These things still happened even though it had been years since she'd published her last book and the books she had written—the two of them—sold fewer and fewer copies until finally they went out of print.

Still my mother had her fans. She'd written two books in a trilogy about a fantasy world called Tirra Glynn. The first book, written five years before I was born, was called *The Broken Pearl*. The second book, written while she was pregnant with me (she always told me that she'd conceived both me and the idea for that book at the same time and that we both took exactly nine months to bring forth), was called *The Net of Tears*. No one ever knew what the third book would have been called because it never appeared. I remember that it was around the time of my sixth birthday that my first-grade teacher asked me if I ever saw my mother writing. When I relayed that conversation to my mother she had me pulled out of the public school and put into a private school in Poughkeepsie. Two years later I was put back into the public school. Sales from my mother's books had dropped precipitously. Who wanted to read the first two books in a trilogy if there wasn't going to be a third book?

Also the hotel had fallen on hard times. It was the 1960s and Americans had discovered air travel and Europe. One by one the big hotels to the south and west of us went out of business. If it hadn't been for a core of faithful clientele—the families whose grandparents had stayed at the Hotel Equinox and the painters who came to paint the view—we would have closed as well. Who wanted to drive three hours to a resort to swim in an ice-cold lake? The Hotel Equinox, perched on a ledge above the Hudson, was too out of the way and too old-fashioned and then, when my mother left, just too sad.

She left for good when I was ten. She'd been invited to sit on a panel of women science fiction and fantasy writers at a two-day conference at

NYU. She was supposed to leave for the city in the morning, but because she couldn't sleep she asked Joseph to drive her across the river to catch the night train. I heard her arguing with my father in the hall outside my room. "But where will you stay?" he asked. "Your reservation isn't until tomorrow."

"They're bound to have a room for the night," she told him, her voice light with laughter. I imagined her putting a hand on his forehead and stroking his hair back, something she always did to allay my fears. "You worry too much, Ben. I'll be fine."

Then she came into my room to kiss me good night and I pressed my face into the dark plushy fur of her coat collar. Her coat was buttoned to her throat and she didn't undo it or let it settle down around her waist as she usually did when she was going to tell me a story.

"Tell me the selkie story," I asked. She pressed her hand against my forehead, as if checking for fever, and brushed my hair away from my face, combing the tangles out with her fingers. I waited to hear her reply, *That old thing?* But instead she said, "Not tonight." She told me to close my eyes and go to sleep and when I had kept my eyes closed for several minutes I heard the clicking of the pearls around her neck falling against the buttons of her coat as she leaned forward and kissed me good night. And then she was gone.

When she got to New York she did not check into the Algonquin where her editor had made reservations for her even though we found out later that they did have rooms available for that night. My mother never went there at all. Instead she checked into the Dreamland Hotel—a run-down hotel in Coney Island near the site of the old Dreamland amusement park. It was the last weekend in September 1973, the weekend that the Dreamland burned to the ground. It was weeks before we knew for sure what had happened to my mother because she hadn't registered under her married name, Kay Greenfeder, or her pen name, K. R. LaFleur, or even her maiden name, Katherine Morrissey. She, and the man she was with, were registered under the names Mr. and Mrs. John McGlynn. The investigating officer who saw the registration guessed who it was because his wife was a fan of my mother's who had read that she was missing and she recognized the name McGlynn because my mother had named her fantasy world Tirra Glynn.

He'd come all the way from the city to show my father a charm bracelet, which my father identified as the gift he and I had given her for Christmas the previous year. They met in the library and I hid in the courtyard outside the library windows and listened to what was said. My father asked him if they had identified the man she was with, but the officer said they hadn't found the man's body. That my mother had died alone.

For years after I could only fall asleep listening to the story of the selkie girl. I would ask my aunt Sophie, who took care of me after my mother left, to tell me the story.

"That old thing?" she would say, using the same words my mother had, but meaning something else entirely, "That morbid story?" She said *morbid* the way she said *dirty* when I was little and tried to eat a treat that had fallen to the floor or a pastry left on the rim of a saucer by one of the hotel guests. Morbid thoughts were what I had when I wasn't attending to my chores or going to bed promptly so she could attend to hers. Morbid was what my mother had been before she went away. But like my mother, my aunt could be convinced to tell me the story if she thought it would put me to sleep. I would fold the felted nap of the blanket against my cheek and imagine it was the fur collar of my mother's coat and I would imagine my mother's hands stroking my hair, just as the selkie's daughter could feel her mother's hands in her hair even as she slept. My aunt could tell the story word for word because, as I knew by then, it was the first chapter in my mother's book, *The Broken Pearl*, but if I squeezed my eyes tight enough I still heard the story in my mother's voice.

"In the morning, when the selkie's daughter awoke she was alone on the beach. She'd heard her mother's voice in her sleep thanking her for returning her skin. 'Now I can go back to the sea where I belong and where I have five selkie children, just as I have five human children on the land, whom you must watch over now. You mustn't weep for me but instead, whenever you miss me, come stand at the water's edge and listen for my voice in the surf. And on the first day of spring each year, and the last day of summer, you'll see me as you know me now, a woman in a woman's skin.'

"The girl went back to her father's house, determined to keep her promise to her mother even though every step she took away from the sea felt heavy as if her feet were caught in a net that was dragging her out with the ebb tide. Even her hair, which had frozen in the night, seemed to drag her down. But still she went home and lit the stove and made the porridge and when her brothers awoke she explained to them that although their mother was gone, she would take care of them now, and that twice a year she would take them to see their mother again.

"It wasn't until later, when she still felt the weight of ice in her hair, that she looked in the mirror and saw her mother's parting gift. She remembered her mother's hands stroking her hair through the night. Her mother— who couldn't knit a stitch, or tat lace, or even tie a knot—had woven a wreath of sea foam frozen into bright stone: caught in its net, a single green tear the color of the sea."

My aunt would turn out the light, then, and straighten the covers and smooth my hair away from my face. I'd feel her dry lips brush my forehead and then I'd be alone in the dark, listening to the sounds of the old hotel settling. On a windy night the beams and floorboards would crack and pop like logs in a bonfire and I'd imagine that the hotel was on fire. But on a still night, if I listened closely enough, I thought I could just make out the sound of the river far below us. I would think about my mother following the river south that last night and I would imagine that the ocean at the end of the river had called to her—that she hadn't died in the fire at the Dreamland Hotel, but that instead she'd gone back to her other family under the sea—that it was only fair that they have their time with her now. I only had to wait and she would come back to me when their time was up.

About the Author

CAROL GOODMAN's work has appeared in such journals as *The Greensboro Review*, *Literal Latté*, *The Midwest Quarterly*, and *Other Voices*. After graduation from Vassar College, where she majored in Latin, she taught Latin for several years in Austin, Texas. She then received an MFA in fiction from the New School University. Goodman currently teaches writing and works as a writer in residence for Teachers & Writers. She lives on Long Island.